D1142317

Bright's Passage

Bright's Passage

A Novel

Josh Ritter

NEW ISLAND

BRIGHT'S PASSAGE
First published 2011
By Dial Press
New York, USA
This edition published 2012
By New Island
2 Brookside Dundrum Road, Dublin 14
www.newisland.ie

PRINT ISBN: 978-1-84840-143-3

Bright's Passage is a work of fiction. Names, characters, places,
and incidents are the products of the author's imagination or are
used fictitiously. Any resemblance to actual events, locales, or
persons, living or dead, is entirely coincidental.

British Library Cataloguing Data. A CIP catalogue record for this book is
available from the British Library

Book design by Rebecca Aidlin
Cover design by Matthew Fleming
Printed by Scandbook

New Island received financial assistance from
The Arts Council (An Comhairle Ealaíon), Dublin, Ireland

10 9 8 7 6 5 4 3 2 1

For Dawn

Bright's Passage

1

The baby boy wriggled in his arms, a warm, wet mass, softer than a goat and hairier than a rabbit kit. He held a blade over a candle flame for some time, then cut the cord and rubbed the baby with a wetted shirt. When this was done he laid the child in a basket near the fire and then stood at the head of the bed and looked down at his wife's face a long moment. Abruptly, he bent low and placed his head near her mouth, staying all the while stone silent, waiting for some whisper from her lips. At last he stood straight once more, seeming to disappear into the still blackness of the low rafters as if he had become just another of the cabin's shadows. The child began to cry, and he turned to look at it lying there by the glow of the dying fire.

The man paced the floor, biting the large front knuckle of his fist. At length he picked the child up from its basket and lifted the flap of heavy hide over the doorway, stepping out into the last of the blue twilight as the rising sun began to gild the topmost trees along the crest of the ridge.

Although he'd lived in its shadow almost his whole life, he stood there watching the sleeping leafy hulk closely as if for the first time. The forest was in the full trembling swell of high summer, the trees clamorous for sunlight, permitting only a few stray drops of gold to fall between their leaves and onto the scraggly undergrowth below. The ridge would offer nothing in the way of hindrance should men take it upon themselves to cross it. He again put his hand to his mouth and could be seen from the dark of the nearby chestnut tree to bite down hard on that knob-knuckled, much-abused fist. When the fit had passed he sat down cross-legged on the ground, his crying baby boy in his lap. The child's eyes were shut tightly, but its paw searched the air waveringly for something until the man put his finger down and the little hand grasped it, held it. The two waited there a while.

By and by the angel spoke from the darkness by the chestnut tree. "She's gone."

"Course she's gone! What am I doing out here with the baby if she ain't gone?"

There was silence.

"Yeah," he said after a while, his voice catching, "she's gone."

"That's how it had to be."

"You didn't tell me that she had to die," the man said accusingly. "You said to do whatever you told me to do and you'd keep us safe . . ."

The silence continued for so long that he knew the angel would not answer him, but he continued to sit there anyway, one arm holding the child close while the other arm worked a stick into the packed dirt. The child had red hair and cried and cried.

Nearby, a hutch held several hens clucking pointlessly at one another, and atop the hutch, white against the still-dark trees, stood the she-goat. Without his mother's rifle he had not been able to hunt that winter, and he had been forced to slaughter the goat's kids, and finally the billy, one by one. Now the white little widow stood atop the hutch all day every day, coming down to the dirt only to forage or to be milked.

4

Even when his wife was hugely pregnant she had milked the she-goat to keep the milk flowing, but yesterday morning her water had broken before she'd had the chance, and the ensuing afternoon and evening had been long and frightful. Now the goat's udder was strained to bursting. He fetched the basket from the cabin, set it on a stump, and laid his son inside it. Then, kneeling by the stream, he washed his hands clean of blood and grime. He rose with much fatigue and made his way slowly across the bedraggled stretch of dirt to the hutch, lifted the goat down, and squeezed the milk into a bucket.

When the bottom of the bucket was covered with milk, he took it to the baby. Dipping his finger in the froth, he held it to the boy's suckling mouth. He sat and fed the baby like this as the last of the dark was drawn away and the dawning sky was revealed, pink and leafed with clouds. When the baby was done eating it seemed to crumble in upon itself, and for a terrible moment he thought that the infant had died, until, by the movement of its tiny fingers, it became clear that the boy was only sleeping.

He went inside and pulled a small black lacquer box off the shelf and from this box removed an ivory comb, yellowed with age and impossibly delicate. The comb's handle was carved in the shape of a kneeling woman, her hands folded in prayer. She wore a long gown with flowers on the fringe, and her hair was plaited into two flowing tresses on either side of her face beneath a tiny crown. It was ancient, this comb, having belonged to his mother and before that to a Queen of England.

He sat near the head of the bed and began to comb the tangles from his wife's hair. She had thrashed all night and the odor of stale sweat hung in the room, mixing with the plummy tang of blood. He spoke softly to her and touched her face often as he ran the comb through her hair, parting it at the scalp and arranging it on either side down her shoulders like the woman

5

on the comb. Then he straightened her body in the bed, arranging her arms across her breasts so that her palms met in an attitude of prayer.

When this was done he took a dead black ember from the fire and, using a nail, mixed it with some of the goat's milk in a tin cup. He pulled the Bible off the shelf, lifted the age-slackened cover of the heavy book, and, using the nail as a quill, beneath the names of long-dead others wrote:

Rachel Bright
1900–1920
Wife of Henry Bright

He lifted the nail from the page and surveyed the grisly black scrawl of the epitaph. Outside, the horse began to slap its tail against the trunk of the chestnut tree. He dipped the nail once more in the ink and added:

Mother to the Future King of Heaven

When this was done he held the Bible open on his knee and read the other names, but, except for his mother and father's and his aunt Rebecca's, they were all strangers to him. As he read, his hand worried absently through the pages and pulled a thistle from between the leaves where it had marked, like new grass over a grave, some passage that had been special to his mother. He looked now for the page, but it was lost to him, and he threw the thistle to the coals.

He went to the cabin door and looked out on the child, then gazed up to the hills again, watching them closely. Nothing but the quantity of the light upon the canvassed green trees had changed. He retrieved the long-handled shovel that he had last used for mucking out the chicken hutch and walked beneath the dark spread of the chestnut tree to where his horse stood.

"Now git," he said. The horse was standing directly above where he wished to bury his wife. "Now *git*," he said again, and pushed himself against the horse's shoulder.

"We have to go from here," said the horse. "We have to take the Future King of Heaven and leave."

"Why?"

"That will be made known to you in due time, Henry Bright. First we have to leave this place. You will burn it down." The horse bent to the patch of timothy grass and pulled up on it, munching with a broad satisfaction.

"Where are we gonna live if we burn it down?" Bright watched the plate-shaped muscles of the big jaws working.

"That will be answered once we leave," said the angel.

Bright's eyes wandered over the cabin he had grown up in. His father had gone away to the coal mines to earn money before Henry was born and had died in a cave-in, leaving his wife to raise their son amid a wilderness of tendrils and gnats that seemed always on the verge of devouring the little house. Much later, after his mother died and Henry had gone off to the War, the chimney had returned itself to the land, becoming a tunnel of vines and birds' nests so thick that the first time he had tried to cook over the fire after he came back, the smoke had driven him outside and the mourning doves had thrown themselves from the eaves to the ground in confused jumbles. Sometimes, as they lay in bed at night, it had seemed to Rachel and him as if the whole cabin was hurtling at great speed through the dark, so loudly did the wind wail through the chinks in the caulking.

"Why do you want me to burn it down?" he asked again. "That's our house. We ain't got any other house."

"Then stay here—"

"My boy needs a roof over his head."

"—and let your son die."

Bright shoved the animal again, to little effect. The horse stood its ground. "We can leave, angel, but I ain't gonna burn it down!" he yelled. "It's all I got left!"

On the stump behind him, the baby began to cry. Bright whirled around, shielding his own tears from the horse's view. He stood with his back to the angel for a long time, his shoulders jerking violently at first and then slowing to a composed rise and fall. He ran the back of a hand across his face and looked at the cabin.

"Henry Bright," the angel said, finally breaking the silence, "do as I say."

The back of Bright's head fell forward as his chin sank to his chest. "I can't believe this," he said. "All right. All right, I'll burn it down."

He ran a hand across his face again and then, turning back, he gave the horse a final push and the animal stubbornly relinquished his ground. Then he set about digging a grave for his wife next to that of his mother. When he was knee-deep in the ground, he heard the baby begin to cry again, and so he climbed up from the hole and moved the basket out of the sunlight. He fed the boy with the goat's milk again and returned to digging. When he had finished the grave, he went inside and cut his wife out of her clothes.

Opening the large trunk, he looked down at what to dress her in. The white dress lay there, its stiff collar holding up determinedly against desperate age and the fungal dampness of high July. He reached beneath this garment to where the slip, with its tiny lace eyelets, waited primly. He had bought the slip for her in Fells Corner, an extravagant wedding gift that was almost the only thing she had worn until she was finally too big with child even for it to fit. It glowed out at him with a spectral

8

whiteness in the ill-lit lowness of the cabin. After that came the brutal, delicate task of getting her stiffening body into the garment, but when he was done he again arranged her beautiful hair on either side of her shoulders, the way he liked it best. Finally, he opened the black lacquer box once more and removed a length of golden ribbon. He tied it around her head like a crown and stood up to survey his work.

He'd dug enough graves to know that she would fit perfectly into this one, but even so he stood there with her body in his arms, a rack of painful hesitation as he considered taking a few planks from the cabin in order to build her a box that would keep her from ending up so dirty.

"There's no time!" the horse nickered behind him, as if it knew his mind, which perhaps it did. "Leave her buried deep and let's go."

He sat at the edge of the grave, his legs hanging into the hole, and dropped her in. He whispered something down at her, then he stood up and began to shovel in the dirt as a preacher might baptize someone in frigid water: quickly, to overcome the shock of the cold. He began to cry again. While he worked, the horse stood nearby, dark and still, perhaps gone to sleep. He filled the grave and then knelt, spreading leaves and sticks over the slight mound. The heat was coming on hard now, and sweat ran over his brow and into his eyes before continuing down his face and neck in the long, dusty canals that had already been carved by his tears.

When he stood up from the grave, he went to the cabin flap and pulled a handful of corn kernels from a sack hanging just inside the doorway where the animals could not get at it. Then he stood in the yard near the chickens. Stock-still, his arms hanging loosely at his sides, he let a few of the kernels fall from between his fingers. The three birds pecked at the kernels and then looked up, pinning him against the sky with their tiny black eyes and waiting for more. He chose the hen he would try for, and when it looked up at him again he let a few more kernels fall. When he and Rachel had been small, they used to play with the chicks in the yard of the elderly couple his mother had cooked for. Rachel liked to hold the little yellow things against the nape of her neck and would laugh as their feathers tickled her. He would lie very still on his back and they would see how many she could put on his chest.

The third time Bright let the kernels fall, the chickens did not look up but busily went about their feeding. He bent quickly, grabbed the hen by its head, and broke its neck. The goat watched on without emotion from atop her perch.

He plucked the body quickly, then went inside and placed it on a spit above the embers of the dying fire. He brought the baby in and laid it on the bed where it might survey the room it was born in. Maybe someday the Future King of Heaven would need to describe his own humble beginnings.

He took off his dirty clothes and put on the uniform that he had worn home from the War. His fingertips touched at the bullet hole in the jacket's shoulder as his eyes searched the cabin for what he would need and what he could carry: a haversack, his woolen blanket and greatcoat, the spare shirt, underclothes, a toothbrush, a cup, matches, a cook skillet, a fork; and his mother's ivory comb. The bucket would hang over the pommel along with the sack of corn. He took a length of fishing line and hooks and tried laying them flat between the pages of the Bible, but upon hefting the heavy book he decided against taking it with him and replaced it on the shelf. He piled the rest of his traveling possessions at the feet of the horse, then looked up at the ridge warily once more, searching the forest for faces. He thought of his mother's rifle, but of course it was gone, so he went back inside and sat in the cabin for the last time, feeding the child with his trigger finger dipped in the goat's milk and waiting for the chicken to finish cooking.

The sun was high above its cradle in the crook of the mountains by the time he was finally ready to depart. The cabin, stripped of his wife and his few possessions, sat there in naked impoverishment, a sorry matchbox devoid even of matches. He had cut the stiff white dress into strips, fashioning the swath that had been its bodice into a sling that he hung around his neck to carry the child. The other strips he had slathered in the grease of the cooked chicken and placed in the corners of the house. He had only a small ration of matches and he had never been the kind to waste a match anyhow, so once he'd placed the rags in the corners of the room, he lit one and carefully carried the guarded flame from one pile to the next until each was aflame. Then he walked out to the yard and stood by his horse to watch the cabin burn.

"It's not going to go."

"It will. I can start a fire without a angel."

"You can't do anything without a angel."

"It'll go," he said. "You watch."

"Get the Bible."

Bright scuffed the ground with a boot. "You're always telling me we don't need the Bible no more! Haven't you been saying that since we met? That the King of Heaven is bad and we need a new one and all that?"

"What you say is true."

"So how'm I supposed to understand you if you keep changing what you say? First we don't need the Bible and now we do?"

"Henry Bright, go back inside and use the Bible to help start the fire. Now."

"Rachel died," he said. He swatted at a fly that was tickling his face.

11

"And you are grieving."

"Yeah." He pulled the child from the basket and put it in the sling around his neck.

"I understand. Now go back in and don't come out until the fire is started."

He stared incredulously at the angel a moment, but the horse just looked placidly ahead at the dark cabin as if waiting for a page to turn. Bright stalked across the dirt yard to the flap, lifted it perfunctorily, and peered inside. The rags sat in the corners of the room, smoking sullenly. He did not look back at the horse but entered the cabin, took the Bible down off the shelf, and began to tear its pages out, crumpling page after page into yellowed knuckles of parchment, finally throwing the ransacked book facedown on the bed when he'd harvested enough. He placed the paper in piles above the smoldering rags and then, twisting a few remaining sheets of Leviticus into a brand, he lit the piles once more.

He rejoined the horse in the yard. It looked at him smugly but said nothing as the dried wood of the cabin popped into flames. Henry Bright bit his fist as the fire took hold. Then, lowering his chin to his chest, he let his eyes rest on the tiny face of his son, the Future King of Heaven.

2

Mud and water and the stumps of trees. In every direction that was all there was. Bodies fell, but the trees died standing up. Nightly they were crucified upon themselves by the zip and whine of machine guns, their leaves corroded by gas, their branches and trunks hacked for kindling, some roots cut by en-trenching tools, others drowned by the ceaseless, steady drip-dripping of blood and rain. Back home, these waning days of September could seem at times like one long sunset, the oak and hickory forest a blaze of yellow, orange, and red leaves. Here, it was impossible to tell by the trees what season it was; any that were still standing had nothing left to give away.

They'd been told that the Argonne would remind them of home, but as they'd moved ever closer to the front line, from transport trains to dirt roads to muddy tracks to brutal gashes in the ground, the greenery had disintegrated around them until finally the only tree that Henry Bright could see from where he was squatting in his trench was a barkless and bone-white totem thirty yards distant. This tree, too, had to go, because someone important far back of the line had decided that German gun-ners must be using it to site their long-range artillery. Perhaps this was so, but the line had been ebbing and flowing around the tree for so long now that it was just as likely that the very same someone important had simply grown tired of looking at it through binoculars all day. Regardless, an order had just come down to Sergeant Carlson that he and three other men were to blow it up when the night was at its pitchest black.

Bright tore a sheet from *The Stars and Stripes* lying nearby where he rested his haunches against the trench wall. He scanned it:

> If we laugh at the cooties when they come, and hunt
> them with the same merriment that the French hunt
> the wild boar, the joke will be on them after all, for they
> do not laugh back. And then they won't seem half so
> bad. Laughter is a good insecticide!

He cleaned himself as best he could and pulled his britches back up, then made his way down the narrow length of trench to the zag. Here he angled a sharp right, squeezing by a lumpy yellow-haired kid named Bert plodding in the opposite direction. A few moments later he heard the boy turn and slosh through the mud to catch up behind him.

"Hey, what's the idea, Bright? That was a paper for all us boys to read! How long's it gonna last anyway, if everybody comes along and wipes their ass with it?" He waited for an answer from Bright and got none. Bert seemed younger than the rest of the men, or if not younger, at least pinker. He seemed made of pinkness. His father was a banker in Wheeling. Around the next zag, some of the others had finished pulling the sandbags from a portion of the trench wall and were now hollowing out a cavity in which to bury McCauliff and Standish. The two men had been shot by a sniper within a few moments of each other, just before noon. Bert squeezed between Bright and the trench wall, raising his voice so that the men digging could hear him. "So, Bright went and wiped his ass with

14

the newspaper again," he said, as if it was some sort of common occurrence for there to be paper of any kind lying about.

"Who's got paper?" one of the others said. "I need a few pages. Let me see 'em, Bert."

"I need pages too!"

"How'd it stay so dry?"

"This is all that's left," Bert said. "I was too late to save the rest." He waved the unused portion of *The Stars and Stripes* above his head for everyone to see. The paper exploded in his hand as a bullet tore through the pages.

"Jee-roosh!" Bert jerked his arm below the lip of the trench. His eyes were the size and shine of quarters as he looked at the remnants of the newspaper in his hand. He let the scraps fall to the mud and turned dejectedly back down the trench in the direction of the latrine. Everyone else, Bright included, finished burying McCauliff and Standish in the wall of the trench. Then they all sat there waiting for something, or nothing, to happen.

Five hours after darkness fell, they sat in lines against the trench wall and listened to the random fire of ammunition for miles to either side. It began to rain again, though at times star shells would brightly illuminate the ground, as if the moon were making bayonet lunges at the earth. The rain slapped at the soil in weary, unwelcome applause. Finally, Sergeant Carlson heaved himself off the trench wall. Bright and two others did the same, dressing themselves in the dung-colored burlap they wore in order to blend in against the hummocked and devastated ground of the battlefield. They climbed over the top of the trench and out into the open, moving slowly on their bellies as if the slurry of mud and bodies, wire and spent casings, were in reality only a thin layer of ice that might at any moment shatter and fall away into an abyss beneath them.

The dynamite was strapped to Bright's back, and Sergeant

15

Carlson had the fuse on a spool tied to his belt. The other two, just in front of them, had wire cutters. They had blacked their bayonets and entrenching tools over a cook flame so that the metal edges would not glint out of the darkness and give them away to the opposite line. They wore no helmets for the same reason. They would dig small holes at the base of the tree and deposit the dynamite. Then they would unspool the fuse, setting a light to it once they were back in their own trench.

It took almost an hour to cover a distance of thirty yards. There were bodies everywhere, mostly from an earlier failed advance on a group of machine-gun emplacements. After the advance had been repulsed, stretcher bearers from both sides had gone into the field to collect the wounded and had been shot; now the bodies lay there in jumbles to be crawled over. There was much wire to cut, and the ground was cratered hell-ishly, but at length they reached the tree as the rain began to ease to a drizzle. Carlson untied the bundle of dynamite from Bright's back and handed the first stick to the next man, so that he could in turn hand it to the next man to place in the hole. Bright lay still on his stomach, his arms outstretched in front of him, his body pressed flat against the earth.

In front of him suddenly the air felt strange, and then without warning one of his hands was cupping a face. Its features froze in his hand for an awful moment before whispering something. It whispered again, louder this time, and at the sound of the voice the others around Bright went still. If the alarm was raised on either line guns on both sides would open up.

"Shoosh," the voice said, almost a sigh. The War seemed to fall silent at the voice of the German soldier and darkness lay around it like a pack of bristling, dreaming dogs.

A star shell hissed upward and turned the sky to tin. Bright did not close his eyes. Instead, he looked directly into the eyes of the man's face in his hand. On either side of the face, four other men were also pressed tightly to the ground. The man looked steadily back into Bright's eyes as the light flared and then subsided.

"Shoosh," Sergeant Carlson himself whispered after a dark age. He said it calmly, and it was returned calmly, the word bouncing quietly around in the darkness until Bright felt the face in his hand speak it as well once more. He pulled away and the party pushed back from the tree, Sergeant Carlson unspooling the fuse as they retreated. Bright made out the scuffle of fabric and the soft tink of metal as the soldiers on the other side did likewise. Less than an hour later, back in the trench, Carlson and the other two men smoked and talked lowly while Bright sat on a wet duckboard and stared at the nothingness of the trench wall.

"Jee-roosh!" Bert, who hadn't gone, said to no one in particular.

They waited perhaps ten minutes more and then Carlson lit the fuse. Even as he did, though, the tree exploded up into the night sky with a tremendous crack. A second and third blast told them that the German dynamite had gone off. They listened to the hooting of the men across the field, and watched their own fuse crawl like a lost lightning bug over the ground, finally detonating its charges beneath the wrecked stump of the tree.

3

Henry Bright had seen many buildings burn in France during the War, but this did not seem to lessen his surprise at the sudden gusts of heat that washed over him and his newborn boy as the cabin blossomed into flames. The roof shingling was first to catch, blazing upward with terrifying speed. The incendiary heat quickly consumed this kindling, and the remainder of the roof collapsed down inside the thick log walls of the cabin, throwing sparks and burning pieces of wood into the air as it did so. The she-goat, who had not been to the War but had earned, by any honest estimation, a hard-won reputation for composure in the last several months, lost the last reserves of her calm and burst out with a serrated bleat of alarm. She tugged against her tether as the horse canted back onto its hind legs in fright. Bright struggled to hold the leads of both animals as he watched the sparks climb into the air. Then it seemed that even the fire caught fire. In the space of a few moments there were three smaller blazes burning at the periphery of the farmyard, one of which had begun to crawl over the chicken hutch on its way toward the graves of his wife and mother. He tried to rush forward in order to stomp out the blaze, but the leads by which he held his frightened livestock were far too short and he could not reach the fire without letting the animals go. The pe-

18

ripheral branches of the big chestnut tree began to wither and brown, falling to the ground like burning feathers. The young chestnuts popped in their spiky shells, exploding in the angry swell of heat. Then, with a howl, the whole tree was aflame.

"What the hell did you make me do!?" Bright shouted at the angel over the roar, but the horse was twisting and stamping at the ground and would not answer. Bright gave a tremendous pull on its lead. The horse fought him for a few seconds, dancing in panic as the goat darted this way and that. He finally got the horse around somehow, tugging it and the goat into the cool safety of the woods to the east.

There was a short rise half a mile away, and he tied the animals to a tree and walked to the top. A steady floral breeze was blowing at his back and had already pushed the fire below from the chestnut tree to a silver maple nearby. The wood burned in a plume of viscous, greasy heat that shot into the sky like a column of dirty water. He turned and walked back down the rise, the familiar, low rumble of combustion beginning its muttering in his ears.

He did not speak as he untethered the horse and goat from the tree, and the horse, for its part, allowed itself to be ridden into the depths of the woods without a struggle. For all its earlier shows of panic, it now seemed deaf to the buzzing alarm that was spreading through the forest canopy. For the next few miles it clomped along with the maddening contentedness of an old dray taking the pumpkins to town. Once or twice it tried to chomp at the clumps of grass along its path, but Bright pulled back sharply on the reins each time, cursing the angel under his breath.

"Last time I let a goddamn angel help me start a goddamn fire," he said. "He makes fun of me, tells me I can't start a fire without a angel, and then that very angel goes and burns the whole goddamn forest down." He rode along in silence for a piece more. "Goddamn it," he added. A voluptuous purple-headed thistle drew the horse off to the right, but Bright jerked it back.

"It was you who started the fire, Henry Bright, not me."

"It's gonna burn the whole goddamn forest! Ain't you gonna do something?"

"What can I do?"

"It was you told me to set it. Now you don't know what to do with it?"

"I didn't tell you to set the whole forest on fire, only the cabin," the horse sighed as it ambled along. "Sadly, there's no stopping it now. But have heart, Henry Bright."

"But ain't the Colonel going to see the smoke? You know he will."

"I know he will."

Bright pulled back on the reins and the horse came to a stop. "You do?"

"Of course I do. I know everything, Henry Bright."

"But we don't want him to see the smoke, I thought. 'Cause he'll know something's on fire and he'll come over the mountain, him and his boys."

"And what will they find?"

Bright looked down at his own son, who had stopped crying for the moment. "He won't find nothing, because the whole goddamn forest is gonna be burned down," he said.

"And what will the Colonel and his sons think then?"

"That we're dead. Both me and Rachel," he said. "Burned up in the fire."

"And your son?"

"Him too. They'll think he's dead too." He bit his fist. "Do you think they'll really think that? That we all just got burned up in the fire?"

"The fire started in the early morning while you and your

20

wife were still asleep. By the time the conflagration had passed over, there was nothing to show that you or she and her unborn child had ever existed. It was a tragedy."

"And you think they'll believe that? The Colonel is gonna believe that?"

"Why would he not?"

"Well, for one thing, he's had Corwin and Duncan watching us."

"How do you know?"

"'Cause I saw them. Up on the ridge in the winter, when there was no leaves on the trees. They were just sitting there looking at me one time. And then even last week I saw Duncan. He was on his belly there in the shadows underneath the ferns by the side of the road. I think the Colonel was waiting for my boy to be born. I think he wants to take my boy away from me."

The angel said nothing to this and Bright mused a while in the saddle, rolling the terrible notion in his mind. The horse made another foray, this time into a stand of nettles, and Bright, lost in his reverie, permitted it.

They rode on for several more hours, the light shifting and dappling, the humidity settling around them like a warm, wet sigh, until at length they came to a rill and followed it down a long hillside to where it emptied itself into a fast-running stream. Here they stopped and he removed the baby from the sling around his chest and placed it on the ground. He stripped off his shirt, and, dipping both shirt and sling in the cool water, he rubbed the fabrics together until the mess the boy had made was gone. The baby wailed as he dunked its hindquarters in the flow, but it quieted some after he laid it upon the woolen blanket. By the time he had milked the goat, the last portion of sunlight was being sopped up by the low moon, and the stars were beginning to show on the plate beneath. He tied the horse to a chokecherry and the goat to a peeling ninebark near the water.

It was muggy, but he unpacked his greatcoat anyway and, sitting on the ground, wrapped himself and the child in the garment, more for relief from the mosquitoes than from any cold. With his finger, he fed the boy from the milk and with his other hand ate a piece of the chicken that he'd wrapped in a few pages from the Book of Jeremiah. Then Henry Bright lay back and thought about Rachel, the delicate shells of her ears, the pinkness of her tongue, the way she laughed in her sleep. The tiny body of his son slept silent and warm in the crook of one arm, and he kept very still lest he should wake the boy.

4

With the tree gone, the world went aimless for the next several days. Shots were taken at whatever happened to rise above the bags that lined the trenches, but even the bodies of the men who were hit seemed bored by the tedium of the killings and fell to the ground with more listlessness than violence. Of course there were always the punctual, workmanlike exchanges of shelling, shooting, and maiming, called "the hate," at the beginning and ending of each day, but by now these were ritual, and no one paid them much mind.

Bright's company was relieved and went to sit in the dirty basements of eviscerated villages under the watchful eyes of old women. Everyone had fleas. Bert argued with whoever would listen to him, mostly about whether chickens could get the cooties. Finally someone had gone out in the yard and killed a bird, brought it in, and inspected it. There had been no fleas. Behind a basket of onions in a nook that served as a kitchen, Bright found a small patch of plaster wall so white that it seemed supernatural, a solitary untouched thing in the whole wet and muddy world. He stared hard at it while the others smoked cigarettes and slept around him. They were moved from the basement back to the reserve trenches, and he resumed watching the treeless early October sky with the same intensity as he had the wall in the old woman's house. Shells burst around him, but they burst around everyone. Many had caught the flu, and there was coughing at all hours. Some suffocated in the night from the infection in their lungs. Men came back from the field hospitals looking sicker than when they had left for them. They died of fevers in the cold, their bodies shivering so violently beneath sodden blankets that it seemed their bones might break. It was not unusual to wake and find the man sitting next to you dead; the War had become something so powerful that it could kill without wounding. On occasion even Henry Bright smoked, but not often.

Back he moved to the front line, and, one morning, the hate was louder and longer than normal, and he began to clean his rifle with his toothbrush and then fix his bayonet in preparation to go over the bags. The word being passed around was that the village in front of them had been relinquished in the night. Some speculated that it was a trap, that this portion of the line was playing possum, luring in as many as they could in order to surround them in one last, desperate attempt to turn the tide of the War. Farther south, another rumor had it, an entire German company of starving old men and young boys had surrendered en masse. Some held that this would be the final push, that the Kaiser had had it and the German army was collapsing. Still, if this was the case, no one in charge was saying so, and until they did say so, the only thing that mattered was the village that lay before them a little ways distant, close enough that the white steeple of its church could be seen peeking out above a small rise of hills.

His mother had died during a windstorm that made the trees bow to one another like ballroom dancers. He had buried her in the whipping rain and then trudged through the mud to Fells Corner for nails with which to patch the holes where the singles had blown off the cabin's roof. The hardware man had measured out the nails, offered his condolences, and then asked Bright if he'd considered signing up to go to the War. The hardware man had been made a registration officer with the responsibility of signing up men to go across the sea to avenge the women and children of the *Lusitania,* to make the world safe for Democracy, to defend France, and, lastly, to aid England. With his mother dead, there was nothing really to stay for. Bright had signed his name, listened wordlessly to the instructions the man gave him, and then headed back to the cabin with an extra portion of nails for being the first to sign up in the book. It had been as easy as falling in a river.

In early March 1918, he hid his mother's rifle in the rafters above the bed, used the extra portion of nails to cover the door frame against the weather and wilderness, and then walked to the train depot in Fells Corner. He was mustered at a camp in Virginia with a company of gangly and goosenecked men and boys. By late April they were on their way to France.

Feeling for the War was high, as was excitement over the ocean voyage. Men showed it in different ways. Some told stories of their valor in advance. Others prayed and gave up vices. Most wrote letters of some kind to be mailed home upon their arrival, and a chaplain assigned to their unit tried to get everyone's soul in order. He was most concerned about the Catholics of France. "You stay the hell out of those churches, boys," he would shout as they went to sleep. "You just walk the other way. There ain't nothing those Catholics can give you except fleas and the clap. You need anything, you want to unburden your soul, you come to me or you go to the YMCA." He was naturally red in the face and, according to Sergeant Carlson, accidentally shot himself during a training exercise, only two weeks after their boat had landed in France.

They entered the War like men stepping out from beneath an awning into a torrential thunderstorm. The first man that Bright saw die fell back down into the very trench from which he'd just climbed. His uniform was still fresh and the tops of his boots had been shined. Only the soles looked muddy.

5

Bright rode on throughout the next day, following the stream and keeping to the hug of a range of foothills where the canopy of hickory was thickest and there was less chance of being seen. He took short breaks to water the horse and to feed the child from the thin skim of goat's milk in the bucket tied to the saddle pommel. As the sun began to slip behind him, he tethered the horse near an ess in the stream. A few deep-brown trout grazed fatly in the dark holds beneath a stretch of half-submerged hemlock trunk that had fallen across the water. He unswaddled his son, walked out on the trunk with the boy, and knelt down as he had done the previous night to dunk the boy's naked hindquarters in the water. The child meeped and mewed up at him as he laid it on the ground. He walked out onto the trunk once again to wash the diaper, but this time as he stooped to the stream he lost his balance and toppled headfirst into the water. He stood up spluttering, thoroughly soaked, and, reaching into his pocket, found the matches ruined.

He stood there, waist-deep and dripping, looking down into his palm at them. Then he let them fall from his hand to float away like tiny boats in the current. He sloshed through the churned silt to the steep lip of the bank and pulled himself up next to his boy. The child's feathery red hair fell thinly across its

27

knobbled head in the style of a middle-aged auctioneer or feed-store man. The same coppery color gave the boy a pair of sharp little eyebrows that scrunched and relaxed and then scrunched again as if, behind those tightly locked eyelids, he was figuring a sum of arithmetic. The intricacy of the boy's ears and the translucence of his tiny nostrils already bore the stamp of Rachel's beauty. His face was so unlike the faces of the infants Bright had seen frolicking among the painted clouds of a certain church back in France. It was a good, open face, without malevolence or mischief. Bright rolled onto his back and re-garded the sweeping trees above. At length he pulled himself to his feet, stripped naked, and hung his clothes up on some low-hanging branches to dry.

When the father and son returned to camp, the horse took one look at Henry Bright's pale, stem-thin body and snorted. Bright ignored the animal and set about clearing a patch of ground, arranging the woolen blanket, and laying the child upon it. Next he set the goat loose and watched her forage, by which way she led him to a mulberry bush, a serviceberry bush with a few precious berries that had somehow escaped the no-tice of the birds, and a gnarled old crab apple tree, loaded down with tight, bitter green fruit. He ate with as little com-punction as the goat. He had fishing line, but without matches there would be no campfire. Perhaps that was just as well; an-other fire, one that might betray their whereabouts to the Colonel and his sons, could be even more disastrous than the fire the angel had made him set in order to burn the cabin down. He ate the unripe crab apples and milked the goat, feed-ing the boy from the bucket and leaving aside a good portion from which to feed him again in the night when the child awoke hungry.

As Bright made ready to sleep, the horse's derisive humor de-scended into contempt. It stared darkly from out of a purple and malignant silence as Bright curled his naked form closely around his son. The boy muzzled into Bright's chest. Bright noticed the angel's scornfulness, and though he said nothing, he stared back at the horse from the darkness with a like animus.

He sat up again suddenly. "What did you call me?"

The horse chuffed the air. "What do you mean?"

"You called me something." Bright flicked the ground with his hand. "You wanna call me names, you just say 'em loud enough for me to hear 'em."

"You are mistaken, Henry Bright."

Bright whipped his jacket over his child's nakedness and then, with a final deathly stare, he rolled over to face away from the animal. Around them in the forest thrummed the ordinary night sounds, but beneath those came the ossiary click as Henry Bright's jaws worked to eat the sounds deep down in his throat that might betray his great grief at the death of his wife, his foolhardy destruction of their home, and the wildfire that had ensued. He thought fearfully of being discovered in the night by the Colonel and his cruel sons and, as he bit the knuckles of his fist, the bitterness of the crab apples he had eaten mixed against his tongue with the sour shame of being mocked by his own horse.

6

"You said we were going to be married?" Rachel asked expectantly out of the darkness. She sat in front of him astride the horse as they left the Colonel's house behind.

"We will," Bright said.

"Oh, good. I hate this thing." She began to tear at her ragged white dress. A bundle of thread tangled out from the shoulder, where a bow had once blossomed. On the other shoulder the bow was still hanging on, but it drooped lifelessly. "Can't wait to get it off." By the motion of her arm he could tell that she was tugging the dirty stretch of silk that ran between her neckline and her breasts.

"Don't you tear at that thing," he said, letting go of the horse's rein to pull her arm down and her hand away from the garment. "We ain't married yet and I ain't got nothing else for you to wear."

"So?"

"So, you can't get married naked, can you? When was the last time you ever heard of anyone getting married naked?"

She giggled at this, as if he hadn't just ridden his horse through the front door of the Colonel's house and stolen her away. "Are we going to get married real soon?" she asked again.

"I said we were, didn't I? Didn't I just tell you that?"

"Real, real soon, then?" There came a ripping sound, and a scrap of white fabric floated to the ground. The horse snorted.

Bright brushed the girl's hands away from her dress once more. "Yes. Now stop tearing at that. Take your hands away and stop messing with it!"

Dawn was breaking as they melted out of the darkness of the woods and into the tenuous circle of habitation that he had reclaimed from the wilderness in the month since he'd returned from the War.

She got down from the horse and stood in the center of it all, surveying the little farmyard expectantly as Bright looped the animal's tether loosely around the chestnut tree and then went to the stream to dunk his head in the water. He came up gasping from the cold.

"You might want to wash yourself too," he said, rubbing an arm across his forehead as he looked at her. "Get cleaned up a bit." The girl stood where she was. He disappeared into the cabin and came back with a clean shirt on.

"You ain't washed up yet," he said. "You're filthy, girl. Goddamn." In the morning light the girl's face and hands had lost the marble whiteness with which they'd glowed in the gloom of the previous evening.

"Stay there," he said. "I'm going to get the Bible. Will you stay right there?"

"I'll stay. I'll stay right here with this tired old horse. He's a nice horse. Aren't you a nice horse?" She reached up to scratch the animal's ears.

"You don't need a Bible," the horse said. "Come here and stand near the bride."

He immediately turned around and came to stand near Rachel.

"I thought you were going to get the Bible," she said.

"We don't need it."

31

"Ask the bride her name."

"Her name's Rachel!" he burst out. "You know that's her name! She's all you been talking about!" Then, remembering that she was standing right there beside him, he ducked his chin to his chest and looked at her bare feet. "I been talking about you to my horse," he said, forcing a chuckle out.

"You have?" The girl giggled as she stroked the horse's head.

"You must ask the girl her full name. This is a sacred ceremony."

"For God's sake." Bright stomped a foot on the ground.

"What?" Rachel asked.

"Nothing." Bright sighed. "What's your name, Rachel? Your full name, is what I mean."

"It's Miss Rachel Stallsworth Murtry Marion Morse," she said, and then, unaccountably, "On account of us being Catholic on the Lady Stallsworth's side."

"What does that mean?" he asked, perhaps to the horse and perhaps to the girl.

"I don't know," the girl said.

The horse said nothing.

"Well, now it's Bright and you're my wife, unless somebody has problems with that," he said significantly, "somebody who makes me go all over the country riding up inside other people's houses, and stealing people's daughters." He spoke expectoratingly into the big face of the horse.

The animal ran its velvet muzzle along the pale floe of the girl's collarbone and paid Bright no mind.

"Well," he said, putting his hands on his hips, "you gonna forever hold your peace, or what?"

The horse snuffled with evident pleasure in the girl's scraggled hair. The girl shied flirtatiously from its attentions.

Bright burrowed his eyes like bullet holes into the animal as it tossed its head for the girl's amusement. After a long moment of silence, he continued. "All right. Then I guess we're married now."

He took Rachel by the hand and pulled her away from the lecherous animal's ears mid-scratch. "Over there"—he motioned toward the cabin—"is where we live. There's where the chickens live. You always been good with them. Those are the goats. This here is a beaten-down old farm horse with no sense in it at all." He was about to point out the stream but she had already begun walking toward it, not even stopping as she pulled the dress over her head and let it fall forgotten on the bank. Then she was wriggling in the icy water. When she stood, the water halfway up her calves, Henry Bright looked upon her naked body for the first time. She bent her head to the stream, dunking it, and then straightened, looking frankly at him as she twisted the water from her hair.

7

You were never to run when advancing. You were to move at a slow and steady pace that allowed the artillery behind you to fire over your head and clear the way for you. Of course, when the ground at your feet exploded it was impossible to tell whether the barrage was coming from in front of you or behind you, so you forgot about slowly advancing and you ran, you ran right into the gun barrels of whoever was there in front of you.

When the order was given, the men climbed the lip of the trench and were soon running across the field. There was always much screaming when this happened, and even Bright would find his mouth hanging open and releasing sounds that he could never quite catch up with and that he could never quite remember afterward. He never looked down no matter what he felt himself stepping on. The fields in between the trenches were wind-whipped ponds of bodies, and even though the bodies were dead they could still pull you down with them; the dead were hungry that way. This morning, with the white beacon of the church in the distance marking the location of the village toward which they were to advance, he climbed out from behind the bags and ran keening and lurching across the dead world of cold limbs and helmets and faces with forgotten names. He had done this before, but this time something felt

34

different. To either side men should have been falling by now. Instead, two had gotten tangled in the barbed wire and a third was frantically trying to cut them loose with a wire cutter. Bright continued on, expecting at any moment to be shot, but as he got ever closer and was not cut down, it became evident that the trenches that lay between them and the village had been surrendered.

After the ragged and slapdash improvisation of their own dwellings, the deserted German trenches were a wonder to behold. Cut much deeper into the ground than the American and French ones, they were reinforced against the shifting mud with concrete. There was a regularity to their construction as well, as if they had been designed dispassionately by some crisp gray architect rather than a panicked animal with a short shovel. A man of average height could almost stand upright in a few of the rooms, and the German soldiers who lived in them, far below the clamor of artillery barrages above, must have experienced, in quieter moments, the same placid satisfaction that brown trout feel as they dream away far beneath the rain-addled surface.

Uniform artillery gaps between the sandbags afforded a clear view of the cavitied village in front of them. The little cluster of buildings seemed far less worthy of defense than the snug bunkers that Henry Bright and his companions now found themselves in.

They scoured the trench for souvenirs but there was little left to take. A couple of large skillets had been abandoned, their weight disqualifying them as items to accompany rapid retreat. There were indecipherable books and a few utensils. Bright was holding an empty cracker tin when a shot rang out. Twenty yards off the trench cut sharply left, then right. Rounding the turn, he saw a wooden door that had swung wide from the trench wall. He crept up to it and, peering around the doorway, found himself looking directly down the black pupil of a pistol barrel. He squeezed the trigger of his own gun reflexively, firing a bullet into the ground between Bert's feet.

"Whoa, Bright! Whoa!" Bert said. "It's me! It's me!" He lowered the pistol he had been pointing at Bright. "Jee-roosh! You trying to kill me or what?"

Three others came around the corner, rifles at the ready. Bright set his own down and sagged back against the trench wall, rubbing his knees and breathing deep.

"It's all right, boys!" Bert called out. "Bright's got an itchy trigger finger is all! Hey, look! I got one! An officer!" Behind him in the room was a man in a wooden swiveling office chair, his head thrown back, his mouth drawn open as if in mid-snore. There was a hole blasted in the side of his head and another one in his stomach.

Carlson pushed through the others in the narrow doorway. "What the hell happened?"

"I came round this corner and found the door open," Bert said. "I crept on up and this big Fritzy in the chair here had his pistol pointed at me. He had a bead on me but I was faster, yessir, I was! I blew him away before he had the chance to pull the trigger!" He held up the officer's pistol that he'd pointed at Bright. "And just look at this! Jee-roosh!"

Carlson took a look at the dead man. "Christ, Bert. How long was this fella dead before you killed him?"

Bert purpled. "You saying I'm lying, Sergeant? You saying I didn't shoot this Fritzy?"

"No. You shot him, Bert." The sergeant started to laugh. "You shot him for sure." He turned to Bright, still leaning leadenly against the trench wall. "You all right?" he asked. Bright nodded his head and took a cigarette one of the other men offered him. "Christ," Carlson sighed finally. "I wish I could be there when you tell this story, Bert." He pushed back through the group of soldiers, and one by one they all turned and followed him up the trench. After a moment Bright, too, stood and made his way to rejoin the others, leaving Bert to stand alone in the doorway, eyes downcast, absentmindedly swinging the officer's pistol at his side.

A short time later the bells in the village church tower began to peal. Bright and the others climbed from the trench and made their way through a pocket of eerie calm toward the clanging. Almost every building had been reduced to rubble. A few thick arches were still standing, and here and there perched the precarious remnants of rooftops, their jagged beams exposed like broken bones. Rising above the chaos of the ruined town, however, stood the church, miraculously spared, its slender steeple chastely white and incongruous with the garish tolling coming from within. A handful of pebble-eyed women and children hid in the shadows, peering out at the new arrivals as they made their way across the town square and toward the source of the bells.

8

Bright lay awake and tried to listen through the night sounds for the vengeful tread of boots. Instead, he was almost sure that he heard the fire, rumbling so low and far off that perhaps it was only the blood rushing in his temples. The baby awoke three times in the night, and each time Bright sat up and rocked the boy in his arms and nursed him with his finger dipped in the goat's milk. The horse stirred where it was tethered and he could see the luminous white goat sleeping beneath the leaves of a bush. He drifted off near dawn, the few clouds overhead blown in mare's tails and limned with an orange light.

He got up sometime later, took up his child and gathered his animals, and continued following the stream that babbled its way eastward at a playful splash, oblivious to Bright's exhaustion and wary sorrow. A little after noon, in a dark green chasm far beneath a railroad trestle, they came across a group of naked young boys swimming in a cauldron made from the large rocks that had tumbled down the mountain and into the stream.

The boys were taking turns swinging on a rope far out into the deep pool. They pretended to ignore Bright while he watered his horse and changed and fed the baby. He set the goat free from its tether and the animal jumped off the bank and into the water, swiping its hooves to keep its head above the

38

slow, glassy current. It swam in several tight circles before clambering up on a large rock that rose above the flow. From here it looked defiantly back at Bright, as the boys smiled like he was some kind of circus man.

While Bright waited for the goat to come back, one of the boys swam across and stood a ways off from him in the water, eyeing Bright's uniform. "Were you in the War?" he asked.

"I was."

"Did you ever kill anybody ever?"

"Yes."

The boy was quiet and looked back over his shoulder at his companions, who made a great show of not returning their friend's glances. The boy turned to face Bright again and shivered, crossing his arms over his bony chest. "Want some blackberries?"

"Can you tell me where a town is at?"

"Why," the boy brightened with his trove of information, "town is just over back that way." He swung an arm over his shoulder, his eyes never leaving Bright's own. "You can't miss it."

"Can you help me fetch my goddamn goat down off that rock?"

The boy smiled a wide, gap-toothed smile. "Sure!" He spun in the water and began to wade deeper, before turning back. "How many Germans did you kill anyways?" he asked, squinting against the glare.

"We won, didn't we?"

9

The Colonel stood at the lip of the grave and looked down at the body of his only daughter, Rachel. He was quiet for a long time. "Well," said Corwin, his fat son, "that's that." The Colonel continued to say nothing. The black embers of the ground squeaked beseechingly beneath his boots as he shifted. Behind him were the charred remains of the cabin where his daughter had died in childbirth. In front of him, across the grave, stood the glass-black trunk of a chestnut tree from which the wildfire had begun its gallop eastward. He looked back down at his daughter. Buried deep, her body had escaped the blaze, and now her skin and the ivory-white slip that she was dressed in dazzled out like a diamond from its soot-black facet of ground.

"Well, that's that," Corwin said again.

"That," said the Colonel, not lifting his eyes from the hole, "is not that. That is your sister. A year ago she was stolen from me and gotten with child. That she is now dead is an insult that will be answered for."

"That's what I meant," Corwin said. "I meant that it was a insult."

Duncan, the Colonel's other son, stood at the head of the grave and looked down. All the way up the ridge from their home, Corwin had been whacking the crystallized black stems

40

of burnt wildflowers, while Duncan trailed silently behind him, a wraith floating over landscape that seemed to have been rendered down into shadows by the flames.

"I told you she was dead," Corwin said to his father. He pushed the shaft of the shovel handle at his brother's chest. Duncan's eyes were the same coal color as his hair. He looked long at Corwin before resetting his gaze on his sister.

His boys had at first dug up the wrong grave. After an hour, the Colonel had stood at the edge of the hole and looked down at the long-dead bones of the rogue's mother. He'd taken the shovel and swung it at his sons for their idiocy. Then, winded, he'd sat down and waited as they dug up his daughter.

The embers he stood upon took to shrieking again as the Colonel turned and looked east, where smoke colored the sky.

"After he buried her, he set the cabin on fire," Duncan said.

The old man looked down at his daughter. "I should have killed him sooner. The many times that I could have shot him down."

"You didn't have any bullets, though."

"In the winter when he went to fetch wood. The days he took the horse to town. When he came out each morning to break the ice from the stream for water. So many times." He shook his head and ground his front teeth. "I let him live, after all. I put aside killing him so that I could do it when his child was born, so that he could see me steal his child, like he stole mine." He turned away from the hole.

"But you couldn't a done it, 'cause you didn't have no bullets."

The Colonel swung aimlessly at Corwin, but he was distracted. "It was vanity," he said. "He would be dead now save for my own vanity. Cover her up."

Duncan began pushing the dirt back into the grave. His eyes were set far back in his head, his thoughts set back even farther.

41

The Colonel walked up to the top of the rise and surveyed the plumes of smoke as if they came from the camps of some mighty army. To the north ran ridge upon ridge of unbroken forest, but off to the south, where these crenulations began to broaden and grow larger, a silver thread of railroad track stretched east and west, glinting out like a necklace along the nape of the mountainsides. The Colonel came back down the slope to find his sons waiting, sweaty and sullen, by the freshly filled hole.

10

Rachel doted on that mangy old horse. She searched out tart wild apples, brought it thistles and fistfuls of stinging nettles and mint from downstream where the ground turned marshy. As September oranged into October and such treats became harder to find, she would harry Bright for bags of sweet dried corn when he went to town so that she might hold handfuls of it lovingly under the horse's greedy snout. Sometimes, in the wood-smoke-blue mornings, he would watch her leaning against its warm flank, one arm thrown up and across its withers, whispering into its ear as she ran his mother's ivory comb through the animal's forelock. Despite all the girl's attentions, however, the horse's thickening pelt took on a shagged and greasy appearance that, along with its baleful gaze and consumptive ribs, made it look like some moss-covered mule wandered in from a fairy tale.

"She spoils you and I don't know what for," he said to the back of the horse's head one early morning after the first frost. "I don't know what kind of hold you got on her." Horse and man were on the road to Fells Corner for supplies and dried corn. "And don't pretend you don't hear me, 'cause I know you hear me." He twitched the reins pettishly.

"Henry Bright, you have a beautiful wife."

"I know it. I married her, didn't I?"

"No need to sound so jealous. I helped you, so it is only right that you should share her with me."

"Helped nothing!" Bright laughed bitterly atop the animal. "I had to *drag* you inside that goddamn house, remember? If you were gonna steal her and marry her on your own, you coulda done it the minute you thought of it, and with my blessing too, but you couldn't, could you? You don't even have no hands! What if there was a doorknob or something?"

"Henry Bright . . ." The angel affected to sound weary.

"Keep it," Bright snapped. "I'm telling you whatever sweet-talking you're doing to my wife, quit it. She don't need those kinds of distractions right now. We're gonna have a baby."

"The child has been conceived."

"That's what I said, isn't it? So quit whatever other mischief you got on your mind for her and remember the promise that you made to me."

"Which was?" The horse's steaming breath swirled numi-nously around its ears in the cold air.

"Which *was* that you were gonna keep her and the baby safe from the Colonel and his boys like you done for me in the War. Remember when you said all that? That you'd protect us and the Future King of Heaven and all that?"

"When did it happen?"

"What?"

"When was the child conceived?"

"What the hell does that matter? It got conceived, didn't it? Don't try to change the subject. You gonna keep your promise to me or what?"

"We have done well."

"What do you mean, 'We'?"

The angel said nothing but clomped along thoughtfully.

"Angel?" Bright snapped the reins. "Angel, what do you

mean by 'We'? You ain't done nothing yet. Angel?" Receiving no answer, he sprang from the saddle and stood in the horse's path, bringing it to a desultory halt before him. "I'd hit a horse," he said. "You probably think I wouldn't, but I would."

The two stood there on the empty forest road, their eyes locked. Finally Bright resumed his place in the saddle and they continued on toward town.

"So fearful," the angel tsked.

"Yeah, well, it's your fault if I am. We're in trouble now," Bright said. "I hope you know what you got us into."

"Trouble?" the horse chuckled softly. "From the old man? From his half-wit sons?"

Bright bit his knuckle. "The things those boys did in that house over there in the War." He shivered in the cold air. "It wasn't half-wits that did all that."

"Which is why it could not have been the Colonel's sons."

"Course it was them!" he said, though he spoke under his breath, almost to himself. "I know it was. I *know* it was them." Bright twisted in the saddle and looked back down the road in the direction of the cabin. He scanned the forest to either side of the road for faces. The motley fall curtain of leaves drifted and swelled in the breeze, but none were revealed.

"I told you to close your eyes as the figures approached you where you lay. How then did you see their faces?"

"I opened them while they were standing above me."

"In the darkness?"

"It was getting to be day—"

"Come now, Henry Bright."

"What?! I'm telling you, it was *them*. Duncan stuck his fingers in my mouth to see if I was still alive, remember?"

"How do you know it was Duncan with your eyes closed in the dark?"

"It wasn't dark!"

45

"It was pitch dark and you know it."

"His fingers."

"You knew it was Duncan by his fingers?"

"They're skinnier than Corwin's. Corwin has those big fat fingers."

"I see."

"Oh, why don't you shut up!" He kicked the horse with his heels. "You ain't blind. You seen how fat Corwin's fingers are." He shivered again at the thought of Duncan's bony fingers in his mouth. "They knew I was alive, but they let me live. I think they let me live 'cause they wanted to torture me later. I told you about the other things those boys used to do when we were kids." He snapped the reins curtly against the horse's neck to dispel the memory. "You were there in the ditch with me, angel. You saw it all happen. You ain't gonna make me think I'm crazy."

"You really think it was them," the angel stated flatly.

"I'm telling you, it was!"

"Well, then, half-wits or not, you should be happy that upon your return from the War I told you to save Rachel from them."

"Yeah, yeah. But it's me the Colonel's gonna come kill, not some angel. Must be nice being you! All you get these days is apples and corn and I get nightmares about what them boys did over there in France." His face turned red and he spluttered, "And I tell you what else, I bet that if the Colonel and those boys came down over the ridge today and did to us what they did to those people in that farmhouse during the War, all you'd have to do would be disappear and it wouldn't be no bother to you no more. You'd be just fine, wouldn't you, angel?"

"Peace," the angel said. "They won't come today."

"How do you know that?"

"Shush."

"Don't you shush me!"

"Shush."

46

11

The boys fetched the goat off the rock in the stream and, shortly after, the baby slung securely around his chest and his livestock in tow, Henry Bright climbed the incline of shale and slate tailings to the road and struck out toward the town to buy a new box of matches. He'd been riding only a few minutes when he heard the growl of an automobile coming around the curve of the mountainside. It swerved to avoid them and then was gone around the next bend, a buff-colored, open-topped blur, its tires spraying his face with bits of gravel, the chemical fumes of its engine exhaust settling in his nose a moment before being picked up by the wind and blown behind him, out across the gorge, through the slats of the railroad trestle and into the sky where it would eventually join with the great veil of smoke that was rising from the forest at his back.

A while later the road changed from gravel to macadam, and the smell of roast chicken and chives, of mint and fresh-baked bread, threaded the air as he and his son rode through drowsing afternoon heat into the town. It seemed a tidy place of dappled white houses and American flags, and he found it almost impossible to keep the greedy animals back from the banquet of flowers spilling down to the street from arbor after shady arbor. Children could be heard, as could the lovely low hum of

leisurely work being done: painting of fences, canning of tomatoes and runner beans, gossip over cooling pies. Even the trees
here seemed to have a kind of deep green and prepossessing
prosperity that the trees of the forest could have no share in.

He found Main Street and tethered the horse and goat under
the sign of the general-merchandise store. Inside was long and
narrow, and he stood with the baby on his chest in the doorway
a moment, allowing his eyes to adjust to the cool darkness of
the aisles. The boards under his feet had been worn to a honey
luster by workboots and linseed oil. To his left, a long counter
supported an ornate brass register, behind which bolts of colored
fabric stood row on row. In front of the till, amid a dawdling,
noisy clutch of hip-high children, a young woman with a round
milky-white face listened to an older woman address the little
ones from behind the counter with an auntly air.

Bright walked down the far aisle, listening to their talk, his son
sleeping warm against his chest. As he approached with his new
box of matches, the two women broke off their conversation
and the younger began to arrange her children about her. He
laid the matches down on the counter alongside a dime.

The girl turned toward him. "Oh! What a beautiful baby!"

Bright made no reply but tilted his chin down against his
chest to peer in acknowledgment at the infant who was just now
waking and thrusting tiny fists aimlessly at the air. She pulled
back the edge of the sling on his chest to peek in at the boy.
"Hello . . . hello," she cooed.

"I believe he needs a diaper," the auntly one said, crinkling
her nose. A bleached and sparkling rag appeared off the shelf
from somewhere behind her and the woman laid it on the
counter, pulling its edges taut and trim with the expert grace of
long service. Next, she reached across and lifted the boy from
Bright's chest. After undoing the esoteric knots of his own efforts, she laid the child flat on the pristine square of fabric and

48

looked the baby over, pinching a foot, pulling its arms to full extension, clucking first to the right and left of the boy's ears, and finally looking straight down into its tightly closed face. The boy twisted on his back like an overturned turtle. "Few mosquito bites," she said, nuzzling its belly. All at once she tilted her head and looked up at Bright, her eyes gone flinty. "Where's his mother?"

"She passed."

The auntly woman looked at Bright for a long moment and then back down at the boy. The younger one leaned in for a closer look at the baby. The children sucked on candies near the door or else fussed around an old tomcat suffering them from a patch of sun by the front window. "Margaret," the older woman asked, "will it be you or I that shows this poor man how to change a diaper?"

"You do it," the girl named Margaret said. "You're so much better at it than me."

The old woman shook her head in disapproval. "Well, if you haven't learned yet I just don't know . . ."

"Oh, I don't have to do any of *that* kind of thing," Margaret said. "They have their own nannies for *that* kind of thing."

The auntly woman shook her head again at this. She looked back up at Bright. "Are you coming from the fire?" It was the first time that Bright had heard someone besides the angel or himself speak of it.

"I saw it yesterday morning," he said finally.

They looked at him expectantly, waiting for more.

"After he was born and"—he paused—"and . . ." He looked at the box of matches there on the counter. "Yes, Ma'am, I saw it," he said.

"Mmm." The auntly woman's mouth set grimly, her eyes roaming over the naked baby. Then, drawing in her breath and pulling herself straight, she said, "Well, it'll be here by tomorrow

49

or the day after if the weather doesn't change." She looked around the store. "We had a fire here when I was a girl," she said. "Well, not here, but next town over. Anyhow, my father took the register out of the store with the help of three men, and they pulled it down the road on slats and buried it in our front yard. My father was a good man, always fair. Half the people in town saw him bury it there, but he knew it would be safe. The fire burned down the whole town, but he came back and dug up the cash register—this very cash register—and we started new right here."

"When did your wife die?" Margaret asked, interrupting the older woman.

"Margaret!" the older woman barked. "Keep your mouth shut, if you don't have any sense at all." She wiped the child's little legs clean with a rag.

"Day before yesterday," Bright said.

"Oh." Margaret looked down at the floorboards. "I'm sorry," she said. "What's your baby's name?"

"Margaret! Tell me I didn't just tell you to keep your mouth shut?"

"He doesn't have a name," Henry mumbled. He watched the auntly lady twist the ends of the diaper so that the whole assemblage seemed to wrap itself around his boy like magic. The spell of white fabric was held by two pins that materialized from the same nowhere that the diaper itself had.

"Well, you need a name for him," the auntly one said. "Have you thought maybe about naming him after yourself?"

"He don't need any kind of name like mine."

"What's that?" Margaret asked.

"Henry Bright."

"Well, what's wrong with a name like that?" Margaret asked. She turned to the auntly lady. "What's wrong with the name Henry, after all?"

50

"Not a thing," the aunly one replied. "What boy wouldn't be proud to carry his father's name? And a man like you who went to war and fought for his country?" She clucked her tongue and reached beneath the counter, pulling out a horse-hair brush that she passed to the girl. "Margaret, reach up there and brush all that dust off his nice uniform. The shoulders there," she said, "and his back," she said, directing as the girl ran the soft brush over his uniform as she might dust a mantel-piece. "There." Margaret passed the brush back to her. "I'm giving you a drop of cinnamon oil here . . . and here." She put a dab of the warm-smelling stuff on either side of the sling hanging on his chest, then gave him back the boy. "Keeps the mosquitoes away," she winked. She stood back from the counter and looked at Bright. "And for you, I have some cheese and crackers. I don't like the looks of how thin you are in that uni-form." She placed a large wedge of hard white cheese in a square of brown paper and laid a package of crackers along-side it.

There arose the sound of an automobile outside, and the girl Margaret looked back toward the door, where her brood was trying to teach the tomcat how to lick a stick of candy. "That's our car. I have to go now," she said. "Mr. Bright, I'm very sorry for your loss. Everyone!" She clapped her hands for their atten-tion and the children piled out of the store.

"Learn to tie a diaper!" the aunly one yelled after her as the door closed.

12

The men spread out as they approached the church, their eyes roving over the village square for any danger that might lurk in the debris. Bright reached the immense doors first, and at a signal from the sergeant, the others spread to either side. The wood was stained almost to ebony by age, and the weighty brass rings that served as handles were polished yellow at their base from centuries of use.

They waited on Sergeant Carlson for the signal to open the heavy doors, and, when he gave it, they grabbed the rings and pulled hard until a small crack afforded Bright a look inside. The sanctuary was narrow, the floor a diamond-checkerboard pattern of slate and marble. The walls had been painted an austere white but were stippled here and there with muted flecks of color as daylight shone through the few remaining stained-glass windows, as through the prism of an icicle. An altar hunkered squatly on a dais at the far end of the room, one corner chipped away, a candlestick fallen to the floor.

Bright signaled that the room was empty, and at another sign from Carlson, he slipped inside. In the single, brief moment before the others crowded in around him, he let his eyes rise to the painted ceiling and, unprepared for what he saw there, found himself falling headlong into the crowded heaven that spiraled into infinity above him.

It was the blue of the sky that caught him first: a rapturous, painfully pure spike of color that hooked his eyes like fish and reeled them upward into the heights. Gone in that instant was the viscous puddle of October light that had dribbled in behind him through the crack in the doorway. Beneath the gracious blue vault of the church it was a fresh and dazzling spring morning at the beginning of the world.

His hand shot out, gripping the brass door handle hard, as if to keep himself from falling upward. He had believed the church to be empty, but, hanging there, Henry Bright realized he was in fact surrounded on all sides by a great gesticulating host of fellow beings. There were thousands of them in the sky around him—men, women, and children, in every conceivable pose and color. Some had the muscular builds of riverboat men and stood proudly astride their cake-white clouds. Others, a species of fat-faced-baby things, seemed to have leavened their way into the clouds themselves and popped their tousled heads at random from out of the billows, wearing expressions of frantic mirth and mischief. Many figures in the assemblage thrummed musical instruments, while others placidly displayed brutal and mysterious wounds. A finely featured woman held a pair of eyeballs on a platter, next to a nearly naked man who was calmly watching his own body being rendered into fat by flames.

Above this crowd and higher still, a circle of bearded and wild men looked down from their perches with electric severity at Henry Bright, though he barely noticed them. His eyes now had come to rest on the figure of a young girl kneeling in prayer there in the highest heavens at the dome's apogee.

She was almost impossibly beautiful, her eyes filled with such

53

reserves of comfort that to Bright it seemed as if, had he come into the church only an instant earlier, she would have been happy to give him all the love and understanding he might have ever needed or desired. Sadly, though, this was not to be, for her face was even now caught in the act of turning toward the other figure who was interrupting her prayers.

This other interloper was an angel, its hair like twists of fire, its wings bejeweled with eyes in all states of opening and closing, its white robes trailing just behind it in this, its moment of arrival. It was impossible to tell what the angel was saying to the girl, but so beautiful was she, so composed and fatalistic was the poetry of her face against the urgency of the angel's, that Henry Bright fell in love with her in that moment and stood staring up at her as if stricken.

"Bright!"

"Bright?"

Bathing in the radiant pool of the girl's beauty, he was deaf to the men behind him and returned blinkingly to himself only to discover that he had been jostled forward by the others as they pushed past him into the church.

"Jesus! Would ya look at that!"

"Jesus my foot! Chaplain was right. Catholics. Nothing here but a bunch of dirty pictures. We oughta—"

The pealing bells above came back to him now and, turning, he found that he was standing before a small stone archway past which a staircase led upward into the bell tower. As the others argued with one another or else stood silently looking up into the blue, Bright stepped through the archway and began to climb the stairs.

54

13

Without his mother's rifle, and with little money left to buy provisions, the winter was very hard. The wind shrieked and the stream froze solid. He melted snow for water in which to boil the dwindling reserves of dried corn and bitter carrots. Rachel had terrible pains and sickness for a while. Her tongue turned a bright red and she ran a fever, but she didn't miscarry.

When the temperature dropped so low that the chickens stopped laying eggs, he brought them inside and they lived with the clucking all hours. The goats dug for forage some, but as the snow got deeper all the animals got thinner. He killed the first kid and they ate the thing down to nothing. Rachel's health made an improvement. He killed another and made a stew with a few potatoes and the last of the carrots. She ate this for a week, and gradually the fever broke and her tongue returned to its normal shade. Now that they were inside the cabin, the hens began laying again. In the mornings there would be eggs in the folds of their blanket, in the bottom of the bucket, in the heel of a boot. She got up often now and would peek out at the horse through the freezing crack between the cabin flap and the door frame.

The horse was enduring the winter only slightly better than the goats. Its thick coat hung loosely over ribs, which showed as plainly as the bars on an empty prison. Except for the times when Bright would rouse it for his rare trips to town, its breaths came slow and deep, as if it was waiting to be revived by a kiss of spring breeze or the chirp of returning birds. Rachel often asked to bring it into the house, something that Bright forbade explicitly. He returned from Fells Corner once to find that she had led the animal inside their cabin anyhow, throwing their quilt over it and stoking the fire. It had been hell getting the stubborn thing out again, but he relented somewhat after this episode and tied the animal to the leeward side of the cabin, where it would be most out of the wind.

They ate the last kid in late February, when the world was at its coldest, and by early March he had butchered the billy. By then they had both developed a rank distaste for goat meat, and this last sacrifice to their hunger and the hunger of the unborn child was the worst. When he cooked it, the room had filled with gamy, clinging steam.

She milked the she-goat every day, though, and somehow, slowly, the world began to get warmer and the slant of the sun began to find their faces when they would leave the cabin and tramp through the melting snow to the hutch where he had resettled the chickens. The horse was moved back from the side of the cabin to its customary spot under the chestnut tree. The she-goat began to get fat again, and Bright suspected that she came down off her perch on top of the hen hutch in the night and foraged, when she could be sure that he would not come out and slaughter her as he had the rest of her family.

By May, his wife's belly was big and they were happy. At night he would hold her close and she would tell him wild stories that came from her own mind. She never talked about her father and brothers. It was as if since her rescue they had ceased to exist for her, and if that was so he saw no need to remind her of them or of the awful threats the old man had made as they turned their backs on him and rode away together. Sometimes he would tell her about the War, but when he did it was always about little things: the finding, once, of a lemon, or the unlikely discovery of a bottle of clear liquor standing untouched in an exploded bar, the thick white towels at the hotel where he had stayed in Paris during his leave from the front. He never told her about the church or the angel or Bert, and if he ever got too close to those things, he would stop mid-sentence. She, sensing something in him, would help him to steer his stories until the tension in his voice was gone and the pounding in his chest had slowed.

"And where were you then?"

"In Saint-Mihiel."

"That's a pretty name. San Maheel."

"Yeah. In a graveyard."

"In a graveyard? You were in a graveyard?"

"Yeah. And we were all on our hands and knees, and the one guy next to me, Ezra, he froze because he saw a gravestone with his last name on it."

"Really? What was his last name?" Her fingertips stroked at the thin hair on his chest.

"I don't remember what it was. Ezra Something-or-Other. He saw it and he just froze there, and all the rest of us, we crawled on and didn't see him. Then someone noticed he was gone so I went back to find him and he was still there, down on all fours, staring at that gravestone like it was telling him something he didn't want to forget." Bright looked up into the ceiling rafters. "I said 'Hey, Ezra, hey, hey,' but he wasn't listening to me, he was listening to the stone, so I reached over and I grabbed him and hauled him around in front of me so that I could get him going. After a bit I got him moving again. He was real young, younger than me. So we were crawling around the stones to join the others when a shell landed right next to me. It shattered another gravestone and there was rock everywhere. I got some in my eyes and I was coughing on dust and for a second I thought that I was dead, but the shell didn't explode."

"Why?"

"I don't know. I guess it was—" He broke off and she waited for him to continue. When he didn't, she helped him finish the story.

"It was because God saw you helping that man and he said, 'Hmm! I like that boy Henry! I'm gonna keep him safe.'" She laughed quietly and held him and kept laughing to herself until she fell asleep. It was a playful laugh that bubbled up around them like a spring of freshwater. Sometimes he thought it was actually the child laughing inside her. He would fall asleep to that music, and some nights he would escape his dreams.

14

He saw the horse caroming wildly about the small chamber as he rounded the final curve of the steeple staircase. Whoever had led the animal up these perilous spiral steps had finished cruelly by tying its tail to one of the ropes that rang the bells above. He stood still in the entrance of the room and allowed the horse to see him. More boots were coming up the stairs behind him. He waved a hand behind his back and the footsteps halted. The whites of the horse's eyes sliced at the air fearfully, its mouth was specked with foam at the corners. Bright stayed at the edge of the room and did not move, and eventually the animal began to quiet. It stamped uncertainly in a pile of dung, but its huffing slowed and it focused on him, watching for what he was going to do.

Bright moved slowly across the room toward it until he was close enough to reach out and rest his palm on the animal's twitching flank. The bells above had fallen silent as it had stopped moving and the rope tied to its tail slackened. The horse whinnied a few times, but Bright kept his hand where it was, and when he judged it finally calm enough, he ran his palm down the length of the shivering body until he was holding the slack of the belfry rope in his hand. He slipped the rifle off his shoulder and, holding it by the stock, sawed through the rope.

Above them in the belfry, the bells jangled loudly at their sudden release from the horse's tail. Hearing the dreaded things unexpectedly once more, the animal spooked clattering across the stone floor and hurtling in headlong panic past the men pressed against the staircase walls. From below them came a frantic whinny followed by a single shot as the horse reached the sanctuary.

Bert stood at the bottom of the stairs, the officer's pistol dangling loosely in his hand. The horse lay a few feet away, nearly dead, its tongue tasting the dusty marble of the floor, its eyes watching the heavens painted above them.

They all stood around it dumbly until Sergeant Carlson stepped forward and shot the horse in the head. The animal lay still. He looked down at it, rasping a hand across his face. "Well," he said, raising his eyes and looking around him at the others, "we're not leaving a dead horse in a church." He removed his helmet and ran a hand through his hair. There were the beginnings of a smile at the edges of his mouth. "Anyone see anyplace to get a drink in this town?" he asked. Then the smile disappeared and he stepped back to survey the problem of the dead horse. "I'm buying for anybody who's ever moved a dead horse before." Bert was still standing by the door, the gun swinging slightly back and forth like a pendulum.

"Bert," he said, but Bert's eyes were far off beneath his yellow hair, as if he were looking at reflections in the pooling blood there on the checkered slabs.

"Bert!" Carlson stepped between the boy and the dead horse. "If I *ever* see that Kraut gun of yours again, I'm going to kick your teeth in."

It took ten of them to push and drag the horse by its legs and neck across the blood-slicked marble floor. Finally they got it down the nave and from there pulled it bruisingly down the steps and out under the full ominous weight of the afternoon sky. Then there was nowhere else to drag it, and so they all straightened and looked around at one another and then around at the shattered village, unsure of what to do next.

Bright took off his helmet and walked back up the steps and into the church for a last look at the girl on the ceiling, but the light through the transept windows had begun to fade and he had to squint now to read her features. Then, hearing the sergeant call his name, he turned and walked out past the immense wooden doors to rejoin the company. He had just replaced his helmet when the air above them screamed and the church exploded.

15

Back in the sunlight, a sack of rag diapers in his arms, a new box of matches in his pocket, and his son clean and dry in the sling on his chest, Bright watched the girl named Margaret as she glided down the street above her throng of children.

"The Future King of Heaven needs that woman, Henry Bright."

Bright said nothing, tying the bundle of diapers to the saddle pommel, where they would hang next to the bucket of goat's milk.

"The Future King of Heaven needs a mother," the angel said again.

He untied the goat and then swung the animals around in the direction from which they'd come into town.

"She will suckle your child. Your son needs a mother or he will die. He will starve."

"He ain't gonna starve. I been feeding him, haven't I?"

"Your child cannot live long on goat milk. See how skinny he is. How slight."

Bright ignored the angel and began to lead the party up Main Street. Off in the distance the smoke from the fire painted the sky a sulfurous gray. The wind picked up, its hot tail whipping against their faces as it sucked past them.

"Bithiah," the angel began.

"You're talking nonsense and I don't want to hear it," Bright said as he watched the darkly spreading wings to the west. "Did you see that car? A girl like that, and all them kids dressed up so pretty, ribbons in their hair? Did you see her?" He coughed. "What would a girl like that need with my boy and me?"

"Bithiah," the angel continued, "was the daughter of the Pharaoh. She found a baby boy floating in a basket of reeds and she raised him as her own. This child was the prophet Moses. He grew up to lead the children of Israel out of Egypt."

"I know all that," Bright said. "My mother read that to me all the time when I was little."

"The Pharaoh's daughter was named Bithiah," the angel said again.

Bright pulled the animal up short. The goat continued on until it reached the end of its lead and came to a stop in the middle of the road. "I said I know all that," he said, exasperated.

"Her name is there in the Bible. Bithiah. You could look it up."

Bright scuffed the macadam with the sole of his boot and turned to look back down the street. Margaret was ushering the children into the big black auto. "Now you're just trying to make me mad," he said. "You know that it *ain't* her name we're arguing about. And," he added, "I *couldn't* look up her name if I wanted to, because you made me go and tear up the Bible to start the fire, remember?" He leaned toward the horse, waving his arm toward the wall of smoke. "Maybe you don't remember this, but my wife *just* died! Rachel? The one you liked so much? The one who gave you apples and corn?" His eyes were watering, and he spit to clear the catch from his voice. "You told me she was gonna be safe!" He gave the lead a jerk and got the animal moving again. It plodded stubbornly along behind him.

"The girl's many children need a father, Henry Bright.

63

When she approaches, you will tell her of the Future King of Heaven. The words will be put into your mouth."

Bright turned and saw the big black auto rolling slowly toward them on its way down the street. The car stopped a few yards away and waited for Bright and his animals to move out of its path.

"Do it now," the angel commanded. "The child must be fed. He must be taken in by a woman and cared for. He will surely die otherwise . . ."

For a moment the horse looked down its nose at the driver and the driver looked across the leather steering wheel and back at the horse. Bright wavered and then left his animals blocking the road and went to bend down level with Margaret's face in the back passenger window.

"I mean to say thank you for your treating Henry so good back there in the store."

The children were up on their knees in the wide backseat, giggling at the funny-looking horse and goat in the middle of the street.

She smiled. "Are you going to name him Henry?"

"I guess I am." She squinted at him against the sunlight, his mouth hanging part ways open as he waited for the words the angel had promised would be given to him. Then he closed it and turned to glare at the horse, but the animal seemed oblivious to his discomfort and continued staring down its nose at the car and its driver.

"Henry needs a mother," Bright said. "He . . . He's . . . an important child," he said. "He's to be important. I think."

He paused painfully again, and waited for any kind of help at all from the angel. "I'm a good man," he said. "Your children need a father."

He pinched the bridge of his nose between a thumb and forefinger and closed his eyes briefly in tribute to his own frustration. "I mean," he said, opening them again and speaking more slowly, "I believe . . . that you and I . . . that maybe you and I could . . ." When the words didn't come he thrust a hand into his pocket, pulling out his mother's ancient ivory comb. He offered it to the girl through the car's window. "I'm sorry if this don't make much sense. My wife died two days ago."

Margaret turned in her seat to look at the children. They were watching the strange man and his animals in rapt fascination, as if a single sound might break the magic spell of their presence there in the middle of the road. The wind peppered stray bits of grit against Bright's face, and the goat began to snuff her nose at some message in the air. The lights in the girl's eyes did not dim but became sadder somehow. She looked at the comb in his outstretched hand and then gently placed her fingertips against his palm and pushed it back at him. "I'm sorry she died," Margaret said. She reached her hand through the window and brushed it against the child's copper-colored head in its sling. She smiled at him, a beautiful smile, like a dream in passing. Then the driver backed up and swung around them, leaving Henry Bright and his livestock to stand dumb, dirty, and still in the rising heat of the afternoon.

16

The concussive shock of the first shell hitting the church was the only one Bright actually felt. After that came the now-familiar feeling of capsized calm in which the world seemed viewed from beneath a great depth of water. It was as if all sound and feeling were gone suddenly, and, within that watery silence, death was not something hurtled from above but more like a meadow of wildflowers that blossomed from the ground in radii of plaster, mud, and dust, swallowing buildings and bodies, chewing them in the air a while and then spitting them back out upon the trammeled ground like the ends of gnawed bones. When the flowers finally stopped blossoming, the earth lay back down again and the senses returned.

After several minutes he began to pick his way through the church rubble in search of the others. Bert and Sergeant Carlson were the only ones that he found alive. Carlson lay next to an avalanche of roofing tile by the enormous splinter of the fallen steeple. He had a hole in his chest that had not yet begun to bleed but hung open in an "O" that looked like a mouth that was about to start screaming. He was breathing, but that was all. Bert was unhurt, though his pale face was pocked with plaster and his eyes were wide and shiny.

"That was really something, huh? Wow!" he said. "I mean, wow!"

Bright stooped next to Carlson. "Help me."

"You bet!" Bert said, but he didn't move. "How you doin', Sergeant? Don't you worry none, you hear me? You're doin' real good, real good!" He laughed to himself in disbelief. "Jee-roosh! We had a tight one today, didn't we, boys?" He was staring at the bodies scattered about; his brow was furrowing and unfurrowing. "Jee-roosh!" he said again. He began to shake.

"Help me," Bright said again, but Bert's whole body was now convulsing in some no-man's-land between laughter and sobs. Bright stood, hauled back, and hit Bert hard with the flat of his hand. "Help me," he said one last time, and Bert's eyes focused and he stopped shaking so much. "We need to move him someplace safe," Bright said. The sergeant's wound had finally begun to bleed.

It was terrible ground to try to carry a man over, and Carlson's feet shambled loosely against the pebble and debris as his legs began the process of forgetting how to walk. They passed the ruins of the church and had made it about a hundred yards down the road before Bright began to wonder if he'd been turned around by the shellings. Without the steeple it was hard to tell, suddenly, which direction they had first entered the village by. It was also beginning to get dark, and so he pulled Bert and the sergeant to the side of the road and down into a ditch by a stone wall. The hate had begun now, and stretching away for miles to either side of them came the sounds of the War.

Artillery passed high above their heads in singsong trajectories that merged and lifted with one another into strange musical chords, like cats crossing pump organs. The gigantic trench mortars were the loudest, the reverberations of their fusillades abating slowly across the night sky, briefly disappearing behind

67

the sound of howitzers before the red-hot shards of metal they had fired into the air came screaming earthward once more.

"We'll go back to the line tonight," he said to Bert. "After dark." They angled Carlson into a sitting position against the wall and Bright put his ear close to the dying man. The sergeant's wound burbled as if a flock of sparrows had made a nest deep in his chest. To their left the road led back into the little town square and, to their right, sixty or seventy more yards down the road, hunched a glowering stone farmhouse.

"Why not take him over yonder?" Bert asked, motioning toward it.

"That's no good for us if someone comes in the night. They'll check the buildings first. We're better here." He looked down at Carlson.

"The hell we are!" Bert snapped. "And, anyway, like we got to be afraid of anything! You and I, we're good old West Virginia boys!" He pulled the German pistol from the waistband of his trousers. It was silver and shiny and seemed to distill, like dew, all the light from the darkening gray sky, so that the sky itself grew darker as Bert rolled the gun first one way and then another in his hands. Its barrel looked as narrow as a knitting needle. Bert pointed it at Bright an uncomfortable second, then laughed. "Boy, didn't I get you good?" He laughed again at the memory of frightening Bright with the gun as he'd come around the doorway of the deserted trench. "You 'bout shit your britches! You thought some big old Kraut had you dead by rights! Pow," he said, puffing the air.

Bright looked steadily at Bert and said nothing.

"I killed that Kraut officer," Bert said with petulance. "I know you all don't think that's so, but I did. He was gonna shoot me dead, but I shot him first." He turned it around so that the handle was to Bright. "And, look at this." He reached to light a match.

"No matches," Bright said.

"I want to show you the carvings and what all that's on the handle. They're something devilish. Dang! It's too dark to see 'em." He made again to strike a match. "Here."

"No matches. No light."

"Fine," Bert sighed. "Anyway, if you weren't so scared, you could see it's got a handle that's pure gold or something and carved with all that crazy Kraut writing. And if you'd let me strike a match, I was gonna show you the dragon with the spear through its neck. So don't you tell me that we got anything to worry about, 'cause if any Kraut Boche Fritzy decides he's gonna scout that farmhouse over yonder while we're in it, he's gonna find out exactly what the last fella found out who thought he could outdraw me." He tossed the gun in the air and caught it with surprising grace. "Now, Bright, let's get the sergeant over to that farmhouse and not say anything more about it."

"We're staying here."

Bert's face fell in the purpling light. "Is that all?" he whined. "Here we are, so close to those stinkers we can smell the pickles, and we're just going to hide out until we can sneak on back with our tails between our legs?" He poked the toe of Bright's boot with the pistol barrel. "Hell! This is as close as we're gonna get to them? What am I supposed to say when I get home? That I didn't kill a German the whole time I was in France?"

"I thought you did kill one."

Carlson coughed wetly then, expectorating blood. He raised his head and banged it against the wall several times like a man fluffing a pillow. There was a gravelly sound from his chest.

Bert looked at the dying sergeant a moment and then back at Bright. He stood up. "Boy, I know you want to, boy," he said to Bright as one might talk to a fire being stoked. "I know you want to go after them too! Ooooh, I can see it! I can see it in your eyes! You're a good old West Virginia boy!"

69

"All right," Bright said finally. "You want to go over to that farmhouse, go on over there. Check to make sure it's safe, and if it is, then we'll all go over. If it isn't, you just go ahead and kill as many Germans as you find in there." He tossed his canteen up at Bert. Bert stood looking at it. "Sergeant's thirsty too. You find any water, you bring plenty back for him." Bright handed him Carlson's canteen as well. "Well, go on," he said. "Git."

Bert looked from the empty canteens in his hands to the farmhouse waiting for him in the failing light. "Well, I ain't going over there alone," he said, and squatted back down again next to Bright. "And don't you go orderin' me to do nothin' either. We do things together."

"We can't leave him here alone," Bright said, nodding at Carlson. "And we can't carry him. And he needs water."

"You go, then," Bert said, and pushed the canteens back at Bright. He unhooked his own canteen and placed it atop the other two. "I'll wait here."

Bright peered through the darkness for signs of danger, but everything around him was a testament to that, so he climbed cautiously from the ditch and headed toward the farmhouse, crouching low as he hurried down the road with the empty canteens in his arms. He slowed as he approached the dwelling. The once-white paint gave off a muted glow against the fields, and the slate shingles were scruffy with lichen. The windowpanes were mostly gone from their frames, save for a few stray shards that glinted viciously out at him from the gloom like fangs. He went to his knees and peered between them into the dwelling, but it was as dark in there as a crack in the earth. He got to his feet and began to search for water. On the far side of the house he found what he was looking for. He held one of the canteens under the spigot but the pump handle dangled uselessly on its hinge. After a minute of pumping, he abandoned it for the stone livestock trough that his eyes now made

70

out dimly, set flush against the house's wall. In the shadow of the farmhouse, the rainwater that came up to the lip of the cistern looked like a sheet of black glass. He knelt down in the mud and quietly set the empty canteens next to one another at his knees before lifting the first one above the still surface of the water.

"Wait."

At the sound of the voice, the world fell silent. There was no night breeze, no rifle fire. Even the large-caliber guns seemed to pause from their thundering and look around themselves, as if the unexpected word had wandered in like a small child and interrupted their supper conversation.

Bright stopped as well, the canteen in his hand frozen above the trough. It was impossible to tell how distant the voice was or even if it had been speaking to him. It had seemed to come from all directions at once, a calm command without emotion. He lifted his eyes to the farmhouse window above the trough, expecting to see a face framed in it peering out at him, but the darkness there was just as still and solid as it had been before. Beneath his hand, the water's obsidian surface reflected the shadow of the canteen against a cold backdrop of stars. He knew then that whoever was speaking must be behind him, training a rifle at the back of his head, a killer whose face he would never see.

"I . . . I'm fetching water," he stammered. "I got a shot man and I'm fetching him some water."

He took the silence that followed as incomprehension or consideration.

"English?" he asked. "American? Water?" He waited for an answer, thinking of the rifle slung on his back. There would be no time. He put his hands in the air, one still clutching the empty canteen, and stood slowly. "Water?" he said again, turning to face the man who had snuck up behind him. There was nothing and no one there. He shifted to the right and left, then made a full circle in the darkness to show whoever had whispered that he was only holding a canteen in his hand. "Water?" Running was hopeless, the voice had been too close. He waited for a reply another minute at least, but the hidden man did not answer. Expecting at any moment to be killed, he stooped to the trough once more and put the canteen to the surface of the water.

"Wait," the voice commanded.

He froze again. "Who are you?" he said, louder now. Compared to the hidden man's voice his own sounded thin and desperate.

A faint scent, insidious and sharp as chopped radishes, rose to his nostrils. In an instant he had thrown the canteen on the ground and dropped his hand to grope at the belt where he kept his gas mask. It wasn't there, and he searched frantically for it before realizing that he'd left it with his jacket back in the ditch by the stone wall. Cold panic held him for an instant, then drifted away like mist. He'd heard no shells fall nearby.

It was still possible he had missed the sound of a gas canister, which traveled at slower speeds than artillery shells and hummed lowly like old men in workshops as they flew. When a gas alarm was raised, you had six seconds to get your mask on or, if not, you had two days in which to experience annihilating agony and then forever to be either dead or terribly wounded. There were many false gas alarms on the line, and men were forever putting on and taking off their masks. Sometimes men would dream the alarm in their sleep and would open their eyes with their masks already on, having put them on without waking. Phosgene, if you noticed it at all, smelled of new-cut grass. The next day, however, you were coughing up pints of thick yellow fluid from your lungs every hour, and the day after that you were headed for a lifetime in some peeling hospital, the helpless ward of aging nurses. Unlike phosgene, mustard gas didn't even

72

need to be inhaled. It was heavy, gangrenous stuff that trundled close to the ground, burning any skin that it came in contact with and causing huge, disfiguring blisters. Eventually the gas would settle, collecting with the rainwater in greasy floating slicks at the bottom of shell craters, potholes, and trenches.

His temples were throbbing and he realized that he had been holding his breath. He let it out slowly and sniffed the air again. The smell of the gas was certainly there but it was very faint. Looking down, his eyes came to rest on the trough. In the darkness, its pale-gray stone shone up around the water it held like the wide mouth of some monstrous fish. Whatever mustard gas had recently drifted through this farmyard was gone now, save for the stuff that had settled in a thin layer over the surface of the water in the trough.

All at once, with a kind of pent-up gaiety, the War started up once more where it had left off. In the distance, explosions strobed haphazardly against whatever poor clouds had wandered into the path of the big guns. Bright stared down into the gape of the great fish's mouth until he'd finally caught his breath and his heartbeat had slowed. Then he picked up the canteen from the ground and replaced its top before stooping to collect the others.

When he got back to the stone wall, Bert was asleep and Carlson was dead. He looked at the sergeant's face a long minute and then sat down again next to his remaining companion and waited.

It was well past midnight when Bright stood again and nudged Bert awake with his boot. He awoke violently, his pistol flashing out in the starlight. Bright knelt and put his hand against Bert's chest to hold him still. "Sergeant's dead."

"Yeah?"

"Time to go."

Bert leaned out over the ditch and looked up and down the

road. "So that's that?" he asked, his voice rising, turning harsher between his teeth. "We're just gonna run, huh?"

"We have to go before it starts to get light. If it gets to be morning and we're on the wrong side of the line, we'll be in worse trouble than we are now."

"We'll make a great sight then, won't we?" Bert jeered. He fumbled angrily in his pocket for a cigarette. "You may not have to impress anybody, but I gotta go and take over the bank, and what am I gonna say when some little old lady comes to my desk and asks me, 'Now, what was you doin' while the whole army got blown to pieces? Boy, you sure are lucky to have made it alive! And not a scratch! Land!' What am I gonna tell her, Bright? I ain't gonna say I sat in a ditch by the side of the road in the middle of the whole German army, am I?" He reached to light a cigarette. Bright pushed the match down once more.

"I told you, no fire."

"Fuck it, Bright. Fuck you." The match flared and Bert began to smoke his last cigarette. When he was half through, he turned toward Bright and said, "You know—" and was shot in the head from somewhere in the dark. Bright rolled over and flattened himself in the ditch, pulling Bert down on top of him. "Whew!" said Bert. "Jee-roosh!" he sighed. Finally he said, "Well," and that was the last he said of anything.

74

17

The car carrying Margaret and her children moved down Main Street, past the coal-company office and a church to where the trees took over and the large houses lulled in the shade of the overhanging elms. Bright watched it until it was gone, then he sagged in the heat. He recognized the kind of smile the girl Margaret had given him. It was the kind of smile that people give to children, and he surely knew what it meant when she gave it to him. Rising up from the sling on his chest now came the smell of his son dirtying his new diaper. He yanked a fresh rag from the sack hanging off the saddle pommel.

"You are a coward, Henry Bright."

"Goddamn it! Why you always got to talk to me when I'm covered in shit? You know I ain't a coward! And, anyways, why didn't you jump in and give me something to say when she was smiling at me like that?"

"Coward," the angel said again.

Bright spit on the ground. "You're a big one to talk," he said. "If you're so brave, why didn't you stay in France? You didn't go and find another church to go be an angel in because you were afraid of getting bombed again, weren't you? That's it, isn't it? You were scared just like everyone else."

"The Future King of Heaven needs his swaddling changed."

"I'm getting to that, so be quiet, 'cause I'm talking now." Bright whipped the white rag in the air before the horse's face. "What about when I needed you on the field after I got shot? Where were you then? You were hiding is what. Scared is what you were! You're the coward, not me." He shook his head as he knelt and spread his jacket on the hot pavement, then laid the new diaper on the jacket.

"Henry Bright, you are so blinded with fear that you refuse to see that I am trying to help you now, just as I helped you then."

"How are you trying to help me?" Bright took his son from the sling and rested him gently on the jacket. As he waited for an answer, he began hesitatingly to tie the new diaper as the auntly woman had taught him to do in the store. "Exactly how you're helping is what I don't know," he said again, looking up once from where he knelt near the horse's hooves.

"I am trying, despite all your best efforts to the contrary, to find you a mother for your son, the Future King of Heaven. As I was telling you before you allowed the girl Margaret to escape, the boy needs a woman who will claim him as her own. You cannot care for him by yourself. Now we must follow her. She must take the boy or all is surely lost."

"What do you care if he's safe anyhow, angel? You weren't so careful with me when I got shot in the War. I lay there for hours and called for you, but you didn't come. And you didn't care any when Rachel was dying either, did you? She was screaming—*screaming!*—and you didn't care. You just stood out there under that chestnut tree like you were asleep."

"You survived. I knew that you would. And Rachel lived long enough to fulfill her destiny as the mother of Jee-roosh. I never assured you of her well-being past that point."

"What's that supposed to mean?"

76

"What's what supposed to mean?"

"Jee-roosh?" Bright replaced his son in the sling. The baby cooed up at him. "What are you saying 'Jee-roosh' for?"

"The time has come to name the child. He shall be named Jee-roosh."

"No, it ain't!" Bright said. "Oh, no, it ain't, angel." He climbed into the saddle. "He's my son and his name is going to be Henry, like me." The angel said nothing, as the horse's big jaws worked a cud. "And Henry's a good name too, angel," Bright continued. "You have a problem with a name like that?" Its ears twitched and it lifted its tail, allowing several large balls of dung to fall to the pavement.

Bright sat up in the saddle. "That's real polite," he said. He gave the horse a sharp kick with his heels to get it moving.

"Very well," the horse said. It swished the argument away with its tail and began to clomp along in the direction that Margaret's car had gone. They passed a group of men loitering around the coal-company office. "For now the Future King of Heaven's name is Henry, but it will be Jee-roosh as the boy grows older, and men will speak the name with awe as the centuries unfold. Your own name will be recalled from time to time."

They went by the church and the spreading elms and through the smell of green onions and pecan pie, roasting chicken, and garden laughter, through the dark mahogany sound of someone playing hymns on a piano and the far-off thrumming of a train. The breeze had dropped as they walked up the street, but now it picked up again, the leaves above beginning to clap against one another as the air blew warmer. The goat, normally so quick to dart this way and that on her tether, now stayed close to the horse and lifted her white nose again to snuff at the black scrolls of smoke garlanding the air.

"Smoke's getting a lot stronger," Bright said.

77

"Yes."

"Fire's gonna burn this place down."

"It would seem so."

The road passed the last of the big white homes and swished through a series of lazy bends as the smell of smoke grew first stronger, then weaker, and then stronger again in the uncertain breeze. Bright let the reins hang loosely in his hand, allowing the horse to slouch unhurriedly down the middle of the road until at last they pulled to a halt before a gigantic gate, its ornate wings swung wide. The road continued on, bisecting a rolling ocean of tight green grass, threading its way between several nickel-colored ponds and curling itself finally around a gushing fountain. Behind the fountain, like a series of new white molars, rose a huge and beautiful palace. Margaret's auto was parked there at the foot of a set of creamy steps that led up to the gleaming golden front door.

"The girl Margaret waits within. Go to her quickly."

"That place ain't hers," Bright said, shaking his head.

"Think again, Henry Bright."

"Even if it was hers, if you think I'm impressed by a palace you can forget it," Bright said. "I seen a hundred palaces in France, all of them just like this one here." His eyes drifted across the expanse of green to the building a long moment.

The wind buffeted again at their backs, as if to push him forward, but before he took a step the driver of Margaret's car emerged from the palace, carrying the bags for a finely dressed couple and a young child. He ushered them into the auto, then arranged their luggage on the car's roof before getting in behind the wheel and circling around the fountain and back down the road, toward the gate where Bright now stood. His path once more blocked by Bright and his animals, the driver slowed to a crawl and stopped until Bright pulled the livestock to the side of the road and let the car pass. As it did, Bright recognized the child within as one from the clutch that had surrounded Margaret earlier. She was a little girl with a wine-colored cap, and she now sat happily on the lap of a woman who was clearly her mother.

"Well," Bright said, turning to face the horse.

"Go to Margaret, Henry Bright."

"She ain't no mother of five children, you idiot! She probably ain't even a mother at all." He swung his arm behind in the direction of the palace. "And that palace over there? That's a hotel! I seen those in France too. I even stayed in one once. Either you're trying to trick me or you don't know what you're talking about."

"I am only trying to help you."

"Some help you are. That girl Margaret minds children for rich folks." He threw a caustic laugh in the horse's face. A touch of spittle landed on the its dark nose, startling the beast. "*You know everything!* I just bet you do!"

The angel was silent.

Bright tied the horse's lead tightly around a tree. Then he went to fill a pail with water from one of the small ponds on the lawn. He came back into the trees and plunked the bucket down in front of the horse. "Everything you told me so far has been wrong," he said, as it lowered its head to drink. "I come back from the War and you show up all of a sudden, tell me I gotta go steal Rachel from her own house, and I listen to you and go on over there and get her in the middle of the night and the old man comes out yelling he's gonna kill me. Then she's having a baby and you don't help us and she dies. Rachel! Now the Colonel and his boys are gonna kill me and take my son—"

"The old man and the half-wits are not chasing you," the angel interrupted.

"You say that, but you been wrong about everything else!"

"They are not chasing you."

79

"I loved Rachel, angel! I loved her! Maybe you don't know about that kind of thing."

"You are being a coward, Henry Bright. Go and—"

"She was my wife!" he screamed. His eyes were red-rimmed and welled with tears. His lower lip trembled. There was a twitch in the skin over his cheekbone and he tried to smooth it out by rasping a hand over his face and looking up into the hazy sky until he had composed himself. "And *now*," he said, once he was able to continue, "you want me to give my boy to that girl Margaret in there because you say she's a mother, and now I find out that she's not even a mother at all."

The goat began to pull on its tether, straining toward a bush. Bright bent and untied it to forage. The horse rumbled deep in its throat.

"You'll get your food when I say you do," he snapped. "And I'll tell you another thing: Everything you tell me is wrong and makes me look like a fool. So why am I supposed to believe you? And don't say something like, 'It's because I know,' 'cause we both know that ain't gonna wash with me no more." He took the baby out of its sling and laid it on his jacket on the ground.

"Go."

"No, no, no! I ain't going. This is a wild-goose chase. Only thing we got to do is stay away from the Colonel, and that's just what we're gonna do. We'll stop here tonight and head out in the morning. We'll ride another piece tomorrow and another piece the next day."

"The boy will die."

"He ain't gonna die. I ain't gonna let him die, but I ain't gonna do everything you say anymore just 'cause you tell me to." He threw himself on the ground next to his son and cast one arm over his eyes. "If you want that girl so much, then *you* should go and ask her to be *your* mother. We'll just leave you behind in the morning, see if we don't." He rolled over. "Go to hell."

He lay there for a while, and the horse held its peace. Eventually Bright got up, emptied the bucket of water, and went to pick the goat up and carry it out of the dark-green leaves where it was munching contentedly. He milked it for a bit, then set up camp and ate the crackers and wedge of cheese that the woman had given him at the general-merchandise store. After a little while, the big black auto came back, empty of its passengers and their bags. The birds began to sing and then they stopped, and the sky began to darken as night fell. Finally the moon rose, nearly full, but its light seemed to be shining down through a trough of smoke-slicked water, and across the lawn the white hotel fell into dark shadow beneath stars that were fainter than they should have been.

18

Henry's mother taught him how to take care of the rabbits and chickens that they kept in a hutch near the chestnut tree. In the late summer the two of them would eat apples and then push the cores through the fencing and sit watching as the two species shared the remainders decorously with one another. In the mornings the hens liked to lay their eggs in the warmth where the rabbits had been sleeping, and they would squabble and squawk the rabbits out of their beds. This always made his mother laugh, no matter how many times she saw it, and when he heard her laugh it would make Henry laugh too.

The garden patch would be thick with vegetables, and when she gave him haircuts she would keep his hair and show him how to tie it up into little bundles which they would hang on the fence posts around the garden to keep the deer away from the vegetables. He would pick runner beans and bring them to her, and she would put them in jars and boil the jars and then put them on the shelf for winter. When they could get to the tomatoes before the birds did, they would preserve those too, but not before they ate some with eggs and bread.

They had summer squash and acorn squash and some stalks of corn. She would make the corn silk into a beard and hold it to her face like a monster and chase him around with it while he screamed in terrified delight and the chickens and rabbits clacked and scampered in their pen.

When he was seven and it was time for him to start going to school in Fells Corner, she got a job cooking for an old couple in town. Each morning, after the chickens and rabbits had been fed, they would head out. Whatever else she took with her, his mother always carried her rifle slung across her shoulders, and he knew to be quiet and not talk while they passed the turnoff to the Colonel's house. She would grip his hand hard then, pulling him along, so that he could never see past the first bend in the drive. He knew somehow that she had used to live there, until something bad had happened.

When the Colonel's little boys, Corwin and Duncan, started to come to school too, sometimes they would all be on the road together at the same time. He knew his mother didn't like them, was maybe even afraid of them the way she was always sure to place herself between them and Henry as they walked.

Sometimes it was the Colonel's little girl, Rachel, who would be standing at the end of the drive of his mother's old house, waiting for them to walk by so that she could join them. His mother liked Rachel. She was a funny one, his mother said. She would tell funny stories about big green monsters and beautiful ladies and knights that lived in castles and chased wild pigs. And she was pretty, his mother said. Her clothes were very bad, though. Her skirts were muddy at the hems, and even the parts that weren't muddy were dirty, like they had never been washed. She never had any food with her and she smelled bad. Her hair was all knotted, and she had a single green ribbon that she always untied from her hair and tied round her wrist because she liked to see it and was afraid to lose it. Even the ribbon was dirty, though.

One time, while he and Rachel were walking ahead of his mother, Rachel made him hold her hand and told him that they were going to get married. He didn't say anything. It was like she had cast a special spell for him, like the women in the stories she told. He didn't want to ruin her spell. Even after the teacher told Corwin and Duncan that they couldn't come to school anymore, for the way they were with the other children, Rachel still came each morning, walking alongside Henry and his mother. His mother put more food in Henry's lunch bucket. She began to bring the beautiful ivory comb with her, and with it she would work the knots out of the girl's hair before they came in view of the schoolhouse.

For the Christmas program, Henry was to be a donkey and Rachel was to be an angel. His mother made him funny brown ears from the fabric of a flour sack and they practiced making donkey sounds for weeks. On the night of the program, they crunched through the snow and met Rachel in the darkness at the end of her drive, and then they all walked together. When they got to the schoolhouse, it was brightly lit and whole sleighloads of people were arriving in their best clothes. Before they went in, Henry's mother tied a new piece of ribbon—bright and glossy gold—around the girl's head.

"There, you beautiful girl," she had said. "Now you look like a real angel with your own halo."

Even from the vantage point of a donkey, Rachel had looked glorious.

Henry was eight years old before he saw the Colonel. He came to their cabin on the very day that the first green blades of corn began knifing through the slush of the farmyard. He had gray hair cut close. His beard was trim and the same color of gray as the hair at his temples. His eyes were flat and spoon-colored, set within an angular face that seemed carved out of a large block of salt. His back, beneath a military uniform much frayed from use, was so straight and sharp of shoulder, and his legs in their black riding boots so thin and knobble-kneed, that the man seemed almost to have been fashioned in a workshop rather than a womb. To Henry, he looked like the monster his mother pretended to be sometimes when she would hold the corn silk to her face and chase him around the yard. Henry knew then that the man was the Colonel, and that the Colonel was a monster too. He waited for Henry to fetch his mother.

When she came, she stood at the cabin flap and looked at the Colonel for a long moment. She put her hands on Henry's shoulders and pulled the boy closer to her. "What can we help you with today, sir?" she said. "Maybe you'll want some tomatoes or some beans and then you'll go on your way." She did not ask the man inside.

"She is dying," the Colonel said. "She has been calling for you."

His mother's tongue caught in her throat with a click until she forcibly cleared it. She let go of Henry's shoulders and wiped her hands on her apron at the words. "All right." She disappeared into the blackness of the cabin, and when she reappeared her hair was tied back and she was no longer wearing the apron. Her knuckles knotted and unknotted themselves around the stock of the rifle that she held between her breasts. "This is loaded," she told the Colonel. Then, to Henry, "Henry, wash your face and fetch a clean shirt. Quick, now, we're going to meet your aunt Rebecca."

Henry did as he was told and came to stand by his mother and the Colonel.

"Good man." The Colonel smiled faintly down at him. "Rum rations doubled." He bowed and swept a courtly arm up the road.

"Don't speak to my son," his mother said. "And we'll walk behind you, not the other way around."

"Chivalry is—"

"Keep it," she said.

As they came up the drive, Henry was happy to see Rachel standing on the porch, but when they got closer he could see that she had been crying. His mother saw the girl too, and she slung the rifle by its strap over her back. It rattled against her shoulder blades as she ran up the steps and pulled the girl close. Only when she saw the Colonel's two boys standing silently in the open door did she become wary once more and release Rachel, pulling the gun back around into her hands so that the barrel pointed at the space of porch between her own feet and the boys'. Corwin, thick-lipped, his eyes cast downward and his fingers kneading themselves into fat fists, refused to acknowledge Henry or Henry's mother. Duncan, yowl-eyed and willowy, regarded them both with the steadiness of an underfed barn cat. Henry's mother turned to the Colonel. "Where is she?"

Henry followed her through the front door and into the gloom of the Colonel's house. In front of them a staircase led to the second floor, but his mother did not ascend it, instead veering left and into a large sitting room festooned with portraits. Here the air was heavy and the light pierced through the gap-toothed slats of the shutters like hot knitting needles. A woman dressed in an old gown lay on her back upon a table in the middle of the room. Henry's mother went to the head of the table and gazed down. That the women were sisters was unmistakable, and yet, while Henry's mother was healthy and strong, her sister's face was sunken, her arms at her sides like sticks, her tiny feet laced tightly within ankle-high black boots. She did not seem able to move save for her eyes, which blinked at a crack in the ceiling plaster above her.

"Colonel," his mother said, as she turned and fixed the man with a look of hatred, "I'll ask you for a few minutes alone with

86

my sister please." The Colonel backed out of the archway, through the front door and down to the yard. When he was gone, she turned and leaned over the woman. "Rebecca?" She said the name very quietly. "Rebecca? Can you hear me?" She laid her hand on the table and then rested it on her sister's hand. "He came and told me you were asking for me." She beckoned Henry to her side. "Henry, come here and say hello to your aunt Rebecca."

Henry had been standing in the center of the room, afraid of the woman on the table in front of him, and afraid of Corwin and Duncan standing with Rachel in the archway behind. He approached slowly. The woman tore her eyes off the ceiling crack and looked at Henry blisteringly. Her pupils were very large in the dimness and they jittered back and forth like birds in shaken cages. He had to look away, and when he looked back her eyes were once more fastened on the ceiling above.

"Last time you saw him was when he was born," his mother said. "He's growing up into a big strong man like our own brother Henry was." The woman's hands were small and seemed covered over with the kind of thin, beautiful skin that frogs have. "It's all right about everything," his mother said to the woman. "I know it didn't turn out like you thought it would. It didn't turn out that way for me either. We both know where things went wrong, but it's no good worrying about any of it now. The world got us all at once. First with our Henry dying in the Philippines, then Mother and Father"—here she turned and looked out the window at the Colonel on the lawn—"then my own husband buried in the coal mine before he could lay eyes on his son." She raised Rebecca's hands a little and then lowered them again as she leaned over her. "Too much," she said quietly. "Too much all at once." She let go of the woman's hands in order to fasten a stray button at the top of the woman's neckline. "We can't blame each other for all the things we said to each other that we didn't mean, but I know we can't say we're sorry either. So I'll just say that I love you. I love you so much. Looks like you have some really fine children here, and I'm gonna pray for them. I'm gonna pray really hard for them and I'm gonna pray hard for you and that we meet again in a better world than this one we've been given." She bent and kissed her sister on each of her cheeks and then, taking the ivory comb from the folds of her skirt, she began to comb the woman's hair. "I'm not gonna leave you here like this," she said, her voice turning as thin and jagged as the crack in the ceiling.

"Children," she said. "If you stay, you need to bow your heads and close your eyes and don't open them again, no matter what you do, until I tell you that you can. Henry, go on over there with Rachel and the boys and bow your head too." They did as they were told and she began, her back to them and standing over her sister. "Heavenly Father, if it is true that you give us sorrow and joy in equal measure according to the strength of our backs to bear the load, have mercy on your daughter Rebecca and give her now the joy in her new life that you withheld from her in this one." Henry opened his eyes to peek at his mother, but he couldn't see her face. "We pray that as she enters your kingdom . . ."

Her voice left off suddenly and her body hunched with some strange effort, her head bowed from sight beneath the line of her shoulders. The rifle slung over his mother's shoulder shifted this way and that as if it was aiming at some high-flying, far-off bird. Rebecca's tiny boots kicked against the table three or four times, then lay still.

In the silence that followed, Henry looked over at Rachel and her brothers. Corwin and Rachel's heads were bowed, but Duncan's eyes were wide open and he was watching Henry's mother as well. After a long while a sigh escaped her lips and she continued, "We pray, Heavenly Father, that as she enters your kingdom you will offer her some explanation for the sorrows that you, in your infinite wisdom, saw fit to visit upon her." His mother's hands dropped to her sides all at once. She turned, the rifle butt clanking hard against the parquet as she sank to the floor. She pulled the gun around and laid it across her lap, leaning back against one of the table legs for support. She closed her eyes. "Amen."

She opened them again. Her hair was mussed, her face as waxen as her dead sister's. Corwin and Rachel still had their eyes closed and their heads bowed. She glanced at Henry and then at Duncan. The boy looked back at her steadily. She looked more exhausted than Henry had ever seen her. She reached behind with one hand and used the lip of the table to pull herself to standing. "Corwin, Rachel, you can open your eyes now. Henry," she said, "come along with me."

She walked through the upper rooms, standing in doorways, trailing her hands absentmindedly behind her along the walls as if her fingertips were collecting old memories. Here and there a few strips of dirty wallpaper had once been printed with lilac bunches and roses. One room had been a nursery, and where there had been a water closet, part of the wall had fallen away, the room dropping off abruptly into open air and the dusty lawn below. The tub and washbasin were filled with old charcoal.

There was a sharp, mildewed odor to the rooms. Plaster pieces lay fallen and cracked everywhere. One room was bare save for a pair of boots lined up against a wall, a broomstick planted stick-down in the hole of one as if awaiting the firing squad. "It didn't used to look like this, Henry," she blurted all at once, standing framed in the crumbling hallway. "It was a beautiful house once. Do you believe me?"

89

He went to take her hand, but she brushed by him now and ran down the stairs. He went to a window and looked down to the yard where she had joined the Colonel. She was leaning forward and speaking to the man's unmoving profile, strands of her hair escaping the knot she had tied it in and puffing into cirri around her face. Henry crept down the stairs to the porch and stood half hidden in the doorway, next to Rachel. The Colonel seemed oblivious to his mother's ferocious presence. He stared off into nothing as she spat words so quietly at him that Henry couldn't make them out.

Just when it seemed he had turned into some Civil War statue the Colonel collapsed from his reverie and walked to the squash patch and pulled a rusty shovel from where it was stuck into the ground. "Boys!" he yelled toward the house, and looked off into the far distance as he waited for an answer. When none came, he did not call again, instead holding the shovel handle toward the open doorway where Henry was standing.

Henry's mother snatched it away from the Colonel and stepped back, the shovel in one tightly clenched hand, the rifle in the other. "What in God's name *are* you?" she hissed. "Henry!"

He was down off the porch and at her side in a moment. She did not look away from the Colonel as she held the rifle down for him to hold. "You remember how to use this, don't you?"

Henry nodded, taking the gun in his hands.

"Yes, you do. And you remember how I taught you to pull the hammer back so the gun is cocked and ready to fire?"

He nodded his head once more.

"Good," she said. "Now, I want you to cock the gun carefully, all right? Pull it back with your thumb like I showed you." There was a click as the hammer locked. "Good, Henry." She seemed to exhale forever. "Now I want you to point it at him, and if you see him move from where he's standing, I want you to shoot him dead." Her eyes flitted quickly down to see if he'd comprehended. "Do you understand me? If he moves while I'm digging this hole, I want you to shoot him dead in the face. You don't even ask me if you should; you just pull the trigger. I need you to protect me, Henry. Can you do that?"

He clenched the rifle so tightly in his hands that his fingers began to tingle and whiten. In answer, he pointed the gun up at the Colonel's head. The Colonel stared hard at Henry, and those spoon-colored eyes frightened him, but he hid the man's face behind the eclipse of the rifle barrel and kept it there as his mother dug the grave.

The early-spring ground was still frozen solid beneath the slush, and digging was nearly impossible. She chiseled away at it nevertheless, steam rising first from her mouth and then from her entire body before she broke down and sat in the middle of the shallow gash she had cut in the yard. When she caught her breath she got up and began again. Henry's arms began to tire and his fingers to feel numb from holding the heavy rifle trained on the Colonel. By the time his mother had dug a trench two and a half feet deep he was nearly weeping from the weight of the thing. She stood back and let the shovel fall on the frozen pile of chipped dirt by the side of the hole. She came and knelt next to Henry. He tried to give the rifle to her but after an hour his fingers seemed locked around it. Her eyes shone as she eased the hammer back down and helped each of his fingers to uncurl from the gun. "That was just fine, Henry. Your father would be proud of you." She kissed his cheek and then heaved herself up with the rifle and walked up the steps into the house. The Colonel followed close behind her.

Standing at the foot of the table, she took her sister's ankles in her blistered hands and made ready to lift them. The

Colonel went to the head and stood looking down into his wife's face. He removed his broad-brimmed hat and ran his hand through the plastered strands of his hair. "Well, that is that," he said. He reset his hat firmly on his head and strode from the room without a second glance, leaving her still holding the dead woman's ankles at the foot of the table.

She set the legs down and came to kneel next to Henry. "I'm going to need your help one more time. This will be hard, but we'll go slowly. Will that be all right?"

Henry looked out the doorway where the Colonel had gone and nodded yes.

"Now, I want you to go to where I was standing and I want you to try to hold those legs up while I pull her off the table. Can you do that?"

He nodded again and went to where she had been standing.

His mother took the body by the armpits and began to pull it slowly down the length of the table. Henry followed the dead woman's feet as they slid down the long plane of wood, and he tried to catch them as his mother finally pulled the last length of the woman's body off the table, but the legs were too heavy and the little black boots passed through his hands and thumped to the floor. His mother caught her breath and considered her sister's body. She looked at the doorway warily before taking the rifle from around her back and nestling it in her sister's arms. They half carried, half dragged the deadweight a few feet at a time until, as they passed into the hallway and neared the front door, his mother gave up trying to carry the body at all. Instead, she grabbed whole ripping handfuls of the woman's gown and heaved her over the threshold and down the porch stairs each step punctuated by the dragging *rat-tat* thump of the boots. At last the body rested in the dirt at the Colonel's feet. She bent and pulled the rifle from her sister's embrace.

"You haven't got a box, have you?"

The Colonel stood erect and did not reply, so she cocked the rifle and handed it back to Henry, who pointed it at the man while she climbed into the shallow grave and pulled the body in after her.

She took a long time arranging her sister in the narrow hole, brushing the dust as best she could off the gown, combing her hair once more with the ivory comb. The arms, which had twisted in their joints from being dragged, did not look right. She tucked them behind the body, so that the dead woman appeared to be clasping her hands behind her as she walked through a doorway from one world into the next.

Finally, she closed her sister's eyes, climbed out of the grave, and, after taking the rifle back from Henry, allowed her gaze to rove the house and the overgrown craze of bramble and crabgrass that lived in its shadow. She put a hand on Henry's shoulder. "We're going now," she said to the Colonel. "She was my sister but she was your wife, and I'll not be the one to bury her. That's for you to do, and I know you know how to do that at least," she said. "It didn't take you long to get my father in the ground. If he'd known what kind of a man you really were, he'd have shot you down like a sick horse. He might not have been a colonel, like you claimed to be, but he fought in a war too, and when he came home he held his head high." She spat on the ground. "Look at you," she said to the uniformed figure, "*Colonel* Morse." She said the name as if it were a bad taste. "They were all so proud of you. She was so proud of you. A colonel. The last man to know my brother." She snorted once with derisive finality. "To think anyone was ever worried about the family name because I married a coal miner."

The Colonel's eyes raked across her face, but he said nothing.

"Rachel," she said to the small girl in the doorway. "I want

93

you to come live with Henry and me now. Just leave your things and come along. This isn't the place for you to live anymore."

"Leave her be," the Colonel said quietly. "That is my daughter."

The girl in the threshold curled her neck around the door frame like a little swan, her body still subsumed by the interior shadows behind her.

Henry's mother raised the rifle with one hand until it was pointing at the Colonel. With the other hand she beckoned to the girl. "Rachel? Just come along now, all right? You're going to come and live with us."

The girl wavered, looking in confusion between the face of Henry's mother and the Colonel. The man did not turn to his daughter but continued to regard Henry's mother.

"It's all right, girl," his mother said. "He isn't gonna hurt you. He knows this is no place for little girls. You know that too, don't you? Come along now."

The girl's dirty face flickered. She unfolded herself from the door frame and came walking slowly down off the porch. The Colonel lunged and grabbed her as she was about to pass. He pulled her close to him, and the girl did not resist, appeared in fact to relax into the surety of her father's grip.

"She is my daughter," the Colonel said. "You dare insult a grieving man."

"Rachel," Henry's mother said. "Little girl, if you ever need anything, if anything ever happens to you, I want you to come find me, do you hear? You know where we live."

All the way back to the cabin, his mother walked facing backward, the rifle gripped so hard in her hands that her knuckles looked as if they might pop out from beneath her skin. Once they were home, she put it up in the rafters where she always kept it and sat down on the footstool by the empty fireplace a long, long time, rubbing her shins beneath her skirt and staring into the charred rocks at the bottom of the flue. Henry went outside and played with the rabbits and chickens through the fencing. As the sun was going down, he went and threw rocks on the road. Only when the sky was as black as the fireplace itself did his mother emerge from the cabin and fetch some wood for a cook fire.

19

The night passed with agonizing slowness as Bright lay in the ditch beneath Bert's body. He thought for a long time about the girl in the church, about her beautiful face and the way that she had looked down from the ceiling at him in the very instant he had put his head through the doorway. It had been as if, in that moment, the girl had wished to go with him but knew that she never could, that her fate was elsewhere. He knew that look well. He'd seen it on Rachel's face the last time she had come to their house.

It had been almost two weeks since the death of his aunt Rebecca, and his own mother had been in the house working to mend a hole in the bed quilt. Henry had been in the yard when he glanced up and saw the girl standing there in the road. He knew immediately that everything was different now. She was not the same girl that he had been walking to school with every morning for two years, not the same one who had told him that he and she would one day be married or who had laughingly piled the peeping golden chicks on his chest. This girl looked as if some giant from one of her own stories had stooped down and whispered the world's largest, worst secrets in her ear. She was barefoot. He could have gone to her, but something, some new kind of law, prevented it. Instead, he had raised his hand to her and she, after a moment, returned the gesture. The golden ribbon was tied around her wrist. She had looked at Henry with the same expression on her face as the girl on the church ceiling. It was a look of farewell, he realized now, lying there in the ditch. She had come to tell him goodbye. She never went to school or came back to the cabin again after that day. Perhaps she didn't even remember who he was anymore.

"She does."

The world once again got very still, very small at the sound of the voice.

"You hear me, Henry Bright." The voice was very close to his ear in the blackness.

"Yes," he said finally. Then, "Who are you?"

"I am an angel, Henry Bright, be not afraid."

"I am." His throat was tight with fear and the words came out with a cracked, whistling sound. "I am afraid."

"Be not," the voice said again.

"Where are you?"

"Henry Bright, be quiet. Look."

He was quiet and he looked. The sky was getting infinitesimally lighter now, and in the farmhouse down the road, through the gaping holes of one of the window frames, he saw something move. It was slight, a kind of rustle upon the eyes that carried no sound, but it was there nonetheless. "Who is it?"

"I am an angel. Be not afraid."

"No," he whispered. "Who is that down there, moving around down there?"

"You must lie very still."

The squat figure of a stoop-shouldered man emerged from the house. He stood there in the door frame and looked up into the blue moonlit sky before walking into the middle of the road and stretching, as if just having risen from a heavy meal. The doorway disgorged another figure, this one much thinner than

97

his companion. The two stood in confab a moment, the silver splinters of rifle barrels glinting down their backs in the moon-light. It was too dark to tell what uniforms they wore, but as the duo began to walk down the road in his direction, their move-ments were animated with a kind of easy contentment, as if whichever side they belonged to, they felt quite safe in their sur-roundings.

He tried to pull Bert's body even farther on top of him.

"Lie still, Henry Bright."

He lay still as they passed him by, but they could not have gone twenty feet when Bert's empty canteen shifted somehow in the dark and fell against the stone wall, making a clinking sound. Bright caught his breath and, as he did, Bert's corpse shifted above him once again, the dead man's head lolling to re-lease a stream of cold, thick fluid onto his face. He coughed quietly once against the wetness.

"Lie still, Henry Bright."

The footsteps pulled up short and stood there in silence. Then the boots came back, mulching and sucking against the mud of the road.

"Close your eyes. Do it now."

He closed his eyes and pretended to be dead. The boots stood there in the darkness a long time. Then there came a cracking of joints and the crunkle of leather as one of the figures stooped to a squat for a closer look. A hand came down softly on Bert's back, resting there like the kind of close friend that it was likely Bert had never had. The hand whispered up and down the fabric of the dead man's back two or three times and then a palm was running along the scalp of Bert's head, and more cold fluid dripped and slid onto Bright's face. The fingers trailed down past Bert's ear and then down the nape of the dead man's neck until they came to rest on the crest of Bright's eyebrow. He held his breath in agony as the hand made its way across the wet, sticky surface of his eyelids, down his cheek, and then slowly pried his lips apart and slid into his mouth. The fingers worked between Bright's teeth and under his tongue as he struggled to hold his breath. Just when he felt that he might explode from lack of air, the fingers pulled away and the figure stood. A metallic sound was followed by a quick punch of pressure from above, and a harsh, sulfurous rip of air escaped Bert's bloating body through the puncture made by a bayonet. The blade came down hard three more times, but due to Bert's girth Bright was untouched. What followed was the kind of long, steady silence that accompanies surveyal, and Bright waited behind closed eyes for the bayonet to come for him, but the awful silence went on for so long that he began to wonder whether the figures had somehow slipped away. When the agony of waiting was too much for him, he found himself, almost against his own volition, opening his eyes a fraction in the moonlight, catching the men's familiar faces in the instant before they turned and continued walking away from him down the road. He did not need an angel to tell him who it was he had seen.

20

Bright couldn't sleep, and so he lay looking at the bilious sky and the hotel, which sat in its pool of electric light there in the middle of the darkened lawn. On occasion the breeze scooped up a few jostling strains of music being played on a piano, and once or twice voices broke out in singing. The infuriating horse shifted lazily on its feet but then slept. It lay down once to dream, but then it got up again. When the baby cried he fed it from the goat's milk and rocked it slowly until it fell asleep again. Later, he woke to find the hotel silent, and he changed the boy's diaper in the darkness. When this was done, he fed it once more. Rachel's nipples had been small, thimbly things, much tinier than his big index finger. On impulse, he dipped his little finger in the milk and offered it to his son. The boy took it in his mouth and suckled greedily.

She had been out milking the goat when her water broke. As usual in warm summer weather, she was naked, the skin stretched tightly across her enormous belly. She stood there in the yard and called to him. The goat was standing near the puddle of fluid, neck craned up at her. Together the goat and the girl looked at Bright. He had tried to pick her up to take her inside, but she had waved him away and finished milking the goat first.

He stood above her, unsure of whether to touch her or not,

and then after a while he went to stand with the horse under the chestnut tree. "Well," he said, "I guess that it's happening now. This is what we talked about, ain't it?" He watched the girl milk. The horse was not watching, but its nostrils flared, pulling in drafts of the new scent and chuffing them out again. "And she's happy, ain't she? I mean, we're going to have a baby. What I mean to say is, thank you for making me go over there and steal her away."

The horse said nothing in reply.

"Angel?" he said, but if the angel was there it gave no answer.

His wife stood then, the bucket in her hand. "Maybe it's time we went in to the bed and see what happens," she said, and held an arm out for him to slip his shoulder under.

He went to her then, the angel forgotten, and carried her feetfirst through the cabin flap, one arm holding the bucket, one arm slung around his neck.

That was the last time she ever put her arm around him. After that had come a feverish nightmare that he could remember only pieces of. The baby's head was large, and he had twisted around sideways. Bright had been forced to reach in, as he'd seen a man do once with a cow, and pull the infant out by its heels. At some point during this time Rachel had died. He wasn't sure quite when. Maybe she had looked at him and tried to say something. Maybe she had said something. She could have been screaming something; he might have been screaming too, but suddenly there was only a single sound in the cabin, and that was the crying of their son, the boy who now lay in a clean diaper against his chest.

21

They had watched the young boys as they fished and played in the swimming hole below the railroad trestle. When the sun was starting to sink, the Colonel and his sons emerged from the trees and made themselves known to the boys, who looked at the Colonel in his tattered uniform as if he were some kind of Confederate ghost. While Corwin and Duncan stood on the bank, the Colonel waded into the middle of the stream up to his waist and stiffly saluted the boys on the far bank.

"Which of you here is the eldest?" he called out to them.

The narrow-chested boy who had examined Bright's uniform lifted his hand. He was perhaps ten years old.

"I see," the Colonel said with a curt nod. "And did you take any part in the recent War?"

The boy was baffled and looked at his friends for some kind of answer to the strange man's question.

"You mean over there?" another boy said.

"That is correct, sir," the Colonel replied. "Over there."

"No," the boy said. He puffed out his chest. "But I woulda gone!"

"Brave boy, brave boy," the Colonel said quietly, as the

stream rushed around him. "Of that I have no doubt. You may observe that I also am a soldier."

The boy nodded.

"A soldier always recognizes a brother soldier. It has nothing to do with uniform. It has to do with bearing." He leaned forward in the flow and lowered his voice conspiratorially. "My own sons, the ones on the far bank back there, are not soldiers, sadly. They have none of your martial bearing."

"We saw another soldier here today," the boy said.

"Yes?"

"Yessir."

"Good man. That was my next question. He must have been my son-in-law. A great war hero."

"A war hero?"

"Oh, yes. And did he have a child with him?"

"Yessir. He had a little baby, and a white goat that climbs on rocks, and a horse too."

"A little baby, did you say?"

"Yessir."

"We were escaping the fire and were separated in the confusion. Can you tell me which way he went?"

Corwin and Duncan had begun to set up camp when he waded back across the stream. "The rogue made his way to a town not far from here. He is bent on some new seduction, no doubt. Probably already visiting whores."

Duncan looked up from a pile of sticks that he was gathering together to build a fire.

"No doubt," Corwin said. "He's probably visiting whole bunches of 'em!"

"Contractions," the Colonel said.

"What?"

"I will not have sons of mine speaking in contractions," the

103

Colonel said very calmly. "'Ain't,' 'dasn't,' 'won't,' 'of 'em'— how many times have I berated you, beaten you both, in the vain hope that you will learn to speak in a manner that does not insult the listener with your ignorance?"

"Lots of times," Duncan said.

"What was that, my boy?"

"Lots of times," Duncan said again. "You've berated and beaten us lots of times."

The Colonel sighed and sat down in his wet boots and trousers. Almost immediately he stood up again.

"We will not sleep here tonight."

Corwin, who had found a patch of blackberries by the bank, looked up pleadingly. "Why not?"

"Because Henry Bright may come back in the night and find us unawares. Also, the fire is coming quite close. Should you prefer death by flames or rogue to a restful night's sleep, you are under no obligation to follow me to my mountainous redoubt."

"So?" Corwin gripped a blackberry bramble to pull himself up the bank and winced as the thorns cut into his hand. "So what if he comes? We'll kill that son of a whore, won't we?"

The Colonel threw a stick at Corwin. "Contractions! And, anyway," he lowered his voice, "how would you propose to kill Henry Bright, who has recently returned from the War and is well practiced in the taking of life?"

"We could shoot him with the rifle?"

"With the rifle? You may remember, my son, how, without permission, you went to shoot with the rifle in the woods, bring- ing it home to me without ammunition?"

Corwin looked down into the stream. "The knife, then?"

"Ah, yes, the knife." The Colonel took the blade out from his belt and held it up. "It *is* a fine blade. At any rate, I will sleep up there tonight." He turned and began walking toward the slope of tailings that led up the steep incline to the mouth of the tunnel.

Duncan stood and looked down blankly at the tinder he had carefully arranged for a fire. He ran a hand through his hair two or three times, then followed his father and brother.

"I bet he was visiting whole bunches of whores!" Corwin whispered again to Duncan after night had fallen and they were safely encamped in the railroad tunnel. "Whole bunches!" Duncan listened to his brother's conjectures without reply. "Whoooooooooo!" Corwin hoot-owled behind him in the dark. "Oooooooooo!" his echo came back.

"Silence!" the Colonel yelled. He lit his pipe with an ember from the fire and listened to the river below. "Mark me well, boys, Henry Bright is not content to seduce and murder only one woman; no, he will do it over and over again. He must be killed and his child taken and raised properly." He talked on like this for a little while, caught up in whores and murder.

At some point in his father's monologue and his brother's hooting, Duncan stepped from the mouth of the tunnel and climbed out onto an outcrop of the cliff face just to the side of the trestle tracks. He curved his thin torso tightly against the rock wall. "Train," he said softly.

It happened very fast. The light of the train filled the tunnel, and the breeze sucked past them; the Colonel left off from his sacred vows and bloody imaginings, and Corwin from his hooting. Both burst out of the tunnel's mouth and onto the moonlit trestle. Corwin found the opposite ledge from Duncan and somehow managed to pull his big body up onto it, hugging the cliff side in terror and leaving his father to stand blinded and trapped on the tracks above the abyss. The Colonel stood agape only a moment before he ripped his belt off. The knife fell away and was swallowed up by the emptiness. For an instant his crouching form was silhouetted by the locomotive's headlight against the slope of the far mountainside. Then he was gone.

He hung there in the cathedral darkness, his belt looped over a trestle tie as the wheels razored deafeningly above him. When the train had crossed over the canyon and disappeared into another tunnel on the far side, he called out for his boys to pull him up. He brushed himself off, patting and straightening his clothes.

"My knife." He looked over the side of the trestle, but the watery dark below was even blacker than the smoke-blotted night sky above. The knife was gone. "The rifle," he said then. "God help the both of you if the rifle is gone." It was not. The gun lay against the tunnel wall and had been untouched by the passing train. All that it needed was bullets.

22

After he was sure that the Colonel's sons were well and truly gone, Henry Bright lay in the ditch beneath Bert's body and waited for the voice that said it was an angel to speak to him again. He waited for a long time but it didn't, so he remained there, unmoving lest he be seen or heard. Bert got colder and stiffened above him. The sky changed color with the same maddening imperceptibility as time's passage.

He was sure that he had not been dreaming when he heard the voice. It had been very clear, had spoken his name, had told him what to do. He stared intently at the sky for a time more. A flock of geese passed overhead—very high up—and then, lower in the sky, the first rays of sun played themselves against the wing of an airplane. In the dawning light it looked like the lost leaf of some autumnal tree, baked golden and blown far afield. Finally, he twisted his torso in the ditch and, getting his palms flat against Bert's chest, he gave a great push until he could look the dead boy in the face. Bert's mouth had been very close to Bright's ear all night. His eyes were open, and in death they looked every bit as confused and angry as they had in life, the childlike glare of one who has grown up suspecting that he's being laughed at. Bright had seen another boy once, about to go over the top of the trenches, suddenly turn white, his hands moving through every pocket and then searching his helmet before looking around in a mute panic at the others as they made their preparations. He had lost the address of a girl that he'd met on leave. Where could it be? Would he ever see her again? It was not a thing to worry about for a boy going almost certainly to death, but there it was, and what it was, it was. Another time, while sitting out a mortar barrage in a muddy, melting trench for almost six hours, Bright watched a man pour a portion of kerosene on a sleeping friend's foot and light the man's big toe on fire. The joke had been far more absorbing to everyone than the hell going on above.

Perhaps it was Bert who had chosen to speak Henry Bright's name as his last words, Bert who had somehow proclaimed himself an angel and warned him of the coming of the Colonel's sons. There were certainly stranger last words in the history of war. But what of the voice he had heard by the animal trough, the one that had told him to wait before dipping his canteen in the poisoned water? Could that voice really have been Bert's as well? There were no answers in that vacant stare. He relaxed his arms and let the body fall back on top of him.

Suddenly he heard voices coming toward him down the road. They were plain, real voices and, most important, they were discussing a Brooklyn Robins baseball game. "American!" he called out, but his voice was far gone from thirst and exhaustion, and it was hard to draw enough breath to yell with Bert's deadweight pressing down on his chest. "American," he said again, more softly.

A long, narrow face came into his vision. "Jesus! Nice place to go lie down! Give me a hand with the big one here," the slight man said to an apple-cheeked, larger man over his shoulder. The two rolled Bert's body off Bright. "They get you?"

"No." He lay there pressed into the mud of the ditch until they pulled him to his feet.

"What happened? Christ, look at your face."

Bright tried to wipe Bert's blood from his face with his jacket sleeve, but it had dried there and his lips were tacky with the stuff. He explained about the shelling of the village, leaving out the parts about the Colonel's sons and the angel's visitation.

The narrow-faced one looked at his bigger companion and they both burst out laughing. "Do you know how lucky you are, kid?" the narrow-faced one asked. "Krauts were only sixty yards away." He shifted a water bucket to his other hand and pointed with his free arm toward the farmhouse. "You slept next to 'em most of the night."

"How many were there?"

"Who knows, but they were busy."

"When did you get here?"

"We got orders to scout the village and find out what happened to you guys about an hour ago. Everyone was dead. Not a soul."

" 'Cept you," the other one said.

"I saw them leave. There was only two of them."

"Bullshit."

"They came out of that house and walked right by here, then one came back and did that." He pointed down at the bloodless bayonet holes in Bert's back.

"Well, however many of 'em there were, there were enough," the shorter one said. "Take my word for it." He pointed over at the farmhouse one more time. "Or don't. Take a look in there and see for yourself."

They turned to continue walking, and Bright reached down to Bert's body and pulled the beautiful silver and gold pistol from where it was tucked in the waistband of the dead man's trousers. In the fresh morning light the gun looked sylvan, magical. The writing on the filigreed handle was in German and he could not read it, but the bullets—coppery nocturnal things

109

asleep in their snug chambers—he understood well. He re-
leased the gate and emptied them onto the ground by the bodies of Bert and Carlson, then he followed the two men to a
water pump that had been found in the square. They waited for
Bright while he drank and washed Bert's blood from his face,
then they went to stand joking by a group of ashen-faced others
while Bright walked back down the road to the farmhouse from
which he'd seen Duncan and Corwin emerge. The forced
laughter of the men in the square followed him, a kind of de-
spairing jollity that faded abruptly from his ears as he stooped
to step inside the doorway. A chaplain was within, also gray in
the face. He looked at Bright pleadingly and then spread his
arms as if trying to encompass the pitiable carnage he stood
in the midst of.

After she had waved goodbye to Henry, Rachel didn't come
to meet him and his mother at the end of the drive for the walk
to school anymore. They waited for her the first couple of days,
but when she didn't come they kept going. His mother began to
grip Henry's hand protectively for the first time in a long while.
He was eight now and he didn't like that, but he let her do it
anyway, because he knew she was scared.

One day after school he went to meet his mother where she
cooked for the elderly couple in town, and the two of them had
walked toward home, his mother's rifle, as ever, over her shoulder. As they neared the turn up to her old house, she gripped
Henry's hand even harder than usual. "Hello, Duncan," she
said. The boy was standing at the mouth of the drive, his head
and thin body swaying slightly like a pitcher plant in the still-
ness. Although the weather was cool and he was still a boy, his
sweat-soaked shirt clung to his chest and there were dark circles
under his arms. Duncan said nothing in reply, but he repaid the
stare Henry's mother gave him with his own implacable gaze,
his thoughts as opaque as his pupils. Henry heard the rifle creak

as she shifted it on her back. "Face forward, Henry," she said. "Chin up. Don't look back."

When they arrived home, they found the chickens dead in a white feathery pile, their necks broken. The rabbits had been killed as well and were now tied in drooping clusters to the fence posts around the garden, fastened with the twine that his mother had used to make bundles of Henry's hair. A few of the rabbits had been skinned, and these lay like enormous overripe strawberries in the middle of the garden, beneath where a stick had been stabbed into the ground. At the stick's top was tied the golden ribbon that his mother had given to Rachel at Christmas.

Bright backed out of the farmhouse and sank to his knees in the middle of the road. He vomited thinly, waited, then fell to all fours and gagged until his chest hurt and the sweat ran out of his scalp, down his face, and onto the ground. When he felt strong enough, he got to his feet and walked back to the town square to stand near the body of the dead horse that he had helped to drag from the church the day before. Fragments of plaster painted as blue as the sky itself lay scattered about. The next morning he was back in a cold, wet trench and November was beginning.

23

After he fell back asleep at the edge of the hotel lawn, Bright
dreamed strange, feverish dreams. In one, he found himself
rolling Duncan, still a young boy, over and over again in the
muck of a field. In that strange currency of dreams, he found
the boy to be weightless and his body spun in the mud like a log
floating in a river. Each time the boy's face resurfaced, it was
frozen in some new expression, sometimes smirking mischie-
vously, sometimes grinning widely or pulled forcefully downward like a carp's yaw. Despite the ever-changing set of the
mouth, however, the eyes were always empty black holes that
bored fiercely into Bright. He became wildly angry. He began
to kick and kick Duncan in the head, to no effect. He smelled
the mustard gas, a tingling around his nostrils and lips punctuated by sharp little bites, as if he was about to be devoured by a
swarm of insects. In his rage he could not stop kicking Duncan.
The burning settled like bees around his mouth, and was followed quickly by an awful pain across his neck and chest; still,
he could not stop kicking. Only when he knew that it was too
late and that he would soon die of the gas did his anger begin
to fold. Then he was simply staring at the thin little body bob-
bing in the muck. Duncan's eyes pulled him downward, and his
awful grin had settled itself into a warm, welcoming smile.

Bright he awoke to the sounds of his son crying and the smell of smoke strong in his nose. It was far too early to be dawn, but the sky had taken on a diseased half-light. He propped himself on an elbow and made clucking sounds to comfort the child, but it continued to wail so loudly that Bright replaced the fragile bundle carefully on the blanket and reached for the bucket. He dipped his little finger in the milk for the boy to suckle, but the child was utterly wild in the darkness. He again went to hold his son close, but the boy's shit was everywhere and there was something frantic to the smell: a sour, unwholesome odor that rose from the child like heat. Bright got on his knees above the infant and struck a match; then, as if burned by what he saw, he fell backward. The match went out. In the gloom he put his fist to his mouth and bit down hard, a small sound escaping from far back in his throat. Sweat was running down his back in skeins. He lit another match and looked again. The child's face was covered in amber blisters the size and shape of pumpkin seeds; its mouth was a welter of pain.

He scurried backward on all fours into a thicket of brambles, tearing the skin of his hands and legs. He scratched the ground, clawing at the dirt in his confusion, aware of neither the piercing thorns nor the burning red wings that had spread themselves across his own face and chest while he slept. He looked up a moment at the sleeping horse, then hurriedly scooped the crazed child into his arms, broke out of the woods, and ran across the darkened lawn toward the hotel.

24

"Henry Bright."

He was digging a new latrine pit fifty yards distant from a row of Red Cross tents. If the voice startled him, he gave no indication and said nothing.

"Henry Bright."

A group of soldiers moved down the road—an exchange of shifts. The relievers were tense and quiet, the relieved looking drawn but laughing loudly as they walked.

"Henry Bright."

"I know who you are," he said at last. "You're the angel from the church." He made again to dig. His shovel had run up against the sodden wool of a buried uniform. There was no telling, with the muck, whose side it belonged to. He gave up trying to cut through it with the shovel blade and bent to pull it out with his hands. The ground sucked back hard and would not budge.

"Yes," said the angel. "Fear not."

"The big one talking to the girl up on the ceiling."

"Yes."

"I knew it was you. Why are you here?"

"Because now I'm talking to you."

He gave another great pull on the sleeve of the buried uniform, the veins on his forehead popping and his face going

114

red with the effort. The jacket came away all at once in his hands and he fell backward against the side of the hole. He rested a moment there, and then threw the heavy mass on the ground before taking up the shovel again. He spoke under his breath, his eyes fixed on the latrine he was digging. "Why did you tell me to be quiet?"

"Because I wished to save your life. I have chosen you, Henry Bright. I saw what you tried to do for the horse in the church. I saw you looking up at us, the girl and me."

"Why are you here now?" he repeated. There was a tooth in the shovelful of dirt.

"The church was destroyed. I needed a place to go. I chose you and I am with you now."

"Was it you told me not to drink the water?"

"The water was poisoned," the angel said. "Mustard gas."

"Is it only you come from that church?"

"Yes."

"Where's the girl then? The one on the ceiling up there with you."

"The girl is gone. You and I will find a new girl."

"I'm just digging a latrine is all I'm doing," Bright said, but to whom he was speaking would have been obvious to no one.

25

Standing naked and willow-kneed there near the hotel fountain, he began to scream along with his child. Whoever woke from sleep to peer down from the hundreds of windows at the disturbance below saw a man who could just as easily have been a ghost. His mouth hung open in a wail, and his silhouette, partially obscured by the darkness of the drive, flickered with an otherworldly translucence in the light cast by the corona of the burning ridge behind him.

A light came on, and then another and another. Men dressed in pajamas or hastily thrown-on shirts surrounded him with their lanterns and loud voices. Tears and spittle ran down his face. He held his son out at arm's length toward the uncertain circle of men, as if blindly searching for an altar upon which to offer up the tiny gargoyle of pain.

And then, parting it all, a small and round female figure in a white apron stepped through the circle. Her hair was pulled back and her face was indistinct, lit dimly as it was by the murky orange sky, the lanterns, and the lights of the awoken hotel. The woman approached Bright and his baby slowly.

"Now," she said. "Now, it's all right, it's all right." She talked to him as if he were a shied horse and held out her arms to accept the child. "Give the baby to me." For a brief flash he thought that it was the girl Margaret, but even in his panic he realized that this woman was different, moved with greater bearing than the girl he had first followed to the hotel. She held his face in her gaze for a moment. Then, with what could only be a supernatural grace, she lifted the boy from his arms. The child pressed itself against her, almost butting at her chest with its head. Bright just stood there, his red-rimmed eyes blinking hard against the brightness of the lanterns. Then his teeth began to chatter and he seemed to discover his own nakedness and the red welts that had capered across his thin white chest. The woman put a hand to his head, still rocking the child, then she addressed the men within the circle of light.

"It's all right, gentlemen, just put down the lights, put down the lights, except for you, Dennis." A tall, sandy-haired man in work boots rubbed sleep from his eyes. "The rest of you, it's all right now, it's all right. Just go on back up to bed." She clucked down at Bright's son in her arms.

"You're going to let these two in the building?" a man asked. He had a burgundy nightshirt on, and he pulled incredulously on a corner of his mustache. "They might have the flu." He stepped forward and thrust his light in Bright's face. "Just look!" Bright shrank away from the sudden brilliance of the lantern, and the woman stepped between him and the man.

"I'll take the responsibility for these two myself," she said. The boy had begun to wail again, but his eyes were cried out. "We have a doctor on call in town. We'll send for him"—she turned to a young man groggily buttoning a tan and red uniform—"unless there's one staying here. Is there a doctor staying with us? Yes? Well, then, please wake and fetch him. Apologize, of course." She turned back to the men. "There. He's gone to fetch the doctor. I'll watch them in the meantime."

117

She looked at the man who had lunged at Bright with the lantern. "And you needn't fear; this isn't the first time someone wandered into a patch of poison ivy."

The men put out their lights, and the glow of the forest fire on the ridge seemed to grow brighter. "By the looks of things, I don't imagine that we'll all be worrying too much about poison ivy soon anyhow," she said. The group turned silently and looked at the flames. "Now, Dennis, help me get these two indoors. Sorry for the disturbance, gentlemen. See you in a few hours at breakfast." She carried the child to a set of steps leading down to a door that stood open in the foundation. Dennis followed her, helping Henry Bright to walk across the gravel drive and down the cool flags of the basement steps. The rest of the men stood in the drive by the fountain and stared at the approaching fire for a long time, the crying child and its raging father forgotten.

Bright was laid in a small bed in an empty white room. He cried out. The light burned his eyes.

The woman came in and placed wet rags on his face. "I've had a cradle brought down to my room," she said. "I'll look after your son until you're feeling a bit better, all right?"

Then he lay there, a sliver of yellow coming in from the hallway, and fell asleep as voices murmured low and soft next door. He woke once more in the night and something was poured down his throat. After that he slept, and if he dreamed, the dream was forgotten.

26

"Check his pockets."

"I know to check his pockets!" Bright was on burial detail.

"In his pockets there is a packet of cigarettes and a lemon."

"I know that already, 'cause I saw him put the lemon in his pocket! You saw me see him put the lemon in his pocket!"

"This one has no flask. That last one had a flask. It was in his boot."

"What do you need any whiskey for?"

"You could still get it. It's still there."

"How do you know?"

"I know everything, Henry Bright."

Henry Bright bent down and reached in the dead man's pocket to retrieve the lemon. Unlike the man, the lemon had escaped the machine guns unscathed. He put it into his own pocket and then began to roll the body slowly into the forty-foot-long hole that he and the others had dug for the bodies.

"The packet of cigarettes."

"Would you—" Bright swiped at his face in frustration; his voice dropped to a hiss between his teeth. "Would you just *stop* talking? I know all about the cigarettes and I was about to get them, but you're always, *always* talking at me. Can you *please* just be *quiet?*"

119

For a moment there was silence.

"Give the cigarettes to Sergeant Matthews."

Sergeant Matthews was his new sergeant, now that Carlson was dead back by the farmhouse near the village. He found Sergeant Matthews digging through another dead man's clothes, putting whatever he found into his own bulging pockets before rolling the body into the hole and standing up. He saluted the corpses. "Hinky, dinky, parley voo," he said. "*Adios,* so long, *adieu.*"

"Sergeant. I thought you might want these." He held the cigarettes toward Sergeant Matthews with solemnity.

"Toss 'em here, Bright. There's a good kid." He lit one of the cigarettes and scoped, squinty-eyed, through the tobacco smoke at Bright. "You need to shave, Bright. You look like a German or a bomb-throwing anarchist." He looked down the line of bodies. There were thirty-six of them. "Or a German anarchist!" he erupted. He laughed for a little while about this. "Hmmmm," he said. Then he smoked the rest of the cigarette. "Well," he said. His eyes were red.

They were taking their time. The brigade had been sent into the woods on information that only the southernmost part of it was held by the enemy, and loosely at that. In reality, machine-gun emplacements were everywhere, and maybe six hundred men had been killed or wounded in the few minutes after the first companies had entered the forest. The advance had been a complete disaster, and the order to fall back came after one endless hour of slaughter. After that it had been two days of sitting in the mud, during which there had been much talk of the supposed armistice. Some said it would happen any day now, that the order would come and they would all rise from their trenches like the dead hearing the last trumpet sound, and head to Paris and eat steak with oyster mushrooms. Others had it on good authority that peace of any kind was as far away as the moon. Regardless of all conjecture, there followed a day and then another day of shells raining blindly into the trees as the enemy slowly relinquished ground. During this time the angel hadn't talked to Bright, though he had called for it several times. Now Bright and ten others were on burial duty. At first they had moved in pairs, picking up soldier after soldier by the boots and arms and placing them on the lip of the grave, but then time and the sloshing mess of it all began to eat away at the last vestiges of formality, and the men began to break from one another so that they could do the numbing job as quickly as possible. There were regulations about the respect to be shown toward American dead, but the numbers were enormous, and in the end the only concession that seemed to matter was that the bodies were rolled, not thrown, into their graves. The rules said nothing about what was supposed to happen to whatever money, chocolate, or cigarettes they might find while doing so.

"You find any lemons, Bright?"

"No."

"Huh. Well." Sergeant Matthews walked upwind of the grave with a few other men in the burial detail and stood there smoking.

Bright touched the lemon in his pocket. He smelled his fingers, smelled them again, and then rolled another man into the hole.

There came a short, sharp whistle, and a tremendous explosion threw Bright sidelong into the brush at the bottom of a tree trunk. After a while he woke up and blinked dozily. Above him in the sky, even the sun seemed to have been jostled from its slow transit by the force of the shell's impact. His ears were bleeding and a boot was resting against his cheek. He shrugged it off. It wasn't his. On the hillside around him, a few of the others raised their heads. He stood and picked up the leg, which he had buried ten minutes before, and tossed it back into the hole that they had almost finished filling when the shell hit. He and the others looked briefly for Sergeant Matthews and the other smoking men, finding only pieces here and there on the trees and scattered about the ground. These also were placed in the grave and covered.

He walked a hundred fifty yards back and lay down on his woolen blanket. His head was angled downhill, but he was too exhausted to change position. There was a mark on his face where the boot had kicked it. He took the lemon from his pocket. It was a small, runty thing with mottled skin. He put it to his nose and inhaled convulsively. Lifting it again above his face to look at it, he turned it over and over between his fingertips before finally putting it to his teeth. He bit a small hole in the rind and began to squeeze the fruit in his fist, gently, as one would milk an animal, coaxing the juice into his mouth. While he slowly pumped the lemon, his eyes turned themselves upward into the blank sky.

"What wreckage this King has wrought."

Bright took the lemon away and spoke softly. "Not now."

"A new King must be found. This one has soaked the world in blood. He has allowed War to become so terrible that it can kill all of mankind. No King of Heaven has ever allowed War to become so powerful."

"I said not now," Bright said again, and continued to suck the diminishing lemon until it was a leathery husk. Then he lay there, licking his teeth, contorting his lips as the sour taste turned somehow to sweetness on his tongue.

27

Light seeped in beneath the moist rags on his face, and he was being scooped up and carried in someone's arms. At first he knew it was the angel. Then he knew for sure that he was about to be rolled into a grave. He began to twist and kick out against the walls of a narrow hallway.

"Shh shh shh. It's all right," a woman's voice came cooing from nearby. "We're moving you someplace you can be more comfortable. Just lie still, lie still."

The arms held him close and he lay still.

They ascended a set of bare wooden stairs and went through a doorway, then the sound of the footsteps changed and they were clicking across stone. The rags fell from his eyes and he was looking into the face of the sandy-haired man who was carrying him, then past the man's face and up into a dome of painted blue sky. The ceiling was gently illuminated from below, as if the sun were about to rise in all directions. Aside from the chance embroidery of clouds, the sky was clear. There were no cherubs, no judges, no dying saints. There were no angels or mustard gas, no smoke or beautiful young girls; the dome was simply, blessedly, empty. He felt that he might like to drift in that sky forever, breathe that clean, cold air, and leave the earth below to consume itself.

They passed by a grand piano, a row of potted ferns lining the curvature of the wall, and finally out from under the dome and into a tight brass elevator. The doors closed and they moved upward. A cool hand rested against his head. "You have a fever," a woman's voice said. "I'm going to put these back over your eyes now."

He closed his eyes and felt the cool rags against his eyelids. The elevator chimed open and he was carried down a quiet hallway. There came a click as a door opened and then he was being laid on cool sheets.

"Thank you, Dennis," the woman said. A moment later the door clicked once more as the man who had carried him left the room.

"Water," Bright whispered. She helped him sit up and the rags fell away again, and he saw her distinctly for the first time. She was about the same age that he was: perhaps twenty, perhaps younger. Her face, like the rest of her, still had the soft glow of baby fat. There was a light-brown birthmark, like the silhouette of a duck's head, between her temple and her hairline. Her eyes were downcast.

"Where's my son?" he said after he had sipped from the glass she held to his lips. His voice was torn. "Where's my boy?"

She placed the glass on the nightstand and crossed the room to where a bowl had been set. "I'm keeping him in my room for the time being," she said quietly. "The doctor has been in to see him. His rash is worse than yours, but we rubbed him with jewelweed. He didn't like that very much, but he'll be all right." Their eyes met, and both looked away. "The doctor," she said. "The doctor gave me some salve and told me to put it on you." She paused a moment, embarrassed. "On your chest."

Bright said nothing and she came to the side of the bed to stand over him. Whatever was in the bowl was pasty and grayish in the low light. She pulled the sheet down slowly, exposing the amber blisters of the rash. "Oh," she said, and bit her lower lip.

"I dreamed that it was mustard gas," he said.

"What?"

"They would put the ones who got gassed in the same tents with everyone who got shot and shelled. The people who got shot didn't make much sound, just lay there feeling bad. The ones who got gassed, though, they cried all the time. Calling out. The nurses would set their sheets up like tents so no one would have to see them like that, but you could still hear them."

She took a dollop of the lotion on three fingers and held it suspended over his chest.

"Go on," he said to her. "Put it on."

"I'm sorry," she said again. She looked into his eyes briefly and then stared at his chest.

"They ain't gas burns," he said. "It won't be as bad as all that."

Still biting her lip, she daubed the cold poultice on the slight cavity below his sternum. He made a low rasp in the back of his throat and craned his neck backward against the pillow. She spread the lotion thickly over the welts and boils. "He said it was poison ivy, the doctor did. But he also said you were just worn out and needed to rest and eat." Her hands were so red and rough that, if it weren't for their size, they could have belonged to a man twice her age.

"I fetched my goat out of some bushes after it was dark. Must have been then. And then I went and fed my boy." He took a deep breath, winced, and let it out through his nose. "I about killed my own boy," he said. His head seemed to sink deeper into the pillow.

"It's not your fault." She took a rag and wiped her hands of

125

the lotion, then began to wash them in the little marble sink. "It's not," she said. "Is that how you were feeding him? With the goat? Where is your wife?"

"She died," he said. He began to push himself up against the headboard. "Then there was the fire."

"It's coming close," the woman said. "Today is going to be a full day. Please lie down." She dried her hands on a towel and lightly pushed him back down with a few fingers on his shoulder.

"My horse and my goat need food and water," he said, staring upward at the white plaster ceiling with its fine cornice and moldings. "I need to go and fetch them."

"Dennis can go."

She began to move about the beautiful room, arranging some flowers in a vase on the mantel, fluffing the pillows, making sure the curtains were drawn tightly against the light. "Was your wife named Angel?" she asked.

"No." He looked at her suspiciously. "Why?"

"I'm sorry." She reddened, brushing a strand of hair behind her ear as she backed toward the bedroom door. "You were crying out in your sleep. I think that Angel is a beautiful name." She put her hand on the doorknob. "I'm very sorry I asked," she said again quietly. She opened the door and turned to leave.

"My name is Henry," he said. "Thank you for taking care of my boy and me."

"Mine is Brigid," she said. "I help to cook here." She switched off the lights. "It's still early. You should sleep more."

"I want to see my boy," he said, out of the curtained darkness.

"I'll bring him in to you once you've had a chance to rest a few more hours. Now sleep." She closed the door behind her, and Bright lay in the room's stately, cool gloom, a delicate floral smell like lavender rising from the medicine that she had rubbed on his chest.

28

The armistice that would end the War was to be signed at eleven in the morning. All fighting was to cease after that. Still, the hate came and went as usual at dawn, and, as the sun began to rise on the last day of the War, he found himself running across the fields a final time toward the coughing guns in front of him. It was then that the hand had reached up and grabbed him as he tried to pass. It held him tightly around his ankle, and Henry Bright did the one thing he had sworn to himself that he would never do. He looked down.

A man was looking up into his eyes. "Henry Bright," the angel said.

And then a bullet from somewhere had hit Bright in the shoulder, knocking him to the ground. Sometime later the War ended, but none of the dead got up and he couldn't get up either. He wondered if he was dead too, and he tried to prop himself up on one elbow. The stretch of pain across his arm was like crucifixion, and he had to lie back down. He began to feel as cold as the hand that had wrapped itself around his ankle.

"Angel!" he called, but if the angel heard him it didn't answer. Keeping his arms very still at his sides, he strained to sit up again. This time the hand still held his ankle fast, giving him something to pull against until he was finally in a sitting position. His teeth began to chatter. The fields around him seemed empty of life in all directions. Here and there, as if fissures had opened up in the crust of the world, puffs of smoke lifted and blew off in the breeze, but this seemed like the only movement. He called out to the angel again, but it gave no reply, and he knew somehow that it was gone.

He pulled the field dressing from the inside of his belt. There was a wax envelope filled with white powder, a bundle of lintin, two pins, and a roll of gauze. His shaking fingers dropped one of the pins on the ground, and his heart went thudding in the back of his head as he twisted to pick it up. He tried to hold the stays between his lips but his teeth wouldn't keep still, so he stuck the pins in the leather of someone's nearby boot heel. He pulled off his punctured jacket and then his bloody shirt. He poured his canteen on the wound, but he couldn't see if it was clean. His good hand looked enormous and tremendously real while it did its work, as if it belonged to a stranger. He watched it pour the waxen envelope of powder into the wound in his shoulder, and he heard the pop and sizzle of the powder as it cauterized the hole. The sound was like the small-arms fire of a faraway front line where nobody knew that the War had ended. It burned badly, the powder, and he pressed the twist of lintin into the wound and watched it turn red before his eyes. He threw it away and applied the other piece, then wrapped the gauze bandage tightly around it, managing for a few seconds to hold the end of the dressing between his chattering teeth to keep it tight until he had it pinned. Then he fell backward again and lay there looking up at a sky that was empty of shells, empty of bullets, empty of gas and planes, empty of bearded old men and beautiful girls, empty of angels.

128

29

The Colonel stood in the general-merchandise store puzzling over his money. On the counter lay the half box of bullets that the lady had counted out. He had spied her working alone through the window and straightened his uniform in the reflection of the glass. He'd removed his hat, run his fingers through his thin gray hair, and told his boys to wait for him outside the establishment.

"I seem to have a few mites less than the purchase price," he said to her.

"Well," the lady tried, "you could just buy fewer bullets." The old man had been standing there looking at the coins in his hand quizzically for almost a minute, as if more money might suddenly appear.

"Yes . . ." His voice trailed off, and he looked up at her as if she might have more to say on the subject.

"The rifle can't hold more than a few bullets at a time anyway, so why don't you just buy a few and then come back if you need more?"

"Contractions," the Colonel said softly.

"What?" She tapped the box of ammunition impatiently. "If it was me, that's what I'd do." A bowl of sugar cubes sat near the register.

"Was there a man in here with a baby yesterday?"

Duncan and Corwin stood watching him through the window as he questioned the lady.

"What?" The lady seemed annoyed to have the subject changed.

"Yesterday," he continued. "A father and an infant. Henry Bright is the man's name."

The lady's face softened a bit. "That poor man," she said. "His wife died, and it's only him left to care for that little boy." She shook her head and sucked in her cheeks against the bitterness of it all. "The world is a cruel place, and there's no denying it."

"A little boy," said the Colonel. "A little baby boy." His eyes drifted off the woman's face and over her shoulder at the bolts of fabric a moment before they snapped back. "It is a cruel place and there is *indeed* no denying it," he agreed.

"You're right about that," the woman said, reaffirming the fact. "Now," she said, tapping the box again, "can I help you with anything else?"

"May I?" The Colonel pointed his finger close to the sugar bowl.

She looked at the man's dirty hands and then at the clean white lumps of sugar. She took one from the bowl and placed it on the counter next to the bullets.

The Colonel took the sugar and turned toward the window, popping it in his mouth and winking for the benefit of his sons. Corwin pressed his face against the pane of glass with a beseeching look in his eyes. The Colonel turned back to the lady, his face gone somber and gray.

"I am seeking that man for something." He fixed the woman with a cold stare. He pointed at the sugar bowl again. "Might I have another lump of sugar?"

Before she could answer, there came a thud against the windowpane and sounds of a scuffle from outside. Corwin and Duncan were surrounded by six men.

The woman looked out the window and then back at the Colonel. "They're from the coal company," she said. "Making sure we don't have the wrong kinds of people staying in town too long. Are you relations?"

The Colonel glanced over his shoulder without interest at the faces of his sons. "With them? No. I have never laid eyes on them in my life," he said.

"I didn't mean with them," the woman said, frustrated. "I meant with the soldier—Henry Bright—and his boy. Are you related to the soldier and his boy?" She asked the question slowly, as if the old man was softheaded.

They both looked at the bullets there on the counter.

"Ah, yes. Henry. The man is my . . ." He chuckled to himself, then smiled thinly at the snooping old thing. "You see, the man murdered my daughter."

She threw a hand over her mouth and stared at the Colonel wide-eyed.

From outside the store rose the quick, scuffling sounds of a nascent mêlée. He listened with quiet satisfaction, but his gaze did not wander from the woman's face.

"That man?" she asked in disbelief. "The war hero?"

"Oh, yes," he said. "The man stole my daughter from me in the black of night, and less than a year later left her for dead after she delivered his child."

The woman looked vaguely off toward the door. "That nice soldier?" she asked.

"Indeed so," he said. "Will you tell me where he went?"

Her eyes watched the fighting outside vacantly.

"Please, will you tell me where Henry Bright went?" the

Colonel insisted. She didn't hear him, so absorbed was she with watching the fight outside her store and weighing the awful claims that the old man had made. The Colonel saw her distraction and snuck another lump of sugar into his mouth and leaned in closer across the counter. "I fear for the infant's life as well. The man is a murderer." He reached out suddenly, grabbing the woman high up on her arm. She looked away from the window and down at the hand clutching her, then up into his face. "I need to find Henry Bright," he said. "Tell me where he—"

The woman yanked back from his grasp. "Get the hell out of here!" Her face had gone purple with rage all at once, and she started around the counter toward him. She took a rake from a milk crate where a number of them were standing and knocked a stack of enameled pie plates to the floor. She swung the thing in a wide arc, missing him but sending a stuffed pheasant flying down the aisle. "I'll give you a beating for talking like that about a war hero!" She pounded the rake's handle on the floor and glared at him as two of the coal-company men entered the store. "Ralph," she said. "Edgar."

"I can see that you are a fine woman and ever the help of those in need," the Colonel said, with the last reserves of his courtly composure. Strong arms pulled him toward the shop door. "If you see that rogue again, tell him that I am going to find and kill him."

The woman followed the men to the doorway and out onto the street as they dragged the old man and his sons down toward the coal-company offices. "Make sure I don't ever see them again or I'm gonna cut them from their ears to their assholes!" She huffed in disbelief at the kinds of people there were in the world, then she dusted herself off and disappeared into the store. In another moment she came back out again and hollered up the street to the roughs. "And when you're done with them, get on back and help me bury my cash register."

The coal-company roughs tied the trio and carried them like spitted heifers out of town, dumping them finally by the train tracks running past a coal depot. They pulled out the men's pockets but found nothing of any interest. One of the roughs drew a long knife from his own belt and held it under the Colonel's nose. "You ain't coming back here again, are you?" The Colonel shifted in his ropes and turned his face away. The rough watched him a beat longer, then laughed and cut the old man's ropes, spun him around, and kicked him hard on the backside, sending him sprawling down the tracks. He threw the unloaded and useless rifle after him. "We don't want your types around here," he said.

The roughs walked, joking among themselves, back down the road the way they had come. The Colonel sat gingerly on the railroad track and watched them go, then looked at his sons where they lay, bloody and straining against the ropes that still bound them.

When he was sure the men were gone, he pulled the long brass bullet out from between his cheek and his teeth. "I thought," he said, holding it up and examining it with a jeweler's eye, "that you would both be better behaved if I left you outside of the store."

He rubbed the bullet on his sleeve and, after inspecting its gleam, he chambered the round in the rifle with a satisfying mechanical clack. Then he laid the rifle aside and looked placidly at his sons.

"Henry Bright is nearby, and I have procured the means with which to kill him." He nodded at the rifle lying by his side. "Since it is growing late and there is nothing more that can be done at present, I feel we are all in possession of a blessed space

133

of leisure time in which I might pass on to you both a few bits of instruction concerning proper manners when residing in town." This he proceeded to do, talking at length as night fell, his lecture interrupted only once when he saw the light of a train coming and he paused so that he could drag his boys one by bundled one from the tracks, lest they be cleaved in two.

30

He lay there on the battlefield with a hole in his shoulder, until eventually he was found and moved boozily to a Red Cross tent. A racket of haphazard marching bands moved up and down the gruel-colored stretch of camp road at all hours. The walls of canvas were stiff and dreary as the sky, still as paint. The nurse came and retreated. He was woken at times by the screams of others. When this happened, the nurse would be there, and sometimes the doctor too. He would be given something for his pain and would go back to sleep, wake, and eat the cool soup that was spooned to him. There were voices outside and commotion at times. Then everything would get dark again and he would lie there and call out to the vanished angel.

He was in the Red Cross tent for so long that it began to seem that he might be the last one to leave the War. He got up but was made to lie back down again. He got up again, and this time he was put on a truck that took him to a train. The train took him to the coast, and at the coast he was placed aboard a steam liner. After four days of sitting in port, the steam liner left. He never saw any of the men he had known in the trenches again. He kept a careful watch for the Colonel's sons, but they weren't on his boat. He found whatever solitude he could on board. He tried closing his eyes or watching the waves as they frothed behind the ship. He took Bert's stolen gun from his haversack and sat staring at the lettering, letting his eyes unfocus and the talk of others blur around him. None of it was any use. The angel seemed gone for good. His shoulder throbbed in the damp air. The boat landed in Virginia. He was given a ticket and got on a train that, after many stops, dropped him at the same empty station he had departed from just over a year previous.

The neglected cabin was in much need of work, but Bright began at the edges. He went into the woods and cut six trees, then spent the next two days fashioning fence posts that he placed around the small garden that his mother had made. Although it was still early in the spring and frost painted the ground each morning, he slept in his army kit in the timothy grass within sight of the cabin. He did not go in. He wasn't quite ready to resume his former life. He ate whatever he had left from his trip. He walked a half day to Fells Corner for a bar of soap, a pound of nails, and tar paper with which to patch the roof of the hen hutch. At first the old man in the hardware store didn't recognize the gaunt, uniformed young man who stood before him. When at last he did, the man came out from behind the counter and put his arms around him, and this time he gave him two full pounds of nails for free before making Bright promise to come to the auction the following week.

He returned home and hacked away the tall grass that had grown up around his mother's grave. Something—the winter snow, wild animals—had pushed inward most of the boards he had nailed over the cabin door to protect the inside from weather. He pried and yanked away whatever splinters remained nailed to the door frame, then he turned in the doorway and looked a while at the homestead he had reclaimed. When he was finally ready, he stepped inside the cabin and sat there on the bed for a very long time, as if waiting to feel something, while the hours passed and the slant of the daylight changed around him. At last he stood on the lumpy straw mattress and felt around in the shadows of the rafters for his mother's rifle. The gun was missing.

31

Come morning, his boys were a travesty to look upon. Swollen lips, black eyes, cheekbones bruised, foreheads and noses bloody and dirty. After untying them, the Colonel made his way a little farther into the forest and then up a small rise. To his left and right the trees went on to the horizon, deep blue-green and gently breathing. Directly in front of him, about a quarter mile distant, the forest of hickory and oak gave way to an enormous rectangle of lawn with several small man-made ponds strewn carelessly about. They reflected a sky that was one part daybreak and two parts smoke. The Colonel paid the impending fire no mind. His eyes were roving over the spectacular white hotel. The building was at least four hundred feet long, with drowsy, darkened windows just beginning to garner the sunlight, as if the morning was one more servant to be admitted into the room along with the coffee and the big-city papers. Tennis courts and a swimming pool were appended to the right side of the hotel, and to the extreme left, on the far side of the great lawn and set slightly back into the trees, stood a large white barn trimmed in green.

"I am going to the hotel to ask for Henry Bright," he announced to his sons when he got back to the train tracks. "I gleaned from the lady in the store that he was very close. I will see what further information I can come by there." Corwin was sitting on one of the rails, throwing small rocks at his brother's back. The struggle had gone out of Duncan, who sat staring fixedly at the sunlight glancing off one of the rails.

"From the rise there you can see a large white barn," the Colonel said, pointing. "While I am away, I want the two of you to scout it for Henry Bright's horse. If by luck you do find the animal stabled there, do not harm it." He looked hard at both of his sons to make sure that they were listening. "Allow me to emphasize. Do not harm the horse! . . . I want nothing to alert the rogue that we are nearby." The Colonel removed his uniform jacket and shook it, releasing clouds of dust into the air. "And you would both do well to otherwise keep to the woods, as you look less than presentable."

He made his way through the woods and down to the road leading through the gates to the hotel. At the foot of the hotel steps, he met a crisply dressed porter who brought him up the wide marble stairs, through an ornate revolving door, and into a large lobby with a sky-blue dome and a beautiful grand piano. Here the ragged old man was passed from the porter to an equally well-pressed bellboy, of whom the Colonel inquired where a proud grandfather might breakfast with his son and new grandson, who happened to be guests of the hotel. The bellboy smiled at him and led the way to the breakfast room. A few reverberant murmurs of conversation met the Colonel's ears from a group of departing guests as he walked by the reception desk.

". . . and so we decided to get out now while the getting out was good . . ."

". . . but I don't believe it . . ."

". . . if it is worse than '09, which they say maybe it will be . . ."

". . . never happen . . ."

The bellboy spoke over his shoulder to the Colonel. "Everything you've heard about the breakfast here is true," he said, as they passed beneath an oaken Tudor arch and into a glassed-in conservatory. The light streaming through the windows gleamed off the polished silver service and scattered brilliantly in all directions, as if the whole room were contained within a bubble in some sunlit brook. "Eggs Benedict, eggs *Florentine*"— the bellboy stretched the word out like he was describing the Grand Canyon—"eggs Benedict *with trout*? Believe me, sir, it's the best there is, and there's plenty of it." With a nod to a passing girl, he returned to the lobby and the girl led the Colonel to a setting for two near the far end of the long glass room. Nearby, a group of four young people—two men and two women—was arrayed around a table. They had stopped their talking as he approached and were now looking at him as if he was some acquaintance of theirs who had dressed in costume. The smiles of the two women were already forming as they turned back around to face the men. A chair was pulled out for the Colonel, and he brushed the seat cushion once with the napkin.

"So then . . ." he heard one of the women say, as she tried to retrieve the strand of the conversation, "so then Amelia went . . ."

"Good morning to you all," the Colonel said brightly.

"Ah, good morning," one of the men said. The other, looking directly down at his crumpet and spearing it absentmindedly with a knife, turned his head and gave the barest, most obligatory of nods before returning his attentions to the pastry.

The Colonel, after nodding respectfully at the women, turned his attentions fully upon his napkin, taking it by the corners and flipping it as if he were taunting a bull before tucking half its length into his collar.

The woman began again, "So then Amelia—"

"*I'll* tell it, Evelyn, if you don't mind, since he did propose *to me*," Amelia laughed.

"She's jealous," the truculent man said into his crumpet.

"I am jealous," Evelyn said. She turned, smiling, to the man with a fine mustache at the end of the table, who had first greeted the Colonel. "Lawrence"—she laid her hand on his arm and batted her eyelashes—"if you'd asked me to marry you, I would have said yes in a second!"

"I recall that I did ask you to marry me once, Evie," he said.

"But that was ages ago. Years. And just moments before, you'd fallen off the railing and into the garden. I chalked it up to a head injury. But if you asked me now—"

"Oh, hush," Amelia said. "He's asked me to marry him and I'm not letting him take it back, am I, Lawrence?"

"What a pleasant day for a walk," the Colonel interjected from over at his small table.

The group paused their conversation and looked at him blankly.

"Yes, it is," Amelia said after a moment, "and you look as if you've already been out walking this morning."

"About a thousand miles," the ill-natured man said with a snort.

"Now, Russell . . . manners . . . How far have you come, sir? Have you had to escape the fire too?" She twisted her hair and leaned toward him as she asked the question.

"Oh, I live just down the road, a mile back in town," the Colonel said.

"Pleasant place," Lawrence remarked. "I've been coming here since I was a boy. I've always loved it." He had on a hunting jacket with a leather patch on the shoulder for the rifle butt.

"It is an extremely pleasant place," the Colonel agreed. He motioned at the extra place setting. "I am meeting my son here for breakfast. He has just had a child." The waiting girl arrived.

141

"Coffee, black," he barked. "And steel-cut oats with canned peaches." She left. "My son is a soldier," the Colonel said, and watched their faces.

"Well, that's wonderful," Evelyn said. "Soldiers everywhere."

"Was he in France?" Amelia asked.

"Yes he was. Fighting the Boche. Am I to take by your comment that there are other veterans here besides myself and my son?"

"Were you in France too?"

"The Philippines," he said, his eyes never leaving Amelia's face. "And you said there were other veterans staying here?"

Not to be ignored, Evelyn leaned in closer. "Early this morning, a veteran in his uniform came in from the direction of the fire. He was out of his senses."

"Shouldn't have let him in," sullen Russell opined. He sat back in his chair and looked in the opposite direction from the Colonel. "He'll get the whole place sick with the mumps. That on top of the fire, on top of them letting the whole pikey hillbilly world come and stay for free until it passes? I won't be coming back here. I don't pay good money to get the mumps and eat possum stew."

"I swear, Russell, you're such a pussy willow sometimes." Amelia cocked her thumb back at her new fiancé. "You're as bad as Lawrence. After all, it was only poison ivy." She turned back to the Colonel. "Lawrence thinks I was crazy to have the man moved up out of the basement and into the hotel, but I had a nice room and he is a veteran after all, so I wanted him moved to a place where he could be absolutely comfortable. It was the very least I could do. We're leaving today anyway."

"What was the room number?" the Colonel asked. "Perhaps I will visit him before I leave. Veteran to veteran, you know."

"Oh, dear, I don't have any idea. There are no room numbers on the top floor, are there, Lawrence?"

"I haven't got the foggiest," Lawrence said, grown bored.

The group drifted back into their own conversation, and the room filled with the boisterous laughter of men about to go out for a last round of golf or shooting before they all got in their cars to drive away and escape the fire. As he ate and drank his coffee, the Colonel listened for further word of Henry Bright, but he heard nothing.

Before the bill could be brought, he stood and bowed to his neighbors. "Have a blessed day," he said sweetly. Holding his paper-white palms out toward Amelia, he took her hands in his and bent low across the breakfast table to kiss them. "May your impending union be as fruitful as my son's has been." He nodded once more at Lawrence, who returned the nod sternly. Then, with great and gathered dignity, he walked across the breakfast-room floor and out into the smoke-filled morning to go find his sons and fetch his rifle.

32

For the next few days after he arrived home, Bright worked steadily at making more repairs. He cleared the garden patch, beating back the intruding tendrils of the wilderness and in the process exhuming nearly a bushel of homuncular carrots. He climbed up on the roof and repapered with the tar paper he had bought at the hardware store, then he chipped some new shingles from the pitchy remnants of the fence posts he had set around the garden. He removed the contents of the cabin and placed them in the yard: the enameled washbasin, the trunk for his mother's clothes, the mahogany credenza, the moldering Bible, and the bed. He swept out the cabin's lantern-blacked interior, then filled the bucket with water and used a rag to work the deep dirt out of the floorboards. When he was done, he stripped off his clothes and washed in the stream. Then he shaved, climbed into his uniform, and set off to Fells Corner for the auction. Though he'd dumped the bullets on the ground back in the War, he held Bert's beautiful stolen gun in his hand, visible to anyone who might be watching him from the woods as he passed the house where the Colonel and his sons lived. Once he was down the road a ways, he tucked the gun back into his haversack.

He was unprepared for the stir he would make at the auction. Since he'd returned from France, he'd spoken to no one but the conductor on the train and the man at the hardware store. After such long silence, the little town at auction time was a nightmare of back slaps, hand-wringing, tears, and canned fruit. A fat little man with a straw hat and a blueberry stain on his shirt turned out to be the mayor. He stood on a crate, clasped Bright's hand above his head, and made a speech. Everywhere Bright went, small boys followed him around, patrolling left and right and using the same kind of talk that Bert had before he was shot in the head. Old men saluted him and young men watched him from the corners of their eyes.

The auctioneer referred to him as "our very own" each time Bright raised his hand to place a bid. He bought the hens first, then the two white goats. He went outside and ate some fried chicken that was given to him and drank a mug of beer and a cup of buttermilk. He ate a piece of pie that had been brought to him by a detachment of flat-chested girls. When he was done, he got up from the picnic table and went back into the sweat and tobacco of the auction hall to examine the horses.

33

The Colonel arrived back at the train tracks near the coal depot where they had spent the night to find his sons squatted around a desultory fire, tearing at an unplucked chicken carcass. He eyed the two boys closely. Corwin glanced up dully, then returned to his meal. Duncan received his father's gaze in his bottomless black eyes. After a moment the old man looked away, then turned to Corwin. "Report," he commanded.

"We found a chicken," Corwin said, his mouth around a bone.

"I can see that. Where?"

Corwin ducked his head in the direction. "The barn. They got a bunch of them there if you want to go get one."

The Colonel sniffed at this. "I am not asking because I wish to pilfer a chicken. I have already taken my breakfast. I had steel-cut oats with peaches and cream."

Corwin's fingers were sticky with down and chicken blood. "Peaches?" he asked. He wiped his index finger and thumb on his pant leg, but none of the grime came away.

"Peaches in syrup, yes."

"I've never had a peach."

"It would be wasted on you."

"No, it wouldn't!"

146

"In any case, you will never have the chance. The two of you could never behave yourselves in such fine company as take their breakfast yonder. Now report," he said again.

Duncan watched his brother throw a chicken bone off into the weeds by the train track. "A man was there. We watched him through the trees. He had Henry Bright's horse and he was brushing it and then he took it into the barn."

"How do you know for sure that it was the rogue's horse?"

"Because he also had his goat there on a rope. I know it was his goat. Corwin and I seen it once."

Corwin nodded at the memory, breathing through his mouth.

The Colonel sighed in contentment over the peaches in his belly, no longer listening to the story. He looked for a while through the trees in the direction of the hotel. Then, as if a great notion had come into his mind, he turned back to his sons. "Would you like some peaches after all, Corwin?"

"You know I do!" Corwin said.

"Of course you do." The Colonel smiled. He stooped to pick up the rifle and began walking down the tracks in the direction of the coal depot. Corwin jumped up and followed his father, leaving what was left of the wretched chicken body to blow forlornly in the morning breeze between the rails.

Duncan looked at the fire gathering strength behind the trees. Then he stood and followed, rubbing the small of his back where it was sore from his relations and other kinds of people kicking him and throwing rocks at him.

147

34

When Bright woke again, the curtains were drawn wide and muted morning light suffused the room. A kind of woman entirely unknown to him sat slung across a burgundy divan.

"*You* have been talking in your sleep," she said. Her darkyellow hair hung heavily about her face as if freshly forged. She looked at him amusedly.

"What did I say?" he asked, his eyes roving about the room for the cook, Brigid. The carpets were thick and beige colored. At either end, body-length mirrors in japanned frames reflected back and forth upon each other.

"Oh, all of your secrets are safe with me, H. Bright," the woman said. She vaulted to her feet and came to stand at the head of his bed, shooting a hand toward him. "Amelia," she said. "My last name is Choate, A. Choate. And you are H. Bright."

The bed squeaked as he took her hand.

"There," she said. "Formalities laid to rest. Now, just lie back and let me talk." She leaned over him, peering closely at the rash on his face. "Cripes. They say the water here is healthful, so maybe you've come to the right place. I see you've noticed my ring. Ha. It's black pearl. Not at all so rare as Lawrence would have me believe, but I don't tell him this, of course, because all that kind of talk is so dull. Anyway, if he really is serious about marrying me this time, which I can't help but think he is, then he'll have to cough up for something much flashier soon enough. I'm talking diamonds, H. Not that I care. I don't wear much jewelry. I'm wearing this at the moment only because he's just given it to me. Now he's out shooting birds with his 'pals.'"

She ran a hand through her hair. "I was invited to join them too, of course. I'm actually quite a good shot, but that would mean me spending more time with his 'pals,' and so I told him that I was going to head back upstairs to make the acquaintance of my war hero, H. Bright." She regarded him with a cocked eyebrow. "Dear H., can't you see that I'm trying to get it through your head that you haven't introduced yourself to me yet? Your last name was easy, it's written on your uniform. I was in school with an Alexandra Bright. We called her Flexy."

"My name is Henry," he said. "Where is my boy at?"

Amelia looked hard at him, as if he'd said something unexpectedly cruel. Then her face changed and she let out a small sigh. "Ah. Henry. I see. Then I hope that you won't mind me calling you H. It's not your fault, it's just that a certain other Henry was the author of a disastrous chapter in my life, and the memory is a bit . . . fresh . . . yet." She gave a short laugh and looked down at the bedspread.

"Isn't it funny, don't you think, how at times one can't escape a name? There was a year when it seemed that every new man that I met was named Albert, or Bertie, or Bert. Large-footed, husky dolts, to a one, but I couldn't escape that name. There's a riddle in it somehow, or perhaps it was my subconscious telling me that I needed to be with a strong, simple-minded, Teutonic sort."

"I knew a Bert," he said. "In the War. Where's my boy?" he asked her again.

"Oh, H.! I'm sorry. I'm going on and on, and all the while the forest fire really is coming close. Well, I'm getting out," she said. "Still, there's a part of me wishes I could stay here and help fight it. Your boy. Yes. Your boy is being cared for by one of the cooks. He'll break hearts for sure." She tapped her ring finger on the wooden headboard and winked down at him. "Like you, H., like you."

"He's all right?"

"Of course he's all right! He's in the pink! The doctor has been in checking on you both. He's from Baltimore. They say he's the best there is in nem-...pom-...I don't know, something-something-ology. Anyway, he said it was poison ivy."

There came a knock at the door. Amelia peered through the peephole and then swung the door open for Brigid to enter. "Ah! The soup! Just put it over there to cool, and you can come in and feed Mr. Bright when I'm through with him."

Brigid set the steaming bowl on a side table and stopped to readjust the covers at the bottom of the bed. Again Bright noticed the rough redness of her hands.

"Thank you, thank you," Amelia said, holding the door open for the departing girl.

"Is my boy all right?" he asked loudly. The exhaustion and anxiety welled up plainly in his voice.

Brigid turned back and nodded. "He's fine." There was a long pause as she stole a glance at Amelia and then back at Bright. "Try to rest now." She turned again to leave. The smoke outside waved across the room at itself in the facing reflections of the japanned mirrors.

"My horse and my goat?" he asked after her.

"They're both fine as well. We've kept them at the barn, but if the fire gets closer, Dennis will make sure they're moved. Now, don't worry. I'll bring your boy up to say hello in just a little bit."

She let the door hang open a crack when she left the room. Amelia crossed the floor and pushed it firmly closed.

"I like her," she said, rapping her ring on the doorknob. "Now, tell me, H." She walked across the room and stood at the foot of his bed. "What was it like?"

"What was what like?"

"Oh, don't be like that. What was *it* like? The War? Come, now, no one gets to be my war hero unless they tell me what it was that they did in the War."

"The War?"

"All right," she laughed. "I'm too proud to wheedle it out of you, H. My things are being packed while Lawrence is out shooting at quails or ducks or geese or whatever, but I'll be back to say goodbye when he's ready to go. When I get back, I expect at least one ripping good yarn. And see if you can work in that Patton fellow," she added. "I think he is absolutely a man."

She put her hand on the knob, but she stood still and did not turn it. "My first husband went, you know," she said, not looking at him. "He wasn't actually my husband, not yet, but we were going to be married. He died. I was there with his family when the man came. He said that Henry—yes, that was his name, H., *Henry*: horrible, isn't it?—had perished a hero. 'Perished?' I asked the man. 'Yes,' he said. 'Perished.' I asked him how and the man said that that was all he could tell me. He told me that he was loved by his men and that he had perished a hero. I said, 'Well, of course he was loved by his men. Of course he perished a hero. How else could he have perished?' "

She toed the plush silver carpet, her face impassive. "Lawrence

151

didn't go," she said. "He has a trick shoulder, but keeping him out of the War is the only trick I've seen it do." She opened the door. "I'm sorry," she said. "I'm spilling my guts all over you."

Henry Bright had had guts spilled on him before, and he said nothing.

35

The fire pushed them all before it, eastward, through the hardwoods to the coal-company town. They carried everything they could with them: heirlooms and axes, tin washbasins and butter churns. Whatever couldn't be carried by hand was lashed to livestock. There were a few spluttering automobiles, but mostly it was mules and doze-eyed oxen dragging wagons, horses carrying the infirm.

Upon arriving in the coal-company town, the refugees found a prosperous place coming apart at its seams. The pale, frightened faces of children peeked out from the shadows behind screen doors. Men soaked their lawns and roofs with water in the hopes that the fire might not be able to catch hold. Women piled precious belongings in the street, torn between what could be taken and what would be left to burn.

Rumors that had been gusting about on the dry wind could now be confirmed by the new arrivals. Fells Corner was gone. Its inhabitants had tried briefly to save it, but what had initially been a small blaze had quickly grown monstrous on great drafts of air and the summer heat. There had followed a chaotic period of making ready to leave, and by the time that they finally abandoned town, the fire was crowning and there was scarcely time for a last look back.

After that it had come down to simply trying to stay ahead of the blaze. They traveled along the train tracks through cold-mouthed railroad tunnels and across the perilous high trestles that seemed to creak and sway with vertigo beneath them. Even as they crossed the final one, the stragglers had seen the flames licking at its stanchions, the rising odor of boiling pitch and creosote like burnt black licorice in their noses.

The coal-company town, racked by a panic of its own, could offer no help or shelter to this smoke-stained group except to point them down the road toward the wide open lawn of the hotel. So they came through the hotel gates in ragged, stumbling clumps of humans, animals, and housewares, casting themselves upon the safety of the great green field, milling about like people awaking from a single shared nightmare.

In the midst of this strange scene, no one took much notice of the three bedraggled men, hands and faces deeply stained with soot, who shambled out of the woods and onto the lawn toward the gushing fountain at the front of the hotel. Once there, the three did not get in line to wash their faces in the water but instead hung closely together. When at last the eldest, a graying man with a rifle slung over his back, did peel away from the other two, it was in order to address a young woman who wore the uniform of a cook. The young woman carried an infant hugged securely against her inside a white sling. She nodded at what the soot-covered man said before motioning him along toward a sandy-haired man who was directing another group of refugees into the hotel. A smile played itself across the old man's blackened face as he bowed low to her, but the girl had already turned away and was now talking with someone else, her hand brushing absently at the birthmark on her temple.

36

When the auctioneer held up Bert's stolen German pistol, the auction hall gasped. The bidding was higher than expected, but in the end a man from Lewisburg, a doctor, purchased it. With the money he made, Bright bought a black horse, about twenty years old with decent teeth, freshly shod hooves, and a back only slightly bowed considering the size of the farmer putting it up for sale. He slept soundly that night in the barn of the hardware-store man, with a full belly, four chickens, two goats, and the horse.

It was raining the next morning as he and his band of animals began the trip homeward. He tied the chicken crates to the horse's back and strung the goats in a caravan behind the horse. The goats were meddlesome creatures and the horse, bored, stupid, or both, didn't resist them when they chose to go their own way. As a result, the big animal's plodding hindquarters would gradually drift sideways toward whatever leafy green the little white goats had a taste for. A passerby would have wondered at the group: a skinny, uniformed young man leading a horse that seemed to be learning the difficult art of walking sideways in a steady downpour. Eventually Bright untied them from the horse and briefly tried pulling them down the road separately, holding their tethers in his free hand. In the end, though, he let them off their leads entirely and left them to follow him as he and his horse continued trudging down the muddy road.

They stayed close at first, but as he passed the overgrown wagon-wheel tracks that were the turnoff to the Colonel's house, the she-goat hung back to munch and nose the tall grass and nettles of the drive. After a hundred yards she had made no signs of rejoining the group. He pulled the horse to a halt and waited for her to emerge. When she did not, he retethered the billy goat and led his remaining animals down the road to stand once more at the turnoff. It was all very quiet, save for the quizzical clucking of the chickens and the raindrops against the leaves. He thought of how his mother always had her rifle with her when they passed the drive. He remembered how they used to meet Rachel here each morning before school and how Duncan had stood in this very spot on that terrible day of the rabbits and chickens. He wished briefly to have Bert's gun back. When he could no longer help it, he let his mind linger on the French farmhouse and the things he had seen inside it.

He began walking up the drive, pulling the animals behind him and clicking his tongue softly for the she-goat as he peered through the dripping foliage. There was nothing around the first bend but the rain and yet another bend. Around this second corner, the road softened into a wet marsh of cattails and devil's walking stick and the house hove into view. The lawn was mangy gray, the brittle needles of grass grown high and spiky. A rust-colored stream ran along the far southern edge of the plot, and what few trees remained between the stream and the house seemed like overgrown twins of the grass. Their branches were hacked crudely away up to forty feet, past which point they spindled outward like finger bones. The wrought-iron balcony listed dangerously out of plumb, the ivy vines hanging thickly from it pulling it to the ground like some waxen

156

green lion. It was here, beneath the balcony, that he saw Rachel. She was standing so motionless in the shadows that at first glance he had taken her for an off-white warping in the moldering clapboard. She was watching something that was happening in the mud-packed wasteland out of view on the other side of the house. He moved farther out onto the drive, hoping for a better angle in which to see the girl, and caught his breath on what he saw instead.

Corwin had scooped up the she-goat in his cumbersome arms, and reedy, underfed Duncan stood close by, holding a clump of yellow grass under her nose. Her tail flicked and looped in the air like a distress flag.

Rachel had noticed him now. He stared back at her, forgetting his goat and the Colonel's sons. She was far too skinny. Around her waist the white dress hung loosely, and her shoulders were scarcely wide enough to keep it from slipping off. Her collarbones were almost avian, painful to behold. When at last the moment passed and he looked over at the two men holding his goat, he thought of them standing above him in the darkness as he lay beneath Bert's body in the ditch during the War.

Together, the group formed a haphazard nativity scene in the rain-soaked yard.

"That's my goat," he said. "I bought her in Fells Corner. At the auction there. There's more like her if you want your own."

The goat began to squirm and kick its stony hooves against Corwin's chest. "I want my goat back," he said again. "Please."

Rachel looked once behind her into the recesses of the house and then at her brothers. "Give it back," she said quietly. "Give it back. That's Henry's goat so don't you be fiddling with it anymore."

Corwin gave his sister a cloying smile and set the goat on the ground with exaggerated care, as if it were a china dish. He backed away from the animal, extending his arms in invitation

157

to Bright. Bright came forward to pick it up, but his eyes never left the two men. "Thank you," he said. He held the goat tightly so that they would not see his hands shaking.

"Henry?" Rachel tilted her head with the question. "Henry, where have you been?"

He didn't know what to say. Her face was so beautiful to him that she made her surroundings look all the more deplorable. "I went to the War," he stammered. "I was in the War." He stole a glance at Corwin and Duncan as he said it.

"Did you get married there, Henry?" she asked. "I bet you did. I bet you got married there."

He swallowed drily. After a pause he said, "No. No, I just stayed there and that's all I did." He nodded to Corwin and Duncan. Neither returned the nod. He nodded at Rachel, then turned and pulled his animals out of the yard, down the drive, and back through the rain to the main road and his cabin.

The angel gave him no peace after that.

37

The Colonel and his sons, another old man, two elderly women, four or five young couples, and an indiscriminate number of children and dogs followed the hotel man named Dennis down a long basement hallway and into a large concrete room. A metallic click came as Dennis flipped a switch, and the few electric bulbs cast their light dimly on rows of mattresses lined up on the stone floor. One of the old women had breathed in too much smoke from the fire, and every time she began to cough, one of the dogs would bark. As soon as Dennis left, Duncan went immediately to a bed in the far corner of the room and lay down, putting the thin pillow over his head to keep out the noise. The Colonel sank down against the wall and pulled his hat over his eyes to think.

He had expected that his army uniform would have more of an effect on the cook he had talked to by the fountain and that, in return for the service he had given to his country, she would have sent him upstairs to rest in one of the resplendent rooms on the top floor, as Henry Bright had been. The young woman had a birthmark on her temple and had been carrying a newborn. He had congratulated her on her beautiful child and had not missed the brief look of confusion there in her eyes. Now he sat on the floor in the basement with the loaded rifle across his knees, pondering how best to find Henry Bright now that he had located both the rogue's horse and his child.

The man who owned the hardware store in Fells Corner stood across the room staring at the Colonel, then walked over and nudged the sitting figure with his boot. The Colonel shifted his hat toward the back of his head and lifted his eyes to return the store owner's glare.

"You don't remember me," the Fells Corner man said. There was spite in his voice.

"Of course I do," the Colonel replied with equal spite.

"We ain't gonna have any trouble with you or them boys. Not today." His voice was flat. "Git."

The Colonel sighed. "Sir, I am a colonel and expect to be addressed with the courtesy due me." He pulled the hat back over his eyes. "As befits my rank," he added.

"If you're a colonel, I'm George Washington," the hardware man said to the brim of the Colonel's hat. An old woman cackled loudly, then began to cough. A dog started barking. "We ain't gonna have your boys in the same room as the children or the women. We all got enough trouble already. Git." He toed the Colonel once again, harder this time.

By the time Dennis returned to the basement room, leading more refugees, three men had ahold of Corwin and another held Duncan's arms behind his back. The hardware-store man was leaning forward on the balls of his feet, jabbing a peglike finger into the Colonel's chest while the Colonel looked derisively at his tormentor over coal-smeared cheekbones.

Dennis stopped in the doorway. "What's this?" The people he was leading went on tiptoe behind him trying to catch a glimpse.

At the sound of Dennis's voice, the Colonel pivoted slowly to face him, showing his back to the Fells Corner hardware man. "There are peasants in my lodgings," he said. "Fleas and the croup are rampant. Children and dogs have overrun the place."

"These ones ain't staying here," one of the men holding Corwin said to Dennis. "Not inside with the children or the women."

"Or the dogs!" someone else yelled.

The hardware-store man went on: "They live over near where we come from. Believe me, there's nothing about these ones that ain't wrong."

"They might even've started the fire," said the big man holding Duncan. He had a thick pink scar running through his right eyebrow. "They ain't staying here." He twisted Duncan's arms hard, as if to emphasize the point. Duncan's body seemed to slacken against the pain, then all of a sudden he jerked back, butting his captor up under his chin with the crown of his head. The man winced in pain and let go of Duncan's arms, grabbing a hank of his black hair and spinning him around. He rammed the heel of his hand into Duncan's nose, releasing a spurt of blood and sending him to his hands and knees on the concrete floor. The man hauled his boot back and kicked him in the stomach. Duncan curled into a gulping, gasping ball at his feet. The man was about to kick once more when Dennis stepped forward and put a hand on his shoulder.

"You do that again, you can all find somewhere else to stay."

The man appeared to consider the option, then lowered his foot.

The Colonel looked at his son there on the cold floor and began to smile faintly to himself. He came to stand by Dennis. "I need my own room," he said. "On the top floor. With the other veteran."

Dennis knelt to help Duncan to his feet. Duncan stood, run-

161

ning a dirty sleeve across his nose. He looked at the red-stained arm as if it did not belong to him.

"I have come to a decision!" The Colonel's voice suddenly escalated to shrill oratory, as if he was reciting epic poetry. "Of my own volition and for no other reason, I will send my boys to stay in the barn. They will be of no trouble to you good people." He pivoted in a martial style to regard Dennis and the hardware man at once. "Is this agreeable to all parties?"

"That's not the safest place for them to be," Dennis said. "The fire will get there pretty quick. I was heading out there soon to fetch the animals closer in."

"My boys are no cowards and are no strangers to livestock. I hope they can be of some assistance in that regard."

Dennis looked at the hardware man, who shrugged back at him. "Not my animals out there," he said. He nodded at the men holding Corwin and they let go of his giant, sloped shoulders.

"Both of you go to the barn," the Colonel commanded loudly. "Stay there until you can either be of use or until the fire burns you out." After a beat he added, "Mind the chickens, but keep special watch over the horse and goat belonging to the veteran." He ran his tongue over his teeth in thought, then added, "I expect them kept safe, do you hear me?"

Corwin made for the basement door. The Colonel fixed Duncan with a dismissive look. The boy looked back at his father, his upper lip still wet with blood, then over at Dennis, and finally at the basement doorway through which Corwin had just passed. Then he walked through the group of Fells Corner men as if he had turned to shadow.

The Colonel returned his attentions to Dennis. "As for myself," he said, "I shall take a room on the top floor, as—"

"Go and talk to Brigid down the hall in the kitchen," Dennis interrupted. "Maybe she can help you like she helped the other fella."

"*Git*," the hardware man said, and spat on the Colonel's boot.

38

It was sometime in the late afternoon when he felt strong enough to rise. His uniform was ready for him on a chair, the freshly pressed trousers and jacket hanging over its back, his underwear, shirt, and socks folded in a neat pile on the seat cushion. Atop the pile lay the ivory comb. Someone had stitched closed the bullet hole in the jacket's shoulder with black thread. He stepped into the trousers and boots, then paused before buttoning his shirt to smell a sleeve. The soap had left a scent behind that he remembered. Lemons.

He pulled the shirt on gingerly over the welts on his chest and then picked up his mother's comb. Somehow the fragile thing had survived the nightmare of the last few days. The ivory woman, whose kneeling, hand-clasped body formed its handle, looked just as composed now as she had when he had run the comb through Rachel's hair for the last time. He held it up and looked for cracks in the delicate tines, but the light was not strong enough and so he took it to the window.

A cursory knock sounded at the door and Amelia strolled into the room. "H.! How wonderful that you're up and about! And just in time too, just in the nick of time. You're watching the fire. How dreadful! Let's watch it together a moment, just you and me." The windows gazed out upon the lawn and the white barn in the distance. The sky was too dark for afternoon, and where the sun should have hung there was now only an undulating black curtain of heat which pulsed through the windowpanes upon his face like the throb of an open furnace. "I'm leaving," she said. "They say the time to leave is now or never, so now that Lawrence is done shooting at birds, he's gone to fetch the car."

He raised a knuckle to his teeth. "Where are you going?"

"Oh, back to Washington. Back to Washington and then to get married. All that. There's no more putting it off." A new crowd of people was coming through the gates on the far edge of the lawn. Carts and horses were laden with family possessions. "He wants to be a diplomat, does Lawrence," she mused. "He will be too, I'm sure. Which means moving someplace dreadful. Indochina, Indonesia, Indiana, who knows." She shook her head. "I mean, really—shooting at birds."

The big pumper engine that they had brought down from the coal mine to fight the fire had gotten stuck in the grass. Henry watched them pushing it forward and back. It belched smoke that was even blacker than the fire as the wheels rocked ineffectually in the soft earth.

It flashed into his mind suddenly that perhaps he had never left the War at all. Maybe, in fact, the War had never ended. It was impossible, standing here, to tell. The flames, the men with shovels, the people who had lost their homes and now stood clutched together, their faces chapped from the heat and windblown . . . He grabbed a hank of the curtain for support and hung on to it. His body still lay on the field where it had fallen. He was floating above it, looking down.

Amelia's voice was lost amid the particulate sift of dust raining down on his helmet, the punch of mortars, the gasp of his own breath as he labored to pull air through his gas mask.

He thought of the Colonel, that looming, constant presence,

and of Duncan and Corwin, whose atrocities had followed him ever since that awful night when they had come out of the French farmhouse and stood above him, jamming dirty fingers in his mouth.

The War, the fire, the Colonel, and the angel: It felt as if some gigantic stone had somehow dislodged itself and begun rolling toward him down the long, slow curve of the world. Soon it would catch up to him, run him and his little boy down, crush them flat, plow them under. He opened his eyes.

Down in the drive, beautiful, shining automobiles were being frantically packed. "I told Lawrence I was going to say goodbye to you and then go find a flask of something for the road. I've been gone so long he probably thinks you've made off with me."

"You've got to take my boy with you," he said suddenly.

"What?"

"When you go, you have to take my son with you," he said again. "Take him away from all of this." He nodded out the window. "He don't need me. He needs a mother."

She looked at him in frank bewilderment.

"Like Bithiah," he added. "She was the Pharaoh's daughter."

"You're talking nonsense, H. I can't do that. I think you need to lie down."

He reached into his pocket and pulled out the comb. "Take him with you. When he's older, give this to him. Tell him it was his grandmother's."

"You're cracked, H."

"Please," he said. "Just take my boy with you. Be a mother to my boy. I can't . . . I can't care for him."

"Listen, H." She pushed the comb away and, reaching up, took his face in her palms. "Listen to me now. Everything is going to be *all right*. It will be *all right*. I don't know what happened to you out there. I won't ever know, but I do know you made it to

166

safety. The fire can't reach you here. You're beyond it now and you're safe, do you hear me? Do you hear me, H.?" She glanced out the window and then back at him. "And *please* don't worry about your boy. He's in good hands and, anyway, even if the fire does come, Lawrence says there will be plenty of caravans to take everyone away."

"You don't understand."

"No, I certainly don't." She smiled sadly and patted his cheek, then took a deep breath. "Anyway, on to business. I've arranged it with the manager, and you can stay here as long as you wish. I'd recommend you do too. You look terrible, H. Get some rest and see how you feel in a few days. Order room service. I have to leave," she said. "Goodbye, Henry."

39

The silver and coffee pantries were deserted, but the Colonel found the girl he was looking for in the food pantry. The wood and metal room was cool and dark, about half the size of a box-car, and lined, floor to ceiling, with shelves and shelves of peach, plum, and cherry preserves; flour and cornmeal; pickles and relish; canned goods of every kind; cheese wheels and sugar cubes; pats, sticks, and baker's blocks of butter; pitchers of cream; bags of salt. To his left the wall was taken up with utensils—bread knives, wooden pails, a sugar dredge, can open-ers, knife polishers, colanders, strainers, a hot-water urn, and various contraptions whose uses were a mystery to the old man. She had her back turned to him as he came to lean against the tin door frame. His eyes wandered over the food before resting on the damp wisps of hair that whorled at the back of the girl's neck. After a time he rapped against the floor with the rifle butt. She started and turned. The infant slept in a sling against her chest.

"The man suggested that I speak with you about being moved to quarters on the top floor of the hotel." She seemed in a spell as she looked at the gun in his hands. He rapped the rifle butt sharply on the ground once more, and she came back to herself. "Are you unwell, child?"

Her face had taken on the soft glisten of candle wax in the light of the nearest ceiling bulb. "I'm sorry," she said. "I'm just worn out. Excuse me." She walked toward the doorway, but he did not step aside. She swallowed twice convulsively, fear flooding her chest. "Excuse me, please."

"It would appear as if my boys and I brought the fire to your very door," he said. "You have been so kind to us and all the other unfortunates—my boys and me, the young veteran and his infant son on the top floor. Such kindness." He stepped across the threshold into the pantry with her, pulling the door gently closed behind him until it latched with a galvanic click.

She looked at the wall of knives, knowing that he had followed her gaze even as she did so. "I . . ." she said, blinking. The blades hung within reach, swaying and winking slightly at her. She could have lunged for one, reached out and grabbed one—she knew each of them, their feel, their balance and weight—but instead she felt her arms wrap themselves protectively around Henry Bright's son.

The Colonel flicked the light switch off. In the sudden darkness she felt him step between her and the knives on the wall. For a long moment the two listened to each other breathing in the blackness.

"A story," he began. "Once there was a good-hearted soldier, a hero, who, having served his country, retired from the battlefield in order to till the land and raise up a family. Having married the beautiful sister of a dearly departed comrade, he settled down with her to raise a family. The other sister, jealous of her fairer sibling, married a vagrant, sometime coal miner and gave birth to a rogue."

She heard the singing sound of the blades as the Colonel leaned back against the wall of knives. "As for the good-hearted man, he and his beloved wife had three beautiful children: two handsome sons and a pretty daughter, who was the man's darling. When his wife died, this good-hearted man, now a widower, found the great solace of his life in watching his children grow, especially the girl, who was beyond compare in beauty and virtue. As the years passed she became ever more radiant, grew up indeed into a beautiful, chaste young woman." He paused and listened for her. "Are you still there, child?"

Her voice came smally. "Yes."

"Good," he said. "Good. Now then, do you remember the rogue born of the ugly sister? Well, the rogue grew up too, but not into a proud young man, no. He grew up into something awful. Into a monster. And then, one night a year ago, without warning, he rode his horse to the old man's house, woke the old man and his children from their sleep, and, with some combination of enchantment and violence, abducted the old man's beautiful daughter and took her away to live with him in the same maggot-strewn ditch where he himself had been raised.

"In the blink of an eye, his dreams of a happy old age vanished and he saw himself for what he really was: just a foolish old man."

He coughed. "I am sorry, Miss Brigid. The smoke of the fire," he said. He flipped on the light switch. The barrel of the rifle was only a few inches from her forehead. She opened her mouth, but no sound came out. He coughed once more. "Would it be too much, do you think, to ask you for a drop of that cognac I saw there? I have not had cognac in a very, very, very long time." He motioned with his head to a dusty bottle sitting low on a shelf. "If it is not too much to ask." He looked at her expectantly. She stood paralyzed, unsure of what he meant for her to do. He cocked his head once more toward the bottle and she knelt slowly to retrieve it. He followed her with the rifle barrel as she stood back up. "The stopper," he said. "Please."

She pulled the stopper from the bottle. At the sound of the release, the baby woke in her arms and began to keen.

He shifted the rifle unsteadily to one hand and held the other out to her. "Hand it to me," he said. He took the bottle and lifted it halfway to his lips. Here he paused, however, and considered her. "Step forward," he said.

Again it was as if she couldn't move.

"Step. Forward." The barrel of the gun was only inches from her. "If you do not step forward, I will kill my grandson."

She came forward an inch.

"Good, good," the Colonel said approvingly. He beckoned. "Forward still. Forward, forward, turn your head just a bit, my dear . . . and . . . good."

When she stopped, the barrel was pressed flatly against the birthmark at her temple. The baby cried. It hurt her to hear it, but she did not move.

"Now," he said. "I have come a long way and I am going to take a drink of this rare old cognac."

He took three long swallows and then held the bottle out to her. "Take a sip yourself, child. You look as though you need it."

The rifle stock appeared to sigh against her skull as she obeyed.

She took the bottle, put it to her lips and sipped.

Abruptly, he switched the lights off again, and the room was submerged once more in blackness.

"The old man made up his mind that he would kill the rogue and bring his daughter back home where she belonged. It was right that the rogue should die. It was strange, though—each time the old man and his sons crossed the ridge with the intention of killing him, something always thwarted them. Once the old man was about to shoot, when the rogue's horse came and stood in the path of the shot. Another time, the old man's sons got into a nest of bees and were stung frightfully. He actually managed to pull the trigger once, only to find that the rifle contained no bullets. The old man would not be deterred, however. He would have his revenge. Then, one day, as he watched his daughter from the woods, he saw that she was with child and a thought came to him."

There was silence. The rifle barrel lifted from her temple in the dark, and the man's voice drew much closer. "He thought to himself, 'As the rogue has stolen my child, so, too, will I steal a child from the rogue.' He decided that he would not kill the rogue until the baby was born. Then, when the child was delivered, he would swoop down and exact his vengeance. The old man made a vow to himself that he would stand victoriously above the rogue, holding the rogue's child in his arms."

"The bottle, please," he sighed. She felt his hand grope down her arm to the bottle. He took it, gulping loudly in the dark.

The pantry could not have been darker had she closed her eyes. She tried to listen through the thick, velvet blackness, through the pantry's stone walls and metal door, for the sounds of someone who might come to her aid. She knew it was useless; the kitchen staff, the coffee and cocoa girl, the dishwashers, the stewards and waiters, had been dismissed to see to their own families, and anyone else who was still here had been set to work out on the lawn. Her thoughts flashed to Dennis, but he was probably gone to the barn to fetch the animals. "Please," she began to whisper. "Please. Please."

"Shush," the Colonel said, his grammar slipping as he drank. "Shush. A little more and then we'll both go, I reckon." He giggled. "Yeah, we'll both get going, I reckon. Anyway, the girl grew and grew with the child in her belly, and then one day she felt the pains."

His breath was at her ear now, the liquor misting on her

172

cheek. She backed up and he moved with her, crowding against her until her shoulder blades were pressed against the shelving on the far side of the room.

"The old man knew it," he said. "When his daughter started feeling the birth pains, he knew. He waited, and the birds of the forest stopped singing and waited with him." His throat clicked drily in her ear. "But he was never to be reunited with his daughter. She died in the early morning, delivering a son. Henry Bright set fire to the cabin and escaped to the east on his horse, carrying the baby boy that is now in your arms."

The bottle shattered against the wall where he threw it among the jars of preserves. "Where is he?" She bolted in the darkness for the door, but the Colonel caught her by her hair, looping it around his fist like reins, forcing her to her knees on the tiled floor.

"I don't know!"

He twisted her hair tightly, as if winding a spring.

"Well," he said. He was breathing hard through his mouth when he put his lips to her ear again. "I found his horse." His grip on her hair loosened for an instant. "And I found his boy." He brought the rifle butt down hard against the back of her head. She slumped, but he held her kneeling body upright by the hair so that she would not fall forward on top of the baby. "I suppose I will find him, too, soon enough." He eased her down against a shelf before switching on the light. He knelt by her, peering closely for the first time at his daughter's child. Its eyes were tightly closed, but it was giving full throat to its displeasure. He lifted the cooking girl's arm so that he could pull the infant in its sling from around her neck and hang it round his own. Then he stood and opened the pantry door to the brightness of the kitchen.

The ridiculous young woman he had met at breakfast was

173

sloshing whiskey into a silver flask over the sink. "Well, hello," she said brightly. "We meet again. I was just finding Lawrence and me a drink to take with us for the road."

Without a word, the Colonel carried the screaming infant past her. He threw open the door of the servants' entrance, and the child's howls folded into the howling of the wind as it whipped around the hotel eaves and into the room, setting the hanging pots and pans to rattling and banging against one another. He stood looking out at the lawn, with its great crowd of people and cars, dogs and horses. In the space above his head, the doorway framed the fire crowning in the treetops. Flames lashed at the trees, tearing branches away, hurling them skyward in great updrafts. The barn stood nestled in their midst, glowing like an in got of white-hot metal. He looked steadily at the far-off building, watching it closely even as a cinder the size of a man's leg fell out of the sky at his feet in the doorway. All at once he seemed to come to a decision, and clamping an arm around the crying child on his chest, he pulled the rifle tightly against his back and started out across the lawn.

Pots were falling off the wall now, and somehow a sack of flour had been knocked to the floor and exploded open. The fine white powder was swept up into the currents of air and swirled angrily around the room like a trapped ghost. Amelia dropped the whiskey bottle and the flask in the sink and grabbed the nearest pot, throwing it under the tap and filling it with water. She ran to the burning branch that had landed in the doorway and doused it. The door itself was blown back on its hinges by the steep wind, and she pushed her shoulder hard against it until it closed and the room fell silent. She rested her forehead upon the wood a moment, then turned to survey the wreckage of the kitchen. Standing unsteadily on the far side of the room was the kitchen girl, Brigid.

40

That night, after retrieving the she-goat from the girl and the Colonel's sons, he made a supper of a few eggs he had brought home with him from Fells Corner. The chickens were clucking their way toward consensus in their hutch, while nearby the billy and she-goat were tucked cozily into a patch of bracken fern. Bright stood in the doorway of the cabin, looking off toward the ridge as if he could tunnel through it with his eyes and see Rachel once more. His fork scraped against the dish as he ate. When he was done, he walked across his little farmyard and stooped to wash his dish in the stream.

"Henry Bright."

He didn't move.

"Henry Bright," the angel said again. "Henry Bright, I found you. Fear not."

He felt the sigh on the back of his neck and the heat of the angel's nearness, but he gave no answer and continued the washing up as if he were completely alone. When at last it seemed he might rinse the plate forever, he twisted his neck around and looked up into the deep pool of breathing black that was his new horse. "Yeah," he said. "You found me, all right." Then he stood up and, turning his back on the animal, walked across the yard to tether the goats.

"Your time has come, Henry Bright," the horse said behind him. "A great work is demanded of you."

"I don't know you," he said. "You'd better git on out of that horse. That's my horse. If you want a horse, there's a auction over in Fells Corner."

"You know me, Henry Bright. The angel from the church ceiling."

"No, I do not know you. And I don't want to know you either." He walked to the cabin and went in and sat there on the edge of the bed. As evening began to deepen, he came back to the door and stood looking out. "Everybody wants my animals," he said, and threw the flap shut again. A little while later, a metallic clatter arose in the yard. It continued for several minutes and Bright, exasperated, finally threw open the cabin flap to investigate the noise. The horse stood in the middle of the farmyard, looking at him expectantly, one of its back feet standing in the bucket Bright had left at the creek side. He went to the horse and lifted its hoof out of the bucket. "Anyway," he said, "how am I supposed to know it's you?"

"You know it's me."

"How'd you find me?"

"Never mind that. Your great work awaits you."

Bright walked to the doorway of the cabin once more. "I don't want any of your great-work talk. I'm going to work in the coal mines."

"You are not going to work in the coal mines. You are going to marry the girl Rachel and have a son."

"I can't believe you," Bright said.

"You have been chosen, Henry Bright. You will marry her and she will bear your child. She has been chosen to be the mother of the Future King of Heaven."

"You're crazy, angel. You talk like you never heard there was a Jesus Christ before."

"Why do you say that, Henry Bright?"

"Because that's what Jesus Christ is, right? He's the King of Heaven."

"Is he?"

"That's what they say, yeah."

"Yes, they do," the horse said, chewing on the thought. "They do say that, don't they?" There was silence. Then, "What about the barbed wire? Is he King of that? And the mustard gas?"

"How do I know?" Bright stood facing the horse head-on. "You're the angel who was always saying he knew everything."

"Or the shells? The trench mortars? The Spanish flu? Do you remember the flu, Henry Bright? The men drowning of it in the trenches? Is Jesus Christ, the King of Heaven, the King of the Spanish Flu? Of the smells? Of the shit and piss? Is Jesus Christ, the King of Heaven, King of all that misery as well?"

"So what if he is?" Bright said. "I don't care anymore."

"You don't mean that, Henry Bright. Please come to one side so that I might look at you when you address me."

Bright stared deep into one of the horse's eyes, as if he were looking through a hole in the world. "You left me when I got shot. We're finished, you and me."

"Answer me, Henry Bright: Is Jesus Christ the King of everything that you've seen?"

"Maybe he is."

"Why do you suppose a good King would let all those things happen? Doesn't a King have the power to stop them?"

"Why are you making me say all these things? I don't know why he does what he does—"

"Nor do I," the horse said. "Nor do I. The cruelty I've seen is beyond my understanding. So I've decided we need a new King of Heaven."

Bright stood a long moment in the darkness, the empty

bucket dangling in his hand. A valedictory stream of urine shot from the horse, drumming hollowly against the ground, as if there were only a thin crust of earth between its hooves and the underworld. Bright peered about him and into the woods, but there was nothing out there. "I don't want to be talking to you anymore," he said finally. "Do you hear me, angel? I didn't ask for you to come around here. You left me out there all shot up and I didn't hear from you for months. Now you're here, just fresh as a strawberry and won't get out of my horse, and talking like you always talked, like nothing ever happened."

"You were never abandoned, Henry Bright. I saved you many times. Remember the graveyard, when the shell landed in front of you and did not explode? And what about in the village? How was it that you kept living while so many others did not? I saved you from drinking the poisoned water and from being discovered as you lay in the ditch. I kept you from being buried along with Sergeant Matthews, and I saved you from being shot in the head on the last day of the War. Who was it but me that grabbed your leg and pulled you to the ground where you would be safe? I saved your life hundreds of times, thousands of times. The bullets that came for you were legion. Tell me truthfully: If not for me, would you have lived?"

"I don't know."

"Yes, you do."

"Well, anyway, I didn't ask you for any of that."

"Of course you did. From the very first moment you heard my voice, you called out to me without ceasing."

"What about all them others? Why was it me you saved and not any of them?"

"Because I chose you, Henry Bright. That day in the church, when you looked up at me, I knew that you alone were the one to help me bring the Future King of Heaven into the world. He is the son you will have with the girl, and, come that great day

178

when the boy takes his throne, men will no longer be forced to kill other men. They will farm, work a trade, marry. They will die in their beds. War will be a thing of the past."

He walked to the creek, dipped the bucket in the water, and set it near the horse for the animal to drink. At the cabin door he lifted the flap, then stood there in the triangle of light for a long moment.

It was four nights later that he saddled the horse and set out toward the Colonel's house to bring back his bride.

41

After Amelia was gone, he held the comb up to the dim light of the window once more. A hairline crack ran grayly up one of the fine white tines. The woman carved into the comb's base looked accusingly at him for this. He held her face up nearer to the window, but the fire had turned the sky the color of engraver's ink, and the only real illumination came from the treetops pluming brightly at the lawn's edge. He pulled her tiny face very close to his own, trying to read her expression, and in doing so the tines seemed to catch a figure running jerkily between them toward the barn. The figure was as thin as a scarecrow, his hat pulled down hard over his pate, his face slanted down against the wind. He wore an outmoded military jacket, and across his back, pulled tight with its tiny burden, hung the sling that Bright had made from Rachel's dress.

42

He threw the door open and stood disoriented in the hallway. It was white plaster and stretched away forever in both directions, the distances measured in potted ferns and musty prints of hunting dogs and prize thoroughbreds. He chose a direction and ran past the numberless doors and flocked wallpaper until he arrived at the brass portals of two elevators. He stood wavering before these, then saw the stairwell beckoning to him through an inconspicuous doorway only a few yards farther on. He threw himself down the steps three and four at a time, holding on to the banisters so that his momentum wouldn't carry him crashing into the plaster busts and knickknacks that crammed the landings. The stairway became more and more crowded with people the closer he got to the ground floor. By the time he rounded the second-floor landing, it felt as if he was wading in a living river of animals, children, nannies, and noise. He pushed his way down into the midst of the confusion and caught a glimpse of the girl Margaret, still directing her brood. He squeezed by her into the domed lobby. Everywhere, trunks and bags were being loaded on large pallets, and porters rushed about, writing on tags and directing one another. Well-dressed men and women stood on the fringes of the activity putting on and taking off gloves, fanning themselves with summer hats, worrying buttons. Children chased one another gleefully through the maze of legs and luggage beneath the dome, climbing on sofas, on hand trolleys, even up on the stately black piano, which stood like a river rock in the middle of the floor.

He wove and jostled his way through the frantic cauldron to the revolving doors and, passing through them, ran down the wide white hotel steps to the drive. Automobiles were backed up fender to fender, adding their own smoke to the air as they vied for space and their drivers shouted at one another. Through the human and mechanical commotion came, at intervals, the velveteen drip of wildlife careening onto the grass from through the gaps in the burning curtains beyond. In the midst of all this, no one seemed to notice Henry Bright as he ran in desperation toward the fire and the barn that it was about to devour.

It looked like the outskirts of the War: carts and horses, huffing engines of all kinds, women and children without homes, and men digging into the dirt to save a piece of ground that only seemed like theirs in that single, desperate moment. The wildfire was a living angry thing in front of him. He could feel the ground itself getting hotter through the soles of his boots, and he was tossed about by gusts of grit-streaked wind. Above its rushing in his ears, he heard another sound and realized that he was screaming, just as he always had when the order came and he fixed his bayonet and climbed up over the sandbags to cross the fields. Then suddenly he was at the lawn's edge, and the world had gotten so atrociously loud and leaden with heat that even the noises coming from his own throat were lost.

Each step toward the incandescent whiteness of the barn became a step into the forge. He skirted a row of rattling cornstalks, moving along the barn's broad side until he came around to the front of the building and could see where its doors hung open. A man's body lay there in the doorway amid a blizzard of white chicken feathers. His neck was a lattice of cuts and scrapes, his dead eyes filled with the same look of insult and terror that crosses an animal's face as it is dragged into the underbrush.

In the midst of the heat, a cold yellow wave of fear sloshed up in Bright's chest. He spun, certain that Corwin and Duncan were behind him, but no one was there. His eyes roved the long row of cornstalks, searching them for faces, but the husks only clapped against each other merrily and gave nothing away. He turned back toward the body lying in the barn doorway and found himself face-to-face with his horse. The animal stood before him, lock-kneed and rigid, its mouth flecked with spittle, its flanks quivering. The black eyes rolled and the big nose snuffed hard against the thick air. The Colonel sat high astride the animal, the baby in the sling upon his chest, the gaping muzzle of the gun pointed down at Bright's head. The horse canted nervously to the left but the Colonel pulled it back to true, hauling viciously on the reins, cutting the bit deep beneath its lolling tongue.

Bright looked up into the black length of the barrel. "That's my mother's rifle."

The old man's eyes glinted. He kicked the horse hard and the animal lunged forward, knocking Bright back against the side of the barn wall with its shoulder. "All your running away," he said, "and you run right to me. A coward always ends up running toward what he wishes to escape. There is no irony in it." He glanced to either side, looking for something. "My goddamn boys are off somewhere," he said. "My useless goddamn boys are off somewhere, but"—he pushed the muzzle of the rifle forward into Bright's face—"it makes no difference to you and me."

Bright looked past the gun into the horse's eyes. "You're gonna let him kill me now?"

"Fear not, Henry Bright." The angel's voice was calm.

183

"But I did everything you told me to!"

"All is well."

Forgetting the rifle pointed down at him, he stepped toward the horse. The Colonel kicked him in the teeth, knocking him painfully back against the barn wall again. His eyes had begun to water hard from the smoke, burning so that it was a struggle to keep them open.

"My daughter." The Colonel, too, was weeping as he ran a sleeve across his mouth. "She was my beautiful girl. You stole her away from me." The tears streamed freely down his face and dropped onto his grandchild as he looked down at the infant. For a moment the old man on the horse seemed to forget that Bright was even there, then his head snapped up once more. "You stole her away from me just like your mother tried to do," he said. "I should have killed you both. I should have shot you down when you were small and buried you where you fell." A thick cloud of smoke enveloped them. The Colonel doubled over, coughing in the saddle. The rifle barrel dipped as he struggled for breath.

"Stay very still, Henry Bright," the angel commanded serenely. "Stay very still and close your eyes."

Another rolling barrage of heat washed over them as the bales of hay inside the barn caught fire. The wind whipped the Colonel's hat off and sucked it behind him into the whirling vortex. He didn't seem to notice. He pulled the rifle hammer back.

Henry Bright looked up into the Colonel's eyes briefly, but the fear was gone, and neither the old man or the waiting infinity of the rifle were of interest anymore. He found that all he wanted to do in the remaining moments of his life was to look at his son. The baby seemed strangely at peace in the conflagration. His coppery hair blew out in all directions. Bright realized that he, too, felt a kind of peace.

If he had lived, it occurred to him, he might have eventually felt that same kind of peacefulness at home, watching his boy grow up. He would have tended to his chickens and rabbits and goats and taught his son the things that his own mother had taught him. And, should he ever again smell the scent of lemons, he might one day have been able to think of sweet tea or lemonade instead of a pile of bodies on the edge of a ragged November tree line.

Maybe, he thought. If he had lived.

He thought about Rachel, whom he had loved since they were small. He felt happy to have held, even for a short while, the son whom she had delivered into his arms. He wondered if his own father had felt such a moment of grace as the earth collapsed around him.

He took one last look at his son and closed his eyes.

The last thing he felt before he heard the gunshot was the breath of the angel on his cheek. After that there was nothing but the heat and the drifting sensation of time continuing to pass in the world beyond his eyelids. He was in hell, he thought. In hell or the War.

He opened his burning eyes to find out which it was.

Above him the Colonel sat erect in the saddle, so still that he could have been posing for his portrait. A purple flower had blossomed beneath his right eye. It bloomed, then wilted and ran down over his cheekbone and into his collar. The old man's face sagged, and then his head drooped and he looked down at his chest as if someone were in the process of pinning a medal there.

The Colonel slumped forward in the saddle. Behind him, a pistol in his outstretched arm, was a man Bright had never seen before. Next to him, faces white and slick with sweat, stood Amelia and Brigid. The Colonel listed in the saddle, his deadweight pulling the horse off balance. Bright pushed away from the barn wall, lunging to catch the old man's body before it toppled off the horse and crushed his son.

The horse began to stamp, but Bright grabbed a stirrup and held the animal where it was as Brigid rushed forward and took the reins. He couldn't reach high enough to pull the sling over the Colonel's head, so he began to ease the body gently down out of the saddle. The buttons of the old man's jacket were hot to the touch.

He saw his mother's rifle only as it slipped from the Colonel's hands. It fell to the ground, firing its single charge. Angel or no angel, the sound of the shot was finally too much for the horse. It went wild, pulling away from Brigid and charging toward Amelia and the man with the pistol as Bright fought hard to hold on. The child bounced crazily in the sling around the dead man's drooping neck.

A second shot sounded, and the rampaging animal, seeming to remember something all of a sudden, went instantly still. It hung there frozen a moment, then collapsed on Henry Bright, pinning him to the ground by his legs. Lawrence reached down and fired a final, merciful shot into its head.

Brigid knelt. "Are you all right?" He answered something, but she was already intent on pulling the infant from the sling.

"You're cracked, H.!" Amelia bent over and yelled down at him. "I tell you to stay put and order room service and this happens?" She watched as Lawrence jammed the Colonel's rifle stock between the horse's hindquarters and the ground. He and Amelia began to lever the deadweight slowly off Bright's legs.

Bright pushed and scraped against the hot ground with his hands and elbows until he'd pulled his feet free and he could stand. They ran from the barn, doubled over, through throes of corrosive soot, washed forward by the percussive *whoosh* of exploding trees, surfacing finally on the great lawn like castaways.

The air was still brutally hot and he struggled to catch his breath as he looked over at Brigid holding his son. She looked back at him, her eyes widening, and yelled something that he couldn't make out. Only when he felt his hair catch fire did he realize that his jacket was burning. He ran to the nearest of the small ponds and threw himself in.

Brigid came to the water too, and he sloshed to the girl's side. She was looking down at the ashen-faced child with deep concern. The boy lay totally still, his expression a mask. Bright reached for the bundle in disbelief, but Brigid slapped his hands away. She bent and dunked the child in the water and, as if reborn, the boy came up howling.

Amelia and Lawrence stood at the pond's edge looking back at the fire. The barn gave way to the flames all at once, as if it had suddenly been transformed into a great swarm of black bees, which at some signal went buzzing heavenward together. Amelia slipped her arm around Lawrence, whom she would marry in the fall, when the weather cooled and the humidity died down. Bright and Brigid looked down at Henry. As she had lifted the infant from the water, the boy had opened his eyes for the first time. They were beautiful and blue, just like Rachel's had been.

They were coming up the bank when the figure of a man staggered out of the fire and stood encased in the dirty-yellow no-man's-land between the trees and the pond as if trapped in amber. Although he made no sound, a serrated cry of alarm came cutting through the roar of the fire from the animal he carried on his back.

By the time Bright reached him, Duncan had sunk to his knees. He tried to pull the goat from his shoulders, but Duncan held the creature's hooves tightly in his fists, unwilling or unable to let go. Bright knocked Duncan to the ground and climbed on top of him, as if he meant to choke him. Duncan made no move either to resist or to let go of the goat, and after a long, tangled moment, Bright grabbed the Colonel's son by his hair and shirtfront and pulled him to his feet. He shoved him, the goat still on his back, to the pond's edge and pushed Duncan in. As he hit the water, the goat finally kicked herself free of Duncan's grip and stood shakily sneezing in the mud.

"I found her," Duncan said, sitting up in the water. "She was running around in the fire and I caught her." He leaned forward and took a drink of water. "Do you have the baby?" Soaked, Duncan looked more like a child than a man. "He's my sister's baby."

"Yes," Bright said. "Come on." The goat was looking at him across the water, as if trying to remember something. A dream came back to him then. In it he was kicking Duncan in the head.

Duncan woozily reached around in the pond for the goat. It made no struggle as he scooped it into his arms again. "I think I need help walking," he said.

"Where did you come from?" He helped the Colonel's son up the bank.

"Corwin and me weren't allowed to stay inside the hotel with the other folks 'cause of some of the things he used to do. They all blamed me too. One of them knocked me down and he was beating me, but a man from the hotel stopped him. We still had to leave, though, so we went to the barn." Duncan coughed. His ribs seemed about to poke through his skin. "And at the barn there was all these chickens. I looked at Corwin. I saw what was in his mind."

Bright looked in those deep-set eyes. "Where's Corwin?"

"That hotel man came across the field just when Corwin was starting in on the chickens. He tried to stop Corwin but it wasn't no use. He didn't know about my brother. Corwin knocked him down and then . . . He wouldn't stop. Finally I took a shovel and I hit Corwin over the head with it real hard and it killed

188

him. That didn't make no difference to the hotel man, though. He was already gone. I saw my father coming across the field, so I dragged my brother over behind the barn. Your goat was standing there. She took one little look at me and just lit out. I said to myself, 'She's gonna run right into the fire.' So I chased after her until I caught her."

He looked around wildly. "Where's he at? My father?"

"He died," Bright said. "I'm sorry," he added.

"I'm not."

They passed a group of men going in the opposite direction, shepherding the big pumper toward the pond. Some were already wearing gas masks. Farther on, others were just setting out for the fire, most still dressed raggedly in the clothes that they had been wearing when they were driven from their homes. Among them were some of the hotel guests in shirt-sleeves, their faces blanching in the temperature. Near the gate, people worked furiously to dig firebreaks with whatever they had. Some used shovels, but others turned the ground with hoes, knives, even spoons. The aunty woman from the general merchandise store was there, ripping great, green chunks of soil and grass from the ground with a pickax. A line of children waited with buckets at a water pump by the kitchen entrance. A hose now ran out of the fountain and was being used to wet the lawn.

"Kill him, Henry Bright."

Bright heard the voice but did not stop walking.

"Henry Bright, you must kill Duncan. Then we will find a mother for the child." Bright glanced toward the goat hanging exhausted in Duncan's arms. Even its ears dangled listlessly. Suddenly it looked up at him, its pupils golden keyholes, its voice serene and confident. "He must die, Henry Bright. The safety of the Future King of Heaven demands it."

Bright looked away and didn't speak. They rejoined Brigid

and his boy in the milling crowd near the fountain. The girl held the child closely and smiled as Bright approached. He reached out and touched his son's hair. "I have to do something," he told her. "I'll be back directly."

He turned to Duncan. "I was in the War. I went to France and I saw some things there." He paused. "No, I saw a lot of things that I wish I'd never seen. Awful things. Sometimes I still see them." Bright's hands clenched tightly at his sides, and he ground his teeth as he fought with some inner thought. Then, suddenly, "Were you there?"

"Where?" Duncan asked.

"Did you go to the War? Did you come out of the farmhouse that night?"

For once, the black stones of Duncan's eyes seemed to register surprise. "Me?" he said. "I never been this far from home."

Bright searched those eyes for any traces of the farmhouse that might be hidden in them. Then his face relaxed and the tautness went out of his shoulders. He reached out to pet the goat in Duncan's arms. "I guess you were right about one thing after all," he said to it.

"What?" Duncan asked.

"I have to take my goat now," Bright said to him. "Don't you worry, she'll be safe. Maybe you and I will find a new goat when this is all over," he added.

Duncan gave the goat to Bright and sat down on the edge of the fountain.

"You must kill him, Henry Bright. If you do, I will help you find a mother for your son."

At his feet, the hotel steps rippled upward like the train of a wedding dress. He ascended them, the she-goat tucked under his arm, and passed through the revolving doors into the silence of the now-deserted lobby. Once inside, man and goat looked up into that domed sweep of beneficent blue sky, so different from the apocalyptic orange world without.

At the center of the great, round room, beneath the eternal early-fall clarity of the painted dome, stood the batholithic piano, impenetrably dark. He carried the creature across the room toward the glossy black slab, turning a slow full circle and checking that the sky above them was as empty as it had appeared earlier. When he was sure that it was, he placed the she-goat atop the piano. Her hooves clicked soundingly against the ebony, causing faint vibrations in the strings. Somehow the sounds were magnified beneath the high ceiling, as if, high above, a discordant orchestra had begun to tune.

"Jee-roosh needs a mother, Henry Bright. The Future King of Heaven needs someone to care for him until he can take the throne."

"Enough of that," Bright said. "Keep it. I've heard enough."

"Do as I say!"

"We've had our differences, you and me, but everyone should have a home, and it weren't a trouble to bring you here. You kept me safe when I was in the War, and maybe I wouldn't have married Rachel if it wasn't for you, and maybe we wouldn't a had a son." He paused to consider the thought. "Maybe that's all true. I don't have any idea one way or the other. But I do know that without you, I wouldn't have burned down our cabin and the whole forest and all those people's homes and let my horse get shot. And," he said, "I wouldn't have let anybody make me believe I couldn't raise my own boy."

He looked at the goat. "I hope that this place will make you happy. If the fire don't reach the hotel I guess you'll be safe enough. There's no one else around you in that sky to bother you, so just get out of that goat and go on up there now. Git."

"Don't leave me here, Henry Bright," the angel commanded.

"Maybe if you're happy here," Bright continued, "you'll just let me go on about my life with my boy." He looked up into the blue and closed his eyes a moment. He was very tired.

"I know you're angry with me," he said, opening them again after a while. The goat was staring at him ponderously, her little teeth sliding back and forth against one another. He smiled at this. "I guess that's all a load of junk you told me about the King of Heaven and everything, but if any of it is the truth, if my son Henry really is the future King of Heaven, then I figure when he gets old enough, if you're still mad at me for leaving you here, maybe he can straighten things out between the two of us."

He leaned over the piano's edge and kissed the goat on her nose. The animal snuffled at the collar of his uniform, and the two of them stayed there a long moment. Then, without looking back, Bright spun on his heels and strode out from beneath the cool light of the dome and through the revolving doors.

At the edge of the lawn, the tumult of flames and smoke was smearing the sky into the ground. Toward the fire's sway marched lines of men and women, holding tiny buckets of water with which to soak the grass. At times throughout the night, they seemed to turn from real, living people into mere photographs of people, and then from photographs into memories, which are like photographs, and finally, as the ground blurred beneath them, whatever parts of them that could be seen from afar seemed to float like ghosts in the rippling air as they went about their work.

He descended the steps and wove his way back through the crowd of refugees. Amelia and Lawrence, arm in arm, were being fretted over by a knot of well-dressed people. Duncan stood near them, looking about him at the world through red-rimmed eyes as if for the first time. Bright found Brigid where he had left her, holding his son in her arms. He smiled at her and

192

she returned the smile. He looked into his son's blue eyes and laughed. It was a strange sound to hear coming from his mouth. He leaned forward to kiss the boy's forehead. With her free hand, Brigid reached out and brushed stiff, white goat hairs from the shoulders of his jacket and then gently pulled him forward by a lapel and kissed his own smoke-stained forehead. He looked at the mother and child together for a long time and then made to join some men heading to fight the fire. Abruptly, though, he turned to face her once more and, drawing from his pocket a small and ancient ivory comb, he pressed it into her hand for safekeeping.

Acknowledgments

This book would not have been possible without my editor, Noah Eaker. Great thanks as well to Scott Moyers. Thanks to my manager and friend, Darius Zelkha, and to Tim Craven, Liam Hurley, Austin Nevins, Sam Kassirer, Zack Hickman, the Ricks, the Leahys, Mary Moyer, Carla Sacks, Maria Braeckel, Kathy Lord, Dave Brewster, Sue Devine, Doug Rice, Dave O'Grady, Dan Cardinal, Brian Stowell, Scott Hueston, Robert Pinsky, Ed Romanoff, Jonathan Horn, and Kathleen Denney.

Much respect is due to Barbara Tuchman for her books *The Proud Tower* and *The Guns of August;* Joseph Persico for his *Eleventh Month, Eleventh Day, Eleventh Hour;* and to William Orpen's *An Onlooker in France, 1917–1919.* These books are requiems.

Most especially, thank you to my family—Robert, Sue, Lincoln, and Chana—the best of the better angels.

About the Author

JOSH RITTER is a songwriter from Moscow,
Idaho. His albums include *The Animal Years*
and *So Runs the World Away*. *Bright's Passage* is
his first novel. He currently lives in New York.

www.joshritter.com

About the Type

This book was set in Baskerville, a typeface which was designed by John Baskerville, an amateur printer and type-founder, and cut for him by John Handy in 1750. The type became popular again when The Lanston Monotype Corporation of London revived the classic Roman face in 1923. The Mergenthaler Linotype Company in England and the United States cut a version of Baskerville in 1931, making it one of the most widely used typefaces today.

Saveurs parfaites
cuisine végétarienne

Parragon

Bath · New York · Singapore · Hong Kong · Cologne · Delhi · Melbourne

Conception et réalisation : Terry Jeavons & Company

Réalisation : InTexte, Toulouse

ISBN : 978-1-4075-1364-5

Imprimé en Chine

Une cuillerée à soupe correspond à 15 à 20 g d'ingrédients secs et à 15 ml d'ingrédients
liquides. Une cuillerée à café correspond à 3 à 5 g d'ingrédients secs et à 5 ml d'ingrédients
liquides. Sans autre précision, le lait est entier, les œufs sont de taille moyenne et le poivre
est du poivre noir fraîchement moulu. Les temps de préparation et de cuisson des recettes
pouvant varier en fonction, notamment, du four utilisé, ils sont donnés à titre indicatif.

La consommation des œufs crus ou peu cuits est déconseillée aux enfants, aux personnes
âgées, malades ou convalescentes, et aux femmes enceintes.

Saveurs parfaites
cuisine
végétarienne

introduction

Le régime végétarien a été longtemps considéré comme un choix excentrique, synonyme d'ennui. Cependant, ces dernières années, le nombre des adeptes du végétarisme s'est accru, pour de multiples raisons. La plus évidente d'entre elles est le désir de ne plus consommer de chair animale ou de poisson. Toutefois, certains aspects médicaux sont également mis en avant : dans la colite chronique par exemple, la consommation de viande est souvent incriminée comme source du mal. La viande et le poisson peuvent se révéler chers, de sorte que même les non-végétariens préfèrent parfois prendre deux ou trois repas hebdomadaires sans viande.

Bonne nouvelle : le regain d'intérêt pour le végétarisme a amélioré son image dans l'univers de la gastronomie. Les chefs ont relevé le défi avec talent et ont concocté des recettes créatives. Les repas végétariens ont cessé d'être monotones !

Si vous venez d'adopter le végétarisme, soyez conscient qu'il ne suffit pas d'exclure la viande et le poisson de vos recettes habituelles. En effet, cette pratique vous priverait de vos protéines et d'autres éléments nutritifs qui sont essentiels à votre

santé et à votre bien-être. La viande et le poisson doivent être remplacés par d'autres protéines et aliments riches en nutriments, comme les haricots, les fruits à coque, le tofu et les produits laitiers. Si vous souffrez d'allergies à l'un de ces ingrédients, prenez conseil auprès de votre médecin ou d'un nutritionniste, afin de vérifier que vous ne porterez pas préjudice à votre santé au lieu de la préserver.

Que vous ayez décidé de devenir un « vrai » végétarien, que vous receviez simplement des végétariens à dîner ou que vous prépariez de temps

à autre un repas sans protéines animales, vous trouverez dans ce livre de fabuleuses idées glanées un peu partout dans le monde. Pour obtenir les meilleurs résultats, utilisez des ingrédients frais et de qualité, qui vous permettront de tirer le plus grand profit de votre alimentation, tout en vous garantissant un goût irréprochable.

entrées

& plats légers

De nombreux plats, parmi les plus célèbres au monde, se composent de légumes ; ce livre contient de superbes recettes de soupes, d'entrées et de sauces d'accompagnement pour les légumes crus. Testez la délicate soupe au cresson, la solide soupe aux haricots blancs et la roborative soupe des moines. Ici, vous ne trouverez nulle trace d'austérité, quel que soit le nom de la recette ! Confectionnez une série de tapas à base d'amandes salées, d'olives marinées, de purée d'aubergine, de champignons à l'ail, et de figues au bleu. Vous pouvez également commencer votre repas par des crudités, mélange rafraîchissant de céleri, de carottes et de betteraves qui chatouillera votre palais.

Certaines de ces recettes sont idéalement légères. Pour un brunch, un déjeuner ou une collation tardive, prévoyez des beignets de courgettes avec une sauce au yaourt, des soufflés au fromage et aux fines herbes ou des galettes de patates douces à la menthe et à la féta. Si vous appréciez la nourriture mexicaine, optez pour le guacamole ou les nachos aux haricots noirs, avant de tester l'houmous du Moyen-Orient et leq falafels au sésame. Ces plats contiennent assez de nutriments pour apaiser votre estomac pendant des heures ! Toutefois, en guise d'entrée parfaite, simple et élégante, servez des asperges avec du beurre fondu. Un régal !

amandes salées

ingrédients

POUR 6 À 8 PERSONNES

225 g d'amandes entières,
   mondées ou avec la peau
   (*voir* méthode)
4 cuil. à soupe d'huile d'olive
   espagnole
gros sel
1 cuil. à café de paprika
   ou de cumin (facultatif)

méthode

1 Les amandes ont plus de goût avec la peau, mais sont plus agréables à consommer une fois mondées. Pour monder des amandes, mettre dans une terrine, couvrir d'eau bouillante et laisser reposer 3 à 4 minutes. Égoutter, plonger dans de l'eau froide 1 minute et égoutter de nouveau. Retirer la peau avec les doigts et sécher sur du papier absorbant.

2 Verser l'huile dans un plat allant au four, répartir dans le fond et ajouter les amandes. Mélanger de sorte qu'elles soient bien enrobées d'huile et étaler en une seule couche.

3 Cuire au four préchauffé 20 minutes à 180 °C (th. 6) en remuant plusieurs fois, jusqu'à ce qu'elles soient dorées. Égoutter sur du papier absorbant et transférer dans une terrine.

4 Parsemer immédiatement de gros sel, saupoudrer de paprika ou de cumin, et bien mélanger le tout. Servir chaud au froid. Ces amandes sont meilleures lorsqu'elles sont consommées le jour même, mais peuvent également être conservées 3 jours dans un récipient hermétique.

olives marinées

ingrédients

POUR 8 PERSONNES

450 g de grosses olives vertes
    non dénoyautées en boîte
    ou en bocal, égouttées
4 gousses d'ail, pelées
2 cuil. à café de graines
    de coriandre
1 petit citron
4 brins de thym frais
4 branches de fenouil
2 petits piments rouges frais
    (facultatif)
poivre
huile d'olive vierge extra
    espagnole, pour couvrir

méthode

1 Répartir les olives sur une planche à découper et écraser légèrement à l'aide d'un rouleau à pâtisserie de sorte que la marinade imprègne bien les olives. À défaut de rouleau à pâtisserie, inciser les olives dans la hauteur jusqu'au noyau. Écraser les gousses d'ail avec le plat d'un couteau. Piler les graines de coriandre dans un mortier. Couper le citron en petits morceaux sans retirer la peau.

2 Dans une grande terrine, mettre les olives, l'ail, les graines de coriandre, les morceaux de citron, le thym, le fenouil et les piments, mélanger le tout et poivrer. Les olives sont naturellement salées, il n'est donc pas nécessaire d'ajouter de sel. Transférer le tout dans un bocal hermétique en tassant bien, couvrir d'huile d'olive et fermer.

3 Laisser reposer 24 heures à température ambiante, mettre au réfrigérateur et laisser mariner 1 à 2 semaines. Secouer le bocal de temps en temps de façon à bien mélanger les ingrédients. Laisser les olives revenir à température ambiante, égouter et servir avec des piques à cocktail.

guacamole

ingrédients

POUR 4 PERSONNES

2 gros avocats mûrs

jus d'un citron vert, selon
    son goût

2 cuil. à café d'huile d'olive

$1/2$ oignon, finement haché

1 piment vert frais, épépiné
    et haché

1 gousse d'ail, hachée

$1/4$ de cuil. à café de cumin
    en poudre

1 cuil. à soupe de coriandre
    fraîche hachée, un peu
    plus pour garnir (facultatif)

sel et poivre

méthode

1 Couper les avocats en deux et retirer le noyau en faisant levier à l'aide d'un couteau pointu.

2 Peler, hacher grossièrement la chair et mettre dans une terrine non métallique. Ajouter le jus de citron et l'huile, et bien mélanger.

3 À l'aide d'une fourchette, réduire en purée grossière ou lisse, selon son goût. Incorporer l'oignon, le piment, l'ail, le cumin et la coriandre hachée, saler et poivrer.

4 Transférer dans un plat de service, garnir de coriandre hachée et servir immédiatement de sorte que l'avocat ne s'oxyde pas.

purée d'aubergine

ingrédients

POUR 6 À 8 PERSONNES

huile d'olive

1 grosse aubergine de 400 g,
    coupée en rondelles

2 oignons verts, finement
    hachés

1 grosse gousse d'ail, hachée

2 cuil. à soupe de persil plat
    frais haché

sel et poivre

1 pincée de paprika

pain frais, en accompagnement

méthode

1 Dans une poêle, chauffer 4 cuillerées à soupe d'huile à feu moyen à vif, ajouter les rondelles d'aubergine et cuire jusqu'à ce qu'elles soient dorées sur les deux faces. Retirer de la poêle et laisser refroidir de sorte que les rondelles dégorgent de l'huile.

2 Dans la poêle, chauffer 1 cuillerée à soupe d'huile, ajouter les oignons verts et l'ail, et cuire 3 minutes, jusqu'à ce que les oignons verts soient tendres. Retirer du feu, ajouter aux aubergines et laisser refroidir.

3 Transférer tous les ingrédients dans un robot de cuisine et mixer jusqu'à obtention d'une purée épaisse. Transférer dans un plat de service, incorporer le persil et rectifier l'assaisonnement. Servir immédiatement ou couvrir et mettre au réfrigérateur 15 minutes. Saupoudrer de paprika et servir immédiatement, accompagné de pain.

houmous

ingrédients

POUR 4 PERSONNES

115 g de pois chiches secs

3 à 6 cuil. à soupe de jus
   de citron

3 à 6 cuil. à soupe d'eau

2 à 3 gousses d'ail, hachées

150 ml de pâte de sésame

sel

1 cuil. à soupe d'huile d'olive

1 cuil. à café de poivre
   de Cayenne ou de paprika

1 cuil. à soupe de persil plat
   frais haché

pain pita, rondelles
   de tomates et mesclun,
   en accompagnement

méthode

1 Mettre les pois chiches dans une grande terrine, couvrir d'eau et laisser tremper une nuit. Égoutter, transférer dans une casserole, couvrir d'eau et porter à ébullition. Laisser bouillir 1 heure, jusqu'à ce que les pois chiches soient tendres. Retirer du feu et égoutter.

2 Transférer les pois chiches dans un robot de cuisine et mixer en incorporant assez d'eau et de jus de citron pour obtenir une consistance souple et homogène.

3 Ajouter l'ail et mixer. Incorporer la pâte de sésame, saler selon son goût et ajouter de l'eau ou du jus de citron pour obtenir la consistance souhaitée.

4 Transférer dans un plat de service, arroser d'huile et saupoudrer de poivre de Cayenne ou de paprika.

5 Couvrir de film alimentaire, mettre au réfrigérateur et laisser reposer au moins 1 heure. Garnir de persil et servir accompagné de pain pita, de rondelles de tomates et de mesclun.

soupe de légumes au pesto

ingrédients

POUR 4 PERSONNES

1 litre d'eau froide

1 bouquet garni (1 brin
   de persil, 1 brin de thym
   et 1 feuille de laurier,
   liés avec de la ficelle)

2 branches de céleri,
   émincées

3 petits poireaux, émincés

4 petites carottes, émincées

150 g de pommes de terre
   nouvelles, grattées
   et coupées en morceaux

4 cuil. à soupe de fèves
   écossées ou de petits pois

175 g de haricots cannellini
   ou de flageolets, égouttés
   et rincés

3 têtes de pak-choï

150 g de roquette

poivre

pesto

2 grosses poignées de feuilles
   de basilic frais

1 piment vert frais, épépiné

2 gousses d'ail

4 cuil. à soupe d'huile d'olive

1 cuil. à café de parmesan
   fraîchement râpé

méthode

1 Dans une grande casserole, verser l'eau, ajouter le bouquet garni, le céleri, les poireaux, les carottes et les pommes de terre nouvelles, et porter à ébullition. Réduire le feu et laisser mijoter 10 minutes.

2 Incorporer les fèves et les haricots, et laisser mijoter encore 10 minutes. Ajouter le pak-choï et la roquette, poivrer et laisser mijoter encore 2 à 3 minutes. Retirer le bouquet garni.

3 Pour le pesto, mettre le basilic, le piment, l'ail et l'huile dans un robot de cuisine, mixer par intermittence jusqu'à obtention d'une pâte épaisse. Incorporer le parmesan.

4 Incorporer les trois quarts du pesto à la soupe, répartir dans des bols chauds et garnir avec le pesto restant. Servir immédiatement.

soupe aux haricots blancs

ingrédients

POUR 4 PERSONNES

175 g de haricots cannellini
  secs, couverts d'eau froide
  et mis à tremper 12 heures

1,6 l de bouillon de légumes
  ou d'eau

115 g de spirali

6 cuil. à soupe d'huile d'olive

2 gousses d'ail, finement
  hachées

4 cuil. à soupe de persil plat
  frais haché

sel et poivre

pain frais,
  en accompagnement

méthode

1 Égoutter les haricots, mettre dans une grande casserole et ajouter le bouillon. Porter à ébullition, couvrir partiellement et laisser mijoter 2 heures à feu doux, jusqu'à ce que les haricots soient tendres.

2 Transférer la moitié des haricots et un peu de jus de cuisson dans un robot de cuisine et réduire en purée homogène. Remettre dans la casserole, mélanger le tout et porter de nouveau à ébullition.

3 Ajouter les pâtes, porter de nouveau à ébullition et cuire 10 minutes, jusqu'à ce qu'elles soient *al dente*.

4 Dans une petite casserole, chauffer 4 cuillerées à soupe d'huile, ajouter l'ail et cuire 4 à 5 minutes à feu doux en remuant souvent, jusqu'à ce qu'il soit doré. Incorporer l'ail et le persil à la soupe, saler et poivrer. Répartir la soupe dans des assiettes à soupe chaudes, arroser de l'huile d'olive restante et servir immédiatement accompagné de pain frais.

soupe au cresson

ingrédients

POUR 4 PERSONNES

2 bottes de cresson
    (environ 200 g),
    bien lavé
40 g de beurre
2 oignons, hachés
225 g de pommes de terre,
    pelées et grossièrement
    hachées
1,25 l de bouillon de légumes
    ou d'eau
sel et poivre
noix muscade, fraîchement
    râpée (facultatif)
125 ml de crème fraîche,
    de yaourt ou de crème
    aigre

méthode

1 Séparer les feuilles des tiges du cresson, réserver les feuilles et hacher grossièrement les tiges.

2 Dans une grande casserole, faire fondre le beurre à feu moyen, ajouter les oignons et cuire 4 à 5 minutes, jusqu'à ce qu'ils soient tendres, sans laisser brunir.

3 Ajouter les pommes de terre et bien mélanger. Ajouter les tiges de cresson, mouiller avec le bouillon et porter à ébullition. Réduire le feu, couvrir et laisser mijoter 15 à 20 minutes, jusqu'à ce que les pommes de terre soient tendres.

4 Ajouter les feuilles de cresson et réchauffer sans cesser de remuer. Retirer du feu et mixer jusqu'à obtention d'une soupe fluide à l'aide d'un mixeur plongeant. À défaut, verser le tout dans un robot de cuisine, mixer et reverser dans la casserole. Réchauffer, saler, poivrer et saupoudrer de noix muscade fraîchement râpée.

5 Répartir dans des bols chauds et servir garni de crème fraîche, de yaourt ou de crème aigre.

bortsch

ingrédients

POUR 6 PERSONNES

1 oignon

55 g de beurre

350 g de betteraves crues,
    coupées en julienne,
    plus 1 betterave crue,
    râpée

1 carotte, coupée en julienne

3 branches de céleri,
    finement émincées

2 tomates, mondées,
    épépinées et concassées

2 grands brins d'aneth frais

1,5 l de bouillon de légumes

1 cuil. à soupe de vinaigre
    de vin blanc

1 cuil. à soupe de sucre

sel et poivre

115 g de chou blanc, ciselé

150 ml de crème aigre,
    en garniture

méthode

1 Couper l'oignon en rondelles. Dans une casserole, faire fondre le beurre à feu doux, ajouter l'oignon et cuire 5 minutes en remuant souvent, jusqu'à ce qu'il soit tendre. Ajouter les juliennes de betterave et de carotte, le céleri et les tomates, et cuire 4 à 5 minutes en remuant souvent.

2 Ajouter le vinaigre, le sucre et la moitié de l'aneth dans la casserole, mouiller avec le bouillon, saler et poivrer. Porter à ébullition, réduire le feu et laisser mijoter 35 à 40 minutes, jusqu'à ce que les légumes soient tendres.

3 Incorporer le chou, couvrir et laisser mijoter encore 10 minutes. Incorporer la betterave râpée et cuire encore 10 minutes. Répartir le tout dans des bols chauds, garnir de crème aigre et parsemer du restant d'aneth. Servir immédiatement.

soupe des moines

ingrédients

POUR 4 PERSONNES

1 litre de bouillon de légumes

1 tige de citronnelle, cœur
   seulement, finement haché

1 cuil. à café de pâte
   de tamarin

1 pincée de flocons
   de piment (facultatif)

140 g de haricots verts fins,
   coupés en tronçons de
   2,5 cm

1 cuil. à soupe de sauce
   de soja claire

1 cuil. à café de sucre roux

jus d'un demi-citron vert

250 g de tofu ferme, égoutté
   et coupé en dés

2 oignons verts, émincés
   en biais

55 g de champignons enoki,
   éboutés

400 g de nouilles udon fraîches
   ou de nouilles aux œufs
   chinoises

méthode

1 Dans une casserole, verser le bouillon, ajouter la citronnelle, la pâte de tamarin et les flocons de piment, et porter à ébullition sans cesser de remuer jusqu'à ce que la pâte de tamarin soit dissoute. Réduire le feu, ajouter les haricots verts et laisser mijoter 6 minutes. Ajouter la sauce de soja, le sucre roux et le jus de citron vert, et rectifier l'assaisonnement.

2 Incorporer le tofu, les oignons verts et laisser mijoter encore 1 à 2 minutes, jusqu'à ce que les haricots verts soient tendres et que le tofu soit chaud. Ajouter les champignons enoki.

3 Ébouillanter les nouilles de façon à les séparer, répartir dans des bols et verser la soupe immédiatement, de sorte que la soupe réchauffe les nouilles.

soupe chinoise

ingrédients

POUR 4 PERSONNES

15 g de champignons chinois
séchés

115 g de nouilles aux œufs
chinoises

2 cuil. à café d'arrow-root
ou de maïzena

1 litre de bouillon de légumes

1 morceau de gingembre frais
de 5 cm, pelé et coupé
en lamelles

2 cuil. à soupe de sauce
de soja noire

2 cuil. à café de mirin
ou de xérès

1 cuil. à café de vinaigre
de riz

4 petits pak-choï, coupés
en deux

sel et poivre

ciboulette chinoise
ou ordinaire ciselées,
en garniture

méthode

1 Dans une terrine résistant à la chaleur, mettre les champignons séchés, couvrir d'eau bouillante et laisser tremper 20 minutes, jusqu'à ce qu'ils soient tendres. Cuire les nouilles 3 minutes à l'eau bouillante ou procéder selon les instructions figurant sur le paquet. Rafraîchir à l'eau courante de façon à arrêter la cuisson, égoutter et réserver.

2 Égoutter les champignons dans un chinois chemisé d'une étamine en réservant le liquide de trempage et émincer les champignons les plus gros. Dans un wok ou une casserole, mettre l'arrow-root et incorporer progressivement le liquide de trempage. Ajouter le bouillon, le gingembre frais, la sauce de soja, le mirin, le vinaigre de riz, les champignons et le pak-choï, et porter à ébullition sans cesser de remuer. Réduire le feu et laisser mijoter 15 minutes.

3 Poivrer et éventuellement saler – la sauce de soja est déjà très salée. Retirer les lamelles de gingembre à l'aide d'une écumoire.

4 Répartir les nouilles dans des bols chauds, verser la soupe et garnir de ciboulette.

champignons à l'ail

ingrédients

POUR 6 PERSONNES

450 g de champignons
   de Paris

5 cuil. à soupe d'huile d'olive
   espagnole

2 gousses d'ail, finement
   hachées

1 trait de jus de citron

sel et poivre

4 cuil. à soupe de persil plat
   frais haché

pain frais, en accompagnement

méthode

1 Brosser les champignons, retirer les tiges et couper les champignons les plus gros en quartiers. Dans une poêle, chauffer l'huile, ajouter l'ail et cuire 30 secondes à 1 minute, jusqu'à ce qu'il soit très légèrement doré. Ajouter les champignons et faire revenir à feu vif sans cesser de remuer, jusqu'à ce que les champignons aient absorbé toute l'huile.

2 Réduire le feu, chauffer jusqu'à ce que les champignons aient rendu leur eau et augmenter le feu de nouveau. Faire revenir encore 4 à 5 minutes sans cesser de remuer, jusqu'à ce que l'eau se soit évaporée. Arroser de jus de citron, saler et poivrer. Incorporer le persil haché et cuire encore 1 minute.

3 Transférer dans un plat de service chaud et servir très chaud ou tiède, accompagné de pain frais pour saucer.

crudités

ingrédients

POUR 4 À 6 PERSONNES

céleri rémoulade

1 gros jaune d'œuf

1 cuil. à soupe de moutarde
de Dijon

$1/2$ cuil. à café de vinaigre
de vin rouge

150 ml d'huile de tournesol

sel et poivre

$1^1/2$ cuil. à café de jus de citron

1 cuil. à café de sel

450 g de céleri-rave

carottes râpées

450 g de carottes, pelées

2 cuil. à soupe d'huile d'olive

2 cuil. à soupe de jus d'orange

sel et poivre

2 cuil. à soupe d'amandes
finement hachées

1 cuil. à soupe de persil plat
frais haché

salade de betteraves

400 g de betteraves cuites,
pelées

2 cuil. à soupe de vinaigrette

1 cuil. à soupe de ciboulette
hachée

tranches de pain frais
et beurre,
en accompagnement

méthode

1 Pour la sauce rémoulade, mettre le jaune d'œuf, la moutarde et le vinaigre dans un robot de cuisine et mixer. Moteur en marche, ajouter l'huile goutte à goutte jusqu'à ce que la sauce épaississe, puis en filet de façon à obtenir une sauce homogène. Saler et poivrer.

2 Dans une terrine, mettre le jus de citron et le sel, râper finement le céleri dans la terrine et bien mélanger de sorte que le céleri ne noircisse pas. Égoutter, sécher et incorporer la sauce rémoulade. Laisser reposer 20 minutes à température ambiante et servir.

3 Pour les carottes râpées, râper finement les carottes dans une terrine, ajouter l'huile et le jus d'orange, saler et poivrer. Couvrir et réserver au réfrigérateur. Incorporer le persil et les amandes juste avant de servir.

4 Pour la salade de betteraves, couper les betteraves en dés de 5 mm, mettre dans une terrine et ajouter la vinaigrette. Couvrir et réserver au réfrigérateur. Incorporer la ciboulette juste avant de servir.

5 Répartir les salades dans des assiettes et servir accompagné de pain frais beurré.

figues au bleu

ingrédients

POUR 6 PERSONNES
amandes
caramélisées
100 g de sucre
115 g d'amandes entières,
   éventuellement mondées

12 figues mûres
350 g de bleu, émietté
huile d'olive vierge extra

méthode

1 Pour les amandes caramélisées, mettre le sucre dans une casserole et chauffer à feu moyen à vif sans cesser de remuer jusqu'à ce que le sucre ait fondu, caramélise et bouillonne – ne plus remuer une fois que le caramel bouillonne. Retirer du feu et ajouter les amandes une à une en les incorporant immédiatement au caramel à l'aide d'une fourchette. Remettre éventuellement sur le feu si le caramel durcit. Étaler sur une feuille de papier sulfurisé légèrement graissée et laisser prendre.

2 Couper les figues en deux et répartir dans 4 assiettes. Hacher les amandes à la main et en réserver un peu pour décorer. Déposer des cuillerées de bleu sur chaque assiette et parsemer d'amandes caramélisées. Arroser d'huile d'olive et décorer des amandes restantes.

asperges au beurre fondu

ingrédients

POUR 2 PERSONNES

16 à 20 asperges, éboutées
    de sorte qu'elles fassent
    toutes 20 cm
85 g de beurre, fondu
gros sel et poivre, pour servir

méthode

1 Peler la base des asperges à l'aide d'un économe. Lier les asperges en botte avec de la ficelle de cuisine ou placer dans un panier de cuisson de sorte qu'elles puissent être retirées aisément de l'eau de cuisson.

2 Porter une casserole d'eau salée à ébullition, ajouter les asperges et couvrir. Cuire 4 à 5 minutes. Vérifier la cuisson en perçant la base à l'aide d'un couteau. Veiller à ne pas trop cuire les asperges.

3 Égoutter les asperges et servir sur de grandes assiettes nappées de beurre fondu. Les asperges et le beurre doivent être plus tièdes que chauds. Servir saupoudré de gros sel et poivré.

beignets de courgettes & leur sauce au yaourt

ingrédients

POUR 4 PERSONNES

2 à 3 courgettes, environ 400 g

1 gousse d'ail, hachée

3 oignons verts, finement
  émincés

125 g de féta, émiettée

2 cuil. à soupe de persil frais
  haché

2 cuil. à soupe de menthe
  fraîche hachée

1 cuil. à soupe d'aneth frais
  haché

$1/2$ cuil. à café de noix
  muscade

2 cuil. à soupe de farine

poivre

2 œufs

2 cuil. à soupe d'huile d'olive

1 citron coupé en quartiers,
  en garniture

sauce au yaourt

250 g de yaourt nature

$1/4$ de concombre, coupé
  en dés

1 cuil. à soupe d'aneth frais
  haché

poivre

méthode

1 Râper les courgettes sur un torchon, couvrir avec un autre torchon et bien presser. Laisser reposer 10 minutes, jusqu'à ce que les courgettes soient sèches.

2 Pour la sauce, mettre le yaourt, l'aneth et le concombre dans un bol, poivrer et couvrir. Réserver au réfrigérateur.

3 Transférer les courgettes dans une terrine, incorporer l'ail, les oignons verts, le fromage, les fines herbes, la noix muscade et la farine, et poivrer. Battre les œufs et incorporer aux courgettes – la préparation doit être épaisse et grumeleuse.

4 Dans une poêle, chauffer l'huile à feu moyen, verser 4 cuillerées à soupe de préparation en les espaçant bien et cuire 2 à 3 minutes sur chaque face. Retirer de la poêle, égoutter sur du papier absorbant et réserver au chaud. Répéter l'opération une fois de façon à obtenir 8 beignets au total.

5 Servir les beignets chauds, accompagnés de sauce au yaourt et garnis de quartiers de citron.

soufflés au fromage & aux fines herbes

ingrédients

POUR 6 SOUFFLÉS

55 g de beurre, un peu plus
    pour graisser

40 g de farine

150 ml de lait

250 g de ricotta

4 œufs, blancs et jaunes
    séparés, plus 2 blancs
    d'œufs

2 cuil. à soupe de persil frais
    haché

2 cuil. à soupe de thym frais
    haché

1 cuil. à soupe de romarin
    frais haché

sel et poivre

200 ml de crème fraîche
    légère

6 cuil. à soupe de parmesan
    râpé

champignons à l'ail,
    en accompagnement
    (*voir* page 30)

méthode

1 Beurrer 6 moules à soufflé de 9 cm de diamètre et réserver. Dans une casserole, faire fondre le beurre, ajouter la farine et cuire 30 secondes sans cesser de remuer. Incorporer le lait et cuire à feu doux sans cesser de battre jusqu'à ce que la préparation épaississe. Cuire encore 30 secondes, retirer du feu et incorporer la ricotta. Ajouter les jaunes d'œufs et les fines herbes, saler et poivrer.

2 Battre les blancs d'œufs en neige épaisse, incorporer à la préparation précédente et répartir dans les moules jusqu'en haut. Mettre dans un plat allant au four, verser de l'eau bouillante dans le plat de sorte que les moules soient immergés à demi et cuire au four préchauffé 15 à 20 minutes à 180 °C (th. 6), jusqu'à ce que les soufflés aient bien levé et soient dorés. Retirer du four, laisser reposer 10 minutes et démouler délicatement. Transférer dans un plat allant au four graissé et couvrir de film alimentaire.

3 Augmenter la température du four à 200 °C (th. 6-7). Retirer le film alimentaire, napper les soufflés de crème fraîche et saupoudrer de parmesan. Cuire au four encore 15 minutes et servir immédiatement, accompagné de champignons à l'ail.

artichauts en sauce vierge

ingrédients

POUR 4 PERSONNES

4 artichauts

$^1/_2$ citron, coupé en rondelles

sel

sauce vierge

3 tomates cœur de bœuf,
    mondées, épépinées
    et coupées en petits dés

4 oignons verts, très finement
    hachés

6 cuil. à soupe de fines
    herbes hachées, basilic,
    cerfeuil, ciboulette,
    menthe, persil plat
    ou estragon, par exemple

150 ml d'huile d'olive vierge
    extra

1 pincée de sucre

sel et poivre

méthode

1 Casser les queues des artichauts et égaliser les fonds de sorte qu'ils soient stables. À l'aide d'une paire de ciseaux, couper le sommet des feuilles. Remplir une terrine d'eau, ajouter 2 rondelles de citron et y réserver les artichauts au fur et à mesure de la préparation.

2 Choisir une casserole assez grande pour contenir les 4 artichauts, remplir d'eau salée et ajouter les rondelles de citron restantes. Porter l'eau à ébullition, ajouter les artichauts et lester avec une assiette de sorte qu'ils restent immergés. Réduire le feu et laisser mijoter 25 à 35 minutes à petits bouillons, jusqu'à ce que les feuilles extérieures se détachent facilement.

3 Pour la sauce, mettre dans une casserole les tomates, les oignons verts, les fines herbes, l'huile et le sucre, saler et poivrer. Laisser reposer de sorte que les arômes se développent.

4 Égoutter les artichauts posés à l'envers sur du papier absorbant et transférer dans des assiettes. Chauffer la sauce à feu très doux et napper les artichauts.

galettes de patates douces à la menthe & à la féta

ingrédients

POUR 4 PERSONNES

600 g de patates douces,
    pelées et râpées

1 œuf, légèrement battu

50 g de farine

70 g de beurre, fondu

100 g de féta, émiettée

3 cuil. à soupe de menthe
    fraîche hachée

sel et poivre

1 cuil. à soupe d'huile

4 cuil. à soupe de crème
    aigre

2 cuil. à soupe de persil frais
    haché, en garniture

méthode

1 Dans une terrine, mettre les patates douces, l'œuf, la farine, le beurre fondu, la féta et la menthe, mélanger le tout, saler et poivrer.

2 Dans une poêle antiadhésive, chauffer l'huile à feu moyen, déposer 4 grandes cuillerées à soupe de la préparation en aplatissant légèrement et cuire sur les deux faces jusqu'à ce que les galettes soient dorées. Répéter l'opération une fois de façon à obtenir 8 galettes au total.

3 Déposer les galettes sur une plaque de four chemisée de papier sulfurisé et cuire au four préchauffé 15 minutes à 160 °C (th. 5-6), jusqu'à ce que les galettes soient croustillantes. Déposer 2 galettes dans chaque assiette, garnir d'une cuillerée à soupe de crème aigre et de persil, et servir immédiatement.

champignons farcis

ingrédients

POUR 4 PERSONNES

12 gros champignons
   portobello, brossés
   et équeutés

huile de maïs, pour graisser

1 bulbe de fenouil, finement
   émincé

100 g de tomates séchées
   au soleil, émincées

2 gousses d'ail, hachées

125 g de fontina, râpé

50 g de parmesan, râpé

3 cuil. à soupe de basilic
   haché

sel et poivre

1 cuil. à soupe d'huile d'olive

copeaux de parmesan,
   en garniture

1 cuil. à soupe de persil,
   en garniture

méthode

1 Huiler un grand plat allant au four et y mettre 8 champignons, côté coupé vers le haut. Hacher finement les 4 champignons restants.

2 Dans une poêle antiadhésive, mettre les champignons hachés, le fenouil, les tomates séchées et l'ail, et cuire à feu doux jusqu'à ce que les légumes soient tendres, sans laisser brunir. Retirer du feu et laisser refroidir.

3 Ajouter les fromages et le basilic dans la poêle, saler, poivrer et bien mélanger le tout. Enduire les champignons entiers d'huile d'olive, garnir chaque cavité de la préparation précédente et cuire au four préchauffé 20 à 25 minutes à 180 °C (th. 6), jusqu'à ce que les champignons soient tendres et que la garniture soit cuite.

4 Garnir de copeaux de parmesan et de persil, et servir immédiatement.

falafels au sésame

ingrédients

POUR 4 PERSONNES

450 g de haricots cannellini
    en boîte, égouttés
350 g de pois chiches
    en boîte, égouttés
1 oignon, finement haché
2 gousses d'ail, hachées
1 petit piment rouge frais,
    épépiné et haché
1 cuil. à café de levure
    chimique
25 g de persil frais haché,
    un peu plus pour garnir
1 pincée de poivre
    de Cayenne
2 cuil. à soupe d'eau
sel et poivre
huile, pour la friture
pain pita, yaourt nature
    ou sauce au yaourt
    (*voir* page 38) et quartiers
    de citron, en garniture

sauce au sésame

200 ml de pâte de sésame
1 gousse d'ail, hachée
1 à 2 cuil. à soupe d'eau
2 à 3 cuil. à café de jus
    de citron

méthode

1 Pour la sauce, mettre la pâte de sésame et l'ail dans un bol, incorporer progressivement l'eau jusqu'à obtention de la consistance désirée et ajouter le jus de citron. Couvrir de film alimentaire et réserver au réfrigérateur.

2 Pour les falafels, rincer les haricots et les pois chiches, mettre dans un robot de cuisine et ajouter l'oignon, l'ail, le piment, la levure, le persil haché et le poivre de Cayenne. Mixer jusqu'à obtention d'une pâte épaisse, ajouter l'eau, saler et poivrer. Mixer de nouveau brièvement.

3 Dans un wok ou une sauteuse, chauffer 6 cm d'huile à feu vif, ajouter des cuillerées à soupe de préparation et frire 2 minutes à 2 min 30, jusqu'à ce que les falafels soient dorés et croustillants. Retirer de l'huile à l'aide d'une écumoire et égoutter sur du papier absorbant. Répéter l'opération jusqu'à épuisement de la pâte et servir chaud ou froid, accompagné de sauce au sésame, de pain pita, de sauce au yaourt et de quartiers de citron.

nachos aux haricots noirs

ingrédients

POUR 4 PERSONNES

225 g de haricots noirs secs
ou de haricots noirs
en boîte, égouttés
175 à 225 g de fromage râpé
1/4 de cuil. à café de cumin
en poudre ou de graines
de cumin
4 cuil. à soupe de crème
aigre
piments jalapeño en saumure,
émincés (facultatif)
1 cuil. à soupe de coriandre
fraîche hachée
1 poignée de laitue ciselée
machos (chips mexicaines),
en accompagnement

méthode

1 En cas d'utilisation de haricots secs, mettre dans une terrine, couvrir d'eau et laisser tremper une nuit. Égoutter, transférer dans une casserole et couvrir d'eau froide. Porter à ébullition, laisser bouillir 10 minutes et réduire le feu. Laisser mijoter 1 h 30, jusqu'à ce qu'ils soient tendres, et égoutter.

2 Répartir les haricots dans un plat allant au four, parsemer de fromage et saupoudrer de cumin.

3 Cuire au four préchauffé 10 à 15 minutes à 190 °C (th. 6-7), jusqu'à ce que les haricots soient bien cuits et que le fromage soit fondu.

4 Retirer du four, garnir de crème aigre et parsemer de coriandre, de laitue et éventuellement de piments.

5 Répartir les machos autour des haricots et servir immédiatement.

haricots, fruits secs & tofu

Les haricots, les fruits à coque et le tofu sont trois des principaux ingrédients du régime végétarien. Les haricots, très riches en protéines, se présentent sous des formes et des couleurs variées, allant du haricot rouge foncé au haricot blanc. Ils constituent une base solide pour les ragoûts et les currys. Les pois chiches se mangent entiers ou écrasés en purée avec de la farine – essayez le curry de légumes et galettes de pois chiches. Les lentilles se substituent avantageusement à la viande hachée, et si vous aimez la cuisine italienne, goûtez la sauce bolognaise avec des lentilles pour vous distraire des plats trop classiques.

Pour tirer un bénéfice nutritionnel maximal, consommez les haricots et les lentilles avec des féculents, comme du riz ou du pain complet. Le risotto aux haricots rouges offre un mélange idéal de nutriments.

Les noix et autres fruits à coque vous apportent une mine de bienfaits, ils sont excellents pour le système nerveux. Servez une terrine au stilton ou un cake salé aux noisettes avec des pommes de terre grillées et un plat abondant de légumes qui remplaceront le rôti de viande.

Le tofu, neutre de goût, se transforme lorsque vous le cuisinez avec de l'ail et du piment. Le tofu est vendu en blocs qui peuvent être détaillés en dés. Cet aliment maigre est parfait pour les végétariens et c'est un délice !

ragoût mexicain aux trois haricots

ingrédients

POUR 6 PERSONNES

140 g de haricots noirs,
de cannellini et de borlotti,
mis à tremper une nuit
séparément

2 cuil. à soupe d'huile d'olive

1 gros oignon, finement
haché

2 poivrons rouges, épépinés
et hachés

2 gousses d'ail, très finement
hachées

1/2 cuil. à café de graines
de cumin, pilées

1 cuil. à café de graines
de coriandre, pilées

1 cuil. à café d'origan sec

1/2 à 2 cuil. à café de poudre
de piment

3 cuil. à soupe de concentré
de tomate

800 g de tomates concassées
en boîte

1 cuil. à café de sucre

1 cuil. à café de sel

625 ml de bouillon de
légumes

3 cuil. à soupe de coriandre
fraîche hachée

méthode

1 Égoutter les haricots noirs, mettre dans une casserole et couvrir d'eau froide. Porter à ébullition et cuire 10 à 15 minutes à gros bouillons. Réduire le feu et laisser mijoter 35 à 45 minutes, jusqu'à ce qu'ils soient tendres. Égoutter et réserver. Répéter l'opération avec les deux autres sortes de haricots.

2 Dans une autre casserole, chauffer l'huile à feu moyen, ajouter l'oignon et les poivrons, et cuire 5 minutes sans cesser de remuer, jusqu'à ce qu'ils soient tendres.

3 Ajouter l'ail, les graines de cumin, les graines de coriandre et l'origan, et cuire 30 secondes sans cesser de remuer, jusqu'à ce que l'ail change de couleur. Ajouter la poudre de piment et le concentré de tomate, et cuire 1 minute sans cesser de remuer. Ajouter les tomates, le sucre, le sel et les haricots, mouiller avec le bouillon et porter à ébullition. Réduire le feu, couvrir et laisser mijoter 45 minutes en remuant de temps en temps.

4 Incorporer la coriandre fraîche, répartir dans des bols chauds et servir immédiatement.

légumes à l'aigre-douce et aux noix de cajou

ingrédients

POUR 4 PERSONNES

1 cuil. à soupe d'huile
   d'arachide
1 cuil. à café d'huile
   pimentée
2 oignons, émincés
2 carottes, finement
   émincées
2 courgettes, coupées
   en rondelles
115 g de brocoli,
   détaillé en fleurettes
115 g de champignons
   blancs, émincés
115 g de pak-choï, coupé
   en deux
2 cuil. à soupe de sucre roux
2 cuil. à soupe de sauce
   de soja thaïe
1 cuil. à soupe de vinaigre
   de riz
55 g de noix de cajou

méthode

1 Dans un wok préchauffé ou une poêle, chauffer les deux huiles, ajouter les oignons et faire revenir 1 à 2 minutes, jusqu'à ce qu'ils soient tendres.

2 Ajouter les carottes, les courgettes et le brocoli, et faire revenir 2 à 3 minutes. Ajouter les champignons, le pak-choï, le sucre, la sauce de soja et le vinaigre, et faire revenir 1 à 2 minutes.

3 Chauffer une poêle à feu vif, ajouter les noix de cajou et griller à sec en secouant la poêle souvent, jusqu'à ce qu'elles soient dorées. Parsemer les légumes de noix de cajou et servir immédiatement.

chili végétarien

ingrédients

POUR 4 PERSONNES

400 g de haricots noirs secs

2 cuil. à soupe d'huile d'olive

1 oignon, haché

5 gousses d'ail, grossièrement
   hachées

1/2 à 1 cuil. à café de cumin
   en poudre

1/2 à 1 cuil. à café de poudre
   de piment doux

1 poivron rouge, coupé
   en dés

1 carotte, coupée en dés

400 g de tomates fraîches
   ou en boîte, concassées

1 botte de coriandre fraîche,
   hachée

sel et poivre

méthode

1 Dans une terrine, mettre les haricots, couvrir d'eau et laisser tremper une nuit. Égoutter, transférer dans une casserole et couvrir d'eau. Porter à ébullition, laisser bouillir 10 minutes et réduire le feu. Laisser mijoter 1 h 30, jusqu'à ce qu'ils soient tendres, et égoutter en réservant 250 ml de liquide de cuisson.

2 Dans une poêle, chauffer l'huile, ajouter l'ail et l'oignon, et cuire en remuant de temps en temps jusqu'à ce qu'ils soient tendres.

3 Incorporer le cumin et la poudre de piment, cuire encore quelques instants. Ajouter le poivron rouge, la carotte et les tomates et cuire encore 5 minutes à feu moyen.

4 Ajouter la moitié de la coriandre et les haricots avec le liquide de trempage réservé, saler et poivrer. Laisser mijoter 30 à 45 minutes, jusqu'à ce que les arômes se développent et que la préparation épaississe.

5 Incorporer la coriandre restante, rectifier l'assaisonnement et servir immédiatement.

ragoût de haricot provençal

ingrédients

POUR 4 PERSONNES

350 g de borlotti secs,
  mis à tremper une nuit

2 cuil. à soupe d'huile d'olive

2 oignons, émincés

2 gousses d'ail, finement
  hachées

1 poivron rouge, épépiné
  et émincé

1 poivron jaune, épépiné
  et émincé

400 g de tomates concassées
  en boîte

2 cuil. à soupe de concentré
  de tomate

1 cuil. à soupe de feuilles
  de basilic ciselées

2 cuil. à café de thym frais
  haché

2 cuil. à café de romarin frais
  haché

1 feuille de laurier

sel et poivre

55 g d'olives noires,
  dénoyautées et coupées
  en deux

2 cuil. à soupe de persil frais
  haché

méthode

1 Égoutter les haricots, mettre dans une casserole et couvrir d'eau froide. Porter à ébullition, réduire le feu et couvrir. Laisser mijoter 1 h 15 à 1 h 30, jusqu'à ce que les haricots soient tendres. Égoutter en réservant 300 ml de liquide de cuisson.

2 Dans une casserole, chauffer l'huile à feu moyen, ajouter les oignons et cuire 5 minutes en remuant souvent, jusqu'à ce qu'ils soient tendres. Ajouter l'ail et les poivrons, et cuire 10 minutes en remuant de temps en temps.

3 Ajouter les tomates avec leur jus, le liquide de cuisson des haricots réservé, le concentré de tomate, le basilic, le thym, le romarin, le laurier et les haricots. Saler, poivrer et couvrir. Laisser mijoter 40 minutes, ajouter les olives et laisser mijoter encore 5 minutes. Transférer dans un plat de service chaud, parsemer de persil et servir immédiatement.

haricots à la mode de Boston

ingrédients

POUR 8 PERSONNES

500 g de cannellinis secs,
   mis à tremper une nuit
2 oignons, hachés
2 grosses tomates, mondées
   et concassées
2 cuil. à café de moutarde
2 cuil. à soupe de mélasse
sel et poivre

méthode

1 Égoutter les haricots, mettre dans une grande casserole et couvrir d'eau froide. Porter à ébullition, réduire le feu et laisser mijoter 15 minutes. Égoutter en réservant 300 ml du liquide de cuisson. Transférer les haricots dans une cocotte et ajouter les oignons.

2 Dans une casserole, verser le liquide de cuisson réservé, ajouter les tomates et porter à ébullition. Réduire le feu, laisser mijoter 10 minutes et retirer du feu. Incorporer la moutarde et la mélasse, saler et poivrer.

3 Transférer la préparation précédente dans la cocotte, mélanger et cuire au four préchauffé 5 heures à 140 °C (th. 4-5). Servir chaud.

champignons portobello farcis

ingrédients

POUR 4 PERSONNES

4 gros champignons
   portobello
200 g de haricots rouges
   en boîte, égouttés
   et rincés
4 oignons verts, hachés
1 piment rouge jalapeño,
   épépiné et finement haché
1 cuil. à soupe de zeste de
   citron finement râpé
1 cuil. à soupe de persil plat
   frais haché, un peu plus
   pour garnir
sel et poivre
85 g de courgettes,
   grossièrement râpées
85 g de carottes,
   grossièrement râpées
55 g de pignons, grillés
40 g de raisins secs
300 ml de bouillon de légumes

sauce

150 ml de yaourt à la grecque
1 cuil. à soupe de persil plat
   frais haché
1 cuil. à soupe de zeste
   de citron râpé

méthode

1 Peler les champignons et retirer délicatement les pieds.

2 Dans un robot de cuisine, mettre les pieds de champignons, les oignons verts, le piment, le zeste de citron et le persil, saler et poivrer. Mixer 2 minutes.

3 Racler les parois du robot de cuisine, ajouter les courgettes, les carottes, les pignons et les raisins secs, et bien mixer le tout. Farcir les chapeaux des champignons.

4 Répartir les champignons farcis dans un plat allant au four, verser le bouillon autour et couvrir de papier d'aluminium. Cuire au four préchauffé 30 minutes à 180 °C (th. 6) en retirant le papier d'aluminium 10 minutes avant la fin de la cuisson.

5 Pour la sauce, mettre tous les ingrédients dans un bol de service et bien mélanger.

6 Servir les champignons très chauds, nappés de sauce et garnis de persil.

curry de haricots rouges & blancs

ingrédients

POUR 4 PERSONNES

85 g de haricots rouges

85 g de haricots blancs

55 g de haricots cornilles

2 cuil. à soupe de beurre clarifié ou d'huile

1 cuil. à café de graines de moutarde noires

1 cuil. à café de graines de cumin

1 oignon, finement haché

1 cuil. à café d'ail réduit en purée

1 cuil. à café de gingembre frais réduit en purée

2 cuil. à soupe de pâte de curry

2 piments verts frais, épépinés et hachés

400 g de tomates en boîte

2 cuil. à soupe de concentré de tomate

125 à 150 ml d'eau (facultatif)

sel

2 cuil. à soupe de coriandre fraîche hachée, un peu plus pour garnir

méthode

1 Dans une terrine, mettre les haricots, couvrir d'eau et laisser tremper 4 heures ou une nuit.

2 Égoutter, transférer dans une casserole et couvrir d'eau froide. Porter à ébullition à feu vif et laisser bouillir à gros bouillons 15 minutes. Réduire le feu, couvrir et laisser mijoter 1 h 30, jusqu'à ce que les haricots soient tendres.

3 Dans une autre casserole, chauffer le beurre clarifié, ajouter les graines de moutarde et de cumin, et cuire 2 minutes à feu doux sans cesser de remuer, jusqu'à ce que les arômes se développent. Ajouter l'oignon et cuire 5 minutes, jusqu'à ce qu'il soit tendre. Ajouter les purées d'ail et de gingembre, la pâte de curry et les piments, et cuire 2 minutes sans cesser de remuer. Incorporer les tomates avec leur jus et le concentré de tomate, allonger éventuellement avec de l'eau, saler et laisser mijoter 5 minutes.

4 Égoutter les haricots, ajouter à la sauce et incorporer la coriandre hachée. Couvrir et laisser mijoter encore 30 minutes, jusqu'à ce que les haricots soient tendres et que la sauce épaississe. Garnir de coriandre et servir immédiatement.

risotto aux haricots rouges

ingrédients

POUR 4 PERSONNES

4 cuil. à soupe d'huile

1 oignon, haché

2 gousses d'ail, finement
　　hachées

175 g de riz complet

625 ml de bouillon de légumes

sel et poivre

1 poivron rouge, épépiné
　　et haché

2 branches de céleri,
　　émincées

225 g de champignons
　　de Paris, finement
　　émincés

425 g de haricots rouges
　　en boîte, égouttés et rincés

3 cuil. à soupe de persil plat
　　frais haché

55 g de noix de cajou, un peu
　　plus pour garnir

méthode

1 Dans une casserole, chauffer la moitié de l'huile, ajouter l'oignon et cuire 5 minutes en remuant de temps en temps, jusqu'à ce qu'il soit tendre. Ajouter la moitié de l'ail et cuire encore 2 minutes en remuant souvent. Ajouter le riz et faire revenir 1 minute sans cesser de remuer, jusqu'à ce que les grains soient bien enrobés d'huile.

2 Mouiller avec le bouillon, ajouter 1 pincée de sel et du poivre et porter à ébullition sans cesser de remuer. Réduire le feu, couvrir et laisser mijoter 35 à 40 minutes, jusqu'à ce que tout le liquide soit absorbé.

3 Dans une poêle, chauffer l'huile restante, ajouter le poivron et le céleri, et cuire 5 minutes en remuant souvent. Ajouter les champignons et l'ail restant, et cuire 4 à 5 minutes en remuant souvent.

4 Incorporer le contenu de la casserole dans la poêle, ajouter les haricots, le persil et les noix de cajou, et réchauffer le tout sans cesser de remuer. Transférer dans un plat de service chaud, garnir de persil et servir immédiatement.

curry de légumes & galettes de pois chiches

ingrédients

POUR 4 PERSONNES

200 g de carottes

300 g de pommes de terre

2 cuil. à soupe d'huile

1¹/₂ cuil. à café de graines
   de cumin

graines de 5 gousses
   de cardamome

1¹/₂ cuil. à café de graines
   de moutarde

2 oignons, râpés

1 cuil. à café de curcuma

1 cuil. à café de coriandre
   en poudre

1¹/₂ cuil. à café de poudre
   de piment

1 feuille de laurier

1 cuil. à soupe de gingembre
   frais râpé

2 gousses d'ail, hachées

250 ml de coulis de tomate

200 ml de bouillon de légumes

115 g de petits pois surgelés

115 g d'épinards surgelés

galettes de pois chiches

225 g de farine de pois chiche

1 cuil. à café de sel

¹/₂ cuil. à café de bicarbonate

huile, pour la cuisson

méthode

1 Pour les galettes, tamiser la farine, le sel et le bicarbonate dans une terrine, creuser un puits au centre et y verser 400 ml d'eau. Incorporer progressivement la farine à l'eau en battant à l'aide d'un fouet, de façon à obtenir une pâte homogène et laisser reposer 15 minutes.

2 Dans une poêle, chauffer de l'huile à feu moyen, verser 4 cuillerées de préparation et cuire 3 minutes sur chaque face, jusqu'à ce que les galettes soient dorées. Répéter l'opération de façon à obtenir 8 galettes au total.

3 Couper les carottes et les pommes de terre en dés, et blanchir à l'eau bouillante salée.

4 Dans une casserole, chauffer l'huile à feu moyen, ajouter les graines de cumin, de cardamome et de moutarde, et faire frire jusqu'à ce qu'elles commencent à éclater. Ajouter les oignons, couvrir partiellement et cuire à feu moyen, jusqu'à ce qu'ils soient tendres et dorés.

5 Ajouter les épices restantes, le laurier, le gingembre et l'ail, et cuire 1 minute sans cesser de remuer. Ajouter le coulis de tomate, le bouillon, les carottes et les pommes de terre, couvrir partiellement et cuire 10 à 15 minutes. Ajouter les petits pois et les épinards, cuire 2 à 3 minutes et servir chaud accompagné de galettes de pois chiches.

pois chiches aux épinards

ingrédients

POUR 4 À 6 PERSONNES

2 cuil. à soupe d'huile d'olive

1 grosse gousse d'ail, coupée
   en deux

1 oignon, finement haché

1/2 cuil. à café de cumin

1 pincée de poivre
   de Cayenne

1 pincée de curcuma

800 g de pois chiches
   en boîte, rincés
   et égouttés

500 g de pousses d'épinard,
   rincées et égouttées

2 poivrons en bocal, égouttés
   et émincés

sel et poivre

méthode

1 Dans une poêle, chauffer l'huile à feu moyen à vif, ajouter l'ail et cuire 2 minutes, jusqu'à ce qu'il soit doré, sans laisser brunir. Retirer de la poêle à l'aide d'une écumoire et jeter.

2 Ajouter l'oignon, le cumin, le poivre de Cayenne et le curcuma, et cuire 5 minutes, jusqu'à ce que l'oignon soit tendre. Ajouter les pois chiches et remuer jusqu'à ce qu'ils prennent la couleur du curcuma.

3 Incorporer les épinards, couvrir et cuire 4 à 5 minutes, jusqu'à ce qu'ils soient flétris. Retirer le couvercle, ajouter les poivrons et cuire en remuant délicatement, jusqu'à ce que le jus de cuisson soit évaporé. Saler, poivrer et servir.

curry de pois chiches

ingrédients

POUR 4 PERSONNES

6 cuil. à soupe d'huile

2 oignons, émincés

1 cuil. à café de gingembre
frais haché

1 cuil. à café de cumin
en poudre

1 cuil. à café de coriandre
en poudre

1 cuil. à café d'ail haché

1 cuil. à café de poudre
de piment

2 piments verts frais

2 à 3 cuil. à soupe de coriandre
fraîche hachée

150 ml d'eau

1 grosse pomme de terre

400 g de pois chiches
en boîte, égouttés

1 cuil. à soupe de jus
de citron

méthode

1 Dans une casserole, chauffer l'huile, ajouter les oignons et cuire sans cesser de remuer jusqu'à ce qu'ils soient tendres. Réduire le feu, ajouter le gingembre, le cumin, la coriandre en poudre, l'ail, la poudre de piment, les piments et la coriandre fraîche, et faire revenir 2 minutes.

2 Verser l'eau dans la casserole et bien remuer.

3 Couper la pomme de terre en dés à l'aide d'un couteau tranchant. Ajouter les pommes de terre et les pois chiches dans la casserole, couvrir et laisser mijoter 5 à 7 minutes en remuant de temps en temps.

4 Arroser de jus de citron, transférer dans des assiettes chaudes et servir immédiatement.

galettes de haricots & leur salsa à l'avocat

ingrédients

POUR 4 PERSONNES

55 g de pignons

425 g d'un mélange de haricots
en boîte, rincés et égouttés

1/2 oignon rouge, haché

1 cuil. à soupe de concentré
de tomate

1/2 piment rouge, épépiné
et haché

55 g de chapelure blonde

1 œuf, battu

1 cuil. à soupe de coriandre
fraîce hachée

2 cuil. à soupe d'huile de maïs

1 citron vert, coupé en
quartiers, en garniture

4 petits pains complets,
en garniture (facultatif)

salsa

1 avocat, pelé, dénoyauté
et haché

100 g de tomates, épépinées
et hachées

2 gousses d'ail, hachées

2 cuil. à soupe de coriandre
fraîche hachée

1 cuil. à soupe d'huile d'olive

poivre

jus d'un demi-citron vert

méthode

1 Chauffer une poêle antiadhésive à feu moyen, ajouter les pignons et cuire sans cesser de remuer jusqu'à ce qu'ils soient dorés. Transférer immédiatement dans un bol et réserver.

2 Dans une terrine, mettre les haricots et réduire en purée. Ajouter l'oignon, le concentré de tomate, le piment, les pignons et la moitié de la chapelure, et bien mélanger. Ajouter la moitié de l'œuf et la coriandre, réduire de nouveau en purée et lier avec l'œuf restant si nécessaire. Façonner 4 galettes, enrober de la chapelure restante et couvrir. Mettre au réfrigérateur et laisser reposer 30 minutes.

3 Pour la salsa, mettre les ingrédients dans un bol de service, mélanger et couvrir. Réserver au réfrigérateur.

4 Dans une poêle, chauffer l'huile à feu moyen, ajouter les galettes et cuire 4 à 5 minutes sur chaque face, jusqu'à ce qu'elles soient croustillantes et bien chaudes. Retirer de la poêle et égoutter sur du papier absorbant.

5 Servir éventuellement les galettes dans des petits pains complets, accompagnées de salsa et de quartiers de citron.

hamburgers végétariens

ingrédients

POUR 4 PERSONNES

1 cuil. à soupe d'huile
de tournesol, un peu plus
pour graisser

1 oignon, finement haché

1 gousse d'ail, hachée

1 cuil. à café de coriandre
en poudre

1 cuil. à café de cumin
en poudre

115 g de champignons
de Paris, hachés

425 g de borlotti
ou de haricots rouges,
égouttés et rincés

2 cuil. à soupe de persil plat
frais haché

sel et poivre

farine, pour saupoudrer

petits pains pour hamburgers

salade, en accompagnement

méthode

1 Dans une poêle, chauffer l'huile à feu moyen, ajouter l'oignon et cuire 5 minutes en remuant souvent, jusqu'à ce qu'il soit tendre. Ajouter l'ail, la coriandre et le cumin, et cuire encore 1 minute. Ajouter les champignons et cuire 4 à 5 minutes en remuant souvent, jusqu'à ce que l'eau soit évaporée. Transférer dans un bol.

2 Réduire les haricots en purée à l'aide d'une fourchette et incorporer à la préparation précédente. Ajouter le persil, saler et poivrer.

3 Répartir la préparation en 4 portions, fariner légèrement et façonner des galettes. Enduire d'huile et passer au gril préchauffé 4 à 5 minutes de chaque côte à puissance moyenne. Garnir les petits pains et servir les hamburgers accompagnés de salade.

couscous de légumes aux pignons

ingrédients

POUR 4 PERSONNES

115 g de lentilles vertes

55 g de pignons

1 cuil. à soupe d'huile d'olive

1 oignon, coupé en dés

2 gousses d'ail, écrasées

280 g de courgettes, coupées
　　en rondelles

250 g de tomates, concassées

400 g de cœurs d'artichaut
　　en boîte, égouttés
　　et coupés en deux dans
　　la hauteur

250 g de semoule
　　de couscous

500 ml de bouillon
　　de légumes

3 cuil. à soupe de basilic frais
　　ciselé, un peu plus pour
　　garnir

poivre et sel

méthode

1 Dans une casserole, mettre les lentilles, couvrir d'eau et porter à ébullition. Laisser bouillir 10 minutes, réduire le feu et couvrir. Laisser mijoter 15 minutes, jusqu'à ce qu'elles soient tendres.

2 Répartir les pignons sur une plaque et passer au gril préchauffé en remuant souvent jusqu'à ce qu'ils soient uniformément dorés. Transférer dans une terrine et réserver.

3 Dans une poêle, chauffer l'huile à feu moyen, ajouter l'oignon, l'ail et les courgettes, et cuire 8 à 10 minutes à feu moyen en remuant souvent, jusqu'à ce que le tout soit tendre et que les courgettes soient légèrement dorées. Ajouter les tomates et les cœurs d'artichauts, et réchauffer le tout 5 minutes.

4 Mettre la semoule dans une terrine résistant à la chaleur. Porter le bouillon à ébullition, ajouter à la semoule et couvrir. Laisser reposer 10 minutes, jusqu'à ce que la semoule soit tendre et que tout le bouillon ait été absorbé.

5 Égoutter les lentilles, incorporer la semoule et le basilic, saler et poivrer. Transférer dans un plat de service chaud et ajouter les légumes. Parsemer de pignons, garnir de basilic et servir immédiatement.

salade de lentilles chaude au fromage de chèvre

ingrédients

POUR 4 PERSONNES

2 cuil. à soupe d'huile d'olive

2 cuil. à café de graines
   de cumin

2 gousses d'ail, hachées

2 cuil. à café de gingembre
   frais râpé

300 g de lentilles rouges

750 ml de bouillon de légumes

2 cuil. à soupe de menthe
   fraîche hachée

2 cuil. à soupe de coriandre
   fraîche hachée

2 oignons rouges, finement
   émincés

200 g de feuilles d'épinards

1 cuil. à café d'huile
   de noisettes

150 g de fromage de chèvre

4 cuil. à soupe de yaourt
   à la grecque

sel et poivre

1 citron, coupé en quartiers,
   en garniture

pain bis grillé,
   en accompagnement

méthode

1 Dans une grande casserole, chauffer la moitié de l'huile d'olive à feu moyen, ajouter les graines de cumin, l'ail et le gingembre, et cuire 2 minutes sans cesser de remuer.

2 Incorporer les lentilles. Mouiller avec une louche de bouillon, chauffer sans cesser de remuer jusqu'à ce que les lentilles aient absorbé le liquide et répéter l'opération avec le bouillon restant – cela prend environ 20 minutes. Retirer du feu et incorporer les fines herbes.

3 Dans une poêle, chauffer l'huile restante à feu moyen, ajouter les oignons et cuire 10 minutes en remuant souvent, jusqu'à ce qu'ils soient tendres et légèrement dorés.

4 Mélanger l'huile de noisette aux épinards et répartir le mélange obtenu dans 4 assiettes.

5 Mélanger le fromage de chèvre et le yaourt, réduire en purée, saler et poivrer.

6 Répartir les lentilles dans des assiettes et garnir d'oignons, du mélange à base de fromage de chèvre et de quartiers de citron. Servir accompagné de pain bis grillé.

sauce bolognaise aux lentilles

ingrédients

POUR 4 PERSONNES

1 cuil. à café d'huile

1 cuil. à café d'ail haché

25 g d'oignon, finement haché

25 g de poireau, haché

25 g de céleri, haché

25 g de poivron vert, épépiné
   et haché

25 g de carotte, hachée

25 g de courgette, hachée

85 g de champignons
   de couche, hachés

4 cuil. à soupe de vin rouge

1 pincée de thym séché

400 g de tomates en boîte,
   concassées, égouttées,
   jus et pulpe réservés
   séparément

4 cuil. à soupe de lentilles
   vertes sèches, cuites

poivre

2 cuil. à soupe de jus
   de citron

1 cuil. à café de sucre

3 cuil. à soupe de basilic
   frais haché, un peu plus
   pour garnir

spaghettis,
   en accompagnement

méthode

1 Dans une casserole, chauffer l'huile à feu doux, ajouter l'ail et cuire sans cesser de remuer jusqu'à ce qu'il soit doré. Ajouter tous les légumes excepté les champignons, augmenter le feu et cuire 10 à 12 minutes en remuant de temps en temps, jusqu'à ce qu'ils soient tendres et que tout le liquide soit évaporé.

2 Ajouter les champignons, augmenter le feu et mouiller avec le vin. Cuire 2 minutes, ajouter le thym et le jus des tomates, et cuire jusqu'à ce que la préparation ait réduit de moitié.

3 Ajouter les lentilles et la pulpe de tomates, poivrer et cuire encore 3 à 4 minutes. Retirer la poêle du feu et incorporer le jus de citron, le sucre et le basilic.

4 Servir la sauce en accompagnement de spaghettis, le tout garni de basilic.

tourte aux lentilles & aux champignons

ingrédients

POUR 6 PERSONNES

175 g de lentilles vertes

2 feuilles de laurier

6 échalotes, émincées

1,25 l de bouillon de légumes

sel et poivre

55 g de beurre

225 g de riz long grain

8 feuilles de pâte filo

2 cuil. à soupe de persil plat
    frais haché

2 cuil. à café de fenouil frais
    haché

4 œufs, 1 œuf battu et 3 œufs
    durs et émincés

225 g de champignons
    portobello, émincés

méthode

1 Dans une casserole, mettre les lentilles, les feuilles de laurier et la moitié des échalotes, verser la moitié du bouillon et porter à ébullition. Réduire le feu et laisser mijoter 25 minutes, jusqu'à ce que les lentilles soient tendres. Retirer du feu, saler, poivrer et laisser refroidir.

2 Dans une autre casserole, faire fondre la moitié du beurre à feu moyen, ajouter les échalotes restantes et cuire sans cesser de remuer jusqu'à ce qu'elles soient tendres. Ajouter le riz et cuire 1 minute. Mouiller avec le bouillon restant, saler, poivrer et porter à ébullition. Réduire le feu, couvrir et cuire 15 minutes. Laisser refroidir.

3 Faire fondre le beurre restant et enduire un plat à gratin. Mettre une feuille de pâte filo dans le fond du plat en laissant dépasser les extrémités de chaque côté, enduire de beurre fondu et répéter l'opération avec les feuilles restantes de sorte que le fond du plat soit totalement couvert. Ajouter le persil, le fenouil et l'œuf battu à la préparation à base de riz. Dans le plat, alterner des couches de riz, d'œufs durs, de lentilles et de champignons, en salant et poivrant chaque couche. Rabattre les extrémités des feuilles sur le tout en les froissant, enduire de beurre fondu et cuire 15 minutes. Cuire au four préchauffé 45 minutes à 190 °C (th. 6-7), laisser tiédir 10 minutes et servir.

dhal au maïs

ingrédients

POUR 4 PERSONNES

225 g de lentilles rouges

2 cuil. à soupe d'huile

1 cuil. à café de cumin
    en poudre

1 cuil. à café de coriandre
    en poudre

1/2 cuil. à café de asa fœtida

1 piment rouge frais, épépiné
    et haché

115 g de haricots verts,
    blanchis, égouttés
    et hachés

1 poivron vert, épépiné
    et haché

115 g de mini épis de maïs,
    émincés en biais

150 ml de bouillon de légumes

2 tomates, épépinées
    et concassées

1 cuil. à soupe de coriandre
    fraîche hachée

1 cuil. à soupe de graines
    de pavot

méthode

1 Rincer les lentilles à l'eau froide dans 2 ou 3 eaux, mettre dans une grande casserole et couvrir d'eau froide. Porter à ébullition, réduire le feu et laisser mijoter 15 à 20 minutes, jusqu'à ce qu'elles soient tendres. Égoutter, remettre dans la casserole et réserver au chaud.

2 Dans une autre casserole, chauffer l'huile à feu doux, ajouter les épices et le piment, et cuire 2 minutes sans cesser de remuer. Ajouter les haricots verts, le poivron et le maïs, et cuire encore 2 minutes sans cesser de remuer.

3 Mouiller avec le bouillon, porter à ébullition et réduire le feu. Laisser mijoter 5 minutes, jusqu'à ce que les légumes soient juste tendres.

4 Incorporer les légumes et leur jus de cuisson aux lentilles, ajouter les tomates et cuire 5 à 8 minutes, jusqu'à ce que le tout soit chaud.

5 Servir immédiatement, parsemé de coriandre et de graines de pavot.

tourtes aux châtaignes, à la féta & aux épinards

ingrédients

POUR 4 PERSONNES

4 cuil. à soupe d'huile d'olive

2 gousses d'ail, hachées

1/2 gros ou 1 petit céleri,
   coupé en julienne

250 g de feuilles d'épinards

85 g de châtaignes, cuites,
   pelées et grossièrement
   hachées

200 g de féta (poids égoutté),
   émiettée

1 œuf

2 cuil. à soupe de pesto

1 cuil. à soupe de persil plat
   frais haché

4 feuilles de pâte filo,
   de 32 x 18 cm

méthode

1 Dans une poêle, chauffer 1 cuillerée à soupe d'huile d'olive à feu moyen, ajouter l'ail et cuire 1 minute sans cesser de remuer. Ajouter le céleri et cuire encore 5 minutes, jusqu'à ce qu'il soit tendre et doré. Retirer de la poêle et réserver au chaud.

2 Ajouter 1 cuillerée à soupe d'huile dans la poêle, ajouter les épinards et couvrir. Cuire 2 à 3 minutes, jusqu'à ce que les épinards soient flétris. Retirer le couvercle et cuire jusqu'à ce que toute l'eau soit évaporée.

3 Dans une terrine, mettre l'ail, le céleri, la féta, les épinards, les châtaignes, l'œuf, le pesto et le persil, poivrer et bien mélanger le tout. Répartir la préparation dans 4 plats à gratin individuels ou dans un plat à gratin de taille moyenne.

4 Enduire chaque feuille de pâte filo avec l'huile restante, froisser et garnir de la préparation. Cuire au four préchauffé 15 à 20 minutes à 190 °C (th. 6-7), jusqu'à ce que la pâte filo soit dorée. Servir immédiatement.

terrine au stilton & aux noix

ingrédients

POUR 6 À 8 PERSONNES

2 cuil. à soupe d'huile d'olive
vierge extra, un peu plus
pour huiler

2 oignons, l'un finement haché
et l'autre coupé en quartiers

3 à 5 gousses d'ail, écrasées

2 branches de céleri,
finement émincées

175 g de châtaignes, pelées
et cuites

175 g de mélange de noix
hachées

55 g de poudre d'amande

55 g de chapelure fraîche

225 g de stilton, émietté

1 cuil. à soupe de basilic frais
haché, un peu plus pour
garnir

1 œuf, battu

sel et poivre

1 poivron rouge, mondé,
épépiné et coupé
en lanières

1 courgette d'environ 115 g,
coupée en rondelles puis
en quartiers

tomates cerises, en garniture

ketchup, pour servir

méthode

1 Dans une poêle, chauffer 1 cuillerée à soupe d'huile à feu moyen, ajouter l'oignon haché, 1 à 2 gousses d'ail et le céleri, et cuire 5 minutes en remuant de temps en temps.

2 Retirer de la poêle, égoutter et transférer dans un robot de cuisine et ajouter la chapelure, les noix, la poudre d'amande, la moitié du fromage et le basilic. Mixer le tout, incorporer progressivement l'œuf de façon à obtenir une consistance épaisse, saler et poivrer.

3 Dans une poêle, chauffer l'huile restante à feu moyen, ajouter les quartiers d'oignon, l'ail restant, le poivron et la courgette, et cuire 5 minutes en remuant souvent. Retirer la poêle du feu, saler, poivrer et égoutter le tout.

4 Dans un moule d'une contenance de 900 ml huilé, répartir la moitié de la préparation à base de noix, lisser la surface et ajouter la préparation à base d'oignon. Garnir du fromage restant, ajouter la préparation à base de noix restante et bien presser le tout. Couvrir de papier d'aluminium et cuire au four préchauffé 45 minutes à 180 °C (th. 6). Retirer le papier d'aluminium et cuire encore 25 à 35 minutes, jusqu'à ce que le tout soit cuit et ferme.

5 Retirer du four, laisser tiédir 5 minutes et démouler. Couper en tranches et servir garni de basilic, de tomates cerises et d'un peu de ketchup.

cake salé aux noisettes

ingrédients

POUR 4 PERSONNES

2 cuil. à soupe d'huile
de tournesol, un peu
plus pour graisser

1 oignon, haché

1 gousse d'ail, finement
hachée

2 branches de céleri,
hachées

1 cuil. à soupe de farine

200 ml de coulis de tomate

115 g de chapelure blonde

2 carottes, râpées

115 g de noisettes grillées,
hachées

1 cuil. à soupe de sauce
de soja noire

2 cuil. à soupe de coriandre
fraîche hachée

1 œuf, légèrement battu

sel et poivre

mesclun, en accompagnement

méthode

1 Huiler un moule à cake d'une contenance de 450 ml. Dans une poêle, chauffer l'huile à feu moyen, ajouter l'oignon et cuire 5 minutes en remuant souvent, jusqu'à ce qu'il soit tendre. Ajouter l'ail et le céleri, et cuire 5 minutes en remuant souvent. Ajouter la farine et cuire 1 minute sans cesser de remuer. Incorporer progressivement le coulis de tomate et cuire sans cesser de remuer jusqu'à ce que la préparation ait épaissi. Retirer la poêle du feu.

2 Dans une terrine, mettre la chapelure, les carottes, les noisettes, la sauce de soja et la coriandre, ajouter la préparation précédente et bien mélanger. Laisser tiédir, incorporer l'œuf, saler et poivrer.

3 Répartir la préparation dans le moule, lisser la surface et couvrir de papier d'aluminium. Cuire au four préchauffé 1 heure à 180 °C (th. 6). Démouler sur un plat de service chaud et servir immédiatement accompagné de mesclun. Il est également possible de laisser refroidir dans le moule avant de servir.

salade de nouilles au tofu fumé

ingrédients

POUR 2 PERSONNES

200 g de nouilles asiatiques

250 g de tofu ferme fumé
(poids égoutté)

200 g de chou blanc,
finement ciselé

250 g de carottes, râpées

3 oignons verts, émincés
en biais

1 piment rouge frais, épépiné
et coupé en fines rouelles

2 cuil. à soupe de graines
de sésame, grillées

sauce

1 cuil. à café de gingembre
frais râpé

1 gousse d'ail, hachée

175 g de tofu soyeux
(poids égoutté)

4 cuil. à café de sauce
de soja

2 cuil. à soupe d'huile
de sésame

4 cuil. à soupe d'eau chaude

sel

méthode

1 Cuire les nouilles à l'eau bouillante salée selon les instructions figurant sur le paquet, égoutter et rafraîchir à l'eau courante.

2 Pour la sauce, mettre le gingembre, l'ail, le tofu soyeux, la sauce de soja, l'huile et l'eau dans un bol, saler et battre jusqu'à obtention d'une consistance crémeuse et homogène.

3 Mettre le tofu fumé dans un panier à étuver, cuire 5 minutes à la vapeur et couper en lamelles.

4 Dans une terrine, mettre le chou, les carottes, les oignons verts et le piment, et mélanger. Pour servir, répartir les nouilles dans des assiettes, garnir du mélange précédent et ajouter les lamelles de tofu. Napper de sauce et parsemer de graines de sésame.

galettes de tofu thaïes & leur sauce au piment

ingrédients

POUR 8 PERSONNES

300 g de tofu ferme
(poids égoutté), râpé
1 tige de citronnelle, couche
supérieure retirée, hachée
2 gousses d'ail, hachées
1 morceau de gingembre frais
de 2,5 cm, pelé et râpé
2 feuilles de lime kafir,
hachées (facultatif)
2 échalotes, hachées
2 piments rouges frais,
épépinés et hachés
4 cuil. à soupe de coriandre
hachée
90 g de farine, un peu plus
pour pétrir
$^1\!/_2$ cuil. à café de sel
huile de maïs, pour la cuisson

sauce au piment

3 cuil. à soupe de vinaigre
de vin de riz
2 oignons verts, finement
émincés
1 cuil. à soupe de sucre
2 piments frais, hachés
2 cuil. à soupe de coriandre
fraîche hachée
1 pincée de sel

méthode

1 Pour la sauce, mettre tous les ingrédients dans un bol, bien mélanger et réserver.

2 Dans une terrine, mettre le tofu, la citronnelle, l'ail, le gingembre, les feuilles de lime kafir, les échalotes, les piments et la coriandre, mélanger et incorporer la farine et le sel de façon à obtenir une pâte épaisse et collante. Couvrir, mettre au réfrigérateur et laisser reposer 1 heure, jusqu'à ce que la préparation se raffermisse.

3 Les mains farinées, diviser la préparation en huit, façonner en boule et aplatir légèrement. Dans une sauteuse, chauffer de l'huile à feu moyen, ajouter 4 galettes et cuire 4 à 6 minutes en retournant à mi-cuisson, jusqu'à ce qu'elles soient dorées. Égoutter sur du papier absorbant et répéter l'opération avec les galettes restantes. Servir chaud accompagné de sauce au piment.

sauté de tofu épicé

ingrédients

POUR 4 PERSONNES

marinade

75 ml de bouillon de légumes

2 cuil. à café de maïzena

2 cuil. à soupe de sauce
    de soja

1 cuil. à soupe de sucre
    en poudre

1 pincée de flocons
    de piment

sauté

250 g de tofu ferme, rincé,
    égoutté et coupé en dés
    de 1 cm

4 cuil. à soupe d'huile
    d'arachide

1 cuil. à soupe de gingembre
    frais râpé

3 gousses d'ail, hachées

4 oignons verts, finement
    émincés

1 brocoli, séparé en fleurettes

1 carotte, coupée
    en julienne

1 poivron jaune, finement
    émincé

250 g de shiitake, finement
    émincés

riz cuit à la vapeur,
    en accompagnement

méthode

1 Dans une terrine, mettre le bouillon, la sauce de soja, la maïzena, le sucre et les flocons de piment, mélanger et incorporer le tofu. Laisser mariner 20 minutes.

2 Dans un wok, chauffer 2 cuillerées à soupe d'huile d'arachide, ajouter la marinade et le tofu, et faire revenir jusqu'à ce que le tofu soit doré et croustillant. Retirer du wok et réserver.

3 Dans le wok, chauffer l'huile restante, ajouter le gingembre, l'ail et les oignons verts, et faire revenir 30 secondes. Ajouter le brocoli, la carotte, le poivron et les champignons, et cuire 5 à 6 minutes. Remettre le tofu dans le wok, réchauffer et servir immédiatement, accompagné de riz cuit à la vapeur.

pâtes, nouilles & riz

Les pâtes, les nouilles et le riz se prêtent admirablement à la cuisine végétarienne. Le choix des sauces est illimité, et vous trouverez dans ce livre plusieurs recettes tout à fait spéciales – celle des fusillis au gorgonzola et aux champignons, par exemple, est riche, élégante et très goûteuse, tandis que les pâtes au pesto sont incontournables. Si vous n'avez jamais préparé de pesto maison, vous serez surpris de constater à quel point c'est facile. Cueillez le basilic à la dernière minute pour qu'il soit le plus frais possible.

Les nouilles structurent merveilleusement les plats de friture, mais si vous voulez innover dans la manière de les servir, essayez les légumes à l'aigre-douce & crêpes aux nouilles ou faites-les cuire dans un bouillon, en même temps que les légumes, mode de cuisson idéal pour les régimes basses calories.

La plupart des cultures du monde disposent d'un plat de riz traditionnel ; en Italie, il s'agit du risotto, réalisé à l'aide d'un grain rond qui libère son amidon à la cuisson pour donner un mets crémeux. Goûtez le risotto primavera, avec des légumes de printemps frais. La paëlla est le plat traditionnel espagnol. Le safran le colore de jaune, et c'est la nourriture idéale pour ce pays de soleil. Si vous êtes friand de cuisine asiatique, essayez le sauté de légumes verts, typique de la Thaïlande ou le biryani de légumes, plat classique originaire de l'Inde. Vous ne serez jamais à court d'inspiration !

lasagnes végétariennes

ingrédients

POUR 4 PERSONNES

huile d'olive, pour graisser

2 aubergines, coupées
en rondelles

30 g de beurre

1 gousse d'ail, finement
hachée

4 courgettes, coupées
en rondelles

1 cuil. à soupe de persil plat
frais haché

1 cuil. à soupe de marjolaine
fraîche finement hachée

225 g de mozzarella, râpée

625 ml de coulis de tomate
en boîte

175 g de lasagnes non
précuites

sel et poivre

55 g de parmesan,
fraîchement râpé

béchamel

300 ml de lait

1 feuille de laurier

6 grains de poivre noir

rondelles d'oignon

1 pincée de macis

30 g de beurre

3 cuil. à soupe de farine

sel et poivre

méthode

1 Pour la béchamel, verser le lait dans une casserole, ajouter la feuille de laurier, les grains de poivre, l'oignon et le macis, et porter au point de frémissement. Retirer du feu et couvrir. Laisser infuser 10 minutes et filtrer. Dans une autre casserole, faire fondre le beurre, ajouter la farine et cuire 1 minute à feu doux sans cesser de remuer. Incorporer progressivement le lait, porter à ébullition et cuire sans cesser de remuer jusqu'à obtention d'une béchamel fluide et épaisse. Saler et poivrer.

2 Huiler un gril en fonte et chauffer jusqu'à ce que l'huile soit fumante, ajouter la moitié des rondelles d'aubergines et cuire 8 minutes à feu moyen, jusqu'à ce qu'elles soient uniformément dorées. Égoutter sur du papier absorbant et répéter l'opération avec les rondelles restantes.

3 Dans une poêle, faire fondre le beurre, ajouter l'ail, les courgettes, le persil et la marjolaine, et cuire 5 minutes à feu moyen en remuant souvent, jusqu'à ce que les courgettes soient dorées. Égoutter sur du papier absorbant.

4 Dans un plat à gratin, alterner des couches d'aubergines, de courgettes, de mozzarella, de coulis de tomate et de lasagnes en salant et poivrant au fur et à mesure. Badigeonner d'huile d'olive, napper de béchamel et garnir de parmesan. Cuire 30 à 40 minutes au four préchauffé à 200 °C (th. 6-7), jusqu'à ce que les lasagnes soient dorées.

fusillis au gorgonzola & aux champignons

ingrédients

POUR 4 PERSONNES

350 g de fusillis

3 cuil. à soupe d'huile d'olive

350 g de champignons
　　sauvages, émincés

1 gousse d'ail, finement
　　hachée

400 ml de crème fraîche
　　épaisse

250 g de gorgonzola, émietté

sel et poivre

2 cuil. à soupe de persil plat
　　frais haché

méthode

1 Porter à ébullition une casserole d'eau salée, ajouter les pâtes et cuire 8 à 10 minutes, jusqu'à ce qu'elles soient *al dente*.

2 Dans une casserole, chauffer l'huile d'olive, ajouter les champignons et cuire 5 minutes à feu doux en remuant souvent. Ajouter l'ail et cuire encore 2 minutes.

3 Ajouter la crème fraîche, porter à ébullition et cuire 1 minute, jusqu'à ce qu'elle ait épaissi. Incorporer le gorgonzola et cuire à feu doux jusqu'à ce qu'il ait fondu. Veiller à ne pas laisser bouillir la sauce une fois le fromage incorporé. Saler, poivrer et retirer du feu.

4 Égoutter les pâtes, incorporer à la sauce aux champignons et servir immédiatement, garnir de persil.

pâtes au brocoli pimenté

ingrédients

POUR 4 PERSONNES

225 g de pennes
   ou de macaronis
225 g de brocoli,
   séparé en fleurettes
50 ml d'huile d'olive vierge
   extra
2 gousses d'ail, hachées
2 piments rouges frais,
   épépinés et hachés
8 tomates cerises (facultatif)
feuilles de basilic frais,
   en garniture
sel

méthode

1 Porter à ébullition une casserole d'eau salée, ajouter les pâtes et cuire 8 à 10 minutes, jusqu'à ce qu'elles soient *al dente*. Rafraîchir à l'eau courante, égoutter et réserver.

2 Porter une autre casserole d'eau salée à ébullition, ajouter le brocoli et cuire 5 minutes. Égoutter, rafraîchir à l'eau courante et égoutter de nouveau.

3 Dans la casserole ayant servi à la cuisson des pâtes, chauffer l'huile, ajouter l'ail, les piments et les tomates, et cuire 1 minute sans cesser de remuer.

4 Ajouter le brocoli, mélanger et cuire 2 minutes sans cesser de remuer de façon à bien réchauffer le brocoli. Incorporer les pâtes et cuire encore 1 minute. Transférer la préparation obtenue dans un plat de service chaud, garnir de feuilles de basilic et servir immédiatement.

pâtes au pesto

ingrédients

POUR 4 PERSONNES

450 g de tagliatelles

sel

brins de basilic frais,
    en garniture

pesto

2 gousses d'ail

25 g de pignons

sel

115 g de feuilles de basilic
    fraîches

55 g de parmesan,
    fraîchement râpé

125 ml d'huile d'olive

méthode

1 Pour le pesto, mettre l'ail, les pignons, 1 pincée de sel et le basilic dans un mortier, piler jusqu'à obtention d'une consistance homogène. Transférer dans un bol et incorporer progressivement le parmesan et l'huile d'olive sans cesser de battre à l'aide d'une cuillère en bois de façon à obtenir une sauce crémeuse. Rectifier l'assaisonnement.

2 À défaut de mortier et de pilon, mettre l'ail, les pignons et 1 pincée de sel dans un robot de cuisine et mixer quelques secondes. Ajouter le basilic et mixer jusqu'à obtention d'une consistance homogène. Moteur en marche, ajouter progressivement l'huile d'olive. Racler les parois, incorporer le parmesan et saler.

3 Porter une casserole d'eau salée à ébullition, ajouter les pâtes et cuire 8 à 10 minutes, jusqu'à ce que les pâtes soient *al dente*. Égoutter, remettre dans la casserole et incorporer la moitié du pesto. Répartir le tout dans des assiettes chaudes, garnir du pesto restant et de brins de basilic. Servir immédiatement.

macaronis au fromage

ingrédients

POUR 4 PERSONNES

225 g de macaronis

2 portions de béchamel
  (*voir* page 104)

1 œuf, battu

125 g de cheddar, râpé

1 cuil. à soupe de moutarde
  à l'ancienne

2 cuil. à soupe de ciboulette
  fraîche hachée

sel et poivre

4 tomates, coupées
  en rondelles

125 g de leicester, râpé

60 g de bleu, râpé

2 cuil. à soupe de graines
  de tournesol

brins de ciboulette fraîche,
  hachés

méthode

1 Porter à ébullition une casserole d'eau salée, ajouter les pâtes et cuire 8 à 10 minutes, jusqu'à ce qu'elles soient *al dente*. Égoutter et répartir dans un plat à gratin.

2 Mélanger la béchamel, l'œuf battu, le cheddar, la moutarde et la ciboulette, saler et poivrer. Répartir le mélange obtenu sur les macaronis de façon à les recouvrir totalement. Garnir de rondelles de tomates.

3 Parsemer le tout de leicester, de bleu et de graines de tournesol, placer le plat sur une plaque et cuire au four préchauffé 25 à 30 minutes à 190 °C (th. 6-7), jusqu'à ce que le gratin soit doré. Garnir de ciboulette et servir immédiatement.

pâtes crémeuses aux épinards

ingrédients

POUR 4 PERSONNES

300 g de pennes ou des
    pâtes de son choix
2 cuil. à soupe d'huile d'olive
250 g de champignons,
    émincés
1 cuil. à café d'origan séché
275 ml de bouillon de légumes
1 cuil. à soupe de jus
    de citron
6 cuil. à soupe de fromage
    frais à 70 % de M. G.
200 g d'épinards surgelés
sel et poivre

méthode

1 Cuire les pâtes à l'eau bouillante salée selon les instructions figurant sur le paquet et égoutter en réservant 175 ml de l'eau de cuisson.

2 Dans une poêle, chauffer l'huile à feu moyen, ajouter les champignons et cuire 8 minutes en remuant souvent, jusqu'à ce qu'ils soient presque croustillants. Incorporer l'origan, mouiller avec le bouillon et le jus de citron, et cuire 10 à 12 minutes, jusqu'à ce que la sauce ait réduit de moitié.

3 Incorporer le fromage frais et les épinards, et cuire 3 à 5 minutes à feu moyen. Mouiller avec l'eau de cuisson réservée et ajouter les pâtes. Saler, poivrer et bien réchauffer le tout avant de servir.

spaghettis aux aubergines

ingrédients

POUR 4 PERSONNES

2 cuil. à soupe d'huile d'olive

1 gros oignon rouge, haché

2 gousses d'ail, hachées

1 cuil. à soupe de jus
    de citron

4 petites aubergines, coupées
    en quartiers

625 ml de coulis de tomate

sel et poivre

2 cuil. à café de sucre
    en poudre

2 cuil. à soupe de concentré
    de tomate

400 g de cœurs d'artichauts
    en boîte, égouttés
    et coupés en deux

125 g d'olives noires
    dénoyautées

350 g de spaghettis

brins de basilic frais,
    en garniture

pain aux olives,
    en accompagnement

méthode

1 Dans une poêle, chauffer 1 cuillerée à soupe d'huile, ajouter l'oignon, l'ail, le jus de citron et les aubergines, et cuire 4 à 5 minutes à feu doux, jusqu'à ce que le tout soit légèrement doré.

2 Verser le coulis de tomate dans la poêle, saler et poivrer. Ajouter le sucre et le concentré de tomate, porter à ébullition et réduire le feu. Laisser mijoter 20 minutes, incorporer les cœurs d'artichauts et les olives, et cuire 5 minutes.

3 Porter une casserole d'eau salée à ébullition, ajouter les pâtes et cuire 8 à 10 minutes, jusqu'à ce qu'elles soient *al dente*. Égoutter, incorporer l'huile d'olive restante, saler et poivrer.

4 Transférer les spaghettis dans un plat de service chaud, garnir de légumes en sauce et de brins de basilic. Servir accompagné de pain aux olives.

radiatore & leur sauce au potiron

ingrédients

POUR 4 PERSONNES

55 g de beurre

115 g d'oignons blancs
ou d'échalotes, très
finement hachés

800 g de potiron
(poids total)

1 pincée de noix muscade

350 g de radiatore

200 ml de crème fraîche
liquide

4 cuil. à soupe de parmesan
râpé, un peu plus pour
garnir

2 cuil. à soupe de persil plat
frais haché

sel et poivre

méthode

1 Dans une casserole, faire fondre le beurre à feu doux, ajouter les oignons, saler et couvrir. Cuire 25 à 30 minutes en remuant souvent.

2 Peler le potiron, épépiner et hacher la pulpe. Ajouter la pulpe dans la casserole, incorporer la noix muscade et couvrir. Cuire 45 minutes à feu doux en remuant de temps en temps.

3 Porter à ébullition une casserole d'eau salée, ajouter les pâtes et cuire 8 à 10 minutes, jusqu'à ce qu'elles soient *al dente*. Égoutter en réservant 150 ml d'eau de cuisson.

4 Incorporer la crème fraîche, le parmesan et le persil à la préparation à base de potiron, saler et poivrer. Allonger éventuellement avec l'eau de cuisson des pâtes si la préparation semble trop épaisse. Incorporer les pâtes et chauffer sans cesser de remuer 1 minute. Servir immédiatement, garni de parmesan.

sauté de légumes au vermicelle frit

ingrédients

POUR 4 PERSONNES

huile de tournesol, pour
   la friture

115 g de vermicelle de riz,
   brisé en tronçons
   de 7,5 cm

115 g de haricots verts,
   coupés en petits tronçons

2 carottes, coupées
   en julienne

2 courgettes, coupées
   en julienne

115 g de shiitake, émincés

1 morceau de gingembre
   de 2,5 cm, râpé

1/2 petit chou nappa, ciselé

4 oignons verts, émincés

85 g de germes de soja

2 cuil. à soupe de sauce
   de soja noire

2 cuil. à soupe de vin de riz
   chinois

1 bonne pincée de sucre

2 cuil. à soupe de coriandre
   fraîche hachée

méthode

1 Remplir à demi d'huile un wok ou une grande casserole et chauffer à 180 °C – un dé de pain doit y brunir en 30 secondes.

2 Ajouter une portion de vermicelle et cuire 1 min 30 à 2 minutes, jusqu'à ce qu'il soit croustillant et gonflé. Retirer de l'huile, égoutter sur du papier absorbant et répéter l'opération avec le vermicelle restant. Vider le wok ou la casserole en y laissant l'équivalent de 2 cuillerées à soupe d'huile.

3 Chauffer l'huile à feu vif, ajouter les haricots verts et faire revenir 2 minutes. Ajouter les carottes, les courgettes, les champignons et le gingembre, et faire revenir encore 2 minutes.

4 Ajouter le chou, les oignons verts et les germes de soja, et faire revenir 1 minute. Ajouter la sauce de soja, le vin de riz et le sucre, et cuire 1 minute sans cesser de remuer.

5 Ajouter la coriandre hachée, bien mélanger et servir immédiatement accompagné de vermicelle frit.

légumes chinois & leurs nouilles

ingrédients

POUR 4 PERSONNES

1,25 l de bouillon de légumes
1 gousse d'ail, hachée
1 morceau de gingembre frais
   de 1 cm, râpé
225 g de nouilles aux œufs
1 poivron rouge, épépiné
   et émincé
85 g de petits pois surgelés
115 g de fleurettes de brocoli
85 g de shiitake, émincés
2 cuil. à soupe de graines
   de sésame
225 g de châtaignes d'eau
   en boîte, égouttées
   et coupées en deux
225 g de pousses de bambou
   en boîte, égouttées
280 g de chou nappa, ciselé
140 g de germes de soja
3 oignons verts, émincés
1 cuil. à soupe de soja noire
poivre

méthode

1 Dans une casserole, mettre le bouillon, l'ail et le gingembre, porter à ébullition et ajouter les nouilles, le poivron, les petits pois, le brocoli et les champignons. Porter de nouveau à ébullition, réduire le feu et couvrir. Laisser mijoter 5 à 6 minutes, jusqu'à ce que les nouilles soient tendres.

2 Répartir les graines de sésame sur une plaque en une seule couche et passer au gril préchauffé en remuant souvent, jusqu'à ce qu'elles soient dorées. Transférer dans un bol et réserver.

3 Dans la casserole, ajouter les châtaignes d'eau, les pousses de bambou, le chou, les germes de soja et les oignons verts, porter à ébullition et laisser mijoter 2 à 3 minutes, jusqu'à ce que le tout soit bien chaud.

4 Égoutter en réservant 300 ml d'eau de cuisson et transférer dans un plat de service chaud. Délayer la sauce de soja dans l'eau réservée, arroser les légumes et poivrer. Servir immédiatement, garni de graines de sésame grillées.

légumes à l'aigre-douce & crêpes aux nouilles

ingrédients

POUR 4 PERSONNES

115 g de nouilles de riz

6 œufs

4 oignons verts, coupés
   en dés

sel et poivre

2$\frac{1}{2}$ cuil. à soupe d'huile

900 g d'un mélange de
   légumes, carottes, mini-
   épis de maïs, chou-fleur,
   brocoli, pois mangetout et
   oignons par exemple, pelés
   si nécessaire et coupés en
   dés de tailles équivalentes

100 g de pousses de bambou
   en boîte, égouttées

200 g de sauce aigre-douce
   prête à l'emploi

méthode

1 Dans une terrine, mettre les nouilles, couvrir d'eau tiède et laisser reposer 20 minutes, jusqu'à ce qu'elles soient tendres. Égoutter, couper en tronçons de 7,5 cm à l'aide d'une paire de ciseaux et réserver.

2 Battre les œufs, incorporer aux nouilles et ajouter les oignons verts. Saler et poivrer. Chauffer une poêle de 20 cm de diamètre à feu vif, ajouter 1 cuillerée à soupe d'huile et verser un quart de la préparation à base d'œufs de sorte que le fond de la poêle soit recouvert entièrement. Réduire le feu et cuire 1 minute, jusqu'à ce que la crêpe ait pris. Retourner en ajoutant éventuellement de l'huile et cuire sur l'autre face jusqu'à ce qu'elle soit dorée. Retirer de la poêle, réserver au chaud et répéter l'opération de façon à obtenir 4 crêpes.

3 Chauffer un wok ou une poêle à feu vif, ajouter 1$\frac{1}{2}$ cuillerée à soupe d'huile d'olive et chauffer jusqu'à ce qu'elle soit fumante. Ajouter les légumes les plus épais en premier et faire revenir 30 secondes. Incorporer progressivement les légumes restants et les pousses de bambou, ajouter la sauce et faire revenir jusqu'à ce que les légumes soient tendres et que la sauce soit chaude. Répartir les crêpes dans des assiettes, garnir de légumes en sauce et servir.

risotto aux noix

ingrédients

POUR 4 PERSONNES

70 g de beurre

1 petit oignon,
    finement haché

280 g de riz arborio

1,25 l de bouillon de légumes
    frémissant

sel et poivre

115 g de cerneaux de noix

85 g de parmesan,
    fraîchement râpé

55 g de mascarpone

55 g de gorgonzola, coupé
    en dés

méthode

1 Dans une casserole, faire fondre 30 g de beurre à feu moyen, ajouter l'oignon et cuire 5 à 7 minutes en remuant de temps en temps, jusqu'à ce qu'il soit tendre et commence à dorer. Ne pas laisser brunir.

2 Réduire le feu, ajouter le riz et cuire 2 à 3 minutes sans cesser de remuer, jusqu'à ce que les grains soient translucides.

3 Mouiller avec une louche de bouillon, cuire jusqu'à ce que le liquide soit absorbé et répéter l'opération jusqu'à épuisement du bouillon. Au bout de 20 minutes, tout le bouillon doit être absorbé et le riz crémeux. Saler et poivrer.

4 Dans une poêle, faire fondre 30 g de beurre à feu moyen, ajouter les noix et faire revenir 2 à 3 minutes, jusqu'à ce qu'elles commencent à brunir.

5 Retirer le risotto du feu, ajouter le beurre restant et bien mélanger. Incorporer les fromages et remuer jusqu'à ce qu'ils aient fondu. Ajouter les trois quarts des noix et répartir dans des assiettes chaudes. Servir parsemé des noix restantes.

risotto aux champignons

ingrédients

POUR 6 PERSONNES

55 g de cèpes ou de morilles
    séchés

500 g d'un mélange de
    champignons sauvages,
    les plus gros coupés
    en deux

4 cuil. à soupe d'huile d'olive

3 à 4 gousses d'ail, finement
    hachées

55 g de beurre

1 oignon, finement haché

350 g de riz arborio

50 ml de vermouth blanc

1,25 l de bouillon de légumes
    frémissant

sel et poivre

115 g de parmesan,
    fraîchement râpé

4 cuil. à soupe de persil plat
    frais haché

méthode

1 Dans une terrine résistant à la chaleur, mettre les champignons séchés, couvrir d'eau bouillante et laisser tremper 30 minutes. Égoutter et sécher. Filtrer l'eau de trempage et réserver.

2 Parer les champignons frais et brosser. Dans une poêle, chauffer 3 cuillerées à soupe d'huile, ajouter les champignons frais et faire revenir 1 à 2 minutes. Ajouter l'ail et les champignons réhydratés et cuire 2 minutes en remuant souvent. Transférer dans une terrine et réserver.

3 Dans une casserole, chauffer l'huile restante et la moitié du beurre, ajouter l'oignon et cuire à feu moyen sans cesser de remuer jusqu'à ce qu'il soit tendre. Réduire le feu, ajouter le riz et cuire sans cesser de remuer jusqu'à ce que les grains soient translucides. Mouiller avec le vermouth et cuire 1 minute sans cesser de remuer, jusqu'à ce qu'il soit évaporé.

4 Mouiller avec une louche de bouillon, cuire jusqu'à ce que le liquide soit absorbé et répéter l'opération jusqu'à épuisement du bouillon. Au bout de 20 minutes, tout le bouillon doit être absorbé et le riz crémeux. Saler et poivrer.

5 Mouiller avec la moitié de l'eau de trempage, ajouter les champignons, saler et poivrer. Ajouter l'eau de trempage restante si nécessaire. Retirer du feu, incorporer le beurre restant, le parmesan et le persil haché, et servir.

risotto primavera

ingrédients

POUR 6 À 8 PERSONNES

225 g de fines asperges
    fraîches
4 cuil. à soupe d'huile d'olive
175 g de haricots verts,
    coupés en tronçons
    de 2,5 cm
175 g de petites courgettes,
    coupées en quartiers puis
    en tronçons de 2,5 cm
225 g de petits pois frais
1 oignon, finement haché
1 à 2 gousses d'ail,
    finement hachées
350 g de riz arborio
1,6 l de bouillon de légumes
    frémissant
4 oignons verts, coupés
    en tronçons de 2,5 cm
sel et poivre
55 g de beurre
115 g de parmesan,
    fraîchement râpé
2 cuil. à soupe de ciboulette
    fraîche hachée
2 cuil. à soupe de basilic frais
    haché
oignons verts, en garniture
    (facultatif)

méthode

1 Ébouter les asperges, couper les pointes et réserver. Détailler les tiges en tronçons de 2,5 cm et ajouter au pointes.

2 Dans unc poêle, chauffer 2 cuillerées à soupe d'huile à feu vif, ajouter les asperges, les haricots, les courgettes et les petits pois, et faire revenir 3 à 4 minutes, jusqu'à ce que les légumes soient tendres et d'un vert brillant. Réserver.

3 Dans une casserole, chauffer l'huile restante à feu moyen, ajouter l'oignon et cuire 3 minutes en remuant souvent, jusqu'à ce qu'il soit tendre. Ajouter l'ail et cuire 30 secondes sans cesser de remuer. Réduire le feu, ajouter le riz et cuire 2 à 3 minutes, jusqu'à ce que les grains soient translucides.

4 Mouiller avec une louche de bouillon, cuire jusqu'à ce que le liquide soit absorbé et répéter l'opération jusqu'à épuisement du bouillon, en réservant 2 cuillerées à soupe. Au bout de 20 minutes, tout le bouillon doit être absorbé et le riz crémeux. Saler et poivrer.

5 Incorporer les légumes cuits, les oignons verts et le bouillon restant, et cuire 2 minutes en remuant souvent. Saler, poivrer et ajouter le beurre, le parmesan, la ciboulette et le basilic. Retirer du feu et servir immédiatement, garnir éventuellement d'oignons verts.

galettes de risotto épicées

ingrédients

POUR 3 PERSONNES

85 g d'oignon, finement
   haché

85 g de poireau, finement
   haché

25 g de riz arborio

550 ml de bouillon de légumes

85 g de courgette, râpée

1 cuil. à soupe de basilic frais
   haché

25 g de chapelure blonde

huile en spray

feuilles de radicchio,
   en accompagnement

garniture

50 g de fromage frais
   à 70 % de M. G.

50 g de mangue, coupée
   en dés

1 cuil. à café de zeste
   de citron vert râpé

1 cuil. à café de jus
   de citron vert

1 pincée de poivre
   de Cayenne

méthode

1 Chauffer une poêle antiadhésive à feu vif, ajouter l'oignon et le poireau, et cuire 2 à 3 minutes sans cesser de remuer, jusqu'à ce qu'ils soient tendres, sans laisser dorer.

2 Ajouter le riz, mouiller avec le bouillon et porter à ébullition. Laisser bouillir 2 minutes sans cesser de remuer, réduire le feu et cuire encore 15 minutes en remuant toutes les 2 à 3 minutes. Lorsque le riz est presque cuit et le bouillon absorbé, incorporer la courgette et le basilic, et cuire 5 à 10 minutes à feu vif sans cesser de remuer jusqu'à ce que la préparation soit collante et sèche. Transférer sur une assiette et laisser refroidir.

3 Pour la garniture, mettre les ingrédients dans un bol et mélanger.

4 Diviser la préparation à base de riz en trois, façonner des galettes et creuser une cavité au centre. Placer 1 cuillerée à soupe de garniture dans chaque cavité, refermer les galettes de façon à enfermer la garniture et refaçonner à l'aide d'un couteau. Enrober chaque galette de chapelure, disposer sur une plaque et vaporiser d'huile. Cuire au four préchauffé 15 à 20 minutes à 200 °C (th. 6-7), jusqu'à ce que les galettes soient dorées. Servir accompagné de feuilles de radicchio.

sauté de légumes verts au riz au jasmin

ingrédients

POUR 4 PERSONNES

225 g de riz au jasmin

2 cuil. à soupe d'huile
d'arachide

1 cuil. à soupe de pâte
de curry verte

6 oignons verts, émincés

2 gousses d'ail, hachées

1 courgette, coupée
en julienne

115 g de haricots verts

175 g d'asperges, parées

3 à 4 feuilles de basilic thaï
frais

sel

méthode

1 Cuire le riz dans de l'eau bouillante salée 12 à 15 minutes, bien égoutter et laisser refroidir. Mettre au réfrigérateur une nuit.

2 Dans un wok, chauffer l'huile, ajouter la pâte de curry et faire revenir 1 minute. Ajouter l'ail et les oignons verts, et faire revenir encore 1 minute.

3 Ajouter la courgette, les haricots verts et les asperges, et faire revenir 3 à 4 minutes, jusqu'à ce que le tout soit juste tendre. Aérer le riz à la fourchette, ajouter dans le wok et cuire 2 à 3 minutes sans cesser de remuer, jusqu'à ce que le riz soit chaud. Incorporer les feuilles de basilic thaï et servir chaud.

pilaf de légumes

ingrédients

POUR 4 PERSONNES

4 cuil. à soupe d'huile

1 oignon rouge, finement
    haché

2 branches de céleri tendres,
    avec les feuilles, coupées
    en dés

2 carottes, grossièrement
    râpées

1 piment vert frais, épépiné
    et haché

3 oignons verts, partie verte
    incluse, émincés

40 g d'amandes entières,
    coupées en deux dans
    la longueur

350 g de riz basmati brun,
    cuit

150 g de lentilles rouges,
    cuites

175 ml de bouillon de légumes

5 cuil. à soupe de jus
    d'orange frais

sel et poivre

feuilles de céleri, en garniture

méthode

1 Dans une poêle, chauffer 2 cuillerées à soupe d'huile à feu moyen, ajouter l'oignon et cuire 5 minutes, jusqu'à ce qu'il soit tendre.

2 Ajouter le céleri, les carottes, le piment, les oignons verts et les amandes, et faire revenir 2 minutes, jusqu'à ce que les légumes soient *al dente*. Transférer dans une terrine et réserver.

3 Chauffer l'huile restante dans la poêle, ajouter le riz et les lentilles, et cuire 1 à 2 minutes à feu moyen sans cesser de remuer, jusqu'à ce que le tout soit bien chaud. Réduire le feu, mouiller avec le bouillon et le jus d'orange, saler et poivrer.

4 Remettre les légumes dans la poêle, bien mélanger et réchauffer le tout. Transférer dans un plat de service chaud, garnir de feuilles de céleri et servir.

paëlla aux artichauts

ingrédients

POUR 4 À 6 PERSONNES

$1/2$ cuil. à café de filaments
    de safran

2 cuil. à soupe d'eau chaude

3 cuil. à soupe d'huile d'olive

1 gros oignon, haché

1 courgette, détaillée en dés

2 gousses d'ail, hachées

$1/4$ de cuil. à café de poivre
    de Cayenne

225 g de tomates, mondées
    et coupées en quartiers

425 g de pois chiches
    en boîte, égouttés

425 g de cœurs d'artichauts
    en boîte, égouttés et
    grossièrement hachés

350 g de riz pour paëlla

1,3 l de bouillon de légumes

150 g de haricots verts,
    blanchis

sel et poivre

1 citron coupé en quartiers
    et persil ciselé en garniture

méthode

1 Laisser infuser le safran dans l'eau chaude quelques minutes.

2 Dans un plat à paëlla, chauffer l'huile, ajouter l'oignon et la courgette, et cuire à à feu moyen 2 à 3 minutes sans cesser de remuer, jusqu'à ce qu'ils soient tendres. Ajouter l'ail, le poivre de Cayenne, le safran et son eau de trempage, et cuire 1 minute sans cesser de remuer. Ajouter les tomates, les pois chiches et les cœurs d'artichauts, et cuire encore 2 minutes sans cesser de remuer.

3 Ajouter le riz et cuire 1 minute sans cesser de remuer, jusqu'à ce qu'il soit translucide. Mouiller avec 1 litre de bouillon, porter à ébullition et laisser mijoter 10 minutes sans couvrir. Ne pas remuer pendant la cuisson mais secouer le plat une ou deux fois en ajoutant les ingrédients. Saler et poivrer, ajouter les haricots verts, et cuire encore 10 à 15 minutes, jusqu'à ce que le riz soit presque cuit. Mouiller avec du bouillon supplémentaire si nécessaire.

4 Retirer du feu dès que tout le liquide est absorbé et qu'une délicate odeur de grillé se dégage. Couvrir de papier d'aluminium, laisser reposer 5 minutes et servir accompagné de quartiers de citron et garni de persil.

paëlla végétarienne

ingrédients

POUR 4 À 6 PERSONNES

1/2 cuil. à café de filaments
de safran

2 cuil. à soupe d'eau chaude

6 cuil. à soupe d'huile d'olive

1 oignon espagnol, émincé

3 gousses d'ail, émincées

1 poivron rouge, épépiné
et coupé en dés

1 poivron orange, épépiné
et coupé en dés

1 grosse aubergine, coupée
en dés

200 g de riz pour paëlla

625 ml de bouillon de légumes

450 g de tomates, mondées
et concassées

sel et poivre

115 g de champignons,
émincés

115 g de haricots verts, coupés
en deux

400 g de haricots borlotti
en boîte

méthode

1 Laisser infuser le safran dans l'eau chaude quelques minutes.

2 Dans un plat à paëlla, chauffer l'huile à feu moyen, ajouter l'oignon et cuire 2 à 3 minutes sans cesser de remuer, jusqu'à ce qu'il soit tendre. Ajouter l'ail, les poivrons et l'aubergine, et cuire 5 minutes en remuant souvent.

3 Ajouter le riz et cuire 1 minute sans cesser de remuer, jusqu'à ce qu'il soit brillant et bien enrobé de matières grasses. Mouiller avec le bouillon, ajouter les tomates, le safran et son eau de trempage, saler et poivrer. Porter à ébullition, réduire le feu et laisser mijoter 15 minutes en secouant souvent la poêle et en remuant de temps en temps.

4 Incorporer les champignons, les haricots verts et les haricots borlotti avec leur jus, cuire encore 10 minutes et servir immédiatement.

paëlla aux légumes

ingrédients

POUR 4 À 6 PERSONNES

1/2 cuil. à café de filaments
de safran

2 cuil. à soupe d'eau chaude

3 cuil. à soupe d'huile d'olive

1 gros oignon, haché

2 gousses d'ail, hachées

1 cuil. à café de paprika

225 g de tomates, mondées
et coupées en quartiers

1 poivron rouge et 1 poivron
vert, grillés, épépinés,
pelés et coupés
en lanières

425 g de pois chiches
en boîte, égouttés

350 g de riz pour paëlla

1,3 l de bouillon de légumes

55 g de petits pois

150 g d'asperges, blanchies

1 cuil. à soupe de persil plat
frais haché, un peu plus
pour garnir

sel et poivre

1 citron coupé en quartiers,
en garniture

méthode

1 Laisser infuser le safran dans l'eau chaude quelques minutes.

2 Dans un plat à paëlla, chauffer l'huile, ajouter l'oignon et cuire 2 à 3 minutes à feu moyen sans cesser de remuer, jusqu'à ce qu'il soit tendre. Ajouter l'ail, le paprika et le safran avec son eau de trempage, et cuire 1 minute sans cesser de remuer. Ajouter les tomates, les pois chiches et les poivrons, et cuire 2 minutes.

3 Ajouter le riz et cuire 1 minute sans cesser de remuer, jusqu'à ce qu'il soit translucide. Mouiller avec 1 litre de bouillon, porter à ébullition et réduire le feu. Laisser mijoter 10 minutes sans couvrir. Ne pas remuer pendant la cuisson mais secouer le plat une ou deux fois en ajoutant les ingrédients. Saler et poivrer, ajouter les petits pois, les asperges et le persil, et cuire encore 10 à 15 minutes, jusqu'à ce que le riz soit presque cuit. Mouiller avec du bouillon supplémentaire si nécessaire.

4 Retirer du feu dès que le liquide est absorbé et qu'une délicate odeur de grillé se dégage. Couvrir de papier d'aluminium, laisser reposer 5 minutes et servir accompagné de quartiers de citron et garni de persil.

biryani de légumes

ingrédients

POUR 4 PERSONNES

2 cuil. à soupe d'huile

3 clous de girofle

3 gousses de cardamome,
   pilées

1 oignon, haché

115 g de carottes, hachées

2 à 3 gousses d'ail, hachées

1 à 2 piments rouges frais,
   épépinés et hachés

1 morceau de gingembre frais
   de 2,5 cm, râpé

115 g de chou-fleur, séparé
   en fleurettes

175 g de brocoli, séparé
   en fleurettes

115 g de haricots verts,
   hachés

400 g de tomates en boîte

150 ml de bouillon de légumes

sel et poivre

115 g de gombos, émincés

1 cuil. à soupe de coriandre
   fraîche hachée, un peu
   plus en garniture

115 g de riz basmati brun

filaments de safran (facultatif)

zeste râpé d'un citron vert,
   en garniture

méthode

1 Dans une casserole, chauffer l'huile à feu doux, ajouter les épices, l'oignon, les carottes, l'ail, les piments et le gingembre, et cuire 5 minutes en remuant souvent.

2 Ajouter le chou-fleur, le brocoli et les haricots verts, et cuire 5 minutes en remuant souvent. Incorporer les tomates, mouiller avec le bouillon, saler et poivrer. Porter à ébullition, réduire le feu et couvrir. Laisser mijoter 10 minutes.

3 Ajouter les gombos et cuire encore 8 à 10 minutes, jusqu'à ce que les légumes soient tendres. Incorporer la coriandre, égoutter et réserver au chaud.

4 Cuire le riz 25 minutes dans de l'eau bouillante salée, égoutter et réserver au chaud.

5 Dans une terrine profonde, alterner des couches de légumes et de riz en pressant bien, laisser reposer 5 minutes et démouler sur un plat de service chaud. Servir garni de zeste de citron vert et de coriandre.

poivrons rouges farcis au basilic

ingrédients

POUR 4 PERSONNES

140 g de riz long grain

4 gros poivrons

2 cuil. à soupe d'huile d'olive

1 gousse d'ail, hachée

4 échalotes, hachées

1 branche de céleri, hachée

3 cuil. à soupe de noix
    grillées

2 tomates, mondées
    et hachées

1 cuil. à soupe de jus
    de citron

50 g de raisins secs

4 cuil. à soupe de cheddar
    frais râpé

2 cuil. à soupe de basilic frais
    haché

sel et poivre

brins de basilic frais,
    en garniture

quartiers de citron,
    en garniture

méthode

1 Cuire le riz 20 minutes à l'eau bouillante salée, égoutter, rincer à l'eau courante et égoutter de nouveau.

2 À l'aide d'un couteau tranchant, décalotter les poivrons et réserver. Retirer les membranes, épépiner et blanchir avec les chapeaux 2 minutes à l'eau bouillante. Retirer du feu et égoutter. Dans une poêle, chauffer la moitié de l'huile, ajouter l'ail et les échalotes, et cuire 3 minutes sans cesser de remuer. Ajouter le céleri, les noix, les tomates, le jus de citron et les raisins secs, et cuire encore 5 minutes. Retirer du feu, incorporer le fromage et le basilic haché, saler et poivrer.

3 Farcir les poivrons avec la préparation obtenue, les refermer et arroser de l'huile restante. Couvrir de papier d'aluminium et cuire au four préchauffé 45 minutes à 180 °C (th. 6). Retirer du four, garnir de brins de basilic et de quartiers de citron.

légumes
& salades

Les légumes sont essentiels et il existe de multiples manières de les accomoder. Les pommes de terre, simples et réconfortantes, se marient très bien avec le fromage. Au gratin ou servies sur un lit de légumes, elles sortiront du four en grésillant. Farcies, elles constitueront un repas familial sans apprêt, particulièrement bon marché.

Dans ce chapitre, vous trouverez la recette riche et crémeuse des champignons stroganoff, qui tire le meilleur parti d'une sélection de champignons variés. Le clafoutis de tomates cerises, la tarte aux pommes de terre à la fontina et au romarin, accompagnée d'un risotto original à base d'un trio de riz, ne manqueront pas d'impressionner.

Pour persuader tous ceux qui croient ne pas aimer les légumes, accompagnez-les de préparations spéciales. Avec une crème d'ail, les pommes de terre qui paraissent souvent ternes paraissent sous un jour nouveau. Le sauté de brocoli est fabuleux avec une pointe de gingembre et une sauce au piment. De même, les choux de Bruxelles accompagnés de châtaignes frits sont originaux et si délicieux !

Les salades de crudités apportent une manne de vitamines, et les avocats sont très appréciés des végétariens, en raison de leur richesse nutritionnelle. Si vous créez un mélange subtil à base d'avocat assaisonné de citron vert, vous irez tout droit au paradis !

gratin de pommes de terre au fromage

ingrédients

POUR 4 À 6 PERSONNES

900 g de pommes de terre,
    pelées et coupées en fines
    rondelles
1 gousse d'ail, coupée
    en deux
beurre, pour graisser
225 ml de crème fraîche
    épaisse
noix muscade, fraîchement
    râpée
sel et poivre
175 g de gruyère, finement
    râpé

méthode

1 Dans une terrine, mettre les pommes de terre, couvrir d'eau froide et laisser reposer 5 minutes. Bien égoutter.

2 Frotter l'intérieur d'un moule à gratin avec une demi-gousse d'ail en pressant bien et graisser légèrement.

3 Dans une terrine, mettre les pommes de terre, ajouter la crème fraîche et la noix muscade, saler et poivrer. Mélanger le tout avec les mains, transférer dans le plat et napper de la crème éventuellement restée dans la terrine.

4 Parsemer de fromage et de beurre, mettre le plat sur une plaque et cuire au four préchauffé 1 heure à 1 h 10 à 190 °C (th. 6-7), jusqu'à ce que les pommes de terre soient tendres et le gratin doré. Laisser reposer 2 minutes et servir directement dans le plat.

tarte aux pommes de terre, au fontina & au romarin

ingrédients

POUR 4 PERSONNES

1 quantité de pâte feuilletée

farine, pour abaisser la pâte

garniture

3 à 4 pommes de terre

300 g de fontina, coupé
    en cubes

1 oignon rouge, finement
    émincé

3 brins de romarin frais

2 cuil. à soupe d'huile d'olive

sel et poivre

1 jaune d'œuf

méthode

1 Sur un plan fariné, abaisser la pâte en un rond de 25 cm de diamètre et mettre sur une plaque.

2 Couper les pommes de terre en rondelles très fines de sorte qu'elles soient transparentes – utiliser une mandoline si possible. Répartir sur la pâte en spirale de façon à ce qu'elles se chevauchent et recouvrent la pâte en laissant une marge de 2 cm.

3 Répartir le fromage et l'oignon, parsemer de romarin et arroser d'huile. Saler et poivrer, et enduire la marge de jaune d'œuf.

4 Cuire au four préchauffé 25 minutes à 190 °C (th. 6-7), jusqu'à ce que les pommes de terre soit tendres et la pâte croustillante et dorée. Servir chaud.

gratin de légumes

ingrédients

POUR 4 PERSONNES

1 carotte, coupée en dés

175 g de fleurettes
de chou-fleur

175 g de fleurettes de brocoli

1 bulbe de fenouil, émincé

75 g de haricots verts, coupés
en deux

30 g de beurre

2$\frac{1}{2}$ cuil. à soupe de farine

150 ml de bouillon de légumes

150 ml de vin blanc sec

150 ml de lait

175 g de champignons,
coupés en quartiers

2 cuil. à soupe de sauge
fraîche hachée

sel et poivre

garniture

900 g de pommes de terre,
coupées en dés

30 g de beurre

4 cuil. à soupe de yaourt

75 g de parmesan,
fraîchement râpé

1 cuil. à café de graines
de fenouil

méthode

1 Cuire la carotte, le chou-fleur, le brocoli, le fenouil et les haricots verts 10 minutes à l'eau bouillante, jusqu'à ce que les légumes soient tendres. Égoutter les légumes et réserver.

2 Dans une casserole, faire fondre le beurre, ajouter la farine et cuire 1 minute. Retirer du feu, mouiller avec le bouillon, le vin et le lait, et remettre sur le feu. Porter à ébullition sans cesser de remuer, jusqu'à ce que la préparation épaississe. Incorporer les légumes, les champignons et la sauge, saler et poivrer.

3 Pour la garniture, cuire les pommes de terre 10 à 15 minutes à l'eau bouillante, égoutter et réduire en purée. Incorporer le beurre, le yaourt, la moitié du parmesan et les graines de fenouil.

4 Répartir la préparation à base de légumes dans un plat à gratin d'une contenance de 1 litre, garnir de purée de pommes de terre et parsemer du parmesan restant. Cuire au four préchauffé 30 à 35 minutes à 190 °C (th. 6-7), jusqu'à ce que le gratin soit doré.

pommes de terre farcies

ingrédients

POUR 4 PERSONNES

900 g de pommes de terre,
   grattées
2 cuil. à soupe d'huile
1 cuil. à café de gros sel
115 g de beurre
1 petit oignon, haché
sel et poivre
115 g de cheddar, râpé,
   ou de stilton, émietté
ciboulette fraîche hachée,
   en garniture

facultatif

4 cuil. à soupe de maïs
   en boîte égoutté
4 cuil. à soupe de courgettes,
   de champignons
   ou de poivrons cuits

méthode

1 Piquer les pommes de terre à l'aide d'une fourchette et mettre sur une plaque. Badigeonner d'huile et saupoudrer de gros sel. Cuire au four préchauffé 1 heure à 190 °C (th. 6-7), jusqu'à ce que la peau soit croustillante et que la chair soit tendre.

2 Dans une poêle, faire fondre 15 g de beurre à feu moyen à doux, ajouter l'oignon et cuire 8 à 10 minutes en remuant de temps en temps, jusqu'à ce qu'il soit doré. Réserver.

3 Couper les pommes de terre en deux dans la hauteur, évider la chair sans percer la peau et transférer la chair dans une terrine. Réserver le peau et la chair. Augmenter la température du four à 200 °C (th. 6-7).

4 Réduire la chair de pommes de terre en purée grossière, ajouter l'oignon et le beurre restant, saler et poivrer. Incorporer éventuellement les ingrédients facultatifs, répartir le tout dans la peau des pommes de terre et garnir de fromage.

5 Cuire les pommes de terre farcies au four 10 minutes, jusqu'à ce que le fromage ait fondu et soit doré. Garnir et servir parsemé de ciboulette.

ratatouille rustique

ingrédients

POUR 4 PERSONNES

300 g de pommes de terre
avec la peau, grattées

200 g d'aubergines, coupées
en dés de 1 cm

125 g d'oignons rouges,
coupés en rondelles
de 5 mm d'épaisseur

200 g de poivrons, épépinés
et coupés en lanières
de 1 cm d'épaisseur

175 g de courgettes, coupées
en deux dans la longueur
puis en morceaux de 1 cm

125 g de tomates cerises

90 g de fromage frais allégé

1 cuil. à café de miel liquide

1 pincée de paprika

1 cuil. à café de persil frais
haché, en garniture

marinade

1 cuil. à café d'huile

1 cuil. à soupe de jus de citron

4 cuil. à soupe de vin blanc

1 cuil. à café de sucre

2 cuil. à soupe de basilic frais
haché

1 cuil. à café de romarin frais
haché

1 cuil. à soupe de thym citron
frais haché

$1/4$ de cuil. à café de paprika

méthode

1 Cuire les pommes de terre au four préchauffé 30 minutes à 200 °C (th. 6-7), retirer du four et couper en quartiers – la chair ne doit pas être totalement cuite.

2 Pour la marinade, mettre tous les ingrédients dans un bol, battre à l'aide d'un batteur électrique ou dans un robot de cuisine jusqu'à obtention d'une consistance homogène.

3 Dans une grande terrine, mettre les pommes de terre, les aubergines, les oignons, les poivrons et les courgettes, arroser de marinade et bien mélanger le tout.

4 Répartir les légumes sur une plaque et cuire au four préchauffé 25 à 30 minutes, jusqu'à ce qu'ils soient dorés et tendres. Ajouter les tomates 5 minutes avant la fin de la cuisson de façon à les réchauffer.

5 Mélanger le fromage frais, le miel et le paprika.

6 Servir les légumes accompagnés du mélange à base de fromage frais et garnis de persil.

gratin de courgettes au fromage

ingrédients

POUR 4 À 6 PERSONNES

55 g de beurre, un peu plus
   pour graisser
6 courgettes, coupées
   en rondelles
sel et poivre
2 cuil. à soupe d'estragon
   frais haché ou de mélange
   d'estragon, de menthe
   et de persil plat
200 g de gruyère
   ou de parmesan, râpé
125 ml de lait
125 ml de crème fraîche
   épaisse
2 œufs
noix muscade fraîchement
   râpée

méthode

1 Dans une poêle, faire fondre le beurre à feu moyen à vif, ajouter les courgettes et faire revenir 4 à 6 minutes en remuant de temps en temps, jusqu'à ce qu'elles soient légèrement dorées. Retirer de la poêle, égoutter sur du papier absorbant, saler et poivrer.

2 Répartir la moitié des courgettes dans un plat de service allant au four, parsemer de la moitié des herbes et de 55 g de fromage, et répéter l'opération une fois.

3 Mélanger le lait, la crème fraîche et les œufs, ajouter la noix muscade, saler et poivrer. Napper les courgettes et parsemer du fromage restant.

4 Cuire le gratin au four préchauffé 35 à 40 minutes à 180 °C (th. 6), jusqu'à ce qu'il ait pris au centre et soit légèrement doré. Sortir du four, laisser reposer 5 minutes et servir directement dans le plat.

clafoutis de tomates cerises

ingrédients

POUR 4 À 6 PERSONNES

400 g de tomates cerises

3 cuil. à soupe de persil plat
   frais haché, de ciboulette
   hachée ou de basilic frais
   finement ciselé

100 g de gruyère, râpé

55 g de farine

4 gros œufs, légèrement
   battus

3 cuil. à soupe de crème
   aigre

225 ml de lait

sel et poivre

beurre, pour graisser

méthode

1 Graisser un plat à gratin, repartir les tomates cerises et parsemer de fines herbes et de la moitié du fromage.

2 Dans une terrine, mettre la farine et ajouter progressivement les œufs sans cesser de battre jusqu'à obtention d'une consistance homogène. Incorporer la crème aigre, verser le lait très progressivement sans cesser de battre, jusqu'à obtention d'une pâte fluide et homogène. Saler et poivrer.

3 Répartir la préparation obtenue sur les tomates cerises et parsemer du fromage restant. Cuire au four préchauffé 40 à 45 minutes à 190 °C (th. 6-7), jusqu'à ce que le clafoutis ait pris et soit bien gonflé, en couvrant éventuellement de papier d'aluminium si la surface brunit trop vite. Laisser reposer quelques minutes et servir chaud ou laisser refroidir à température ambiante.

tarte aux oignons caramélisés

ingrédients

POUR 4 À 6 PERSONNES

100 g de beurre

600 g d'oignons, finement
   émincés

2 œufs

100 ml de crème fraîche
   épaisse

sel et poivre

100 g de gruyère, râpé

1 fond de tarte prêt à l'emploi
   de 20 cm de diamètre

100 g de parmesan
   grossièrement râpé

méthode

1 Dans une poêle, faire fondre le beurre à feu moyen, ajouter les oignons et cuire 30 minutes en remuant souvent, jusqu'à ce qu'ils soient bien dorés et caramélisés. Retirer de la poêle et réserver.

2 Dans une terrine, battre les œufs, incorporer la crème fraîche, saler et poivrer. Incorporer le gruyère, bien mélanger et ajouter les oignons.

3 Répartir la préparation obtenue dans le fond de tarte, saupoudrer de parmesan et placer sur une plaque. Cuire au four préchauffé 15 à 20 minutes à 190 °C (th. 6-7), jusqu'à ce que la garniture ait pris et soit légèrement dorée.

4 Retirer du four et laisser reposer au moins 10 minutes. La tarte peut être servie chaude ou à température ambiante.

fritatta au brocoli & au sésame

ingrédients

POUR 2 PERSONNES

175 g de brocoli, séparé
    en fleurettes

85 g d'asperges, émincées
    en biais

1 cuil. à soupe d'huile d'olive
    vierge extra

1 oignon, coupé en petits
    quartiers

2 à 4 gousses d'ail, finement
    hachées

1 gros poivron orange,
    épépiné et haché

4 œufs

3 cuil. à soupe d'eau froide

sel et poivre

25 g de graines de sésame

15 g de parmesan,
    fraîchement râpé

3 oignons verts, finement
    émincés

méthode

1 Cuire le brocoli 4 minutes à l'eau bouillante
et ajouter les asperges après 2 minutes de
cuisson. Égoutter, rafraîchir à l'eau courante
et égoutter de nouveau. Réserver.

2 Dans une poêle, chauffer l'huile à feu doux,
ajouter l'oignon, l'ail et le poivron, et cuire
8 minutes en remuant souvent, jusqu'à
ce que tous les légumes soient tendres.

3 Dans un bol, battre les œufs avec l'eau, saler
et poivrer. Verser dans la poêle, ajouter le
brocoli et les asperges, et mélanger délicatement.
Cuire 3 à 4 minutes à feu moyen en ramenant
les légumes vers le centre de sorte que l'œuf
qui n'a pas pris coule vers les bords.
Préchauffer le gril.

4 Parsemer la fritatta de graines de sésame
et de fromage, et passer au gril 3 à 5 minutes,
jusqu'à ce qu'elle soit dorée et ferme. Parsemer
d'oignons verts et servir chaud ou froid.

œufs au plat aux épinards & au parmesan

ingrédients

POUR 2 PERSONNES

30 g de beurre, un peu plus
   pour graisser
125 g de pousses d'épinard
1/2 cuil. à café de noix muscade
   fraîchement râpée
4 petits œufs
50 ml de crème fraîche
   liquide
2 cuil. à soupe de parmesan
   fraîchement râpé
sel et poivre

méthode

1 Graisser légèrement 2 plats à gratin individuels avec un peu de beurre.

2 Dans une poêle, faire fondre le beurre à feu doux, ajouter les épinards et cuire 1 minute en remuant à l'aide d'une cuillère en bois, jusqu'à ce qu'ils soient flétris. Ajouter la noix muscade et répartir dans les plats.

3 Casser délicatement 2 œufs dans chaque plat, napper de crème fraîche et saupoudrer de parmesan. Saler et poivrer. Cuire au four préchauffé 10 minutes à 160 °C (th. 5-6), jusqu'à ce que les blancs d'œufs aient pris mais que les jaunes soient toujours coulants. Servir immédiatement.

champignons stroganoff

ingrédients

POUR 4 PERSONNES

550 g de mélange
    de champignons

1 oignon rouge, coupé en dés

2 gousses d'ail, hachées

425 ml de bouillon
    de légumes

1 cuil. à soupe de concentré
    de tomate

2 cuil. à soupe de jus de citron

1 cuil. à soupe de maïzena

2 cuil. à soupe d'eau froide

115 g de yaourt nature allégé

3 cuil. à soupe de persil frais
    haché

poivre

riz et mesclun,
    en accompagnement

méthode

1 Dans une casserole, mettre les champignons, l'oignon, l'ail, le bouillon, le concentré de tomate et le jus de citron, et porter à ébullition. Réduire le feu, couvrir et laisser mijoter 15 minutes, jusqu'à ce que l'oignon soit tendre.

2 Délayer la maïzena dans l'eau et incorporer dans la casserole. Porter de nouveau à ébullition sans cesser de remuer et cuire jusqu'à ce que la sauce ait épaissi. Réduire le feu et laisser mijoter 2 à 3 minutes en remuant de temps en temps.

3 Juste avant de servir, retirer la casserole du feu et incorporer le yaourt en veillant à ce que la préparation ne soit pas bouillante – le yaourt prendrait un aspect caillé. Incorporer 2 cuillerées à soupe de persil et poivrer. Transférer dans un plat de service chaud, garnir du persil restant et servir immédiatement, accompagné de riz et de mesclun.

curry de légumes à la noix de coco

ingrédients

POUR 4 PERSONNES

1 oignon, grossièrement haché

3 gousses d'ail, émincées

1 morceau de gingembre frais de 2,5 cm, émincé

2 piments verts frais, épépinés et émincés

1 cuil. à soupe d'huile

1 cuil. à café de curcuma en poudre

1 cuil. à café de coriandre en poudre

1 cuil. à café de cumin en poudre

1 kg d'un mélange de légumes, chou-fleur, courgettes, pommes de terre, carottes et haricots verts, par exemple, coupés en gros morceaux

200 g de lait de coco

sel et poivre

2 cuil. à soupe de coriandre fraîche hachée, en garniture

riz cuit, en accompagnement

méthode

1 Dans un robot de cuisine, mettre l'oignon, l'ail, le gingembre et les piments, et mixer jusqu'à obtention d'une consistance presque homogène.

2 Dans une sauteuse, chauffer l'huile à feu moyen, ajouter le mélange précédent et cuire 5 minutes sans cesser de remuer.

3 Ajouter le curcuma, la coriandre et le cumin, et cuire 3 à 4 minutes en remuant souvent. Ajouter les légumes et bien mélanger de sorte qu'ils soient enrobés d'épices.

4 Mouiller avec le lait de coco, couvrir et cuire 30 à 40 minutes, jusqu'à ce que les légumes soient tendres.

5 Saler, poivrer et garnir de coriandre hachée. Servir accompagné de riz.

curry de légumes jaunes thaï & riz basmati

ingrédients

POUR 4 PERSONNES

50 g de poivron jaune

50 g de céleri

50 g de mini-épis de maïs

85 g de poireau

100 g de patate douce

100 g de pak-choï

50 g de courgette

50 g de mange-tout

300 ml de jus d'ananas

200 ml d'eau

3 cuil. à soupe de jus
  de citron vert

2 cuil. à soupe de maïzena

4 cuil. à soupe de yaourt allégé

4 cuil. à soupe de coriandre
  fraîche hachée

150 g de riz basmati complet
  cuit

mélange d'épices

1 cuil. à café d'ail haché

$1/4$ de cuil. à café de curcuma

1 cuil. à café de coriandre
  en poudre

1 cuil. à café de citronnelle
  hachée

3 feuilles de lime kaffir

1 cuil. à café de piment vert
  finement haché

méthode

1 Pour le mélange d'épices, piler les épices dans un mortier jusqu'à obtention d'une pâte.

2 Couper le poivron en carrés de 1 cm, couper le céleri, les mini-épis de maïs et le poireau en tronçons de 5 mm et couper la patate douce en dés de 1 cm. Ciseler le pak-choï, couper la courgette en dés de 5 mm et couper les pois mange-tout en fines lanières.

3 Dans une casserole, mettre le poivron, le céleri, les mini-épis de maïs, le poireau, la patate douce et le jus d'ananas, ajouter la pâte d'épices et porter à ébullition. Réduire le feu, écumer la surface et couvrir. Laisser mijoter 15 minutes.

4 Ajouter le pak-choï, la courgette et les pois mange-tout, et cuire encore 2 minutes. Ajouter le jus de citron vert et la maïzena délayée dans l'eau froide. Cuire sans cesser de remuer jusqu'à obtention de la consistance souhaitée.

5 Retirer du feu, laisser refroidir 2 à 3 minutes et incorporer le yaourt en veillant à ce que la préparation ne soit pas bouillante – le yaourt prendrait un aspect caillé. Ajouter la coriandre et servir le curry accompagné de riz.

purée de pommes de terre à l'ail grillé

ingrédients

POUR 4 PERSONNES

2 têtes d'ail

1 cuil. à soupe d'huile d'olive

900 g de pommes de terre,
   pelées

125 ml de lait

55 g de beurre

sel et poivre

méthode

1 Séparer les gousses d'ail, mettre sur du papier d'aluminium et arroser d'huile. Bien envelopper et cuire au four préchauffé 1 heure à 180 °C, jusqu'à ce que l'ail soit très tendre. Laisser tiédir.

2 Couper les pommes de terre en dés et cuire 15 minutes à l'eau bouillante salée.

3 Presser les gousses d'ail hors de leur peau, presser au travers d'une passoire et transférer dans une casserole. Ajouter le lait et le beurre, saler et poivrer. Chauffer à feu doux jusqu'à ce que le beurre ait fondu.

4 Égoutter les pommes de terre, réduire en purée lisse et ajouter dans la casserole. Chauffer à feu doux sans cesser de remuer, jusqu'à ce que les ingrédients soient bien mélangés. Servir chaud.

quartiers de potiron grillés

ingrédients

POUR 4 PERSONNES

200 g de potiron, pelé,
    épépiné et coupé
    en 4 quartiers

1 cuil. à café d'huile

100 g d'oignons, finement
    hachés

1 cuil. à café d'ail haché

70 g d'un mélange de 3 riz
    pour risotto

300 ml de bouillon de légumes

225 g de pointes d'asperges

2 cuil. à soupe de marjolaine
    fraîche hachée, un peu
    plus pour garnir

3 cuil. à soupe de fromage
    frais allégé

2 cuil. à soupe de persil frais
    finement haché

sel et poivre

méthode

1 Répartir les quartiers de potiron sur une plaque antiadhésive et cuire au four préchauffé 20 minutes à 200 °C (th. 6-7), jusqu'à ce qu'ils soient tendres et dorés.

2 Dans une casserole, chauffer l'huile à feu moyen, ajouter les oignons et l'ail, et cuire sans cesser de remuer jusqu'à ce que les oignons soient tendres, sans laisser dorer. Ajouter le riz, mouiller avec la moitié du bouillon et laisser mijoter en remuant de temps en temps, jusqu'à ce que le bouillon ait réduit. Mouiller avec le bouillon restant et cuire en remuant de temps en temps jusqu'à ce que les grains de riz soient tendres.

3 Couper 175 g d'asperges en tronçons de 10 cm et blanchir 2 minutes à l'eau bouillante. Égoutter et réserver au chaud. Couper les asperges restantes en rondelles de 5 mm et ajouter au risotto les 3 dernières minutes de cuisson.

4 Retirer le risotto du feu, ajouter la marjolaine, le fromage frais et le persil, saler et poivrer. Ne pas laisser bouillir.

5 Répartir les quartiers de potiron dans des assiettes chaudes, garnir de risotto et ajouter les tronçons d'asperges réservés. Parsemer de marjolaine et servir.

sauté de brocoli

ingrédients

POUR 4 PERSONNES

2 cuil. à soupe d'huile

2 brocolis, séparés en fleurettes

2 cuil. à soupe de sauce
de soja

1 cuil. à café de maïzena

1 cuil. à soupe de sucre

1 cuil. à café de gingembre
frais râpé

1 gousse d'ail, hachée

1 pincée de flocons
de piment

1 cuil. à café de graines
de sésame grillées,
en garniture

méthode

1 Dans un wok, chauffer l'huile à feu vif jusqu'à ce qu'elle soit presque fumante, ajouter le brocoli et faire revenir 4 à 5 minutes. Réduire le feu.

2 Mélanger la sauce de soja, la maïzena, l'ail, le sucre, le gingembre et les flocons de piment, ajouter dans le wok et cuire 2 à 3 minutes sans cesser de remuer, jusqu'à ce que la sauce épaississe légèrement.

3 Transférer dans un plat de service chaud, garnir de graines de sésame et servir immédiatement.

oignons grillés

ingrédients

POUR 4 PERSONNES

8 gros oignons, pelés

3 cuil. à soupe d'huile d'olive

55 g de beurre

2 cuil. à café de thym frais
    haché

sel et poivre

200 g de cheddar, râpé

méthode

1 Inciser les oignons en croix du sommet vers la base sans désolidariser les quartiers ainsi obtenus. Mettre dans un plat allant au four et arroser d'huile d'olive.

2 Répartir le beurre dans les oignons, parsemer de thym, saler et poivrer. Couvrir de papier d'aluminium et cuire au four préchauffé 40 à 45 minutes à 180 °C (th. 6).

3 Sortir du four, retirer le papier d'aluminium et arroser les oignons de jus de cuisson. Cuire au four encore 15 minutes sans couvrir, jusqu'à ce que les oignons soient dorés.

4 Sortir du four, parsemer de fromage et cuire au four encore quelques minutes, jusqu'à ce que le fromage ait fondu. Servir immédiatement.

choux de Bruxelles aux châtaignes

ingrédients

POUR 4 PERSONNES

450 g de choux de Bruxelles

115 g de beurre

55 g de sucre roux

115 g de châtaignes cuites
et pelées

méthode

1 Parer les choux de Bruxelles et retirer les feuilles qui ne sont pas bien attachées. Porter à ébullition une casserole d'eau salée, ajouter les choux et cuire 5 à 10 minutes, jusqu'à ce qu'ils soient tendres, sans être mous. Égoutter, rafraîchir à l'eau courante et égoutter de nouveau. Réserver.

2 Dans une poêle, faire fondre le beurre à feu moyen, ajouter le sucre et chauffer sans cesser de remuer jusqu'à ce que le sucre soit dissous. Ajouter les châtaignes et cuire en remuant de temps en temps, jusqu'à ce qu'elles soient bien enrobées de beurre et commencent à dorer.

3 Ajouter les choux de Bruxelles, bien mélanger et réduire le feu. Cuire 3 à 4 minutes à feu doux en remuant de temps en temps, jusqu'à ce qu'ils soient bien chauds.

4 Retirer du feu, transférer dans un plat de service chaud et servir immédiatement.

taboulé

ingrédients

POUR 4 PERSONNES

175 g de boulghour

3 cuil. à soupe d'huile d'olive
vierge extra

4 cuil. à soupe de jus
de citron

sel et poivre

4 oignons verts

1 poivron vert, épépiné
et coupé en lanières

4 tomates, concassées

2 cuil. à soupe de persil frais
haché

2 cuil. à soupe de menthe
fraîche hachée

8 olives noires, dénoyautées

menthe fraîche hachée
supplémentaire,
pour garnir

méthode

1 Dans une terrine, mettre le boulghour, couvrir d'eau froide et laisser reposer 30 minutes, jusqu'à ce que les grains aient doublé de volume. Égoutter en pressant bien de façon à exprimer l'excédent d'eau. Répartir les grains sur du papier absorbant et sécher.

2 Transférer le boulghour dans un saladier. Mélanger l'huile d'olive et le jus de citron, saler et poivrer. Arroser le boulghour du mélange obtenu et laisser mariner 1 heure.

3 À l'aide d'un couteau tranchant, hacher finement les oignons verts. Ajouter les oignons verts, le poivron, les tomates, le persil et la menthe dans le saladier, et bien mélanger le tout. Parsemer d'olives, garnir de menthe hachée et servir immédiatement.

salade à la papaye, au poivron & à l'avocat

ingrédients

POUR 4 À 6 PERSONNES

200 g de mesclun

2 à 3 oignons verts, hachés

3 à 4 cuil. à soupe de coriandre
fraîche hachée

1 petite papaye

2 poivrons rouges

1 avocat

1 cuil. à soupe de jus
de citron vert

3 à 4 cuil. à soupe de graines
de courge, grillées
(facultatif)

sauce

jus d'un citron vert

1 pincée de paprika

1 pincée de cumin en poudre

1 pincée de sucre

1 gousse d'ail, finement
hachée

4 cuil. à soupe d'huile d'olive
vierge extra

sel

1 trait de vinaigre de vin
blanc (facultatif)

méthode

1 Dans une terrine, mettre le mesclun, les oignons verts et la coriandre, bien mélanger et transférer dans un saladier.

2 Couper la papaye en deux, épépiner à l'aide d'une petite cuillère et couper en quartiers. Retirer la peau et couper la chair en lamelles. Répartir sur la salade. Couper les poivrons en deux, épépiner et couper en lanières. Ajouter dans le saladier.

3 Couper l'avocat en deux autour du noyau, retirer le noyau en faisant pivot à l'aide d'un couteau pointu et peler. Couper la chair en dés, ajouter le jus de citron vert de sorte que l'avocat ne s'oxyde pas et ajouter dans le saladier.

4 Pour la sauce, mettre le jus de citron vert, le paprika, le cumin, le sucre, l'ail et l'huile, bien battre le tout et saler.

5 Napper la salade de sauce, mélanger et ajouter éventuellement 1 trait de vinaigre de vin blanc et parsemer de graines de courge.

salade d'avocat & sa sauce au citron vert

ingrédients

POUR 4 PERSONNES

60 g de mesclun

60 g de roquette

4 oignons verts, coupés
   en dés

5 tomates, coupées
   en rondelles

25 g de noix, grillées
   et hachées

2 avocats

1 cuil. à soupe de jus
   de citron

sauce au citron vert

1 cuil. à soupe de jus
   de citron vert

1 cuil. à café de moutarde
   de Dijon

1 cuil. à soupe de crème
   aigre

1 cuil. à soupe de persil
   ou de coriandre frais
   hachés

3 cuil. à soupe d'huile d'olive
   vierge extra

1 pincée de sucre

sel et poivre

méthode

1 Laver et rincer le mesclun et la roquette.
Ciseler les feuilles et répartir dans un saladier.
Ajouter les oignons verts, les tomates et les
noix dans le saladier.

2 Dénoyauter, peler et émincer les avocats.
Arroser de jus de citron de sorte qu'ils ne
s'oxydent pas, ajouter dans le saladier
et mélanger délicatement.

3 Pour la sauce, mettre tous les ingrédients
dans un bol, bien battre et arroser la salade.
Servir immédiatement.

salade de poivrons grillés

ingrédients

POUR 8 PERSONNES

3 poivrons rouges

3 poivrons jaunes

5 cuil. à soupe d'huile d'olive
vierge extra espagnole

2 cuil. à soupe de vinaigre
de xérès ou de jus
de citron

2 gousses d'ail, hachées

1 pincée de sucre

sel et poivre

1 cuil. à soupe de câpres

8 petites olives noires
espagnoles

2 cuil. à soupe de marjolaine
fraîche hachée, plus
quelques brins pour garnir

méthode

1 Mettre les poivrons sur une grille et passer au gril 10 minutes à chaleur maximale en les retournant souvent, jusqu'à ce que la peau noircisse et se plisse.

2 Transférer les poivrons dans un sac en plastique ou mettre dans une terrine et couvrir d'un torchon humide. Laisser reposer 15 minutes, jusqu'à ce qu'ils soient assez tièdes pour être manipulés.

3 À l'aide d'un couteau tranchant, inciser la base des poivrons et réserver le jus qui s'en écoule. Retirer délicatement la peau noircie avec les doigts. Couper les poivrons en deux, retirer le pédoncule et les membranes, et épépiner. Couper en lanières et répartir sur un plat de service.

4 Mélanger le jus des poivrons réservés, l'huile d'olive, le vinaigre de xérès, l'ail et le sucre, saler et poivrer. Battre le tout et arroser les poivrons.

5 Parsemer la salade de câpres, d'olives et de marjolaine hachée, garnir de brins de marjolaine et servir à température ambiante.

salade de haricots verts à la féta

ingrédients

POUR 4 PERSONNES

350 g de haricots verts

1 oignon rouge, haché

3 à 4 cuil. à soupe de
   coriandre fraîche hachée

2 radis, coupés en fines
   rondelles

75 g de féta (poids égoutté),
   émiettée

1 cuil. à café d'origan frais
   haché, un peu plus
   pour garnir (facultatif),
   ou 1/2 cuil. à café d'origan
   haché

poivre

2 cuil. à soupe de vinaigre
   de vin rouge

80 ml d'huile d'olive vierge
   extra

3 tomates cerises, coupées
   en quartiers

tranches de pain frais,
   en accompagnement

méthode

1 Mettre les haricots dans un panier à étuver et cuire 5 minutes à la vapeur, jusqu'à ce qu'ils soient tendres.

2 Transférer les haricots dans une terrine, ajouter l'oignon, la coriandre, les radis et la féta.

3 Parsemer d'origan et poivrer. Dans un bol, mettre le vinaigre et l'huile, battre et ajouter aux haricots verts. Bien mélanger.

4 Transférer dans des assiettes, garnir de tomates cerises et servir accompagné de pain frais.

salade à la grecque

ingrédients

POUR 4 PERSONNES

4 tomates, coupées
en quartiers

1 oignon, émincé

1/2 concombre, émincé

225 g d'olives kalamata,
dénoyautées

225 g de féta, coupée en dés

2 cuil. à soupe de feuilles
de coriandre fraîche

brins de persil plat,
en garniture

pain pita, en accompagnement

sauce

5 cuil. à soupe d'huile d'olive
vierge extra

2 cuil. à soupe de vinaigre
de vin blanc

1 cuil. à soupe de jus
de citron

1/2 cuil. à café de sucre

1 cuil. à soupe de coriandre
fraîche hachée

sel et poivre

méthode

1 Pour la sauce, mettre l'huile, le vinaigre, le jus de citron, le sucre et la coriandre dans une terrine. Saler, poivrer et bien battre le tout.

2 Ajouter les tomates, l'oignon, le concombre, les olives, la féta et la coriandre. Mélanger le tout, répartir dans des assiettes et garnir de persil frais. Servir accompagné de pain pita.

desserts

Les végétariens s'intéressent en général de près aux vertus nutrition-
nelles de leur alimentation. Souvent, ils ont à cœur de soigner leur
santé et ont choisi ce mode alimentaire dans cette perspective. Cela
ne signifie pas, cependant, qu'ils boudent systématiquement les
desserts !

Ce chapitre présente une série de recettes de desserts, dont certaines très saines et
d'autres plus indulgentes, à une époque particulièrement intransigeante sur bien des
points. Si vous suivez un régime basses calories, optez pour les granités de fruits, le sorbet
aux abricots et au fruit de la passion, ou le yaourt glacé aux myrtilles, qui convient bien
aux personnes diabétiques. Les abricots rôtis au miel et le fromage frais de chèvre et aux
figues sont aussi des spécialités tout à fait adaptées.

Et si vous voulez lâcher la bride, craquez pour la crème glacée à la framboise ou au citron,
pour la crème brûlée à la mangue ou pour le pudding estival.

Pour le cas où vous voudriez vraiment larguer les amarres, trois choix
s'offrent à vous : les petits banoffees, la tarte du Mississipi et la tarte
au chocolat et au fudge. La crème caramel à l'espagnole sera de
circonstance, et si vous souhaitez briser tous les tabous, laissez-vous
tenter par une tarte aux pommes traditionnelle et de la crème glacée
à la vanille. Deux desserts pour le prix d'un !

crème glacée à la framboise

ingrédients

POUR 6 PERSONNES

85 g de framboises
   fraîches ou surgelées
   ct décongelées, un peu
   plus pour garnir
2 cuil. à soupe d'eau
2 œufs
1 cuil. à soupe de sucre
300 ml de lait, chaud
1 cuil. à café d'extrait
   de vanille
300 ml de crème fraîche
   épaisse

méthode

1 Régler la température du congélateur au minimum. Dans une casserole, mettre l'eau et les framboises, porter à ébullition et réduire le feu. Laisser mijoter 5 minutes à feu doux, retirer du feu et laisser refroidir 30 minutes. Transférer dans un robot de cuisine, réduire en purée et passer au travers d'un chinois en nylon de façon à éliminer tous les grains. Réserver.

2 Incorporer le sucre au lait, battre les œufs dans une jatte et verser le lait sucré en filet sans cesser de battre. Filtrer, transférer dans une casserole et cuire 8 à 10 minutes, jusqu'à obtention d'une crème épaisse qui nappe la cuillère. Ajouter l'extrait de vanille, retirer du feu et laisser refroidir.

3 Fouetter légèrement la crème fraîche, ajouter délicatement à la préparation précédente et transférer le tout dans une jatte adaptée à la congélation. Congeler 1 h 30, jusqu'à ce que les bords commencent à prendre. Retirer du congélateur et remuer de façon à briser les cristaux de glace.

4 Remettre au congélateur, laisser prendre encore 1 heure et retirer de nouveau du congélateur. Incorporer délicatement la purée de framboises, mettre au congélateur 1 heure et servir garni de framboises entières.

crème glacée à la vanille

ingrédients

POUR 4 À 6 PERSONNES

300 ml de crème fraîche
    liquide et 300 ml de
    crème fraîche épaisse
    ou 625 ml de crème
    fouettée
1 gousse de vanille
4 gros jaunes d'œufs
100 g de sucre en poudre

méthode

1 Dans une casserole, verser les crèmes fraîches ou la crème fouettée. Ouvrir la gousse de vanille, gratter la pulpe et incorporer le tout dans la casserole. Porter au point d'ébullition sans laisser bouillir, retirer du feu et laisser infuser 30 minutes.

2 Dans une jatte, mettre les jaunes d'œufs et le sucre, battre jusqu'à ce que le mélange blanchisse et fasse un ruban. Retirer la gousse de vanille de la casserole et ajouter la crème vanillée progressivement dans la jatte à l'aide d'une cuillère en boissans cesser de remuer. Filtrer le tout, transférer dans une casserole propre et cuire 10 à 15 minutes à feu doux sans cesser de remuer, jusqu'à ce que la préparation épaisse et nappe la cuillère. Veiller à ne pas laisser bouillir. Retirer du feu et laisser reposer 1 heure en remuant de temps en temps de façon à éviter la formation d'une peau.

3 Transférer la préparation dans une sorbetière et procéder selon les instructions du fabricant. Servir immédiatement ou transférer dans une jatte adaptée à la congélation, couvrir et conserver au congélateur.

crème glacée au citron

ingrédients

POUR 4 À 6 PERSONNES

2 ou 3 citrons

625 ml de yaourt à la grecque

150 ml de crème fraîche
    épaisse

100 g de sucre en poudre

zeste d'orange coupé en fines
    lanières, en garniture

méthode

1 Presser le jus des citrons de façon à obtenir 6 cuillerées à soupe, verser dans une jatte et ajouter le yaourt, la crème fraîche et le sucre. Bien mélanger le tout.

2 Transférer le tout dans une sorbetière et procéder selon les instructions du fabricant. À défaut de sorbetière, transférer la préparation dans une jatte adaptée à la congélation et congeler 1 à 2 heures sans couvrir, jusqu'à ce que les bords commencent à prendre. Transférer dans une autre jatte et battre à l'aide d'une fourchette ou mixer dans un robot de cuisine. Remettre au congélateur 2 à 3 heures, jusqu'à obtention d'une crème glacée homogène. Couvrir, réserver au congélateur et servir garni de lanières de zeste d'orange.

granités de fruits

ingrédients

POUR 4 PERSONNES

1 ananas

1 gros morceau de pastèque,
    épépiné et coupé en dés

225 g de fraises ou autres
    fruits rouges, équeutés
    et éventuellement coupés
    en lamelles

1 mangue, nectarine
    ou pêche, pelées et
    coupées en lamelles

1 banane, pelée et coupée
    en rondelles

jus d'orange

sucre en poudre

méthode

1 Chemiser 2 plaques de papier sulfurisé,
répartir les fruits, sauf l'ananas, dessus et mettre
au congélateur 2 heures, jusqu'à ce qu'ils
soient fermes et bien glacés.

2 Mettre l'ananas dans un robot de cuisine
et mixer jusqu'à ce qu'il soit grossièrement
haché.

3 Ajouter un peu de jus d'orange et de sucre
selon son goût, et mixer jusqu'à obtention
d'une consistance granuleuse. Répéter
l'opération avec les fruits restants et répartir
dans des coupes glacées. Servir
immédiatement.

yaourt glacé aux myrtilles

ingrédients

POUR 4 PERSONNES

175 g de myrtilles fraîches

zeste finement râpé et jus
 d'une orange

3 cuil. à soupe de sirop
 d'érable

500 g de yaourt nature allégé

méthode

1 Dans un robot de cuisine, mettre les myrtilles et le jus d'orange et réduire en purée. Filtrer et transférer dans une jatte.

2 Mélanger le sirop d'érable et le yaourt, et incorporer aux myrtilles.

3 Transférer dans une sorbetière et procéder selon les instructions du fabricant et congeler encore 5 à 6 heures. À défaut de sorbetière, transférer la préparation dans une jatte adaptée à la congélation, congeler 2 heures et retirer du congélateur. Transférer dans une autre jatte, battre jusqu'à obtention d'une consistance homogène et remettre au congélateur. Laisser prendre totalement et servir, garni de zeste d'orange.

sorbet aux abricots & au fruit de la passion

ingrédients

POUR 6 PERSONNES

sorbet

100 g d'abricots secs

250 ml d'eau

2 cuil. à soupe de jus
de citron

2 cuil. à soupe de jus
d'orange

7 cuil. à soupe de pulpe
de fruit de la passion,
filtrée

biscuits au sésame

1 cuil. à soupe de graines
de sésame

1 cuil. à soupe de sirop
de glucose

3 cuil. à soupe de sucre
en poudre

2 cuil. à soupe de farine

méthode

1 Pour le sorbet, mettre les abricots et l'eau dans une casserole et porter à ébullition. Réduire le feu, laisser mijoter 10 à 15 minutes, jusqu'à ce qu'ils soient tendres, et retirer du feu. Transférer dans un robot de cuisine, ajouter l'eau et réduire en purée. Ajouter les jus de fruits et 3 cuillerées à soupe de pulpe de fruit de la passion, et mixer.

2 Ajouter 2 cuillerées à soupe de pulpe de fruit de la passion, transférer dans une jatte adaptée à la congélation et mettre au congélateur 20 minutes. Battre le sorbet de façon à briser les cristaux et remettre au congélateur 2 heures, jusqu'à ce que le sorbet ait pris, en battant toutes les 20 minutes de façon à obtenir une texture fluide.

3 Pour les biscuits, mettre les graines dans une poêle, et faire griller à feu vif jusqu'à ce qu'elles soient dorées. Retirer du feu, ajouter le sirop de glucose, le sucre et la farine, et mélanger à l'aide d'une cuillère métallique de façon à obtenir une pâte collante. Retirer de la poêle et laisser tiédir. Les mains mouillées, façonner un boudin, couper en seize et rouler en boule. Aplatir et déposer sur du papier sulfurisé.

4 Cuire au four préchauffé 6 minutes à 180 °C (th. 6) et laisser refroidir sur une grille. Servir le sorbet nappé de pulpe de fruit de la passion et accompagné de biscuits au sésame.

crème caramel à l'espagnole

ingrédients

POUR 6 PERSONNES

50 ml de lait entier

1/2 orange avec 2 morceaux de zeste retirés

1 gousse de vanille, ouverte, ou 1/2 cuil. à café d'extrait de vanille

175 g de sucre en poudre

beurre, pour graisser

3 gros œufs entiers, plus 2 jaunes

méthode

1 Dans une casserole, mettre le lait, le zeste d'orange et la gousse de vanille, porter à ébullition et retirer du feu. Incorporer 85 g de sucre et laisser reposer 30 minutes.

2 Dans une autre casserole, mettre le sucre restant et 4 cuillerées à soupe d'eau, chauffer à feu moyen à vif jusqu'à ce que le sucre soit dissous et porter à ébullition sans remuer jusqu'à obtention d'un caramel doré. Retirer immédiatement du feu et ajouter quelques gouttes de jus d'orange de façon à stopper la cuisson. Répartir dans un moule à soufflé légèrement graissé d'une contenance de 1,25 l.

3 Remettre la casserole contenant le lait sur le feu et porter à ébullition. Dans une jatte, battre les œufs eniers et les jaunes, incorporer progressivement la préparation à base de lait sans cesser de battre et filtrer dans le moule.

4 Mettre le moule dans un plat à gratin et verser de l'eau dans le plat de sorte que le moule soit immergé à demi. Cuire au four préchauffé de 1 h 15 à 1 h 30, jusqu'à ce que la crème ait pris. Retirer le moule du plat et laisser refroidir. Couvrir et mettre au réfrigérateur une nuit. Pour servir, passer une spatule métallique le long des parois du moule et démouler sur un plat de service.

crèmes brûlées à la mangue

ingrédients

POUR 4 PERSONNES

2 mangues

250 g de mascarpone

200 ml de yaourt à la grecque

1 cuil. à café de gingembre
en poudre

zeste râpé et jus d'un citron

2 cuil. à soupe de vergeoise
blonde

8 cuil. à soupe de cassonade

méthode

1 Couper les mangues dans la hauteur de chaque côté du noyau, jeter le noyau et peler la chair. Hacher et répartir dans 4 ramequins.

2 Battre le mascarpone avec le yaourt, ajouter le gingembre, le jus de citron, le zeste et la vergeoise blonde. Répartir la préparation dans les ramequins, lisser la surface et mettre au congélateur 2 heures.

3 Parsemer de cassonade de façon à recouvrir la préparation et passer au gril 2 à 3 minutes, jusqu'à ce que le sucre ait fondu et doré. Laisser refroidir et réserver au réfrigérateur. Consommer le jour même.

crèmes au mascarpone

ingrédients

POUR 4 PERSONNES

115 g de biscuits amaretti,
    émiettés

4 cuil. à soupe d'amaretto

4 œufs, blancs et jaunes
    séparés

55 g de sucre en poudre

225 g de mascarpone

amandes effilées grillées,
    pour décorer

méthode

1 Dans une jatte, mettre les miettes de biscuits, ajouter l'amaretto et laisser tremper.

2 Battre les jaunes d'œufs avec le sucre jusqu'à ce que le mélange blanchisse, incorporer le mascarpone et les miettes de biscuits.

3 Battre les blancs d'œufs en neige ferme, incorporer progressivement à la préparation précédente et répartir le tout dans 4 coupes à glace. Mettre au réfrigérateur 1 à 2 heures, parsemer d'amandes effilées et servir immédiatement.

crème dessert au chocolat

ingrédients

POUR 4 À 6 PERSONNES

175 g de chocolat à 70 %
   de cacao, cassé
   en morceaux
$1^1/_2$ cuil. à soupe de jus
   d'orange
3 cuil. à soupe d'eau
30 g de beurre, coupé en dés
2 œufs, blancs et jaunes
   séparés
$^1/_8$ de cuil. à café de crème
   de tartre
3 cuil. à soupe de sucre
   en poudre
6 cuil. à soupe de crème
   fraîche

praliné
pistache-orange
huile de maïs, pour graisser
55 g de sucre en poudre
55 g de pistaches
   décortiquées
zeste finement râpé
   d'une orange

méthode

1 Dans une casserole, mettre le chocolat, le jus d'orange et l'eau, chauffer à feu doux sans cesser de remuer jusqu'à ce que le chocolat ait fondu. Retirer du feu, ajouter le beurre et remuer jusqu'à ce qu'il ait fondu. Transférer dans une jatte, incorporer les jaunes d'œufs battus et laisser refroidir.

2 Battre les blancs en neige ferme avec la crème de tartre, incorporer le sucre, 1 cuillerée à soupe à la fois, en battant bien après chaque ajout, jusqu'à obtention d'une meringue brillante. Incorporer 1 cuillerée à soupe de meringue à la préparation précédente et ajouter la meringue restante.

3 Dans une autre jatte, fouetter la crème fraîche, incorporer à la préparation et répartir le tout dans des coupes à dessert ou un grand plat de service. Couvrir de film alimentaire, mettre au réfrigérateur et laisser reposer 4 heures.

4 Pour le praliné, graisser une plaque et réserver. Dans une casserole, mettre les pistaches et le sucre, chauffer à feu moyen jusqu'à ce que le sucre soit dissous et remuer jusqu'à ce qu'il se transforme en caramel et que les pistaches commencent à éclater. Verser immédiatement sur la plaque, parsemer de zeste d'orange et laisser prendre. Hacher grossièrement et garnir les crèmes au chocolat.

pudding estival

ingrédients

POUR 6 PERSONNES

675 g d'un mélange de fruits
   tels que groseilles, cassis,
   myrtilles ou framboises
140 g de sucre en poudre
2 cuil. à soupe de crème
   de framboise (facultatif)
6 à 8 tranches de bon pain
   blanc rassis, croûte retirée
crème fraîche épaisse,
   en garniture

méthode

1 Dans une casserole, mettre les fruits et le sucre, porter à ébullition à feu très doux sans cesser de remuer délicatement jusqu'à ce que le sucre soit dissous. Cuire 2 à 3 minutes à feu très doux, jusqu'à ce que les fruits rendent leur jus, sans se déliter. Incorporer éventuellement la crème de framboise.

2 Chemiser un moule à pudding d'une contenance de 875 ml avec quelques-unes des tranches de pain en les recoupant aux dimensions si nécessaire et répartir le contenu de la casserole dans le moule en réservant un peu de jus.

3 Couvrir le tout avec les tranches de pain restantes, ajouter une assiette et lester. Mettre au réfrigérateur et laisser reposer 8 heures.

4 Démouler le pudding, napper avec le jus réservé de façon à colorer les zones de pain restées blanches et servir garni de crème fraîche épaisse.

abricots rôtis au miel

ingrédients

POUR 4 PERSONNES

beurre, pour graisser

4 abricots, coupés en deux
    et dénoyautés

4 cuil. à soupe d'amandes
    effilées

4 cuil. à soupe de miel

1 pincée de noix muscade
    ou de gingembre en poudre

crème glacée à la vanille,
    en accompagnement
    (facultatif)

méthode

1 Beurrer un plat allant au four assez grand pour contenir les moitiés d'abricots en une seule couche.

2 Répartir les abricots dans le plat, côté coupé vers le haut, parsemer d'amandes effilées et arroser de miel. Saupoudrer de noix muscade ou de gingembre.

3 Cuire au four préchauffé 12 à 15 minutes à 200 °C (th. 6-7), jusqu'à ce que les abricots soient tendres et les amandes dorées. Sortir du four et servir immédiatement, garni éventuellement de crème glacée à la vanille.

tarte aux pommes

ingrédients

POUR 6 PERSONNES

pâte

200 g de farine, un peu plus
    pour saupoudrer
100 g de beurre, coupé
    en dés, un peu plus
    pour graisser
50 g de sucre glace, tamisé
zeste finement râpé
    d'un citron
1 jaune d'œuf, battu
3 cuil. à soupe de lait

garniture

3 pommes à cuire
2 cuil. à soupe de jus
    de citron
zeste finement râpé
    d'un citron
150 ml de miel liquide
175 g de chapelure blanche
    ou blonde
1 cuil. à café de poudre
    de quatre-épices
1 pincée de noix muscade
    fraîchement râpée
crème fraîche épaisse fouettée,
    en accompagnement

méthode

1 Pour la pâte, tamiser la farine dans une jatte, incorporer le beurre avec les doigts de façon à obtenir une consistance de chapelure et ajouter le sucre, le zeste de citron, le jaune d'œuf et le lait. Pétrir brièvement sur un plan fariné et laisser reposer 30 minutes.

2 Abaisser la pâte de sorte qu'elle ait 5 mm d'épaisseur et foncer un moule à tarte de 20 cm de diamètre.

3 Pour la garniture, évider 2 pommes, râper et transférer dans une jatte. Ajouter 1 cuillerée à soupe de jus de citron, le zeste, le miel, la chapelure et la poudre de quatre-épices, mélanger et répartir sur le fond de tarte.

4 Évider la pomme restante, couper en lamelles et répartir sur la garniture. Enduire du jus de citron restant, saupoudrer de noix muscade et cuire au four préchauffé 35 minutes à 200 °C (th. 6-7), jusqu'à ce que la garniture soit ferme. Retirer du four et servir accompagné de crème fouettée.

riz au lait

ingrédients

POUR 4 PERSONNES

1 cuil. à soupe de beurre,
   pour graisser
85 g de raisins secs
5 cuil. à soupe de sucre
   en poudre
90 g de riz rond
1,25 l de lait
1 cuil. à café d'extrait
   de vanille
zeste finement râpé
   d'un citron
1 pincée de noix muscade
pistaches concassées,
   en décoration

méthode

1 Beurrer un plat allant au four d'une contenance de 875 ml.

2 Dans une jatte, mettre les raisins secs, le sucre et le riz, ajouter le lait et l'extrait de vanille, et bien mélanger le tout. Transférer dans le plat, parsemer de zeste de citron et saupoudrer de noix muscade. Cuire au four préchauffé 2 h 30 à 160 °C (th. 5-6).

3 Sortir du four, répartir dans des ramequins et décorer de pistaches concassées.

petits banoffees

ingrédients

POUR 4 PERSONNES

2 boîtes de lait concentré
    sucré de 400 ml chacune

6 cuil. à soupe de beurre
    fondu

150 g de petits-beurre,
    émiettés

50 g d'amandes, grillées
    et hachées

50 g de noisettes, grillées
    et hachées

4 bananes mûres

1 cuil. à soupe de jus
    de citron

1 cuil. à café d'extrait
    de vanille

75 g de copeaux de chocolat

450 ml de crème fraîche
    épaisse, fouettée

méthode

1 Dans une casserole, mettre les boîtes de lait concentré, couvrir d'eau et porter à ébullition. Réduire le feu et laisser mijoter 2 heures, en ajoutant de l'eau au fur et à mesure de l'évaporation de sorte que les boîtes restent immergées. Retirer de la casserole et laisser refroidir.

2 Beurrer 4 moules à tartelettes à fond amovible. Dans une jatte, mettre le beurre restant, ajouter les miettes de biscuits, les amandes et les noisettes, et bien mélanger. Presser le mélange obtenu dans les moules et cuire au four préchauffé 10 à 12 minutes à 180 °C (th. 6). Sortir du four et laisser refroidir.

3 Ouvrir les boîtes de lait concentré et répartir le contenu sur les fonds de tartelettes. Peler les bananes, couper en rondelles et mettre dans une jatte. Ajouter le jus de citron et l'extrait de vanille, bien mélanger et répartir le tout sur le lait concentré. Garnir de crème fouettée, parsemer de copeaux de chocolat et servir immédiatement.

tartelettes aux myrtilles

ingrédients

POUR 2 PERSONNES

4 feuilles de pâte filo

huile en spray

200 g de mascarpone

1 cuil. à café de miel

1 cuil. à soupe de zeste
    de citron

3 cuil. à soupe de jus de citron

1 cuil. à café de sucre

100 g de myrtilles fraîches

méthode

1 Découper un rond de 14 cm de diamètre dans chaque feuille de pâte filo, huiler chaque rond et les superposer deux par deux. Foncer 2 moules de 10 cm de diamètre et piquer le fond à l'aide d'une fourchette.

2 Placer un ramequin au centre des moules de façon à mettre la pâte en forme et cuire au four préchauffé 5 minutes à 180 °C (th. 6). Retirer les ramequins et cuire encore 4 à 5 minutes, jusqu'à ce que la pâte soit cuite. Sortir du four et laisser tiédir dans les moules. Réserver dans un récipient hermétique de sorte que les fonds de tartelettes restent croustillants.

3 Mélanger le mascarpone et le miel.

4 Dans une casserole, mettre le sucre, le jus de citron et le zeste, chauffer à feu doux jusqu'à ce que le liquide soit évaporé et ajouter les myrtilles à l'aide d'une cuillère métallique. Retirer du feu et réserver au chaud.

5 Disposer chaque fond de tarte sur une assiette, garnir de mascarpone au miel et ajouter le mélange à base de myrtilles.

tarte du Mississippi

ingrédients

POUR 8 PERSONNES

pâte

250 g de farine, un peu plus
    pour saupoudrer
2 cuil. à soupe de cacao
    en poudre
140 g de beurre, coupé
    en dés
2 cuil. à soupe de sucre
    en poudre
1 à 2 cuil. à soupe d'eau
    froide

garniture

175 g de beurre
250 g de sucre roux
4 œufs, légèrement battus
4 cuil. à soupe de cacao
    en poudre, un peu plus
    pour décorer
150 g de chocolat noir
300 ml de crème fraîche
    liquide
1 cuil. à café d'extrait
    de chocolat
425 ml de crème fraîche
    épaisse fouettée
    et copeaux de chocolat,
    en garniture

méthode

1 Pour la pâte, tamiser la farine et le cacao dans une jatte, incorporer le beurre avec les doigts de façon à obtenir une consistance de chapelure et ajouter le sucre et assez d'eau pour obtenir une pâte souple. Envelopper de film alimentaire et mettre au réfrigérateur 15 minutes.

2 Sur un plan fariné, abaisser la pâte et foncer un moule à tarte à charnière de 23 cm de diamètre. Chemiser de papier sulfurisé, garnir de haricots secs et cuire à blanc au four préchauffé 15 minutes à 190 °C (th. 6-7). Sortir du four, retirer le papier sulfurisé et les haricots, et cuire encore 10 minutes.

3 Pour la garniture, battre le beurre en crème avec le sucre et incorporer progressivement les œufs et le cacao. Faire fondre le chocolat noir, incorporer à la préparation précédente et ajouter le crème fraîche liquide et l'extrait de chocolat.

4 Réduire la température du four à 160 °C (th. 5-6). Répartir la garniture sur le fond de tarte et cuire 45 minutes, jusqu'à ce que la garniture ait légèrement pris. Laisser refroidir complètement et transférer dans un plat de service.

5 Couvrir de crème fouettée et de copeaux de chocolat, et réserver au réfrigérateur jusqu'au moment de servir.

tarte aux châtaignes & aux noix de pécan

ingrédients

POUR 6 PERSONNES

pâte

115 g de farine, un peu plus
pour abaisser la pâte

1 pincée de sel

75 g de beurre froid, coupé
en dés, un peu plus pour
graisser

eau froide

garniture

1 kg de crème de marron

300 ml de crème fraîche
épaisse

2 cuil. à soupe de beurre

2 cuil. à soupe de sirop
d'érable

175 g de noix de pécan

méthode

1 Graisser un moule à tarte à fond amovible de 22 cm de diamètre. Dans un robot de cuisine, tamiser la farine et le sel, ajouter le beurre et mixer jusqu'à obtention d'une consistance de farine. Transférer dans une jatte et ajouter juste assez d'eau froide pour obtenir une pâte souple. Sur un plan fariné, abaisser la pâte en un rond de 30 cm de diamètre, foncer le moule et retirer l'excédent de pâte à l'aide d'un rouleau à pâtisserie. Chemiser de papier sulfurisé, garnir de haricots secs et mettre au réfrigérateur 30 minutes.

2 Cuire au four préchauffé 15 minutes à 190 °C (th. 6-7), retirer le papier sulfurisé et les haricots, et cuire encore 10 minutes.

3 Fouetter la crème fraîche, incorporer à la crème de marron et répartir sur le fond de tarte. Mettre au réfrigérateur 2 heures. Dans une casserole, mettre le sirop d'érable et le beurre, porter à ébullition et ajouter les noix de pécan. Chauffer encore 1 à 2 minutes sans cesser de remuer, étaler sur du papier sulfurisé et laisser refroidir. Répartir les noix de pécan sur la tarte juste avant de servir.

tarte au chocolat & au fudge

ingrédients

POUR 6 À 8 PERSONNES

farine, pour saupoudrer

350 g de pâte brisée prête
   à l'emploi

sucre glace, pour saupoudrer

garniture

140 g de chocolat noir,
   finement haché

175 g de beurre, coupé
   en dés

350 g de sucre semoule brun

100 g de farine

1/2 cuil. à café d'extrait
   de vanille

6 œufs, battus

sucre glace

150 ml de crème fouettée
   et de cannelle, pour
   décorer

méthode

1 Abaisser la pâte sur un plan fariné et foncer un moule à tarte de 20 cm de diamètre à fond amovible. Piquer à l'aide d'une fourchette, chemiser de papier sulfurisé et garnir de haricots secs. Cuire au four préchauffé 12 à 15 minutes à 200 °C (th. 6-7), jusqu'à ce que la pâte ait perdu de son humidité. Retirer le papier sulfurisé et les haricots et cuire encore 10 minutes, jusqu'à ce que la pâte soit ferme. Sortir du four et laisser refroidir. Réduire la température du four à 180 °C (th. 6).

2 Pour la garniture, mettre le chocolat et le beurre dans une jatte résistant à la chaleur, disposer sur une casserole d'eau frémissante et remuer jusqu'à obtention d'une consistance homogène. Retirer du feu et laisser refroidir. Dans une autre jatte, mettre le sucre, la farine, l'extrait de vanille et les œufs, mélanger le tout et incorporer le chocolat fondu.

3 Répartir le tout sur le fond de tarte et cuire au four 50 minutes, jusqu'à ce que la garniture ait pris. Transférer sur une grille et laisser refroidir complètement. Saupoudrer de sucre glace et garnir de crème fouettée et de cannelle.

fromage de chèvre aux figues

ingrédients

POUR 4 PERSONNES

200 ml de yaourt au fromage de chèvre

$1/4$ de cuil. à café de poudre de quatre-épices

1 cuil. à café de sirop d'érable

$1/4$ de cuil. à café d'extrait de vanille

15 g de figues sèches, très finement hachées

1 blanc d'œuf

4 figues fraîches, $1/4$ de cuil. à café de sirop d'érable et feuilles de menthe fraîche, pour décorer

méthode

1 Dans une terrine, mettre le yaourt, la poudre de quatre-épices, le sirop d'érable, l'extrait de vanille et les figues sèches, et bien mélanger le tout.

2 Dans une autre jatte, monter le blanc d'œuf en neige, incorporer au mélange précédent à l'aide d'une cuillère métallique et répartir le tout dans 4 ramequins allant au four.

3 Mettre les ramequins dans un plat, verser de l'eau bouillante dans le plat de sorte que les ramequins soient immergés à demi et cuire au four préchauffé 15 minutes à 140 °C (th. 4-5), jusqu'à ce que la préparation ait pris.

4 Retirer du four et servir garni de figues fraîches, arrosé de sirop d'érable et parsemé de feuilles de menthe fraîche.